THE
TANGLEWOOD
MURDERS

THE
TANGLEWOOD
MURDERS

DAVID WEEDMARK

RendezVous
Crime

Cover design by Emma Dolan

Le Conseil des Arts du Canada | The Canada Council for the Arts

We acknowledge the support of the Canada Council for the Arts for our publishing program. We acknowledge the financial support of the Government of Canada through the Canada Book Fund for our publishing activities.

RendezVous Crime
an imprint of Napoleon & Company
Toronto, Ontario, Canada
www.napoleonandcompany.com

Printed in Canada

14 13 12 11 10   5 4 3 2 1

Library and Archives Canada Cataloguing in Publication

Weedmark, David
    The Tanglewood murders / David Weedmark.

ISBN 978-1-926607-09-2

    I. Title.

PS8595.E37T35 2010   C813'.6   C2010-904973-X

For Michael,
Emily &
Amanda

PROLOGUE

In her dreams the river is always thick and bloated, its surface cast in the familiar blues of twilight. Along its flooded banks, thick gnarled willows are intertwined with scrap pine and coarse dead brush. As she approaches the water, the willows lean towards her, their branches like wet tangles of hair brushing across her bare shoulders. The pine trees shift in jagged angles. The bushes crowd towards her and obstruct. Hearing again the muffled cries of her friend, Jennifer wades into the water towards them, but she can see no trace of the girl, no movement in the shadows. As her nightgown rises around her thighs, the water chills her legs. Her steps are slowed by the thickness of the water and the grip of the mud around her feet. Waist deep in the water, Jennifer calls out to her friend, but the cries have faded. Her own voice is absorbed by the growing silence, which is now as thick as the water and the shadows themselves.

She turns around, and around again, searching the shoreline for any sign of the girl, scanning the water for an extended hand, or a rising face gasping for breath. But the river is overcome with silence. She sees only her own black silhouette rippling on the surface. Then the remains of a crow float slowly towards her, one wing spread upon the skin of water, the other submerged. Slowly, it circles past her and fades into the shadows. Jennifer is alone.

She calls out again, but the silence, dark and cold, has a weight, has a substance now all of its own. The water rises around her, and the shadows cover her eyes and ears. The silence fills her open mouth.

She awakes in her bed choking, gasping for breath.

From the window, a bright wash of moonlight cascades across her pale legs and onto the splash of white cotton sheets around her feet. Breathless, panicked and alone, Jennifer shivers in the air-conditioned chill and draws the sheets around her body.

It is the first clear night in a week. The moon, pale and bloated, sheens down through the silence. She rolls away, grasping the sheets in her hands and drawing her knees to her chest. She begins to sob silently, shaking with remorse and fear. The dream continues to play out as her thoughts ebb and flow between wakefulness and sleep. The girl's frightened, lonely cries echo in her mind, even as the silence pulses in her ears.

After her dreams, Jennifer begins to count, as she used to when she was a child. She counts quickly, silently, her lips barely moving, as she feels herself trapped between her desire to lose herself in sleep and her fear that the nightmare will return. When she reaches one hundred, her breathing still has not calmed. She is too afraid to close her eyes. Exhausted, she begins to count again, backwards now, winding down to zero.

ONE

It had been a quiet summer morning in the warehouse. Ben Taylor had just finished repairing a loose conveyor belt on the tomato sorter in preparation for the day's run when Randy Caines, the warehouse manager, arrived. Taylor was still on his knees beneath the steel rollers when Caines told him to hitch a wagon to the old Kubota tractor, empty the old pump-house, then tear it down.

"Get a move on," Caines bellowed, pointing a meaty finger at Taylor. "I want that piece a shit torn down by the end of the day."

"What for?" Taylor asked in surprise, crawling out from under the conveyor belt.

"In case ya didn't notice," Caines said, "it got hit by lightning. Night before last. It's a mess and it's gonna take you most of the day to take it down."

"No, no." Taylor rose to his feet, shaking his head. "That thing's mostly brick and stone. Even for two men, that's a couple days work."

Taylor towered above his turnip-shaped manager. He wiped the oil from his hands with an old rag he had found jammed under the sorter's fuse box. Covered in grease and what appeared to be dried blood, the rag was still cleaner than his hands.

"Where the hell is Scotty then?" Caines demanded.

"I've no idea," said Taylor, patting the dust from his jeans.

"Fine," Caines snorted, turning to Juan Reger, who had just punched in and was sliding his time card back in its metal slot. "You're late!" he shouted across the warehouse floor.

"Like hell," said Juan, angling his thumb at the clock. "It's still a minute to eight. I haven't even started yet."

Caines turned back to Taylor. "Take the kid with ya. It'll do him good to try some real work for a change, instead of tinkering with his toolbox all friggin day long."

Taylor grinned once Caines had turned away. After a week of steady drizzle, the prospect of working in the sunshine where the flowers were beginning to bloom was a welcome reprieve from another monotonous day inside, packing boxes and loading trucks with a forklift.

Juan was not nearly as pleased. He kicked the steel support of the conveyor belt with his torn running shoe. "I wanted to help with the bottling today," he muttered.

Taylor grinned at his young friend. The bottling room was where the young girls Juan's age would be working today.

"You'll have more fun with me," said Taylor. "It's demolition work."

"There aren't any girls out there," Juan said. "Just bugs and weeds."

Taylor grinned. "Girls just get you in trouble anyway. Trust me on that, okay?"

Juan was still sullen after they'd finished hooking the wagon to the small Kubota tractor. His interests were limited to fixing machinery and girls. More precisely, he enjoyed taking machinery apart and trying, with limited success, to put it back together again. As far as the girls went, he enjoyed watching them and doing things to try to get their attention, but did not yet have the confidence to have a genuine conversation with them. At the prospect of doing anything else, he reacted with undisguised boredom or contempt.

While Juan maintained that he was eighteen years old, Taylor figured sixteen was closer to the truth. Juan had come to work at

Tanglewood Vineyards when his parents had signed him out of school a year ago, just a few months before Taylor had arrived. With blonde hair, blue eyes, and a Spanish first name, Juan was a German Mennonite whose parents had moved to Canada from the drought-ridden region of Chihuahua, Mexico, three years ago. His first name was Johann, but because he spoke Spanish so well, the Mexican workers on the farm had always called him Juan. He had happily adopted his Spanish name as an act of defiance to his father, who was the mechanic at the Weber farm a few miles down the road, and whose name was Johann as well.

Taylor piled two long chains into the wagon as Juan dropped a sledgehammer beside them.

"Why do we have to waste our time tearing that stupid thing down for?" Juan asked, "No one uses it."

"Well," Taylor began as he looked for more tools to load. "I guess it got hit by lightning the other night, so now they want it taken down."

"I don't remember any lightning," said Juan.

"It was probably after you went to bed. It was late. Sunday night."

Taylor remembered the storm. It had been the violent climax to a week of daily showers, as cool western winds fought with a warm front coming up from Lake Erie. Before the warm front finally prevailed, the first thunderstorm and tornado watch of the year were announced. There were no actual tornados reported, but the wind and rain had been violent at times, waking Taylor throughout the night with long swells of thunder stretching out from the south until they finally faded towards the east around three in the morning. Ben had heard of a few lightning strikes and some toppled tree branches in Thamesville and Ridgetown, but he hadn't heard of any damage here.

The pump-house lay at the end of a narrow gravel laneway that separated the vineyard from a few dozen old apple trees. It had been constructed at least sixty years ago, at a time when both sides of the lane had been used for tobacco and when a river could still be trusted as a healthy source of irrigation. In recent years it had been used only to store irrigation pipes and a few supplies that came in handy when workers were this far from the winery and the warehouse. The pump-house was situated in a remote corner of the vineyard, hidden behind the small apple orchard. There was no reason for any of the workers to come by this area so early in the season. If it had been hit by lightning, it was doubtful anyone would have known for a day or two, unless they had seen the flames that night.

"So why make us take it down if it's wrecked already?" Juan complained. "Doesn't make any sense. Just let nature take its course, and it'll all fall down anyway."

"I imagine they'll plant some more vines there, or a couple more apple trees. Besides, if the building is structurally unsound, they'll want to make sure it's down before some school kids sneak inside and have it collapse on them."

"School kids would have to be pretty stupid to go into a shack that's half-burned down and falling apart," Juan said.

"Well, school kids aren't as smart as us," said Taylor, without realizing he had winked.

They loaded a couple of crowbars and a rusty hatchet onto the wagon.

"Did you ever like school?" Juan asked. As sullen as he tried to be, he was not comfortable with silence unless he was busy repairing equipment.

Taylor considered the question. He had graduated from university twelve years ago. Memories of high school had seemed to grow more fuzzy, but much warmer with each passing year.

"It was fun," he answered finally.

"It's boring," the teenager said with a shrug. "My mom used to make me go. But they'd kick me out. And then they'd pull my Dad into the office to tell him how bad I was. And I'd get some time off and I'd go to work, which was what I wanted anyway. I hated it there."

"You'll have to finish high school if you want to get to college, you know."

"I don't see what good that does either. You used to work here when you were my age. And then you went to university, right? And now you're back. If school is so great, why are you here with me? Right back where you started from."

"You can't gauge your life by what you think other people are doing," Taylor said, staring at the youth with all the seriousness he could muster. "You're good with machinery, you know. With a little education or an apprenticeship, you could get yourself a good job. There's more to life than working for farm minimum wage, you know."

"I like farms," Juan replied. "It's better than working in a factory. Besides, I want to go back to Mexico one day and work on my own farm."

"But with an education…"

"I don't care about an education. And if an education is really so great and working on a farm is really so bad, what are you doing here?"

Taylor paused for a moment before answering. Of course he could not tell his young friend the truth, but he wondered for a moment how it would sound to any ears but his own: You see, I killed someone. A boy. It was an accident, but I took his life away, and knowing what I did took all the life from inside of me as well. I came here to escape the silence it filled me with, so I could work my body to exhaustion and so I could sleep again through the nights…

Taylor shook his head. "I like it here too," he said. "But don't expect me to be here for long. I have another life, you know. Some people take cruises. Some people go to Florida for a few months. I just wanted to get out of the city and get away from the stress for a while. And with an education, I can go back anytime I want. And that's the point."

"But we're both here the same. I like it here better than school, but I didn't have to go to classes to get here. That's *my* point."

Juan beamed at himself, clearly proud of his reasoning. He glanced up at Taylor's face to see if he had succeeded in irritating the older man.

"If we're both the same," said Taylor, "why is it I'm driving the tractor and you're standing in the back?"

This wiped the smile from Juan's face. He fished a pack of Black Cats from the pocket of his plaid shirt and lit a cigarette with a wooden match. He lumbered onto the back of the tractor, standing on the hitch that joined the wagon and holding onto the back of Taylor's seat.

"All set. Let's go!"

Taylor started up the engine, and the old tractor bucked and groaned to life. The exhaust pipe rattled and spewed a blue cloud of diesel smoke which lingered in the still air. As he eased the tractor into gear, Taylor stood in his seat to avoid the cloud of smoke until he had passed through it.

Emerging from the shadow of the warehouse, Taylor immediately felt the soft caress of the morning sun on his back. He was looking forward to taking off his shirt soon. He longed to feel the full weight of the sun on his skin.

Juan was soon grumbling and battling his grip on the seat as the tractor crossed the first series of ruts and potholes in the dirt path. Taylor decided to take it easy on Juan and drove slowly in second gear between the blossoming grape vines as he edged his way towards the river. He savoured the smell of the wet grass, and even the smell of the diesel exhaust mingling with the smoke from his cigarette, which he held between two fingers on the top of the steering wheel.

As he rounded into the clearing and the river came into view, Taylor could smell the green stagnant water and the lingering odour of dead fish that seemed to always follow a long, hard rain. The river odours soon began to blend with the smell of charred wood and wet ashes as they neared the pump-house.

And then another smell took him by surprise. Taylor tossed his cigarette aside to let it sizzle out in the damp grass. He took the tractor out of gear, denied the engine fuel, and turned off the engine. He stood in his seat to avoid the last gasp of exhaust fumes as he listened through the sudden silence that lingered in the eerily still morning air.

"Don't move," he said to Juan.

Taylor inhaled deeply through his nose a second time. As soon as he filled his lungs, he grimaced with the realization of what he had just breathed in. Thick and acrid, it stung his nose and throat. He knew this sickly, familiar smell all too well. It was already deep in his lungs, in his own body. Mingling with the odour of burnt lumber was the stench of charred human flesh.

Already Taylor's thoughts were on Anna Wagner, the young girl who had disappeared the week before. He turned his head away, exhaling forcefully to get it out of his body, but it was too late. The odour was deep inside him now. His stomach clenched as he brought his hand to his mouth and started to cough—a deep hack that brought the blood to his head and made his sides ache with the strain.

Juan had already scrambled down from the wagon hitch and

was walking towards the old pump-house a dozen yards away. He stopped and spun around, stepping back towards the tractor, covering his nose with his shirt collar.

"Gawd! It reeks!" he shouted. "What is it?"

Taylor wiped the sweat from his face with the sleeve of his plaid shirt. "I told you to stay back, Juan."

The sullen teen stepped behind the tractor. "Shit," he groaned.

Taylor sat back in his seat, taking deep, measured breaths. The smell coming from the pump-house left little doubt as to what was inside, but as long as he stayed on the tractor and didn't approach any closer, he could hold onto the last flake of hope for a few more seconds. He could hope he was wrong, that it was some dead animal inside. As the seconds quickly passed, however, his hope could not last against the certainty of what was waiting for him inside the blackened pump-house.

Taylor glanced at his watch. It was a quarter to nine. Only a few minutes ago, it had promised to be a beautiful day. Much more than just the day had been shattered, Taylor was certain of that. He directed his gaze to the riverbank where the willows, pines and poplars framed a small patch of goldenrod and purple liatris. A large crow was perched on the branch of a nearby maple. It crowed once with a deep, guttural squawk. Black, with a purple sheen in the sunlight, it looked too large to be a crow as it rose into the air and soared behind the more distant trees. A raven, perhaps. Taylor watched the slow, easy movement of the water reflecting the green of the trees on either bank. He wanted to look at anything, simply anything, but this burnt-out shack.

The building had been constructed, it seemed, with little or no planning. It was less than ten feet high and about the size and shape of a single car garage. The thin beams of the flat roof had begun to sag some time ago under the weight of at least a half dozen layers of asphalt shingles. Composed of mostly red brick, shorter brown bricks appeared near the top of the south and east walls, where someone had evidently run out of supplies. Several fieldstones and rough mortar had been used above the doorframe, giving it a rustic look. These would have been used out of convenience or necessity rather than for esthetics. Most probably, the builders had run out of bricks. Fieldstones, a farmer's curse, which worked their way up through the soil with every spring thaw, were always in plentiful supply.

Taylor noticed the frame around the single broken window was black and charred, as were the edges of the shed's only door. The red bricks near the window and door were blackened as well. The door itself, however, was quite intact. Looking closer, he saw about half of the sagging roof had now completely collapsed. He focused on the ground and now saw the shards of glass that littered the gravel. There was another odour here too, just below the surface of wet ashes and human flesh. He should have recognized it before. Gasoline.

"What is it?" asked Juan.

"Just step back for a minute."

Juan did as he was told at first, but as Taylor approached the doorway, the youth was soon crowding him. His hands were on Taylor's back, peering at the doorway from behind Taylor's arm.

"Maybe a raccoon died in there?" said Juan.

Taylor said nothing, motioning to Juan to step back. Dead raccoons and squirrels the teenager was used to, but not this smell.

"Or maybe a stray cat?" Juan offered.

"We'll see soon enough." Taylor pulled the ball cap from his head and wiped his forehead with his sleeve.

They approached the small brick shed. Fallen shingles, fallen metal shelves and several wooden crates filled with rusted tools were blocking the window, preventing him from getting a good look inside. The door was padlocked shut.

"Do you know anything about this lock?" Taylor asked. "Or who has the key?"

"No," said Juan. "But I'm pretty sure it's supposed to be locked. The Mexicans used to sneak in here to sleep when no one was watching."

"Hand me a wrecking bar."

Juan hurried over with a crowbar. Taylor wedged the end of the bar under the rusty latch. After a couple of quick tugs, the latch came free from the door. As he opened the door, the hinges squealed like nails being pulled from green wood, making Juan wince. A dozen or so steel irrigation pipes, each six inches thick and eight to twelve feet long, had fallen from their racks on the wall and were now blocking their way inside.

Warm, moist air wafted from the open doorway. The stench was now much worse. The smell of gasoline was stronger too. Because of the pipes blocking the doorway, Taylor could not get his head far enough into the doorway to see what exactly awaited them inside.

"This can't be good," said Taylor. "But let's get at it."

They made short work of the pipes, moving them onto the trailer quickly, silently. Juan tried his best to keep the collar of his t-shirt over his mouth and nose, handling the far end of each pipe to keep as far from the doorway as he could. Inside, beyond the pipes, flecks of gold buzzed and swarmed, illuminated by the large hole in the roof of the shed. Taylor had only to take a couple of steps inside before he could see what awaited him in the far corner of the shack, behind a stack of charred crates, covered by fallen shingles. Blow flies, with sheens of silver and gold, buzzed frantically, creating a morbid halo above the charred remains of Anna Wagner.

Taylor motioned Juan away. Flies swarmed around Taylor's face as he stepped further into the shed. His skin crawled.

"Gawd, it reeks," Juan whispered behind him. "What is it?"

Taylor gave the youth a sharp look. "Get to a phone. Call the police."

Juan's eyes widened as he pressed forward. "Let me see."

"You don't need to see this."

"Why? What is it?"

"Juan." Taylor leaned forward. "Juan. Call. The. Police."

The boy tried to crane his neck over Taylor's shoulder. Whatever sense of fear and revulsion Juan had been feeling a moment ago was now eclipsed by an intense curiosity.

"*You* go call the police," Juan snapped. "You're not the boss of me. I wanna see."

Taylor was an inch over six feet tall, with a solid, muscular build. The boy was not going to move him. Eagerly, Juan moved towards the doorway. With one hand, Taylor grasped the teenager's shoulder and held him back from the doorway.

"You can't go inside. Call the police. Tell them we've found Anna."

Juan's shoulder slumped in Taylor's grasp, and he stopped pressing forward. He looked up at Taylor with shock, like he had just been punched in the stomach.

"It's her, Juan. Now please call the police."

Juan nodded, but his feet were not moving. His arms were limp at his sides, and his gaze was fixed on the darkened doorway ahead of him.

"But she ran away to Mexico," Juan whispered. "Everyone said she ran away."

"I know what they said. But she's not in Mexico, Juan. You have to call the police."

Juan took a deep breath, as if preparing himself to go back to the tractor, but lurched forward instead with a speed that caught Taylor by surprise. By the time Taylor had his hands on the boy again, Juan had already gained entry to the shack. He did not take more than a step or two inside before he stopped on his own, gasping at the sight inside.

Quickly, Taylor slipped his arm around Juan's waist to prevent him from advancing any farther. His aim for the moment was not to drag the boy out, but to just hold him in place. Juan would leave easily enough in a few seconds, and Taylor could not let a scuffle disturb this crime scene more than they already had by trying to clear the doorway a few minutes ago.

"You've seen her," Taylor said calmly. "Now give her some respect, and let's go back outside."

He gently pulled Juan back into the sunlight and, positioning himself between Juan and the doorway, he loosened his grip on the boy.

Juan gasped once more and began to run towards the tractor, bent forward, one hand on his mouth, the other on his stomach. His legs bent like rubber in his long strides before he fell forward onto his hands and knees. In the tall weeds alongside the shed, he began to spasm and vomit.

Taylor gave him a minute before approaching. Juan was on his hands and knees, fighting for breath. He looked up at Taylor with wide, mournful eyes. Behind his own calm expression, Taylor was burning with rage. He was pissed with himself for letting Juan catch him off-guard as he had, for not protecting him from the sight inside, and for not protecting Anna Wagner from Juan's morbid curiosity.

"Feeling better?" Taylor asked, without showing a trace of his pity for the kid and the harsh lesson he had just learned.

Juan looked up, wiping his mouth. His face was pale. He looked now to be only ten years old.

"Want another peek?" Taylor asked.

Juan shook his head as he climbed to his feet.

"I tried to tell you. But now you know. So get to a phone. Call 911. Get the police here. Don't talk to anyone else on the way to the phone."

Taylor patted his shoulder. "Do it now, Juan."

Juan nodded and turned away. He began to run.

"Save your legs. Stop. Save your legs. Take the tractor."

Juan stumbled back and tried to start the tractor.

"Give it some fuel."

The boy nodded absently and opened the fuel line. The Kubota fired up and hitched as he popped the clutch, steering it around in a tight circle, before bouncing off in high gear between the rows of grapevines and the early blossoming apple trees towards the main warehouse. The right tire hit a deep rut on the side of the laneway, and several tools bounced and fell from the wagon.

Taylor looked at his watch. It was a few minutes after nine. It might take at least a half hour for the police to arrive. As he turned back towards the shed, he recognized in himself the warning signs of shock.

This isn't the same. Isn't the same at all, the echo of a detached voice said to him. *Don't go numb. Compose yourself.*

He let his legs take him towards the water. The dams downstream had not been opened enough for the rain that had come down in the last several days. The river was full, brown and slow. A large branch, still clad in green maple leaves, floated near the shore, barely moving in the swell, looking to Taylor like another body face down in the water. He closed his eyes and for a moment was only aware of the sun, now too hot on the back of his flannel shirt, and the feel of his wet shoes and the wet cuffs of his jeans from the dew on the tall weeds. He opened his eyes and took another step towards the river, but the tranquil scene was marred by the knowledge of what lay behind him. A loud buzzing insect released a steady high-pitched tone from the trees. Fifteen years ago, Taylor would have known its name. An early cicada, perhaps, he thought vaguely.

He rubbed his eyes and walked back to the pump-house, looking at every detail, from the sprinkles of broken glass mixed in with the gravel, to the scorched bricks and mortar around the window and door. There were no discernable footsteps in the dry mud surrounding the doorway. The rain would have washed them away several times over by now. No matches visible, no cigarette butts or weapons. No monogrammed handkerchiefs left behind by a masked villain.

Taylor rolled his eyes at his ridiculous thoughts and circled around the shed before approaching the doorway.

Careful not to touch anything, he stepped inside. Flies buzzed and swarmed around his face, and Taylor became conscious again that he was breathing death into his lungs. He took light, shallow breaths, feeling particles of her corpse entering his body with every breath. He swallowed hard several times as the reflex to retch came over him. A ruptured metal gas tank, visible beneath the fallen shingles and plywood, lay on the floor near the far wall. The red and yellow lettering was still legible on its side, but the metal was torn and blackened where the burning fuel had kicked its way out.

In the corner, he could see a pile of clothes. There were the remnants of a yellow dress with a pattern of blue wildflowers, singed from the fire and wet from the rain. Two white canvas tennis shoes, one singed and melted, the other untouched, lay lopsided on the dress. Protruding from the bottom of the pile of clothing was the edge of a cotton bra that had once been white but was now brown from the fire.

Against the wall were more six-inch irrigation pipes, each about ten feet long, stacked horizontally on metal shelves. Next to the pipe were several wooden pop bottle crates containing several dozen steel and aluminum connectors; shorter pipes with clamps, each about ten inches long. A rusty red toolbox sat unopened beside the crates.

Only when Taylor was certain he had taken in every other detail in the shed did he finally turn his focus towards Anna's body. He took another breath. She was naked, black, grey and white, her burned face staring up from the metal cot. The cot, he imagined, had been used over the years by workers while they waited to move irrigation pipes or just needed to hide from the boss. Her hands were above her head, held by heavy handcuffs now blue and black from the heat of the fire. Her legs were spread open, nylon rope melted into the flesh of her ankles. He could smell the residue of gasoline most strongly from her body now. Several flies still swarmed her mouth and nose, lighting on her open eyes, but there were no maggots visible. Taylor had no desire to look more closely. She had not been dead for much more than two days. Her torso was burned badly, but her face and limbs still recognizable. Her neck had been cut ruthlessly. Most of her hair had been charred. Her mouth was open.

She must have died screaming, he thought as he took another step forward. No, something was in her mouth. A cloth had been pressed deep in her mouth. He pulled his utility knife from his back pocket and prodded lightly at the cloth. White cotton panties with pink flowers, singed by the flames.

Taylor put his knife back in his pocket, careful now to keep his eyes away from her face. The human mind cannot accept chaos. It will play tricks on you, trying to rearrange the details it is seeing into something it can make sense of. Lifeless open eyes seem to blink. Lifeless lips seem to smile then to sneer. It was hard enough when it was a stranger's body you were looking at, when you could detach yourself from the knowledge that the body before you was once a living, animated person. It was nearly impossible, however, when it was someone you knew. Taylor blinked his eyes, again and again, trying to keep his mind focused, and looked around the shed once more.

It was shoddy work, he decided. He looked at the hole in the roof, at the broken glass of the window. More flies, buzzing loudly, lighted on his shoulders, his face and his ears. As he stepped back towards the door, he noticed an old hammer on the floor in the corner, rusted, the wooden handle scorched and split down the centre. Beside it was a small sickle about six inches long with a foot long handle. Taylor crouched down and looked for blood on the hammer and on the rusty serrated blade. There was none. He surveyed the room again, memorizing every aspect of her body and the items surrounding her.

Finally, he let his eyes pass over her face one last time: the mouth open in a silent scream; the disfigured bulging eyes staring at him; and the flies, the endless flies climbing over the once beautiful face. He turned his head away before his feet could move again. Once outside, he leaned against one of the apple trees until his head cleared. He let himself fall against the tree, sitting with his back against the rough trunk, and closed his eyes to the leaves and the blue sky above.

Taylor opened his eyes and looked down the orchard for any sign of Juan. How long, he wondered, would it take the boy to find a phone to call the police. How long before this crime scene became a circus of police, reporters and farm workers? He thought of heading towards the warehouse himself, just to be sure Juan had made the call he was supposed to make, but he fought that reaction. It was best to let the urges come and go as his mind tried to fight the memories of Anna as she had been, of Anna as her body was now. Memories of her blonde hair flashed before him now, so beautiful when she was alive.

Anna Wagner was only eighteen years old. She had disappeared ten days ago. Her boyfriend, David Quiring, was also missing, and the Andover Police, after a three-day investigation, had decided that the two had run away together, either to Mexico, based on what his family had said, or to Alberta, based on what her few friends had said. Anna's father, Abe Wagner, had rejected this theory, adamant that his daughter would never leave without telling him, but his protests to the police had gone largely ignored. Whether she had run away with her boyfriend or not, Abe Wagner wanted her home. To this end, Michael Voracci, Wagner's employer and the owner of Tanglewood Vineyards, had posted a five thousand dollar reward for information leading to her safe return.

One of the last times Taylor had seen her, she had been having lunch outside at a picnic table on a sunny day much like today. She had smiled and waved as he walked by. He could still hear her voice, see her smile and her expressive blue eyes. She was such a beautiful, carefree soul, one of those girls who could have been sixteen or twenty-five depending on the expression on her face. He could hear her laugh now. Taylor dug his heels into the ground as the sound of her laughter turned into a sob then a muffled scream.

Again, he fought the urge to get up, to go to the warehouse, to find out what had become of Juan. He needed to be here, to protect the crime scene, in case Juan returned with some curious workers before the police arrived.

For a moment, he considered covering her naked body with his flannel shirt. But these emotions pass, he reminded himself. It was best just to sit here against the tree. He had seen enough. There was nothing he could do to help her now except to ensure no one else went inside before the police arrived. He clenched his jaw when he remembered how easily Juan had stepped past him to get inside to satisfy his morbid curiosity. What had he been thinking of, letting down his guard like that? Perhaps he had been here too long. Perhaps he had spent so much effort trying to convince himself that he was just another farm hand that he had actually come to believe it.

Taylor shook his head with a surge of self-disgust. What had he been thinking of, coming here, trying to convince himself that he was something he was not? Just two nights before—the night of the thunderstorm in fact—he had been thinking of quitting this job and returning home to Ottawa, thinking of putting the pieces of his own life back together, and finally leaving this fantasy of a simpler life behind. Why had he not come to his senses a few weeks earlier, he demanded of himself now, when he could have done something to help Anna before it was too late?

He knew the answer to this, of course. He had fallen in love and had become too busy trying to find a new place for himself in an old, over-used fairy tale—the white knight trying to save the damsel from a tower of her own making. *Dammit, Ben.* So he had entrusted Anna's fate to the local police—men, it turned out, who had put less thought into her case than they did trying to decide what to order for lunch.

When Taylor had told the Andover Police Chief, Tom McGrath, that he did not think Anna was the kind of girl to run out on her father without saying a word, McGrath had scoffed at him.

"And who are you again?" McGrath had asked, amused. "These Mexican Mennonites, they're just like the migrant workers. They float from place to place. In fact, they're worse than the Mexicans because they don't carry any papers. They're just blonde-haired, drug-selling gypsies." McGrath had grinned at him, the sun reflecting from his sunglasses into Taylor's eyes. "Don't worry. Her dad will get a postcard from her in a few weeks. Just you see."

Taylor understood well enough the prejudice against the farm workers. Tanglewood Vineyards employed over a dozen migrants from Mexico and sixteen Mennonites, most from Mexico, one family from Alberta, and Anna and her father who came from Argentina.

To everyone in town they were all from Mexico. They lived the same simple lifestyle. The men were all thin, and all seemed to wear the same cheap brands of fertilizer caps. The women all wore hand-made dresses, black shoes, white socks, and handkerchiefs tied over their hair. They lived and worked in a world of their own, apart from anyone who lived in town. There was nothing Taylor could say to McGrath to dispel a lifetime of prejudice. Many of them in town dealt in drugs, yes, but not the ones who worked twelve to sixteen hours a day on the farms, and certainly not Anna, or her father. There was nothing Taylor could say to show McGrath that Anna Wagner deserved as much respect as any girl from town.

He closed his eyes, and saw her face again, burned. Silently screaming, staring at him.

Help me, she seemed to say. *You found me. I'm inside you now. You breathed my body into yours. You denied me before, but you can't deny me now. You are responsible.*

Taylor closed his eyes. There was no escape from this voice. There was no escape from these thoughts. He knew that all too well.

You are responsible.

TWO

Taylor was becoming restless. This was taking far too long. Looking at his watch, he realized that only fifteen minutes had passed since he had sent Juan to call for the police, but it seemed to be twice as long.

Still sitting beneath the apple tree, he pulled a cigarette from its pack and slipped it between his lips. His stomach turned as soon as he lit the paper, and he forced the smoke from his mouth with disgust. He squeezed out the smouldering ember between his fingers, letting it drop into the grass next to his knee. He stared at the small brown shreds of tobacco jutting from the end of the broken paper. Even from this distance, he would catch an occasional smell of smoke and charred flesh.

Taylor was watching where the sunlight fell in splinters on the leaves when the sound of muted rock music began to waft towards him along with the sound of an engine and the sound of tires rolling across packed gravel. A gleaming white Ford Dakota pickup rounded the corner at the edge of the orchard, approached the pump-house and idled to a halt beside Taylor.

Michael Voracci opened the driver's door and stepped onto dried earth and gravel. Looking around, Voracci slid his cell phone into his back pocket, hoisted his pants up, then pulled a slightly crushed pack of Marlboros from the front pocket of his red golf shirt. As his eyes locked onto the pump-house a few yards away, his shoulders drooped, and he began to rock from his heels to his toes.

A gold bracelet flashed as he lit his cigarette with a blue disposable lighter, the flame invisible in the bright sunlight. He leaned against the white hood of his truck with a hand as fleshy and soft as a toddler's. He smoked his cigarette and occasionally looked at his watch with distraction as he surveyed the burnt pump-house.

"Taylor!" he called finally and took a step forward. "You in there?"

"Here." Taylor came from behind the truck.

Michael Voracci patted Taylor's shoulder. "You okay, pal? You look pale."

"Better than she is."

"What the hell happened?" Voracci asked.

"Looks like someone cut her throat then tried to cover it up by setting fire to the place. Too much rain, or too little gasoline, I'm not sure. But it didn't work."

Voracci nodded. "Juan told me, but he wasn't very clear. He was pretty panicked. You sure it's her?"

"Yes. Are the police on the way?"

"Of course. I called them right away. I was just getting into my truck when I saw the kid coming up the road on the tractor like his hair was on fire." Voracci shook his head. "It's an awful thing." He took the last drag from his cigarette, threw it down and ground it into the gravel. "I suppose I should see for myself."

"That's for the police, isn't it, Michael?"

As good-natured as he usually was with his employees, Michael Voracci was not accustomed to being addressed by his first name, let alone being told his place. He tilted his head and squinted thoughtfully at Taylor before replying.

"She was a family friend," he said. "Her father is my employee and my friend."

Taylor listened without expression, standing close enough to

23

him that Voracci had to look up to address him. "And it's a crime scene," he said.

"And it's my property." Voracci's voice was soft. "I appreciate your loyalty to her. I'm not going to touch a thing. But I am going to look. And you aren't going to stop me, *Mr.* Taylor. In fact, I think it's time you went back to work now. I'll wait here for the police myself."

Taylor froze for a moment then stepped back. He did not have a badge, so he had no right to stop Voracci. However, there was no way Taylor was going to leave the crime scene to anyone until the police arrived.

Where the hell were the police, anyway?

Michael Voracci, the owner of Tanglewood Vineyards, was the eldest son of Senator Anthony Voracci, former cabinet minister and a one-time hopeful for the leadership of the Liberal Party and the office of Prime Minister. Michael Voracci had been something of a celebrity himself in the late Eighties, known for his nightclub exploits and his outspoken conservative views on politics, which contrasted sharply with his father's liberal stance. Now in his late forties, the boyish good looks the young Michael Voracci had exhibited in his youth seemed to have been stretched and exaggerated with age, making him a caricature of his younger image. With thick thighs, rounded shoulders and a belly that had taken on the shape and texture of bread dough, he was in the midst of a fast, hard slide through middle age.

"Just don't touch anything," said Taylor as he watched Voracci approach the doorway. "The police will want to look for fingerprints."

"I know that."

Voracci stepped into the shadows of the pump-house, emerging a few moments later, pale and visibly shaken. A gold fly clung to the collar of his red golf shirt.

"Horrible," he said. "Just fucking horrible."

24

Taylor nodded.

Voracci's nod mirrored Taylor's. He began to rock on the balls of his feet. "We should cover her up."

"That's a nice sentiment," Taylor replied. "But tampering with evidence won't help her at all."

"No, no. I suppose that's true." Voracci kicked a stone. "Had you seen anyone around here?"

"Not a soul."

Voracci rested his back against the front fender of his Dakota. Reaching into the front pocket of his shirt, he pulled out his cigarettes. After lighting one, he offered the pack to Taylor.

Taylor shook his head. "No, thanks."

"If she'd been alive, I'd have happily paid you the reward, you know. All five thousand. Every penny." He exhaled a plume of smoke high into the air as he shook his head.

"I wasn't worried about that," Taylor said.

"The reward I posted was for finding her safe, remember?"

"I remember."

Taylor turned away and clenched his teeth against the smell of the smoke. He fought to stay focused, fought to keep Anna's face from appearing in front of his eyes again.

Voracci turned towards the front fender of his vehicle and unceremoniously unzipped his pants.

"My grandfather built that shed himself, you know," he said, looking over his shoulder. A thin stream of urine splashed against the tire.

"He was a good man," Taylor said, keeping his eyes from his employer. "I liked him a lot."

"That's right," Voracci from over his shoulder. "I forgot. You used to work here in the old days."

"When I was in school. For the summers."

"Then you would remember him." Voracci rolled his shoulders as the stream of urine slowed before zipping up his pants and turning around. "He started all this with a ten-acre potato field. Worked until his body was beaten. And he taught my father everything there was to know about wine and growing vines. But my father's talent was business. He turned the farm into an empire. And now it's my turn..."

Taylor let the words mingle with the scent of urine. He did not care to hear Michael Voracci's self-advertisements. He had heard the speech before. It had been well-rehearsed, with much of it taken, nearly word for word, from the marketing pamphlets that were shipped with each case of Tanglewood wine. The family farm and wine operations had been successfully marketed as a longstanding family operation for the last thirty years.

Voracci's grandfather, Antonio, a potato farmer, had started the winery as a hobby to keep himself busy in the fall and winter months. His skill with the vines and his love for wine had made him successful. Voracci's father, Anthony, had replaced the potatoes with tobacco, planted more vines and turned the modest family business into a small empire that owned leasing properties, a chain of travel agencies, a trucking company and a wholesale distribution company.

When Anthony had retired fifteen years ago, he'd divided his businesses into parcels, giving most of the shares to his two sons, Vic and Michael, and keeping a small portion for himself. The farm was divided down the centre, the orchards and fields going to Vic, the vineyard and winery going to Michael.

The brothers soon began investing their family fortune into several technology companies and a host of other ventures that had very little to do with wine or farm produce, the pillars of the family's original business. These investments had not fared well when the dot-com bubble of the Nineties had burst, and the brothers had returned their business interests to the family roots.

Vic, with the help of some solid federal financing, had begin covering the fields with plastic, and venturing into hydroponic greenhouse tomatoes. This had not been the gold mine he had anticipated, due to increased competition from California, but it had been steadily profitable over the years. The winery thrived as well, Michael Voracci leveraging the family name through intensive advertising and wine competitions in both Canada and the United States. While they were extremely competitive with each other, the brothers operated both the greenhouses and the vineyard under a single joint holding company, through which they shared their equipment, trucks, water, power and warehouse facilities. Even the employees were hired under this holding company, Ben Taylor included, so they could be used each day wherever they were needed most, at the discretion of Randy Caines.

While Michael and Vic enjoyed the glow of their success, Taylor had some inside information few of the other workers would ever suspect—that most of the family fortune had been squandered. While Michael Voracci and his wife still lived on the farm, he spent more time on the golf course and travelling from one wine event to another than he did on the vineyard. Vic had bought a house a few miles away in Andover but spent most of his time in Toronto, enjoying a condo on the waterfront while managing a series of ever-shifting companies few on the farm knew much about. Abe Wagner, whose daughter Anna now lay less than twenty yards away, had once told Taylor it was a typical path of three generations. The first generation starts the business. The second generation builds the business. The third generation squanders the business. However, Abe Wagner had been quick to point out that this was not a hard and set rule. The aging wine master was hopeful this would not be the fate of the Voracci family business. His own livelihood, after all, depended on it.

Shortly after Voracci had finished his speech, Taylor realized this was already the longest conversation he had ever had with his employer. The few times Voracci was in the warehouse, or touring the vineyards with potential clients, he did not interact very often with his employees. He would wink as he passed, or give a thumb up, and call out with a grin, "Keep smiling!" before disappearing into his office. Taylor could not help but clench his teeth each time he saw Voracci smile.

The trademark grin was far away at the moment as Voracci ran his fingers through his stiff black hair and looked over the damage to the pump-house. "I was going to bulldoze it a couple years ago," he said, "but never got around to it. We could have planted six more trees there."

"Or some more vines," Taylor offered without interest, looking down the orchard for signs of the police.

"No, no," said Voracci, crossing his arms. "I want to keep all the grapes on that side of the lane. Keep this for the fruit trees. Of course, it was all trees in this part when you used to work here, wasn't it?"

Taylor nodded.

"I remember you," Voracci said. "You were just a kid. It's awful strange to see you back here, Taylor. It's nice, of course. Just strange."

"You too," said Taylor. "I'd have expected you to be living in Toronto or New York. Back then you were going to law school, weren't you?"

"Yeah, but life got in the way. You don't understand family business, Taylor. Not just our family. Any family business. You just don't walk away. It keeps you here, tied to the ground." Voracci forced a smile. "I'll tell you, it's a damn good thing I love this land."

Taylor nodded impatiently through Voracci's monologue as he watched a white police cruiser quickly make its way up the gravel laneway, approaching slowly. Rising dust formed a small trail behind it. The cruiser stopped behind Voracci's Dakota. Tom McGrath, the Andover Police Chief, was in the passenger seat. Pat Patterson, one of his six constables, and McGrath's son-in-law, was driving. Taylor knew them all by sight.

McGrath was sixty-four and looking towards the retirement his body desperately needed and his ego could not face. The Chief closed his door, lifted both arms in the air and yawned loudly. Watching the grimace on the Chief's face as he stepped from the car, Taylor understood the yawn was to mask the back pains that came from too many hours behind the wheel of a cruiser, too much weight on his aging spine.

Patterson was in his mid-forties, about the right age to have gone to school with Voracci, Taylor realized, if he had grown up in Andover. Taylor watched the way Patterson would not make eye contact with Voracci or even shake his hand the way McGrath now did, and decided he must know Voracci quite well to warrant such a slight in etiquette. Both officers stood with their hands on their hips, looking over the scene from behind dark sunglasses.

McGrath squinted into a smile behind his glasses, dentures white in the sun. "What's going on, Mikey?" he asked in an amiable, grandfatherly manner. The tone was well practiced and came easily to the Chief after years of pulling over drunk drivers and moving teenagers from the sidewalk in front of the pool hall.

"We found the girl," Voracci answered, looking to the ground. He pointed behind him with a thumb. "She's in there. Anna Wagner."

McGrath drew a long loud breath. "Hell of a thing. Thanks, Mike. You'd better stay over by the vehicles now. We'll take it from here." He did not seem to notice Taylor.

"Of course," said Voracci.

Patterson looked sideways at Taylor as Chief McGrath

disappeared inside the pump-house. The constable did not seem to give Taylor much importance either. He was just another farm worker to them, another set of eyes ogling the scene of a crime.

McGrath stepped out into the sunlight. He pulled a blue linen handkerchief from his pocket and wiped his face and neck. The Chief seemed more annoyed with the additional workload than upset for the girl's fate. Taylor found himself wishing he had covered her body after all.

The Chief nodded at Patterson. "It's her, all right. Not very pretty. It's a damn shame."

Patterson opened the trunk of his cruiser and began rooting around with his equipment. Taylor stepped forward.

"It's a damn shame," McGrath said to Voracci. "You have to think he kept the poor girl in there all this time we were looking for her. Right under our noses. Had anyone looked for her here?"

"I don't think so," said Voracci.

"Wasn't that your job?" Taylor interrupted, glaring at the police chief.

McGrath turned and looked Taylor up and down, as if he had not seen him until this very moment.

"Who's this, Mikey?" McGrath asked. "One of your workers?"

"Yes. This is Taylor. Er..."

"Ben Taylor," said Taylor.

"Yes. Taylor. He was one of the workers to find her."

"And what were you doing out here this morning?" McGrath asked.

"We were going to tear this shed down," Taylor replied. "We were told it had been struck by lightning two nights ago, and we were told to tear it down."

"Did you touch anything inside?"

"Just some pipes that were against the wall. The door was locked.

We broke the locks. It's there beside the door."

McGrath nodded, satisfied, but far from pleased.

"But you should know," Taylor added, "that a few of us searched all around here last week. A couple days after she disappeared, but we didn't see or hear anything to make us think she was in here."

"No one uses this shed," Voracci added. "I was just saying I should have had the thing bulldozed years ago."

"Well, it's a damn shame. She was a beautiful girl. But you can't blame yourself, Mikey." McGrath turned to his constable. "Piss poor time for this to happen, Pat. I'm glad we invested that training in you. The OPP are all working on that big case in Sacketville. And I don't know how long it will take to get the coroner out here today." He looked up at the blue sky. "I don't want the body baking in this heat, so we might have to take her out of here ourselves. We'll have Doc Logan come out here just to be sure. But I want pictures of everything before we touch this body."

Constable Patterson cocked his head. "But he's retired…"

"No, no," said McGrath. "He's semi-retired. Just get him out here, okay?"

Patterson nodded wearily and began to unpack his camera and equipment from the trunk of the cruiser.

Taylor had heard enough. He took a step towards McGrath and positioned himself alongside the two men. He cleared his throat, staring into McGrath's sunglasses.

"Have you notified the provincial police?" Taylor asked.

"All in due time," said McGrath. "All in due time."

"You can't move her until you've notified the OPP."

"Like I said, son, there's no one available right now. Step aside. This isn't a TV show. Leave this to the professionals."

Taylor took another step, putting his face within eighteen inches of McGrath's. He spoke deeply, deadly serious, and intent on getting his point across. "That's what I'm telling you. Leave this for the professionals. Do not touch that girl's body until you've called the OPP."

"Okay now! Calm down." Voracci stepped up and came short of putting his hand on Taylor's shoulder. "That's enough, I think. Let the police do their job, Taylor. I'm sure they know what they're doing."

"I think I know what is and what is not within my jurisdiction, young man," McGrath said, ignoring Voracci's intervention. "Step away."

Patterson closed the trunk of the car and held up his camera for Taylor to see. "That's why we're documenting everything before we remove the body. The rest of this area will not be disturbed."

McGrath turned angrily to Voracci. "Everyone's a goddammed authority these days. Doesn't this man have something to do other than hang around here?"

"Yes," Voracci replied. "Yes, he does. Taylor, thanks for your help here. You can go now."

"This is a homicide, Mike," McGrath continued. "Not just a runaway girl. I'm going to have to make this building off limits to everyone. You and your worker here included. And I'm going to want a list of every worker's name. And I'm going to want to talk to everyone who had access to this building. That includes your family, the workers, this man here, your father, everyone else you can think of."

"Of course," said Voracci. "Taylor, I appreciate your concern, but I told you to go now. Give Scotty a hand setting up the line for this afternoon's shift. And you better make sure Abe doesn't come out here."

"You're too late," said Taylor, pointing over Voracci's shoulder.

Michael Voracci turned around. An electric golf cart was making its way towards them, a sixty-year old man in faded bib overalls behind the wheel. Abe Wagner. His face was ashen. His hand trembled as he pointed at the pump-house.

"Is she in there?" he shouted. "Is she there?" He stepped out of the cart, nearly falling as his foot got tangled in the pedals. "Let me see! Let me see my girl!"

Moving quickly, Constable Patterson set his camera on the hood of the police cruiser and was within arm's reach of Abe Wagner by the time the man had begun to walk towards the pump-house. Taylor, surprised by Patterson's speed, was only a step or two behind him. It took a few minutes for them to gently persuade Wagner to get back in the golf cart and let Taylor take him home.

Taylor had just helped the trembling man sit down in the cart when a black pickup pulled up behind the police cruiser. Michael Voracci's brother Vic and his famous father, Anthony Voracci, climbed out of the cab. Each carried a tray of coffee. Vic, a shorter, thinner version of his brother, balanced a box of doughnuts on the palm of his hand.

"Coffee and doughnuts?" Wagner said with tears running down his face. "Is this some sort of party?"

Taylor started the golf cart and put it in reverse to turn it around. "No," Wagner said as he placed his hand on Taylor's arm. He leaned forward in the passenger seat, watching intently at the action in front of him and at the pump-house. "No. It is all wrong. She wasn't there."

The Voraccis had settled against their vehicles as the two policemen continued their work. McGrath was securing the area around the shed with yellow tape. Patterson was testing the flash on the camera. "She wasn't there last week."

Taylor eased the golf cart into drive, and just before they rounded the corner at the end of the tree-lined road, he looked back.

The three Voraccis, coffee and doughnuts in hand, leaned

against the side of the white Dakota and looked as though they had begun to swap stories. The police disappeared inside the burned pump-house that contained Anna's body. Wagner, sitting beside Taylor, dropped his arms on his knees and buried his face in his hands. The last of the morning dew evaporated from the grape leaves under the brightening summer sun.

Three

The forty acres of Tanglewood Vineyards, owned by Michael Voracci, and the sixty acres of Tanglewood Farms, owned by his brother Vic, existed side by side, north and south, divided by the lane that led to the river. The river, which curled around the farm, marked the eastern and northern edge of the properties, while the highway marked the southern edge. To the west, a long, thin hedgerow divided the Voraccis' farms from the cornfields of their neighbour. The hedgerows were the trimmings left behind of the vast forest that had once covered this region before the first Loyalist settlers had arrived from the United States and assumed upon the land the harsh geometry of their farms and their grid of roads dug out mile by mile by mile.

In the centre of the brothers' farms stood the warehouse, the winery, and the bungalow of Abe Wagner. The warehouse was constructed of corrugated steel, as was much of the winery. Within the core of the winery building, however, one could still make out the architecture of the farm's original barn, with its foundation of fieldstones and large square timber beams. The migrant workers, all of whom were from Mexico, shared a small bungalow on the far southeast corner of the vineyard, where the highway crossed the river on an unnamed bridge. Ben had been there only once, driving an injured worker home to rest, and had been appalled to find the men slept in bunk beds without sheets, six to a room. There was a stove in the kitchen, but no fridge. The shower did not have a curtain, and the bathroom did not have a door. There was not even a seat on the toilet. When he asked Randy Caines about their living conditions, Caines had shrugged. "I don't go there. Beats me why they don't have a shower curtain. They know where the hardware store is."

While Vic Voracci had kept a portion of the apple orchard intact, most of his land had in recent years been covered with plastic and concrete—hydroponic greenhouses. Vic had begun this construction about eight years before, when the peach orchard had been decimated by a particularly harsh spring freeze. That portion of the orchard was bulldozed out and, with the help of some generous grants from the federal government, Tanglewood's hydroponic greenhouse operations were launched. Within a couple of years, nearly all of Vic's portion of the farm was covered with plastic and concrete. Gone were the green fields. Gone were the dark starry nights, masked now by the orange-green glow of the greenhouse lights. Gone as well was the annual Apple Festival, which had been a tradition at Tanglewood Farms for as long as anyone could remember, but which the Voracci brothers had always openly despised.

Taylor parked the golf cart beside the back porch and led Abe Wagner by the arm to his door. Wagner's burning pain and outrage had exhausted itself within moments of leaving the pump-house, and now there was the subdued anguish of knowing a child was lost forever. On his porch, Wagner stared vacantly at the torn screen door until Taylor opened it for him and, hand on Wagner's back, gently led him inside to the sunlit kitchen table.

"Thank you," Wagner said. "But I should check on the vines."

Ben understood this statement was a symptom of shock and grief, complicated by the prospect of going into an empty home. Wagner was a widower. His only son had been estranged from the family for more than a decade. His only daughter, the child he had once held in his arms and had watched bloom from an infant nearly to full womanhood, was dead. Inside his house there was no one to hold, no one to share his grief with or to console. He was alone.

Wagner stared at the table before sitting down on a worn wooden chair. A plate of half-eaten toast, a jar of jam, a jug of milk and a cold cup of coffee waited on the table before him, remnants of a world that had been eclipsed for him less than an hour ago. That these items appeared to be within arm's reach was an illusion. The world Wagner had known this morning was forever separated from him, Taylor understood.

"You should try to get some rest, Abe."

"No," said Wagner after a long, bewildered pause. "I need to keep busy. Keep my mind busy with work." He pushed back the plate of toast and rested his elbow on the table. "I knew she didn't leave. No one believed me. I should have tried harder to find her. She was here somewhere all the time. You know, if I'd been working harder, I would have found my way out there. I might have seen her. I might have heard her…"

Wagner's head and shoulders began to shake.

"Try not to think of these things. You did everything you could." Taylor stood behind him and rested his hand on the man's shoulder until his silent, shaking subsided.

Wagner began to speak softly in German for several minutes, whispering more to himself than to Taylor before coughing and settling into a stunned silence. He stared at the food on the table, leaning forward, concentrating on the plate of toast and the few crumbs surrounding the plate, bewildered as if he were expecting the morning's breakfast would scamper away if left unobserved for a moment.

Taylor patted Wagner's shoulder before stepping outside and walking across the compound to the warehouse, the place he had been this morning when the world had seemed a bit brighter and much less distressing place. He passed the warehouse altogether and stepped inside the first greenhouse. It was quiet here. The pickers would not reach this end of the greenhouse for at least another hour. But picking they were. Outside of this momentary pocket of calm Taylor now found himself in, outside of the pumphouse where Anna's body lay, and outside of Abe Wagner's home, the gears of the world continued to turn.

Taylor gazed down the length of the greenhouse. Within the white arched walls were hundreds of rows of hydroponic tomatoes. The vines were strung by wire eight feet from the ground and fed intravenously with a solution to promote the growth. The fruit which sagged like plump water balloons never saw the ground, which was coated with plastic splash sheets. Even the roots were denied earth. They grew in white fist-shaped blocks of rock wool to keep the vines weighted down.

Taylor wondered to himself if Antonio, Vic and Michael's grandfather, would have ever allowed this type of farming. He doubted if any man with an appreciation for the land could have condoned such a solution. It seemed to Taylor too sterile, too automated and too precise for any man who truly loved the earth.

Taylor had grown up in Buckingham, a twenty minute drive from Andover. He had known very little about the town of Andover, but had spent four of his best summers working at Tanglewood Vineyards—long, satisfying summers. He had had the pleasure of talking to Voracci's grandfather, Antonio, many times. He remembered very well sitting at a picnic table—white table cloth weighted with stones to keep it from blowing away in the breeze—with a dozen or so other students enjoying sandwiches made by Antonio's wife, Juliana, and jugs of cold water brought up from the nearby well with an old iron hand pump. Often she would bring out fresh oatmeal cookies or slices of freshly-baked pie. More often than not, Antonio would take lunch with the students and would ask them about their plans for the future and tell them stories about his life. These were some of Taylor's fondest memories. They were, in fact, a large part of his reason for returning here.

The vineyard and the farm seemed to be more profitable today, but it was no longer the happy place to work that Taylor had known as a student. As he looked now at the plastic walls, the concrete floor, and the plastic all around him, he shook his head; this was not the same farm at all.

Antonio Voracci had begun the vineyard as a hobby sometime in the early Sixties. Until then, it had been a potato farm and orchard, which he had purchased for a modest sum in 1968, after selling the menswear store he had established in Andover twenty years before. Both Antonio and Juliana had been raised on small farms in the mountains of southern Italy. While life in the city had not been bad to either them or their children, Antonio had craved the touch of fresh earth. In the city, they cultivated a large garden in their backyard, at the expense of any grass, where they'd raised their own potatoes, tomatoes, zucchini, grapes and a host of other vegetables, herbs and flowers. It was the garden that Antonio daydreamed about during his long hours handling cotton and silk at his store. He longed for the touch of fresh earth in his hands.

Juliana tended the garden each day, but thoughtfully left behind a small patch of the garden untouched for her husband to work on for a few minutes each evening. When he arrived home, he would put on his overalls and an old shirt to step into the backyard to happily pull some weeds in his garden. He would then lift a fist full of soil and rub it slowly between his palms with a tranquil softening of his eyes.

When he sold his store in the late Sixties, Juliana asked him while sitting on the swing in their garden one afternoon if he would consider buying a farm of his own. Antonio put his arm around his wife's shoulders, threw back his head and sighed happily. At that moment, it was as if his life had suddenly been punctuated with exclamation marks, with an honest life with the land marking both ends.

He had purchased the farm from a man named John Harris whose wife of nearly fifty years had recently passed away. John Harris, whose family had traced their ownership of the farm to the years following the War of 1812, had been alarmed at the amount of residential development he saw around his land. He was happy to pass his farm to Antonio, with only one stipulation: the property was to remain farmland or allowed to grow wild. No houses or shopping centres were to be constructed here. Antonio, from the depths of his farmer's heart, had insisted that stipulation be put in writing, even though John Harris had been satisfied with his word and a handshake.

Under the Harris name, the land had been used to grow potatoes and turnips with a modest allotment of fruit trees, mostly apple and peaches, a few rows of corn and some grazing land for a few dairy cows. Antonio Voracci continued this heritage for several years; except for the sale of the cattle, which he spurned as stupid, unsanitary creatures. He planted potatoes for the most part, with a large vegetable garden for his family and some grape vines for his own wine. As he began to get a feel for the land, he found it uniquely agreeable for wine, due to the quality of the soil, its proximity to the river and its placement in the valley. As the farm straddled the snow belt of southern Ontario, the winters in this stretch of land made it hard for the vines, but not impossible if they were cared for properly.

Tanglewood Vineyards still grew the same varieties that Antonio had established twenty years before, after years of testing and experimentation: Chardonnay, Cabernet, Vidal Blanc, Riesling and Pinot Noir. The unique weather of Canada's most southern region, which gives the grapes a cooler summer than anywhere in the United States, also gives a longer warm period in the fall. The climate, Antonio had always believed, was similar to the Rhine Valley in Germany and the Loire Valley in France (neither of which had he ever visited) and the wines this land produced were, in his admittedly biased opinion, similar, if not superior in quality to anything ever produced in California's Napa Valley.

Twelve years before, as a teenager, Taylor had worked primarily in the vineyard, but now with the new setup, he was spending most of his time working in the tomato portion of the operation, with little time in the vineyard. For most of the fall and winter he assisted with the construction of the three new greenhouses and renovations to the warehouse and offices. During the late winter and early spring, he'd helped pruning the vines outside, planting new tomato plants inside, and helping with the bottling operations.

The efficiency of the hydroponics required eight men to collect a day's harvest. It was hard work for meagre pay, and the picking crew consisted of those who could find nothing better, newly arrived Puerto Ricans for the most part, who began work at dawn each morning. They would pick tomatoes until one or two in the afternoon then work the afternoons maintaining the greenhouses and orchards, finishing their day at sundown. They stacked plastic baskets full of perfect, dirt-free ripened tomatoes on wooden palettes which adorned the edge of each narrow concrete path that ran through the length of each greenhouse.

It was usually Taylor's mid-morning task to remove the palettes with a forklift and stack them beside the sorting line near the coolers and shipping area. There, the girls, who worked for even poorer pay than the pickers and who were nearly all Hispanic as well, would sort them according to size, colour and quality and repack them to be shipped out. This morning, Scotty Doherty had been tasked to take Taylor's place on the forklift. As he pulled himself up to the loading dock through the bay door, Taylor could see all three forklifts motionless on the platform.

Randy Caines sat behind a small desk, filling out a logbook.

"Did Juan talk to you?" Taylor asked.

"Yeah. It sucks, but I'm not surprised," said Caines with a dismissive shrug. "It's about fuckin' time you showed up. Where the hell is Doherty?"

"How would I know? You're the manager."

Caines peered up at him. "Don't tell me you want time off too. Juan already asked."

"I'm fine."

"Good. So get to work. It's backing up out there. The packers are going to be here soon, and they damn well need something to pack, don't they?"

Most probably, Taylor surmised, Scotty had slipped into one of his many hiding places in the back of the warehouse or one of the older glass greenhouses to smoke a joint and doze the morning away. Taylor stepped through the warehouse and opened the doors leading to the first greenhouse. A quick glance inside assured Taylor that his suspicions were correct. Scotty was nowhere to be seen, and dozens of full palettes, each neatly stacked with baskets of tomatoes, lined the walkways in the greenhouses for as far as he could see.

Taylor, vaguely relieved at having something to occupy his mind, quickly hopped onto a forklift, fired it up and began to submerge himself into the warm routine of his usual daily duties. However, the stale smell of propane exhaust, the smooth touch of the steering wheel and the levers beneath his fingers did nothing to ease his thoughts away from the morning's ghastly discovery. His fingers and mouth yearned for the touch of a cigarette, but he had tried to light three cigarettes since taking Wagner home. The tobacco tasted of ashes, burnt wood and flesh. Time slowed down around him, and Taylor felt as if he were moving underwater. He pulled the watch from his wrist and pushed it into his front jeans pocket, lifted the forks by wrenching down on the hydraulic lever and accelerated away.

He tried to summon some anger towards Scotty, his scrawny, good-natured co-worker, but could not find the energy. Each time his thoughts began to drift back to Anna, he would try to envision Scotty crouched and hiding, or asleep, in the rear of the smallest greenhouse, where the Voracci family kept their prized orange and lemon trees. Instead, he would see Anna Wagner, scorched and naked, exposed, staring at him with an open mouthed grimace.

Taylor hit the brake and made the forklift skid-stop on the concrete platform. Her image came to him again, and he snapped his head to refocus his attention and to escape the memory of her blue-grey eyes, the curve of her smile, her shining blonde hair. Such a beautiful girl she had been, shining bright with the possibilities of a full life.

Taylor wiped his eyes and turned his head to the side, staring pointedly at one of the pickers, a Mexican named Manuel, who had his sleeves rolled up to his elbows and was washing his hands in the pale, soapy Pine Quat solution to remove the green stains of the tomato stalks from his hands. He seemed to feel Taylor's gaze on the back of his head; he flinched, stopped washing then carefully moved away, as if a bee had lighted on his shoulder.

"Lot of tomatoes today," said Taylor.

Manuel was one of the few pickers who could speak English. He searched Taylor's face, his eyes soft with sadness, before replying with a simple nod.

"You've heard about Anna," Taylor said.

"It's a very sad day, yes."

"Does anyone know how she got there?"

"No. But my friends, they are all very upset. And they are afraid. They are afraid the police may not believe us that we did not know."

"I'm sure the police will be fair."

Manuel cocked his head and looked as if he had not understood Taylor's words. "I hope so," he said. "I hope they find the one responsible. For her sake, yes. But for our sake as well. I would not want to pay for the blood of another."

With that, he dropped his head, offered Taylor a humble, uncertain smile and walked away.

Taylor drove the forklift a dozen feet forward and expertly slipped the forks beneath the palette. Working methodically, he stepped down and wound a single piece of nylon twine around the top layer of boxes, looped it into itself and tied a simple knot to secure the stacked black plastic boxes from jostling. Lifting the load six inches from the concrete floor and tilting it back a few degrees, he sped in reverse to the end of the greenhouse.

The door that protected the greenhouse environment from the warehouse had to be opened manually. As Taylor slid open the large plastic door, he realized for the first time what was missing. The workers weren't singing, as was their custom. No one was talking. No one was laughing or smiling. They had all heard the news.

Once his load was in place with the other palettes, Taylor put his forklift in park. His fingers moved once again towards his shirt pocket, tapping his chest, reaching for a cigarette, his thoughts on the girl's image again... He could not bear to say her name, not even silently in his thoughts, even though his tongue would press against the roof of his mouth to form the first syllable of her name each time he pictured her in his mind.

By the time he had placed two dozen pallets in the processing area, the crew of young women had begun to step up to their platforms on the sorting line. After one more trip, Juan had returned as well. Without a word, Juan started up the conveyor belts and graders and began dumping tomatoes onto the conveyor belt. The girls were silent, grim; Juan had told them the news.

Taylor drove up to Juan and looked at him pointedly. "I thought you had the day off."

Juan shook his head. "I asked. He said I could go home as soon as I finish here."

Taylor leaned towards him and whispered, "I told you not to talk to anyone but the police."

"Mr. Voracci told me he'd call the police," the youth replied, crossing his arms. "He's the boss. Not you."

"Did you have to tell Caines?"

"He wanted to know why I came back. He'd find out anyway. Why are you mad at me? I had nothing to do with it. It wasn't my fault, you know."

Taylor drummed his fingertips on the top of the steering wheel. "I'm not pissed off with you. I'm just pissed off."

"It sucks," said Juan. "We're all pissed off." He cocked his head, adding quietly, "And the girls are really scared."

"They should be."

After that, Taylor resolved to keep to himself for the rest of the day.

He worked through his lunch hour, lifting pallets and bringing them to the processing area. He was at the far end of the greenhouses when his forklift slowed and sputtered to a stop. Methodically, he unclasped the propane cylinder from the rear of the machine and, carrying it with one hand, he kicked open the steel door to take a short cut across the gravel driveway. He stopped in his tracks as the door slammed shut behind him and stared up in surprise at the bruised and darkening sky of dusk. He pulled his watch from his pocket and hesitated before putting it back on his wrist. Instead he shoved it back in his pocket. It was just after seven o'clock. The compound was silent. All the pickers and packers and truckers had gone home.

"What the hell am I doing here?" he whispered.

Just a few days ago, he'd been preparing to leave, to go home, go back to his job in Ottawa and pick up the pieces of his life. Yet now, everything he had hoped to escape from for a few months had followed him. This was not the peaceful, carefree place he had sought. It stank with the same senseless violence he had turned his back on last autumn, and with the same despair. It had a voice now—the soft young voice of Anna Wagner.

You are responsible, she said.

Taylor walked silently towards the shipping bay and rested the empty cylinder on its rim, twisting it into the gravel a bit to ensure it did not topple over. He climbed up onto the loading bay, where the backs of trucks would couple with the warehouse, and waited. His fingers picked at the black rubber padding that protected the frame from the more reckless drivers and stared out across the gravel parking lot as he listened to the sound of music in the far distance and then the sounds of quiet tires on gravel approaching the loading dock.

Taylor quietly stepped back a few feet into the dark shadows of the loading dock and positioned himself behind a stack of wooden pallets. From between the slats he watched a beige electric golf cart, with Randy Caines at the wheel, round the corner of the greenhouse and continue past.

Caines was a large man, about three hundred pounds, but less than five and a half feet tall. He seemed to own only three shirts and two pairs of pants, and these were all black—golf shirts and track pants; his hair was slick, shiny and black as well. He was the one person Taylor had met since he started working at Tanglewood that he felt himself capable of hating without reservation. Every pound of Caines seemed to be riddled with malice and hatred. Anyone unfortunate enough to cross his path, let alone be placed under his authority, was liable to pay the price for his wrath. As the Warehouse Manager, there was no employee at Tanglewood who did not fall under his shadow.

Taylor eased himself around the pallets and watched Caines stop his cart in front of a white plastic greenhouse then carefully unlock the two padlocks that kept its contents safe and secret. This was the only greenhouse Taylor had never entered, because Caines kept it strictly off limits to everyone. Caines had explained during Taylor's first week at Tanglewood that Michael Voracci grew rare flowers inside as gifts to his wife. Anyone entering the greenhouse, he had gruffly explained, would be fired immediately. Opening the door would disturb the pollination process.

It did not take long for that lie to be exposed. Taylor had overheard someone's remark during dinner break the following night, "Just like Voracci's flowers!" echoed by a chorus of laughter.

"So those aren't flowers growing in there?" he asked.

No one answered him, but the continued laughter made it clear this was a standing joke amongst the workers. As his first days passed, it became obvious that the workers all believed Caines was growing marijuana in there. No one had ever seen Voracci bringing flowers to his wife. For that matter, no one had ever seen him kiss her.

Taylor decided not to concern himself with that greenhouse, at least until it was time for him to leave. For one thing, the greenhouse was quite small, no larger than what a hobbyist would keep in his backyard. For another thing, Ben Taylor was not exactly a narc.

47

But today, he wondered what other secrets besides marijuana might be hidden inside.

Everyone has secrets, of course. Taylor knew from personal experience that most secrets are only interesting to the person harbouring them. Strangers usually don't care if you have a drug or alcohol problem, if you have financial problems, if you are cheating on your spouse, or have a sexual fetish, or were caught shoplifting when you were fourteen. However, that rule flipped like a coin when someone nearby died violently. Strangers, namely the police detectives who would inevitably arrive, would soon search for and isolate any secret they found relevant to their case. Lives were turned over, secrets exposed, and reputations often destroyed, in the search for a killer. Caines' greenhouse would not be sacred territory to anyone once the provincial police began probing around.

There was some comfort in that, at least, knowing that the OPP would now be involved instead of the town police, who had written off Anna's disappearance as a runaway. Taylor would not longer have to sit on the sidelines while the local chief muddled through this case.

Taylor felt just a hint of satisfaction in that when he saw Randy Caines emerge from the greenhouse. He was emptyhanded, and Taylor wondered what the purpose of this visit had been. He smiled. He was going to take a personal interest in watching each of Randy Caines' secrets brought to the light of day.

Now standing in fading twilight, Caines looked left and right before locking the greenhouse door and pocketing the keys. Like a black paunchy thundercloud, Randy Caines cut a conspicuous figure against the white plastic of the greenhouse as he boarded his personal golf cart and hummed away.

Once the golf cart was out of sight, Taylor walked across the loading dock and picked up the telephone, asking the operator for the local OPP dispatch office.

"Just in case you haven't been notified yet," he said, before briefly giving the details of the crime.

With that done, he went outside. The air already felt much cooler now that the sun had set behind the hedgerow at the edge of the vineyard. He listened to the gravel shift beneath his feet as he walked, looking up at the large, expansive clouds, draped in hues of orange and purple, gently wafting across above him. The clouds, it seemed to Taylor as his thoughts rose skywards, were nearly within reach of his hand if he were to merely stretch towards them. It was then that he began to hear the music softly flowing through the air.

Beyond the blue garbage hopper at the edge of the parking lot, perhaps a hundred yards from the loading dock, stood an eight-foot cedar privacy fence that separated the vineyard and farm from the private residence of Michael and Jennifer Voracci. From beyond the fence, from an open window on the side of the two-storey gabled home came the gentle sound of a piano, magically keeping tempo with the cascading white sheer curtain that danced in and out of the open window. Taylor seemed to recognize the piece but could not think of the name. Something classical, obviously, the quick steep notes played by talented fingers. Perhaps at one point in his life he could even have named the composer, but this evening nothing came to mind as he gazed up at the dark purple clouds above the rooftop and the grey, unlit, dancing curtain of the main floor of the Voracci home. It seemed to be a difficult piece, and the pianist would stop suddenly in mid-bar then start from the beginning again. She would play for thirty or forty seconds then suddenly stop to begin all over again. Mrs. Michael Voracci. Ginny to her husband. Jennifer to Ben Taylor.

Taylor had to smile at her persistence—the first time he had smiled since he had stepped down from the tractor this morning. And while he felt like a musical illiterate these days, he had not lost his love for music. If he were to guess—and as he listened more attentively now, he was inclined to guess—she was playing Chopin. The music felt thoughtful, reflective, and Taylor wondered if anyone playing such a nostalgic piece was mindful of the events of this morning or still happily unaware. He watched the darkening clouds bend towards the open window as Venus and Mars peered from behind the orange bending light of the setting sun. He took a breath of the cooling air and listened to her begin the piece once again.

Few of the workers had ever spoken to Michael's wife. Indeed, few people working at the farm had seen her for more than a few moments as she went into or out of her house. She had the reputation of a recluse. During his first month working here, Ben had not seen her at all. At the time, he knew nothing about her. None of the other workers, with the possible exception of Anna Wagner, knew much about her either, but the rumours were abundant. The stories invariably contradicted each other and cancelled each other out: that she had been a model, that she was a distant cousin; that she was shy; that she was a cold and heartless bitch. That she was a simpleton; that she was a Russian bride who spoke no English; that she was the brains behind her husband's success. Most of the rumours were based on fantasy. The souls around him would volunteer anything they knew of anyone to help pass the time more quickly.

The first time Ben had caught a glimpse of her, she had been across the compound getting out of her yellow Volkswagen Beetle with bags of groceries in hand, and he had seen only the back of her head, her long brown hair tied in a ponytail. Still there was something familiar about the curve of her shoulders, her slender arms, the way she wore her hair, and her long slender neck. The next time he saw her, a week or so later, she had been standing at the gate of her small fenced yard, her husband's arm around her waist, as they said goodbye to some guests. That was when he was certain he recognized her. Jennifer Voracci had been Jennifer Spender, Ben's girlfriend in university, his first love.

Not a single worker, trucker, manager or interloper had ever mentioned the sound of a piano coming from the Voracci household. It was as if Taylor's ears alone detected the music, like the scent of a discreet perfume intended for only the most sensitive or closest witness.

Jennifer Voracci's piano had now escaped the practice chords and played smoothly, beautifully for a while. The yard was immersed in darkness before the music stopped. A light had been turned on on the main floor of the house, and the billowing curtain was seen no more. Taylor sat on a small stack of broken pallets and watched the window, willing her with his heart to look outside. The light went out, but she did not come to the window. Then from inside the house, he could hear Michael's voice, calling for his wife.

Ben clenched his fist and turned his attention towards the river, expecting to see the glow of car headlights, flashlights and searchlights from the area around the pump-house. But there were no lights reflected from the apple trees or glowing in the air. The area around the river was dark and silent.

Four

Jennifer Voracci steadied herself on one leg and opened the screen door as wide as its spring would bear. Balancing the basket of towels on her bent knee, she brushed the hair from her cheek and readied herself to run inside. For the five years she had lived here, the spring on the wooden door had always been too tight. It reminded her of a giant mousetrap, poised at any time to catch an errant arm or leg coming through the threshold. With a sudden breath, Jennifer pushed hard against the door and took two quick steps into the kitchen, her white running shoes squeaking on the floor, before the door slammed shut behind. The sudden thwack of the door always made her flinch.

She clenched her teeth as a cool wave of relief slid down her spine. She was inside. Safe in her home.

Yes, it really was a silly game she played racing past the screen door. While she understood that, she still couldn't seem to help herself. Perhaps it was because she had been treated as a child by Michael, her husband, for so many years that she now felt free to play the role. As ridiculous as it might be, it certainly wasn't hurting anyone, and as long as it didn't cause any harm, then it couldn't really be that bad, could it?

More importantly, right now, the small thrill, if for even a few moments, had distracted her from the question that had been seeping up through her thoughts all day: What was going on near the river?

The question had been gnawing at her all day, ever since she'd seen the blonde teenager racing up to Michael on his tractor this morning. Jennifer had been in the kitchen, scraping egg yolk from Michael's plate when she'd seen the tractor racing up the path from the direction of the river. Michael had been outside, cleaning his golf clubs in preparation for a morning tee-off with his brother Vic. From the kitchen window, Jennifer watched her husband put down his golf club and approach the boy, talking with both hands raised, calming the youth down. The teenager climbed down from the tractor, speaking quickly, very excited about something, while Michael nodded and listened before putting his hand on the boy's shoulder, quieting him. The boy stopped chattering. His head fell and his shoulders slumped. Michael said a few words to him, his hand still on the boy's shoulder. Then, with a final nod, the teenager climbed back onto the tractor and drove towards the warehouse.

When Michael came back inside, he was silent, his jaw set the way it usually was when plans were not going as expected. He took his cell phone and his golf hat from the table and paused at the door to say to Jennifer over his shoulder, "Something's come up, Ginny."

"What is it?" she asked, seeing the seriousness in his eyes.

"Nothing to concern yourself with," he replied. He winked and tried to smile. But she could see something was wrong.

Michael never let the door slam. He always let it close slowly, the palm of his hand pressed against the wooden frame, controlling its force in the cautious manner that somehow defined in her mind the type of man he was. Unlike herself, he was a man who had grown up and who was always in control. So it was disturbing to see the worry in his eyes as he tried to wink at her. Nothing ever troubled him.

As she watched Michael direct his truck down the path towards the river, Jennifer knew in her heart what had happened. They had found Anna's body, most likely washed up on the bank of the river, caught in the reeds somewhere near the old pump-house. Jennifer had no idea how long she'd stood at the sink, the water running before her, staring out the window. When the police cruiser drove past, she shook her head, turned off the water, and tried to put her thoughts behind her.

In small bursts and starts, memories of her dream came back to her, and of the last conversation she'd had with Anna.

Anna had been on her way to the warehouse that morning, and Jennifer had called to her from her gate to share with her one of the croissants she had baked. Anna's tired eyes looked into Jennifer's own as she complained about her lack of sleep. "Those trucks are so loud at night," Anna had said. "And they shine their headlights right into my window. It was like they were having a party. Can't they at least be discreet about it?"

Jennifer had promised to look into it and had asked Michael that weekend to make Randy at least have the trucks turn their lights off if they were going to be parked near Anna's bedroom window all night.

Michael had nodded in his detached, methodical way. "That won't be a problem," he had told her. "Haven't you heard? Anna and her boyfriend. It seems they ran away together."

It had taken several minutes for the news to really sink in before Jennifer could reply. "I can't believe she'd run away," she had said, to what was by then an empty room.

Now, this afternoon, almost a week later, standing in the kitchen, with her laundry basket balanced on her hip, remembering that news, and remembering how certain she had been that Anna could never have done such a thing as to run away from home, Jennifer trembled. She shook her head and tried to clear the thoughts from her mind before pressing her toes to her heels, left and right, to pull off her sneakers. On her way upstairs, she looked at the mantle clock above the stone hearth. It was three thirty. The towels still needed to be put away. The beds were still unmade. The bathroom still needed a cleaning.

She had spent the entire day trying to ignore what was obviously going on down the lane. Perhaps it would have been better if she had stepped outside and taken a walk towards the river just to ask what was going on. But the thought of doing that was even worse. She really did not want to know the truth, not yet. If she could keep herself from knowing for certain what had happened, then she could still hold on to her hope that Anna was safe and sound, in the arms of her boyfriend somewhere in the warmth of Mexico.

To that end, she had absorbed herself in the piano for most of the day, playing straight since nine in the morning with no thought of lunch and only two bathroom breaks somewhere in the mix, until she remembered she had left the laundry on the line outside. Her beautiful piano was the focus of her life when she was alone. It had been hard getting into it today, but once she'd connected with the music and found the place that exists between the tips of her fingers and the touch of the keys, she'd escaped from the day. She did not want to think about what the men were doing by the river. Flashes of her dreams intruded on her, but she was able to keep them at a distance by changing the piece, always progressing to something with a different tempo, a different taste and feel, something more difficult, requiring more effort, more concentration, until she was able to forget what might be going on down by the river. A piece of her, anyway. Only a portion of her mind had been aware of the passing of the day, or what might have been going on down the pathway, just out of view of her window. She was aware of only the distant chime of the mantle clock every half-hour, the steady movement of the shadows of her pictures and candles on the top of her beloved baby grand, changing direction and length as the sun passed from the east to the south to the southwest. She now remembered several cars, including police cars, no doubt, going past her window today, moving towards the far end of the vineyard, towards the river.

Standing on the stairs now, Jennifer gave her head another shake. *You could at least put the towels away and clean up a bit,* she heard Michael's calm and unsympathetic tones in her head. *It doesn't take long to clean up after yourself.*

With the first murmurs of growing guilt, she bolted up the stairs, basket still on her hip, and carefully stacked the towels into the hall closet. She closed the door and put the basket in her own bedroom closet.

A few items of clothing littered the floor of her room. Like the unwashed evidence of a wasted day, the garments seemed to wait between her and her piano. Dropping her shoulders with defeat to her own guilt, Jennifer quickly stepped back into her room and scooped up the clothes, tossing them into the basket. She walked backwards towards the door then hesitated. Her blue cotton dress, worn for only a few hours for dinner with Michael last evening, was still draped across her chair. She hurriedly placed it on its hanger, straightened it, then straightened it again with a few slides of her hand to ensure the fabric was unwrinkled.

She stepped back now, surveying the room before pulling the sheets back over her bed and straightening the white pillows. Too many pillows, she reminded herself. Then the reply came like an echo: too big a bed, the pillows make it less lonely.

Stepping backwards to the door for the third time, she bent down to pick up a loose white thread that stood out on the dark green carpet. Forward again, to pick up her oversized t-shirt and track pants that were bundled and curled at the foot of her bed like a faithful sleeping dog. She stuffed them under a pillow, straightened the sheet once more and backed away. It looked fine. Everything looked fine, she told herself, before she stepped back into the hall.

What she wore now, faded jeans, white socks, a dark t-shirt, felt much more her style than any of the dresses Michael preferred her to wear.

At the top of the stairs, she paused to look across the vineyard towards the small apple orchard, where much of the day's activity seemed to be centred. She did not tremble this time. After avoiding it all day, she already knew what had happened. There was only one explanation—they had found Anna's body somewhere in the river.

Now, as she peered out between the slats of blinds at the top of the stairwell, she wished she could see at least a part of the river from here. Then, as the memories of her dream began to emerge and her hands felt, just for an instant, that icy blackness, she was thankful that she could not see the water. And she realized something else: even as she played, a portion of her mind had been playing out tragic scenes. Glimpses of sorrow and death faded in and out with every chord. It was odd how she thought the music could help her hide, when it was the music itself that evoked the truth.

Descending the stairs, Jennifer approached her piano once again. It was nearly four o'clock. She sat down and took a breath, pleased that she had at least another hour to play before it was time to think about dinner. She looked at the keys, which were waiting, teasingly, for her fingers.

Thoughts of Anna and the river, Michael, the police, and what they were doing at the back of the property began to run in and out of her mind as she played. She closed her eyes, trying to connect to that part of herself beginning to stir, trying to feel through her heart to discover what was trying to emerge. It felt warm and wonderful, dark and terrifying, bound to her heart, her dreams and her nightmares.

She opened her eyes and began to caress her beloved keys and, as if of their own volition, her fingers began to play Chopin's Waltz in A flat, Opus Sixty-Nine. She never played it well, but it called to her. It was the piece that her fingers were most likely to travel to when left on their own. Jennifer continued to play while the sun descended and the planets became visible to anyone who might be listening to her music from the forgotten open window behind her arched back.

Although she seldom caught a glimpse of him when she looked out the window, she knew there was one man out there who could sometimes hear her play. For that reason, she played so much more often then she ever had before. In her heart, every song she played was dedicated to him.

She played long after the shadows around her had lengthened to encompass the entire room, until she heard her husband's familiar footsteps at the kitchen door. She quickly sat up and went into the next room to meet him with the smile he expected. It was a smile, she reminded herself, that for all he had done for her, he most probably deserved.

Jennifer watched with dismay from the edge of the living room as Michael, Vic, and Anthony all filed into the kitchen and pulled out chairs at the kitchen table.

"Some dinner, please, Ginny," Michael called to her over his shoulder. "We all missed lunch today."

She wiped her hands on her jeans and put on a smile as she entered the kitchen. Jennifer gritted her teeth each time he said her name. He used to call her "Jennifer" until they were married. Then he had begun calling her Jenny, for short. And then, when her drinking started to get out of hand again, he had revised it by calling her Ginny. It started out as a joke, but the name had stuck. He used it exclusively now and insisted to everyone that was the name she preferred, whether Jennifer liked it or not.

"I hadn't planned—" she began. "I had pasta salad prepared."

"That's fine," Michael said.

"But I don't think there's enough for all of you. Would sandwiches be okay with the salad on the side?"

"Sandwiches are fine," said Michael.

"And some coffee," said Anthony Voracci with a wink.

Michael's father could never seem to look at her without taking a moment to look her up and down. Regardless of what she was wearing, she always felt underdressed in front of him. It made her feel dirty.

Lately, every time she saw him, she saw more and more similarities between Michael and his father. They had the same long nose, the same cheeks and the same receding chin. They had even had the same haircut for the last year, cut long, combed high, and she could not remember which of them had started the new style, the father or the son. Anthony's hair was all silver now, whereas Michael's was only starting to become grey. And he was certainly in better shape than Michael, with broader shoulders and not a sign of a pot belly, but other than that, Michael was looking more and more like his father every day.

Poor Vic was at least fifty pounds overweight, and except for his weak chin, had not inherited any of his father's physical characteristics, or his father's mental acuity. She would catch Vic staring at her breasts, or at her butt when he could, but she only felt sorry for him. He did not have the predatory nature that his father and brother had in abundance. Vic was a weak man.

As she prepared their dinner, none of them spoke about the events of the morning, and Jennifer didn't ask about the police cruiser or the other vehicles that had passed by the house. No one offered to bring her into the conversation. As Jennifer pulled the bread from the cupboard and began making sandwiches, the three men discussed Michael's odds at the upcoming wine contests and his plans for a wine show in Michigan. Anthony and Michael chuckled with each other; Vic did not say much at all. Compared to his father and brother, he looked grim, shaken. His light-blue golf shirt was stained dark below his armpits; his eyes were red. Despite his tan, he looked pale. He would not look Jennifer in the eye, and when she walked by, he did not make a point of staring at her breasts, as he usually did.

Across from Vic, there was the empty chair, where none of the men ever sat. Antonio's chair. He had passed away almost three years ago. Jennifer missed Antonio. Of all Michael's family, it was only his grandfather that Jennifer had ever bonded with. He had been the heart and soul of the family. Widowed for five years, he had given Michael and Jennifer his home as a wedding present. He had planned to move himself into a retirement home, but Jennifer had insisted he stay with them. He had lived with them for two years before he too had fallen ill. She missed him a lot.

"Busy day?" Jennifer asked.

"A bit," said Michael.

"Are you in town long?" she asked Vic.

"Just for the rest of the day," Michael answered for his brother. Vic didn't look up. "He's got to be heading back to Toronto."

"Does she know?" she heard Vic whisper. Then, "You should tell her."

Jennifer turned to her husband and saw a momentary uncertainty pass across his face. When his eyes met hers, it was gone.

"She already knows," he said.

"It's Anna," she said.

"Yes," said her husband. His father and brother stared at their plates.

"They found her," she said.

"She's dead."

"But how…"

60

"Don't worry yourself with that," he said. "Dead is dead."

"But she eloped…"

"She's gone, Ginny. You've been trying to convince me for days that she died. And I'm sorry to say you were right all along."

"But someone killed her!"

"I didn't say that."

"But it's true. Do they know who did it?"

"Ginny."

His practiced stern tone silenced her. Jennifer pulled the tea towel between her fists, fighting back the tears. She watched the men slowly returned their forks to their plates, tapping steady rhythms on the floral stoneware. The silence of the kitchen resonated with the sounds of their chewing, dry swallows of food, and slow measured breaths.

Jennifer retreated to the living room. She sat at the piano bench for a half hour, listening to the murmur of their words until she heard the men rise from the table, followed by the sound of the screen door gently closing by the effect of Michael's firm hand.

Jennifer went to the window, looking towards the loading dock, hoping in vain to catch a sight of Ben. As tears filled her eyes, running down her face, she knew only one thing now. She needed Ben to finally take her away from here.

Five

Scotty Doherty wore two silver hoops on his left ear, eight on his right, and long pork chop side burns. On his left shoulder he had a tattoo of a hawk, but only the talons were visible beneath the sleeve of his beige t-shirt. On his right arm he had a tattooed ring of barbed wire.

Scotty kicked down on the brake of his faded blue Camry and cranked his steering wheel around as the tires dug into the loose gravel, stopping six feet in front of Ben Taylor. He turned to face Taylor and folded both arms on the ledge of his open window.

"Hey!" he called to Taylor. "Where you been all day?"

Taylor stopped, thumbs in his front pockets, and raised his eyebrows quizzically.

"Ohhh, I'm just yankin' ya," said Scotty. "Where you off to, all on your lonesome?"

"Off to get some dinner," Taylor said with unconcealed irritation. He was annoyed that the day had ended so early. It was only seven o'clock. Eleven hours without a cigarette had slit open and exposed every nerve.

"Straight up. Wanna ride?"

Taylor walked behind the Camry and, once Scotty remembered to unlock it, opened the passenger door. Metal ground against metal near the hinges as he forced the door closed.

"Where were you today?" Taylor asked.

"Hiding from that pig," Scotty laughed. He pursed his lips and added needlessly, "Caines really busts my ass."

Taylor buckled up and rolled down the window. Scotty spun his steering wheel round and kicked down on the gas pedal, wheels pulling up gravel. Once he passed the Voracci house and approached the end of the laneway, Scotty turned up the radio. Tom Petty was "Running Down a Dream" at top volume.

The old Camry had seen better days. Specks of rust elbowed their way through the dust on the blue paint. Exhaust escaped through the holes in the muffler. Inside, the car smelled of tobacco, grease and sweat. Crumpled Burger King bags and empty cans of Coke littered the passenger's side of the floor. A faded paper pine tree swung impotently from the rearview mirror. Yet the black vinyl seats, dashboard and steering wheel had been treated with Armor All religiously once a month for the last two years. This was Scotty's home and his only refuge through the busy season. It was the place he lived, ate and slept when he worked sixteen to eighteen hours a day from June to October.

"That fat slob Caines really screwed up my day," Scotty said as he approached the highway. He turned the wheel and directed the car towards town. "I'll tell ya, I thought I'd never get out of there."

"Could be worse." Taylor slid back in his seat and looked across through the driver's side window at the steady line of trees bordering the road.

"Oh, yeah!" Scotty turned his head to Taylor with a sudden grim realization. "Did you hear they found Anna? Just fucking awful."

"I know."

"I found out just after lunch. Maria was crying at the picnic table and told me. Just awful. When did you find out?"

"When Juan and I found her this morning."

"This morning?" Scotty did a double-take, trying to keep his eyes on the road. "That was you? I thought it was Juan and Michael

Voracci. That's fucking awful. I'm so glad I wasn't there." He whistled, loud and piercing. "I don't even want to imagine!"

Scotty pushed in his cigarette lighter and pulled a cigarette from the pack between them. Taylor was craving a cigarette, but the smoke was still nauseating. His increasing irritability from the nicotine withdrawal combined with the smell of the smoke made his stomach turn. He clenched his fist and stared at the road ahead. A dead raccoon lay torn on the gravel shoulder.

"And you're sure you want to eat?" asked Scotty. "I don't think I could eat for a week after seeing something like that. You really saw her, right? Was it the first time? I mean, have you ever seen a dead body before?"

Taylor nodded.

"Not me," Scotty continued. "Just my grandfather and my mom's aunt. Those were both in a funeral home, and that was bad enough. I'll tell ya, I don't want to go near that end of the orchard ever again. I don't like cops, but that's not why." He wiped his forehead with his bare forearm. "That's where she died, ya know? I couldn't ever go around there again. Not even if you paid me."

"Why not?" Taylor asked, already suspecting the reason.

"It's just, I don't know…all tainted now."

"Do you believe in ghosts?"

"Nope." Scotty, annoyed by the force of the wind in the car now, cranked the window closed, his arm vigorously pumping the handle to move the stiff gears. "Never seen one. Never want to."

Beck's Tavern was on the edge of Andover, about three miles southeast from Tanglewood Vineyards. Any traces of the farms that had dominated the area here when Taylor was a child had all but vanished in a ten-year frenzy of suburban building. Occasionally the skeletons of a couple of abandoned barns, or the remnants of split rail fences could still be seen from the highway in the midst of vinyl-clad split-level homes, and the maze of winding drives, streets and crescents, all enclosed by row upon row of cedar privacy fences.

The tavern was generally empty this early in the evening. The pre-dinner crowd had gone home, and the drinking crowd was still finishing dinner. With orange formica tables and vinyl chairs, it felt more like a diner than a tavern to Taylor. The seating area was the shape and size of a boxcar, but without as much character. The walls had been recently dry-walled, painted white, with beer posters tacked neatly between each of the four windows facing the parking lot. Two grey-haired farmers, dressed in green overalls, sat at the bar eating fish and chips. Scotty came here regularly, several times a week, when he had money in his pocket, enamoured as he was by Cindy, the blonde waitress.

The pair had their choice of seats and took the table closest to the door. They ordered two burgers and two beers. Cindy smiled at Ben but refused to look Scotty in the eyes. She either frowned or looked to the floor each time he grinned at her, showing his teeth.

 Scotty never realized that she refused to look at him. He averted his own eyes each time she appeared to look in his direction, but he watched her carefully when she walked away. When he noticed Taylor watching him, Scotty huffed and began to slide the salt shaker from left to right and right to left across the table in a self-conscious game of catch.

"Any idea," Taylor began, "what Caines is up to in that locked greenhouse?"

"Who knows?" replied Scotty. "Who cares?"

"Ever see anyone else in there?"

"Nah." Scotty shrugged. "Caines is the only one with keys. I think he worked out a deal to have a place to do his own gardening or something. Oh. Carl might have a key."

Taylor nodded. Carl Avery was the horticulturist and a friend of the Voracci family. He worked only a few hours each week to measure and test the use of pesticides and fertilizers. The hydroponic tomatoes were fully dependant on the chemical fertilizers pumped into them. While Abe Wagner handled most of the care for the vineyard, Carl Avery was the only one who knew how to care for the tomatoes.

"Last year," Scotty said after some thought, "you know, when they closed it off, I asked Carl what they were doing in there. He said it was just a new kind of grape. Hydroponic grapes, he said."

Taylor squinted at Scotty. "Hydroponic grapes. For wine? Was that a joke?"

Scotty shrugged and stared back without blinking.

"Soil is important for wine," said Taylor. "Hydroponics won't work."

"But you'll get more grapes," Scotty said, staring at Taylor as if he were an imbecile. "They'll be bigger too. More grapes means more wine. Isn't that a good thing?"

"No, it isn't good," said Taylor. "You want to make the fruit work to get the best taste. You don't want the vines to be full of fruit. Less fruit means better taste. Why do you think we spend so much time pulling at them? That's why some of the best wines in the world grow on the soil no one else wants."

Scotty continued to stare.

"Didn't that strike you as being a bit odd?" Taylor asked. "I think Carl was pulling your leg, kid."

"I never thought much about it," Scotty said, looking bored now. "I don't go in Michael's house. I don't go in his truck, less he asks. I don't go in Caines' greenhouse, less he asks. I just work there, y'know?"

Taylor could see this was getting too heavy for Scotty. He nodded until he was certain Scotty's thoughts had begun to wander.

"I think..." Scotty began to grin, "it's pot." He popped with a short, unexpected laugh. "That's it. They'll put hash in the wine. Like…like…Voracci Weed Wine."

"Tanglewood High Vine."

"Wonder Wine!" Scotty snorted, putting his hand over his mouth a second too late.

Scotty was still laughing as Cindy set the two plates of burgers and fries down on the table. Scotty abruptly stopped laughing as soon as he saw her. Taylor thanked her and returned her smile.

"Did the cops talk to you?" Scotty asked once she had left.

"Not really. Not yet. They will. They'll want to talk to you too, I'm sure."

"Why me?"

"They'll want to talk to everyone," Taylor said as he pulled the onions from his burger.

"Dammit." Scotty shook his head back and forth as he talked. "I really don't want to talk to them. I don't want to. I hate cops. I won't do it."

Scotty pushed his plate away, looked at it thoughtfully, pulled it back and began to pick at his fries.

"Why are you upset?" said Taylor. "Something you don't want to tell them?"

"No."

"Something you don't want them to find out?"

"Hell, no!"

Taylor stared at him thoughtfully as he bit into a fry. "You've got me curious about something," he said. "You know, as we're laughing and joking about all of these things, there's something that I'd like to know."

"What's that?"

"Is there anything else bothering you about this besides ghosts and talking to the police?" Taylor asked.

"Isn't that enough?"

"For starters," Taylor said pointedly, "what about the fact that a girl you worked with is dead?"

Scotty shook his head, holding a french fry in front of his mouth, and whispered, "I know."

"And that someone killed her."

"I know," Scotty whispered even more faintly. He did not put the fry in his mouth, but did not put it down. He held it there, poised in front of his lips, forgotten, as he stared at Taylor's eyes.

"And that it might be someone you work with?"

"What are you saying?" Scotty whispered almost inaudibly. The french fry tumbled from his fingers. "You think I had something to do with this?"

"Did you?"

"Of course not."

"I know you didn't do it. I'm sure they know it too. But something's wrong. What is it?"

"I mean..." Scotty shook his head. "I know I joked about her when she was alive. Who didn't? I mean, except you. But everybody else, y'know? It's just cuz she was so stuck up sometimes. Even when we thought she ran away. But that's just talk."

"Yes." Taylor stared at him pointedly. "Just talk. But you said something about her yesterday, Scotty. Remember what you said?"

Scotty's eyes bulged. "What? I didn't say anything about her."

Taylor nodded. "You didn't really want to get her drunk. And lure her father out of the house for a night. Or get her into the cooler for a few hours. And you didn't say anything about the old mattress in the pump-house?"

"That was just talk. That doesn't mean I'd really do it."

"Maybe. Maybe not."

"And if I thought for a second she was dead, do you really think

68

I'd talk about her like that? Sheesh!" Scotty shivered. "That just makes my skin crawl. I wouldn't say anything like that..." leaning forward and whispering now, "especially about the pump-house…" sitting back again, "if I had any idea she was dead. You know I couldn't do anything like that."

"Maybe not," Taylor conceded.

"That just proves you don't know anything about me, man," Scotty continued, speaking as fast as the words formed in his thoughts. "If you did, you'd know I wouldn't be able to hurt a fly. Do you think I'd waste my time working here and sleeping in my fucking car if I could cut it as a criminal? And if I did hurt someone, do you really think I'd stick around for even ten minutes before I blew this fucking lousy dump forever? And if I did hurt anyone, I'd take out Caines first. You know that."

Taylor smiled.

"So!" Scotty sighed with touch of triumph. "So that proves I didn't do it."

Taylor leaned forward. "Sure. Or it proves you wanted to throw everyone off the scent."

"No! That's stupid."

"Then why are you afraid of the police?"

"I just don't like cops, okay?" Scotty shook the ketchup bottle to no avail.

"But it won't be the local cops now," Taylor said. "It'll be the OPP."

"Why?"

"She was murdered," Taylor said without expression.

"But the town police handle this side of the townline…"

"So what? This is a serious crime."

"Get real. To us it's serious. To everyone else she was a Mennonite."

"She was murdered. What does being Mennonite have to do with it?" Taylor demanded. He drank some of his beer, knowing he had to

69

be patient if he was to find out why Scotty was so afraid. "I'm sure you don't want anyone to get away with this. It could be someone you work with, for all we know. Someone you drink beer with."

Scotty picked at his fries, deliberating. "Look," he said, "I don't want you thinking anything that ain't true."

Taylor sipped his beer, listening. He had no idea why Scotty cared about Taylor's opinion of him, but he was not going to question that now.

"I owe some money," Scotty continued, whispering, leaning close to the table. "That's all it is. It's my old lady. She put the cops on me a while back. She doesn't know where I am. I'm supposed to pay her five hundred a month for my kid. But she never let me see him, and I didn't have the money. So she put the cops on me. She's living with her parents in Brampton now. I can't afford to pay her that kinda cash. Not in the winter. You know what we make here. Besides, her parents have money. But she hates my guts, and I gotta hang low till she backs off. That's all."

Taylor understood that as confidential as Scotty's story sounded, it was certainly a cover for something else. He could not imagine Scotty ever having a job that required him to pay more than a hundred dollars a month in child support. Again, that didn't matter right now. At this point, Taylor only wanted to know if Scotty was hiding anything about Anna's disappearance and murder.

"It's hard enough," Taylor offered as he sipped his beer, "to take care of one person on these wages. I can't imagine taking care of a whole family."

Scotty chewed a fingernail.

"How old's your kid?" Taylor asked

"Three or four now."

"Boy or girl?"

"Girl."

"Does she have a name?"

"Of course." He sipped some beer. "Kendra."

"Kendra."

"Kendra Sue."

"Pretty name." Taylor grinned. "Do you have any pictures?"

"Not any more. I used to. But it was ruined when I fell into the septic pond last summer. It was in my wallet and it ruined my wallet." He gulped his beer. "You sound like a cop now too. What does this have to do with Anna?"

"Nothing. Just wondering if you had a picture of your little girl."

"Nope." Scotty finished the last of his fries. "Do you think it was someone we know?"

"The killer? Could be."

"That sounds so weird," said Scotty.

"What."

"The killer. Like it's a movie or something."

"This isn't a movie."

"I know. It just sounds weird to say it out loud. It doesn't seem real." Scotty hooked his fingers as quotation marks, "'The Tanglewood Killer.'" He pretended to shiver. "I was thinking." He sat forward then looked around to ensure there was still no one within earshot. "I think it was that Mexican."

"Which Mexican?"

"What's his name. You know, that mean little guy with the switchblade. The one who hit Michael Voracci the other day…you know…Miguel!"

"Miguel has a switchblade? Are you sure it was Miguel?"

"Sure. I saw it once."

"You're talking Michael Voracci?" Taylor watched as Scotty nodded. "When did all this happen?"

"A couple days ago, remember? Oh, maybe you were in the cooler then. Voracci told him to move his boxes out of the aisle, and Miguel punched him in the head. I know. I was right there."

"You saw him hit Voracci?" Taylor asked.

"Sure. I was just coming in. I guess he was breaking down some old boxes. They were all over the floor, and Voracci slipped on one, and he got sore. I guess he yelled at him and Miguel took a swing at him. Cut his face a bit, cuz he had the box cutter still in his hand."

"He cut him?"

"Just a bit. Right here." Scotty touched his temple near the hairline. "Saw him today though. You can barely see it. He doesn't have a black eye or anything. I think he got off pretty lucky. Miguel is a crazy fuck. Everybody knows that."

"He seems quiet to me," said Taylor.

"Sure. Ever see him smile?"

"Not really."

"There you go. I think he did a lot of drugs. His eyes were always red and glassy, y'know?"

"Yes. I noticed that."

"I think he's an illegal too. Voracci said he was going to call the cops, but I don't think he ever did. He can't tell the cops he used an illegal, y'know."

"I guess not." Taylor had finished with his burger. The bun was hard, and the meat was burnt on one end. He pushed his plate to the side.

"The cops should find him, though—especially with this thing with Anna. I don't think Miguel is his real name though. The migrant workers, the Mexicans, all called him something else, I think."

"Maybe you should tell the cops."

"Why me?"

"Like you said, Voracci may not want them to know about

Miguel. And if you think he had something to do with Anna, you have to tell the police."

"Maybe. I don't want to get Voracci in trouble though," Scotty said quietly as the waitress came to pick up their plates. He smiled at her again, but she did not seem to notice.

Scotty watched her black skirt sway as she walked away.

"She's cute," Taylor said.

"She's hot. I'd love to take her out some night."

"Why don't you ask her?"

Scotty guffawed. "Are you kidding me? She wouldn't have anything to do with us. We're farmhands."

"Come on, she's a waitress. She's cute. Kind of grumpy, but that might just be at work. Give it a shot."

"No way," said Scotty.

When the waitress returned, writing out their bill, Taylor pretended to notice her name tag for the first time. "Nice meal, Cindy."

"I'm glad you like it," she said with a flirtatious smile.

"You're not Beck's daughter, are you?"

"Nope."

"That's good." He sat back, crossed his arms and grinned at her. "I've been wanting to ask you something since the first time we met a couple weeks ago."

Cindy seemed to be bracing herself, suddenly nervous. "What's that?"

"Who the hell is this Beck guy, anyway?"

"Becky," she grinned. "The owner's daughter."

"Is that her nickname, or did someone lose the 'Y' on the sign?" asked Scotty.

"That's her name," she replied. Then she shrugged and picked up their plates.

Taylor nodded. "Anyway, that's real sweet. How old is she?"

"Now? Probably in her sixties. This place has been here a long time…sir."

Taylor grinned. "Are you open for the long weekend?

"Canada Day? Yes."

"But they're giving you the day off, right?"

She held their plates on a tray on the counter behind her and began to add up their bills. "Nah, I'll be working all day."

"Do they pay you overtime for that?"

"Yeah, they are…in a way. I get all of Saturday and Sunday off."

"Going out with your boyfriend?"

She smiled again, anticipating the direction of the conversation. "Nah. I broke up with him after Christmas."

"Then maybe you could go out with me…or my friend here," Taylor continued.

Scotty glowed.

"That depends," she said, ignoring Scotty. "What did you have in mind?"

"How about a movie?"

"What kinda movie?"

"A bad movie."

She laughed. "I'm not seeing no bad movies!"

"Bad movies are best."

"Oh yeah? How come?"

"If it's a bad movie, you won't mind me distracting you through the best parts." He beamed at her.

"I don't think so." She tore his bill from her pad and put it on the table in front of him.

Taylor picked up the bill and reached for some money. "You're absolutely right," he said. "I'll pick you up at seven. Here or at your house?"

She leaned towards him, whispering softly. "Here. Wait out front."

"That's the spirit." He winked and slid out of the booth, Scotty following his lead.

Outside, Scotty walked slowly, chewing his nail, thinking. "That was smooth," he said. "But how the hell did you do that?"

"You just have to be confident," Taylor said and waited for Scotty to get in the car and unlock the passenger door.

"I have bad luck with women," Scotty said as Taylor slid into his seat. "Besides, I don't get to meet too many good-looking women once the summer starts up. There's the waitress there, but she likes you. There's Voracci's wife, and he's got her. And there's the Mennonite girls at the winery, but I'd have to go to church…"

"Ever meet his wife?" Taylor asked.

"Whose wife?"

"Voracci's wife. What's she like?"

"Ginny?" he said. "She's pretty. Not a model. Younger than you, older than me, I'd say. Nice tits. Nice legs."

Taylor forced a smile at Scotty's attempt to describe her.

"Brown hair. Big brown eyes," Scotty continued. "Canadian, not Italian. She wears dresses and jeans, I guess. She never comes out. When she comes out, she never goes far, 'less Voracci's with her."

"But have you seen her lately?" Taylor asked.

Scotty shook his head. "Nope. She won't talk to the workers either. She comes out for the company picnic every July. Other than that she stays in the house. I think she travels a lot too. She's nice to look at, but I heard she's really stuck up. A real bitch."

"No kidding," said Taylor. "That shouldn't surprise me."

"Me neither. The pretty ones usually are."

"That's one hell of an attitude," said Taylor. "I can't imagine why you're on your own."

Scotty shrugged and made the car thunder down the darkened highway.

"You should go into town more often," Taylor shouted over the wind. "Or go to the beach. There are lots of girls there."

"Yeah, right. Those girls aren't interested in anyone like us. They're looking for college guys."

"I'm serious. Just shave, get a haircut, and you won't have a problem at all."

"That your secret, Taylor?"

Taylor shrugged. "I guess."

"Then why don't you shave?" Scotty laughed. It had been a joke.

As a reflex, Taylor touched his chin. He was surprised when his fingers felt three or four day's growth on his face. "Guess that's not my secret."

"So how did you know?"

"What?"

"That she wanted to go out with you when she said she didn't."

Taylor laughed and flashed Scotty the bill. On the top, she had written: "You're bad!" and included her phone number.

Scotty dropped his head and shoulders in surrender. "Well, I'll be damned."

Taylor laughed, and crumpling the piece of paper, let it stream out the window and into the night.

"You bastard," laughed Scotty. "I'd have called!"

"She didn't give it to you."

"So you should call!" Scotty shouted.

"Why?" asked Taylor. "I know where she works. She's at Beck's more than she's home anyway."

"Still..." Scotty began until "Highway to Hell" came on the radio, and he lost his train of thought.

"We go back to work in eight hours," said Taylor. "Just get me home."

Six

Randy Caines was not a drinker of coffee. He liked tea—black and sweet. As he pressed the back of a spoon against a bloated teabag, he watched with pointed attention as the dark brown fluid leeched into the stained saucer. He squeezed honey, thick and yellow, generously into his cup as he stirred it around. Then, as his thick fingers held the cord of the dangling teabag, he lifted the saucer, tipped it, and watched the bitter remains drizzle into his cup.

Caines ran his portion of the Tanglewood empire from an old steel school-teacher's desk in the corner of the shipping platform, just outside Michael Voracci's private office.

His desk was covered with scattered papers, crumpled Kleenex, invoices, shipping documents and a couple of twenty-year-old copies of *Swank* and *Hustler* magazines. In the centre of this were a grimy computer keyboard and a dusty monitor with an amber screen. To everyone's surprise, Caines could find any paper he needed on his desk, almost by touch. It was a mess, but it was *his* mess. He owned it.

He looked up and glared as Taylor approached him. It was nearly six a.m.

"Don't punch in," he growled, punctuating each word with a tap of his pencil on the edge of the desk.

Ben adjusted his ball cap. "Why the hell not?"

"No one is working today. You know why."

"Why?"

"Because they found Wagner's girl," Caines said with a glare. His eyes were piercing and cold—filled with hate. It was not something Taylor could take personally. He knew Caines well enough to know he would not cancel a day of work for just anything. Caines enjoyed displaying aggression on every occasion.

"I know about her," said Taylor, refusing to give her a name in Caines' presence. He doubted Caines could remember Anna's name without serious effort. "Now tell me why I'm not working today."

"The fucking cops. They're interviewing everyone today. Everyone. So no one is working."

Taylor nodded thoughtfully before sliding his time card into the punch clock. The sound of the bolt inside the clock echoed through the warehouse.

"I don't see any cops here," said Taylor without expression. "When they come to see me, I'll punch out."

Caines nodded dismissively as he sat back in his chair. "Make sure you do. I swear, you're the only guy here with a friggin' head on his shoulders."

"I'd have to agree," Taylor nodded, "seeing as we're the only two here."

Caines stood up. "You know I meant everyone here but me."

Taylor suppressed a grin.

"Now get to work."

Taylor turned away and climbed into his forklift. He hit the gas and leaned on the horn as he passed Caines' desk. Caines lifted his middle finger in the air without looking up from his paperwork.

Randy Caines took nothing personally. That the world was harsh to everyone was a lesson he had learned long ago. Most of that education had come at the hands of his father, Lenny Caines, an underemployed truck driver who had battled, with little success, addictions to alcohol, narcotics and amphetamines for most of his short hard life. Caines' decision to deal with the world in the same manner it had always dealt with his father had come several days after his father's funeral, when Caines was seventeen.

He remembered the day with the vividness of a favorite old Technicolor movie, which he played back to himself nearly every day. It was nearly lunchtime when his English teacher, Mrs. Sibley, had placed on his desk his essay with a large red F written on the cover page. Caines was furious. It had been copied word for word from a paper she had awarded a B the year before. He had been up most of the night typing the paper. In fact, he had never worked so hard on a school assignment as he had on that paper. Three hours. Fifteen pages. Word for word. Typed with two fingers at a time.

"You know my dad just died," he said as she walked away down the aisle.

"I'm sorry for that," she replied. "But it's still plagiarized. And you submitted this *before* your father passed away."

As she finished depositing papers on the desks at the end of the aisle, she turned around to find Randy Caines standing behind her, his acne-ridden face glaring at her.

He had never punched a woman before, except his sister when they were kids. His sister had been a lot younger and tougher and had always been able to brace herself for the punch. Caines could still remember how soft the woman's slender belly had been and the look of surprise on her face as his fist connected. He could vividly recall the scent of spearmint gum mixed with the pleasant odour of her perfume, her breath wafting into his face as she cried out in surprise and pain. The sound of her fingers sliding across the formica desk as she tried to keep her balance. The soft thud of her shoulder striking the tile floor. The sight of her bare legs as the green dress rode up her thighs. It was probably a good thing he'd held back, he later decided, or he might have killed the bitch.

He had been arrested outside his house that afternoon when

he'd returned home, but the charges were dropped within hours. He was expelled. Randy Caines would never have to take shit from anyone ever again.

The following afternoon, he'd followed the railroad tracks to a small ravine, climbed down the slope and sat down near the creek. There, while smoking Marlboros and drinking from a half-empty bottle of Jack Daniels his father had left behind, he charted a new direction for his life. It was obvious that he was not a scholar. He possessed no talents; he was not an athlete; he possessed no skills or trades. So he decided to enlist in the armed forces and in the end he spent four years with the military. He served in Cyprus and Rwanda but spent most of his time in Canada, on base at Trenton and Petawawa. When he left the military with no more than his corporal stripes, a little more weight, and two tattoos, Caines found himself in the same position he had been in before he'd enlisted. Like the slow-moving freight train that rumbled above his head, he decided to make use of the one thing he had in common with that train, honed by his time in the army: fearless brute force.

When Caines was on track, there was no stopping him. His mother had called it determination, but Caines preferred to call it what it was: he was bullheaded. He always did what it took to get the job done. It didn't matter what the job was. Like a freight train, all he had to do was pick a direction and keep moving.

With his stint in the military behind him, Caines set out to find himself a career. He responded to the first Help Wanted sign he saw, on the side of County Road 22, and began working at Tanglewood Vineyards the next morning.

At the time, Michael Voracci was the General Manager of his father's company and decided to give the kid a chance. Although he was gruff and hostile, Randy Caines also proved to be a viciously hard worker who never seemed to want to take a break. He nearly always worked through lunch and worked every overtime hour that was asked of him, averaging well over a hundred hours a week during the busy season.

Within a few seasons, when Michael Voracci became the sole owner of Tanglewood Vineyards, Caines had become entrenched in the daily operations. He knew every company secret and had a hand in engineering at least three quarters of the secrets himself, including the ones even Michael Voracci knew nothing about. He was eventually promoted to warehouse manager, where his ruthless lack of concern made him the man to be holding the bullwhip. He could get more work out of fewer people for less money than the operation had ever known. Most of the loyal employees quit when he took the reins, but new immigrant workers from Mexico were easy to find and would put up with more demands for less money. Caines was in charge of the hiring and firing of the work crews. When men came in to apply, he never read the job application form. When he saw the desperation he was looking for in someone's eyes, they were hired without hesitation.

What was most important to Caines was that, as long as he produced the needed results, he had a free hand to do as he pleased. While the vineyard and winery were directed and supervised by Abe Wagner, the daily operations of the warehouse and the new greenhouses were run by Randy Caines.

This morning, Caines worked at his desk until the girls who ran the packing machine began to file in shortly before nine o'clock. There were whispers and drawn faces. Juan was yawning beside the loader. Taylor and Scotty had placed several pallets of tomatoes beside Juan, ready to be dumped into the sorting line. Caines had toyed with the idea of shutting down production for the day. He had no intention of letting everyone talk to the police today on company time, but he also had a lot of tomatoes ready to be sorted and put in the cooler. When the cops arrived, he would let the workers eat their lunch while they gave their statements. He figured they would be grateful enough not to miss the day of work, so this would be a fair compromise.

At two minutes to nine. Caines set down his pen and, with mug of cold tea in hand, approached the girls.

"I'm sorry for your loss," said Caines. "I know she was friends with a lot of you. But we have work to do."

"When is the funeral going to be, Mr. Caines?" asked one of the girls.

"How would I know? I'm not her daddy."

Turning away, Caines shook his head, sounded the air horn and pressed the green button that fired up the line. He grinned as he watched red and green tomatoes shake and bounce firm as young breasts down the line and straight into the company ledgers. This was shaping up to be a good day after all.

Then he turned around and saw a man standing on the loading dock, talking to the driver whose truck had just been loaded with wine and was due in Cleveland before the end of the day.

"Stevie, you get that fuckin' truck out of here! You can stand around with your thumb up your ass when you get to Cleveland!"

The driver shrugged and held his open palms in the air.

The man, who had been leaning against the wall beside the sign that warned "Guard Dogs on Duty Nightly", pushed away from the wall and walked casually towards the production line where Caines stood. He was middle-aged, dressed in a dark blue suit. His shirt collar was open and his blue striped tie pulled away from his throat. Because he had a dark complexion and thick, wavy black hair, for a moment Caines considered that he might be Italian, and hence a relative of the Voraccis. But as he approached, Caines saw that the man's eyes were grey. He decided he looked more Arabic than

Italian. There was no doubt he was a cop. Shit.

"Are you Randall Caines?" the man asked.

"That's right." Caines pointed a meaty finger at the man standing in the middle of his shipping zone. "Now who the fuck are you?"

"Inspector Walter Kumar. Ontario Provincial Police." The man extended his open wallet, briefly exposing his badge for Caines to see.

Caines turned away. He did not like cops. Not in the slightest.

"You want to talk to Ben Taylor and Juan Reger," he said. "I'll get them here for you toot-sweet."

The inspector stood firm. "I'm here to talk to you."

"I'm too busy right now. You'll have to come back later."

Caines began to turn away, but Kumar stepped forward, quickly closing in on him. Caines looked up at him, surprised the cop had blocked his path so quickly.

"You are going to talk to me now," said Inspector Kumar. "And then you are going to give me a list of every person who has worked at these facilities, legal or otherwise, for the last five years, starting with everyone who has worked here in the last three months. Do you understand?"

"Five years? What the hell are you investigating? She's only been gone a couple weeks."

"That's just for starters, Mr. Caines. This is not open for debate."

Caines was taken aback. This cop was not playing around. He wondered if someone had warned him about Caines the hardass. He was secretly impressed.

"Yeah?" was the best he could muster before he took a gulp of his tea.

"Do you understand?" the cop repeated.

"I don't have time for that kinda bullshit paperwork. I have perishables that have to ship by the end of the day. Give me a break, will ya?"

The inspector nodded, expecting this reply, it seemed. "In that case, you'll need to get me that list now. Nothing enters or leaves these facilities until I get it. After I get it, that truck will be searched thoroughly before it is permitted to leave. And then I am going to speak to you and every person here today—on your time, not theirs—about what happened, where they were, and who they have been with in the last thirty days. And if you have a problem with that, then we will start playing hardball. Do you understand me?"

"No shit," said Caines. His jaw dropped, and a drop of sweet dark tea dribbled from the corner of his lips.

Inspector Kumar nodded at Caines. "No shit, indeed."

SEVEN

Ben was in no rush to speak to the police today. The nicotine craving was in full bloom now, with soft pointed petals of irritation all around him, whichever way he turned. Caines had directed the pickers to keep the day's tomato harvest short, picking only the ripest fruit, and the packing line had finished shortly after noon. Skipping lunch, Ben loaded a truck with Riesling and Chardonnay bound for Detroit then crossed the parking lot to help with the bottling.

Juan, kneeling beside the bottling machine, was refitting a tank of nitrogen when Ben arrived. The bottling line had been stopped while he worked, as the corks could not be inserted into the bottles until they were given a shot of nitrogen gas to displace the oxygen in the neck. Five Mennonite girls, in their hand-made floral dresses, were sitting on their stools, rubber gloves off, wiping the sweat from their faces and adjusting their hairnets. They were usually such happy girls, and they always seemed to be giggling and whispering to each other in German. Today they were silent. None of them looked as if she had slept last night. Anna Wagner's cousin, Therese, sat in the middle. Her eyes were red, and her face looked swollen from crying. When she looked up at Ben, he turned away. He could not meet her sorrowful eyes.

"Abe's not here today?" Ben asked as he bent down beside Juan.

"He was here for a while," the youth said as he fitted an adjustable wrench to a bolt on the valve. "He left before lunch."

"Is he coming back, or is he taking time off?"

"No idea. I'm glad he went home for a while. He's making everyone nervous."

"It's rough for him," Ben said. "He's still in shock. And the winery is more his home than his house is."

"Yeah, his home is right here over my shoulder," he said, pointing with his thumb. "Watching everything I do. But it's like he's in a daze today."

"Give him some slack," said Ben. "He's always been there for you. I seem to remember a day when you had the flu, and he let you sleep while you were still on the clock. Would someone like Caines have let you do that?"

Juan looked at the cement floor. "No."

"I heard he let you sleep on his own couch so no one would know."

"I was working hard! And I couldn't afford to take a day off."

"The point is," Ben continued, "he's a good man. And he deserves some understanding too. So have a heart."

"I do. I know. I'm sorry. Honest."

"Listen." Ben softened his tone. "I know it's hard to know what to say. Just give him some space. Try to relax around him."

Juan nodded. "That's the hard part." After several more minutes of tinkering with the valve, he stood up, suddenly grinning and pleased with himself. "Had to refit that valve," he said. "It'll work now."

Without a word, the girls slowly rose and began putting on their yellow rubber gloves.

"Time for a smoke after I fire this baby up?" Juan said.

"No," Ben answered. "I'm not smoking."

Juan shrugged. "Well, I'm having one. Where's Scotty?"

"Haven't seen him. I thought he was here with you."

"He's such a loser. I don't know why they keep him around. He doesn't do a damn thing." Juan's eyes opened wide. "Maybe he's with the cops. Did they talk to you yet?"

"Not yet," said Ben.

"There's a detective here."

"Provincial Police?" Ben asked. "An inspector?"

"The OPP, yeah. Anyway, he came here this morning, asking a ton of questions."

"Good. What did he ask you?"

"Same stuff as the other cops asked last month when she disappeared. Then he wanted to know what we saw the other morning. Didn't take very long, really. He seemed bored by the whole thing. Didn't write down a word I said, either. I don't think he really cares one way or another, y'know?"

"Maybe he didn't have to write it down if you gave him the same answers."

"Maybe. But I don't think they care. Except that it's happened here. I think they want to keep it all quiet. Keep the attention away from the vineyard. Caines wants to keep it quiet, I'm sure. Remember that guy who got chewed up by Caines' dogs? They kept that quiet."

Ben had overheard whisperings of the story, in morsels during lunch and dinner breaks, shared between those who knew. It was true that no one was supposed to talk about it. Sometime during the summer before Ben started working at Tanglewood, one of the migrant workers had been attacked by Caines' guard dogs in the warehouse. Instead of having charges pressed against Caines or Voracci, the rumour was that the police helped them get the worker deported back to Mexico. Ben considered telling Juan that murder was far more serious than a dog attack, but he could see the argument.

"No matter what you might think about the local police," Ben said. "This is the OPP now. They're not going to brush it off."

"Politics is politics. And cops are cops. I don't care who it is."

Ben stiffened, straddling a line between anger and amusement. "You think all cops are the same?"

"No. I'm sure there are lots who know what they're doing and aren't going to let themselves be pushed around. I just never heard of any around here before. You heard the story about that cop a few years ago who arrested Vic Voracci for drinking and driving?"

"No. Tell me."

"It was a long time ago. Before drinking and driving was a really big deal. He pulls over Vic and arrests him for a DWI. It's going to court. A few weeks later, he's transferred way up north. The case is dismissed. The Voraccis' pull a lot of weight."

"Don't you think they want the person responsible to go to prison?" Ben asked. "Why would they interfere with something like this?"

Juan shrugged. "I don't think they give a damn as long as it goes away. They'll take care of Anna's boyfriend themselves if they have to. You don't piss in their wine and get away with it, know what I mean?"

Ben declined to say anything. The last thing Juan needed was more fuel to be added to his conjectures. And the last thing Ben needed right now was an argument about rumours and stereotypes. He was tense enough as it was. He wanted a cigarette but refused to give in to the urge.

Juan shrugged and started up the bottling line. Two girls began feeding empty bottles onto a conveyor belt on one end, a third girl monitored the flow of wine from the barrels, while another girl ensured each bottle was properly labelled before they were cased. With marginal interest, they watched the two men talking.

Ben and Juan took turns lifting each case of wine from the conveyor belt and piling them on a pallet. The red and black

Tanglewood logos on the sides of the boxes made each side of the pallet look like a checkerboard. Ben shrink-wrapped each finished pallet and Juan moved it with a hand lift to the back of the room. With a resounding bang, Juan would let a new pallet fall to the floor beside Ben, grinning shamelessly as he startled Ben each time.

Ben bit into his anger, dropping each box a little harder, wrapping each pallet a little tighter, as he tried not to think about Anna, the police, cigarettes, or the calm with which everyone but he and Abe Wagner worked today. He glared across the machinery at the girls who used to share lunch with Anna and who now worked efficiently and without expression. Of course, he knew he was fabricating their apathy. The nicotine withdrawal, the grief and the anger were distorting everything around him. Even the white paint on the brick walls seemed too bright.

Ben clenched his jaw when the buck-toothed girl with the labels seemed to wink at him. Of course she didn't wink, he told himself. He had imagined it. He needed to get outside. He turned around. There were almost twenty pallets of wine ready to go to the warehouse.

"Time to get the forklift," he said and stepped out the side door.

The afternoon sun hit his eyes hard. The parking lot was nearly empty; Caines' pickup truck and a dusty blue Pontiac were the only two vehicles remaining. Caines had sent everyone home early before they could get their ten-hour shift. It was almost six o'clock. It seemed he had lost some sense of time as well. He jumped down from the stairs, landing hard on the gravel and savouring the momentary pain from the soles of his feet to his ankles. Any distraction was a relief. He walked quickly to the warehouse and pulled open the steel door.

The two men inside lifted their heads at the sound of the door.

Caines was standing over a large box of papers on the corner of his desk, face pale and pasty, large pit stains under the arms of his black shirt. Another man, in a dark blue suit and brown tie, was sitting in Caines' chair, his feet on the desk, showing the worn leather soles of his black brogues. Ben had never seen anyone sit in Caines' chair before.

As Ben entered the warehouse, the OPP inspector pulled his feet from the desk and spoke to Caines. His grey eyes seemed to look right through Ben as he spoke to Caines. "Who's this?"

"A worker here," Caines replied in a tone that sounded far too polite to be coming from this particular mouth. "Ben Taylor."

The inspector stood up and looked him over once with steel grey eyes. "I want to talk to you, too."

Ben extended his hand. After a moment's hesitation, Kumar accepted it. As they shook, their eyes met, and Ben realized now what was so penetrating about them. He had never seen a man with such dark features but with such light eyes. The grey was nearly luminous.

"Ben Taylor," said Ben.

"Inspector Walter Kumar. Ontario Provincial Police."

"You're here about Anna?"

"Yes. I'm the lead investigator in this case."

Inspector Kumar picked up his notebook from the table and leafed back a couple pages. In contrast to Juan's insistence that the inspector had not made any notes, from the looks of it, this had been a busy day. "Benjamin Taylor. You were at the pump-house yesterday morning when the local police arrived. I do want to talk to you." He looked at his watch, then looked at the box of papers. "Mr. Caines, I'd like to pick up these papers first thing in the morning. Is six a.m. too early for you?"

"No, sir," said Caines.

The word "sir" was not one Ben could have imagined coming

from the mouth of Randy Caines. Ben smiled with impunity, and Caines, spotting the grin, glared at him.

Inspector Kumar led Ben up the steps to Michael Voracci's office and closed the door behind them.

"Have a seat."

Ben had rarely been in Michael's office. It was like stepping into a world that had nothing to do with the day-to-day life of Tanglewood. The rough pine stairs and the cement floor outside his office were a sharp contrast to the hardwood and Persian rug in here. A large oak desk occupied the centre of the room; behind, a bay window had been fashioned to overlook the vineyard. The window reminded Ben of the captain's quarters in an ancient galleon. A brass bell rested on the corner of the large desk, and the sextant mounted on the wall made it obvious that Michael wanted to play on that theme. The rich cream walls were adorned with framed pictures from the covers of magazines such as *Food & Wine* and *Connoisseur* that featured either Tanglewood Vineyards or the Voraccis. More than a dozen portrait photographs lined the wall to the right with inscriptions to either Michael or his father, Anthony. Ben did not recognize a single face.

A television set occupied the facing wall with a cabinet featuring at least fifty bottles of Tanglewood Vineyard wines. A reproduction of an antique map detailing the Talbot Trail had been hung behind the desk, illustrating the trail that ran from the Niagara Peninsula to the Detroit River, placing what would later be Tanglewood Vineyard in the centre of this map.

Unlike Caines' desk in the warehouse below, there was no sign of paperwork here, not even an in-basket or a computer monitor. Other than a pad of paper on the tooled leather inset, a yellow pen, and an antique brass bell on the corner, the desk was bare.

Inspector Kumar left the high-back leather chair where it was and pulled two smaller chairs towards the large desk, facing them at angles across the front corner.

"Sit down," he said, dropping his notebook onto the desk and taking the chair on the side near the window.

Ben eased himself into the second chair. "I've never seen anyone handle Caines like that."

"I know his kind," Kumar replied.

"I liked it," Ben grinned. "I liked it a lot."

Inspector Kumar seemed to relax. He leaned back, crossing his ankles under the chair.

"Mind if I ask you a question, Inspector?"

"Shoot."

"Why did you come here today?"

"What do you mean?"

"Anna's body was found yesterday morning. Where the hell were you yesterday?"

Kumar raised his chin and inhaled deeply. He rubbed his face with both hands as he exhaled deeply with frustration.

"I got here as soon as I heard about it. The coroner notified us when he received the body yesterday, late afternoon."

"McGrath didn't call you earlier?"

"I can't comment on that. I can only tell you I came here as soon as I was notified of the case. As for the delay…well…other authorities will be dealing with that."

Ben nodded, thinking this through, before he replied. "So everyone here was right. It would take a lot of gall for a town cop to interfere with a murder investigation. He would have to be either highly inept, or highly motivated, to screw around with a murder investigation."

"Do you have any other questions, Mr. Taylor? Because I have some questions for you."

"Certainly. Go ahead."

"How long have you worked at the vineyard?"

"Eight months."

"Let's get to it, shall we? Tell me everything that happened yesterday morning."

Ben related the details, from the moment he heard that the pumphouse had burned, through his discovery of Anna's body inside, to the arrival of the local police and Abe Wagner's arrival.

"Where were you two nights before?"

"The night of the fire?"

"Yes."

"I worked until eight o'clock that night. Then I played cards with Scotty in the warehouse for an hour or so. Then I went home."

"Where is home?"

"I live at the Innes Road Motel. It's a ten minute walk from here if you cut through the vineyard."

"Past the structure where Anna Wagner was found?"

"No. That's the other side of the vineyard, close to the orchard."

Inspector Kumar leaned forward, elbows on the desk. Ben realized he had not recorded a word in his notebook. "What did you do for the rest of the night?"

Ben continued to look around the room as they spoke. This office gave him no sense of Michael Voracci, aside from the fact that he was the company president. There were no personal items here at all. No photographs of his wife or brothers, no trace of his father or grandfather, not even an ashtray on the desk.

"I watched the storm approach from the doorway," Ben said. "When it started raining, I went to bed."

"What else did you do?"

"That's it. I took a shower when I got home."

"No television?"

"Not that night."

"Did you notice anything unusual that night? Anyone you never noticed before? Any changes in anyone's normal routine?"

"No."

"What about the next day?"

"I worked on the forklift. Helped with the bottling. Took out some trash."

"Did you notice anything unusual? Details that might not seem important to you often help us put together the pieces we need to uncover just what the hell happened."

"I didn't see anything. I heard one of the pickers took a swing at Michael that morning and was fired. But I didn't see it."

"I heard about that. Anything else?"

"Nothing."

Inspector Kumar pulled a black pen from his jacket pocket and tapped it on the desktop, pursing his lips in consideration for a half minute. "Do you find it odd that a young girl could be kidnapped and held against her will right under your nose without you noticing anything unusual?"

"Is that what happened?" Ben asked.

"You must have walked right by her a few times a day. You didn't hear anything? Didn't see anything? Not even a scream in the distance you might have later written off and ignored?"

Ben stiffened and pushed back his chair an inch. "It makes me sick to think she might have been here all this time. I've thought about that a lot. The police were convinced she ran away. I assumed that's what had happened. But still, I should have noticed something. Anything. But I didn't."

"It's not your fault," Kumar said. "We don't really know how long she was there. Or how long she was alive."

"She wasn't dead long."

"How do you know that?"

"I saw her. I saw her face. I saw her skin. I saw her. She hadn't been burned that badly. She seemed to have been dead only a day or two at the most."

Ben stood up walked to the window, looking down at the vineyard through the slats of the wooden blinds. "I notice you haven't asked to look at my shoes," he said.

Inspector Kumar frowned. "No."

"I assume then that the local police didn't leave you much to work with. You know I was at the scene. But you've not tried to separate my footprints from anyone else's at the crime scene."

"I'll have the autopsy report tomorrow," Kumar said. "We have pictures…"

"For what it's worth, I suggested they should be careful with the crime scene," Ben said. "They didn't think it warranted too much care. The local police, I mean."

Kumar said nothing. He picked up his black notebook and read through a few pages. He tapped his pen on the edge of the desktop as he read. "You seem to have a head on your shoulders, Taylor. Why do you work here?"

"Because they hired me."

"No. I mean, why this job?"

"I'd say it had to be the chance to travel as well as the great retirement benefits." Ben sat down, leaned back and stretched his legs out, arms folded. "I needed a job. So I came here."

"What did you do before?"

"Similar work."

Inspector Kumar watched him without expression. "Do you have a record, Taylor? Have you been in prison?"

"Not yet."

"Have you been charged?"

"No."

"Have you been arrested?"

"No." Ben gritted his teeth. His irritation was growing. If he had a cigarette, he would have lit it now.

"Did you kill Anna Wagner?"

"No."

"You were the first to find her body?"

"Yes."

"Why didn't you call the police right away?"

"Juan was with me. I sent him for the police. I stayed there to make sure no one interfered with the crime scene until they got there."

"McGrath says it was Michael Voracci who discovered her body."

"Voracci likes to be the centre of attention. McGrath, I imagine, is eager to please the Voraccis."

"You don't like being the centre of attention?"

"Not very often."

"Did you tell the Andover Police that you went inside the pump-house?"

"Yes. I told McGrath exactly what I found. We smelled that something had been burned besides tools and lumber. We cleared out some of the debris. I went in. Then Juan looked through the door. I sent Juan to call for help. Then Voracci went inside. Then your guys... the local police, I mean. I kept an eye on things. I don't think anyone touched anything until the local police did. The Chief did everything but put her in a wheelbarrow and cart her off."

"Actually, he did. They removed her body an hour after they arrived."

"Unbelievable." Ben shook his head. "At least they took some snapshots. Hope when they're developed, they're not all thumbs."

He paused, uncertain how to handle this moment, though he was certain this was the right time to tell Kumar the truth. The inspector was obviously a good cop. His frustration with the local police was obvious. He wanted to solve this case, and he was not going to let the Voracci's influence, Randy Caines' belligerence, or Chief McGrath's incompetence stand in his way. Ben reached into his wallet and pulled out a white, dog-eared card from behind his driver's license.

"Here," he said. "Please call Bob. I can't discuss it. But he'll vouch for me."

Kumar stared at the card with obvious disinterest, unwilling to take it yet. "What do you mean you can't discuss it?"

"I'm not allowed to discuss it. Not with anyone. Including you, I'm afraid."

"I don't understand."

"Just give him a call, please."

Kumar took the card. "Robert Krall. Assistant Commissioner. Federal and International Operations. RCMP. Hmmm. So you *do* have a history."

"History, yes. But not a record. I used to work for him."

"What? You were a Mountie?"

"Yes. I've been temporarily off duty for the last nine months. But that's all I can say."

"You're not undercover, are you?"

"Not at all. I'm not on active duty."

The inspector frowned. "Don't screw around with me, Taylor. If you have something to tell me, you'd better tell me now."

"This has nothing to do with your investigation," said Ben. "Krall will vouch for me. Even if I could tell you, you'll need to call him anyway."

Ben looked away towards the window. From his position, he could see only a field of blue. Kumar leaned forward, about to press for the details but he must have read the expression in Ben's.

"Whatever it is, it can't be good," said Kumar. "I'll call him."

"Thanks for that," said Ben. "If there is anything else I can tell you, I will."

"Yes, there is. Who killed Anna Wagner?"

"That I *don't* know."

"How well do you know David Quiring?" asked Kumar.

"Not well at all."

"What do you know of him?"

"He was Anna's boyfriend. He works for a trucking company out of Chatham. I don't know which one. I spoke to him a few times. He isn't much of a talker. He's around twenty years old. Drives a truck. Spends a lot of time on the road."

"So you know where he was that night?"

"No."

"So, if I told you he was missing, would you have any idea where to find him?"

"None at all." Ben thought for a moment. "I'd look for him around here. When is the funeral?"

"Probably in a few days. Do you know Miguel Gonzalez?"

"I heard he's the one who took a swing at Michael Voracci. I know him to see him. Not a popular man. I've heard he was dangerous."

"We're looking for him too. Let me know if you hear anything about him or the boyfriend."

"Do you think it was the boyfriend? Quiring?" Ben looked at Kumar searchingly. "You think he had a hand in this?"

Kumar nodded. "I don't know. I want to talk to him. But I also want to talk to every other able-bodied man who knew her, knew of her, drove, walked, paddled or flew by that pump-house." He seemed to drift off in thought.

"Do you think it was Quiring?"

"Hard to tell," Kumar replied. "For now, we don't really know—I don't know. I'll know more when I get the autopsy report."

"I did try to warn McGrath..."

Kumar rose from his chair, tapping his closed notebook on the desk. "When they said, 'keep it simple, stupid', McGrath knew he had better keep it simple."

"How well do you know McGrath?" Ben asked.

"Not well." Kumar pursed his lips and looked at the floor.

"I'd say he's your biggest handicap. He really trampled the crime scene."

"I know." Kumar handed over his own business card. "But that's between you and me."

"As long as you know it was him. I didn't touch a thing."

"Thanks for telling me who you are."

"You'd have found out anyway if you ran a check on me."

"True enough. But I still appreciate it. You know to stick around. I'll be in touch."

"I'm not going anywhere," said Ben.

Downstairs, the warehouse was empty. Caines had left, and most of the lights were shut off. Ben saw the inspector to the door of the shipping dock before hooking up the electric forklift to the recharger and locking up. He didn't know if Caines would be returning or not, but he had to assume he would be. He usually came in later to let the guard dogs out to roam in the greenhouses.

Outside, the sun had slipped behind the line of trees in the hedgerow beside the warehouse. Ben could hear cars rushing by on the highway a half-mile to the east. He took a deep breath of the cool evening air. The breeze was refreshing, but his nerves were raw, and he was very aware of his hands and arms as he walked. His muscles itched.

A raven squawked loudly from the hedgerow behind him. As he cut across the orchards toward the room he called home, the breeze picked up, getting stronger and shifting direction from north to west then back again.

EIGHT

That same morning, Jennifer Voracci emptied the dishwasher as her husband ate his regular weekday breakfast: two fried eggs over easy, bacon, crispy and dark brown, and two slices of lightly toasted white bread with butter on both sides.

Michael had come home late the previous night and had gone to his room and to bed, while Jennifer sat in the living room pretending to watch TV. This morning, before sitting down for breakfast, he had kissed her cheek and wished her a good morning. He said nothing about the discovery of Anna's body yesterday morning, or anything about the police who had come and gone and went yesterday. Not a word was spoken of the coroner's van that had passed within a few yards, slowly, solemnly past her window. Before she could ask about Anna's death, before her mouth could open to utter the words, he had shot her a look, then looked at his watch.

"You should take your pill," he said softly, rubbing his eyes rather than looking at her. "It's getting late."

"But I'm not tired…" she began.

"I know," he replied. "That's because you didn't take your pill yet."

She had gone upstairs, disappointed with herself for letting him intercept the issue so easily. It was because, she decided this morning, she really preferred not to know what had happened to Anna. Not yet, at least. It was just as well for Michael's sake that she did not ask him about it. Anna's death was troubling him too. She could see the heaviness in his face, in the tightness of his mouth and the darkness around his eyes.

After he finished his breakfast, Michael wiped his mouth with a paper napkin, pushed his chair back from the table and walked to the door.

"I'll be back in a few hours," he said without turning. "For lunch, Ginny."

Jennifer listened as he closed the door quietly behind him. The coffee swirled down the sink as she listened to the door of his pick-up open then softly close. She listened to the engine start and, through the sheer drapes of the kitchen window, she watched him drive to his morning tee-off at the Pines. She went upstairs to the window, hoping to catch a glimpse of Ben. He was not to be seen. After twenty minutes, Jennifer returned her thoughts to the dishes and her other daily chores.

The first hour of the morning was always the hardest. Nights were difficult too—coping with the loneliness—but the nights were always softened by the inevitable need to sleep. The mornings were much harder. Once her eyes were open, it was all there in front of her to deal with: the worry, the fear, the pain and regret.

The continual, repetitious dreams of the river had returned again last night. This time, however, the crow, which had always been dead and floating in the water, had come alive and was much larger than before. It had been perched in the treetop above her, looking down and calling loudly to her. And in that dream she was certain that the girl she was looking for was Anna Wagner.

Jennifer poured herself a coffee and sat down at the piano. Fingers to keys, she soon lost herself in the touch of the ivory, the feel of the wires beneath the keys, the sensations of Bach's mechanical precision working their way through her hands and into the air all around her. Each moment evolved into hours through the music.

She paused only to empty her cold coffee into the kitchen sink and to eat an apple. It was not until well after five o'clock that she noticed that Michael had not returned for lunch as he had promised. She was relieved he had not come back, that he had spared her, for whatever reasons of his own, the embarrassment of suddenly hearing him step into the house and realizing that she had lost herself in her music. She played for a while longer as the sun began to dip beneath the tops of the trees and the mild summer breeze began to gain force. Looking out the window, she finally remembered the clothes she had hung out to dry before breakfast.

Quickly, before it slipped beneath her attention again, she found the laundry basket beside the couch in the living room and stepped outside, the screen door snapping shut behind her as she reached the first step from the back porch.

It had been a beautiful warm day. She could still feel the heat rising from the wooden steps as she descended to the back lawn. The overgrown lawn was much cooler on her bare feet, and she smiled as she trailed her toes through the long cool blades. The breeze passed across her cheeks and played with her long, loose hair. She looked up into the darkening clear sky, relieved that there was no sign of rain tonight.

One by one, she began to pull down the sheets and towels from the line, smelling them, folding them neatly, and looking left and right for any activity between the slats of the cedar privacy fence that bordered her yard. Jennifer was acutely aware of the role she played in the drama of her husband's life. It was hard to relax when Michael's employees were about, even from behind her fence. But still she hoped to catch a glimpse of Ben Taylor through the crack between the cedar boards. After she put each towel in the basket, she would step forward to peer towards the warehouse, hoping to see him.

She pulled a white towel from the line and dropped the clothespins

102

into the fruit basket between her feet. She glanced up at the house as she began to fold the towel. It was a wonderful old home, the original homestead house, the kind of home she had dreamed of as a young girl, with white wooden shingles, decorative blue wooden shutters, gabled roofs, a small turret and just the right amount of gingerbread trim along its eaves. She remembered the days when, as a teenager working for Antonio in the winery gift shop, she had walked by this same house each day, wondering what it would be like to live in such a beautiful home. Compared to the small bungalow in town where she'd grown up—with its postage stamp yard, faded blistered paint on its wooden siding, and curling shingles on its roof, and her bedroom window only a few yards from the sidewalk—the Voracci house had been magical to her. It had been a house of Christmas lights and roaring fires in the winter; a house of lemonade and porch swings in the summer. She had wondered every day as she walked by what the world inside such a house must be like. That now seemed like a lifetime ago and, in many ways, perhaps it was. Now Jennifer was the woman inside the house that others would wonder about as they walked by on their way between the winery and their own bungalows.

Now, feeling very much the picture-perfect wife of the picture-perfect husband of a picture-perfect public family, Jennifer took down the sheet of her husband's perfect king-sized bed and tried to remember the last time he had shared a bed with her. It had been months. Last December, to be precise, the night before he had left for California. He had come to her room just after she had turned down the sheets. He had pressed himself between her legs for a few minutes before settling down to sleep beside her. It had been a heartbreaking experience. She had watched him in the faint light as she fought to go to sleep, unsatisfied but not aroused, unhappy but hopeful this was his attempt to reconcile. She watched the dark creases of his eyelids and listened to his breathing through the night. In the morning, still restless and with a grogginess that made all her motions feel as if she were underwater, she had watched him silently eat his breakfast. As soon as he had left, Jennifer had changed the sheets and pillowcases.

The breeze had picked up, and the top of the tall maple above her was swaying. She stood and savoured the sound of the wind through the branches and the tug of the wind as it descended behind her fenced wall and circled around her, lifting her hair. The breeze always gave her a sense of freedom. She wiggled her toes in the coarse grass before pulling the last clothespin from a large white sheet.

Suddenly, caught by the whirling breeze, the sheet pulled itself from her fingers, billowed above her head then was lifted past her grasp above and beyond the cedar fence. Jennifer, surprised and momentarily delighted by this seemingly deliberate theft, laughed aloud then turned and ran for the gate, tripping as she knocked over the basket of clothespins. She opened the gate, and suddenly stopped, amazed at the sight before her.

There he was, no more than two feet from the gate, the man she had been hoping to see from the window just a few minutes before. She looked into his warm green eyes and felt her heart stirred by the warmth of the smile that lay poised beneath his lips, before she noticed the bed sheet he had pulled down from the sky and which was now bundled in his arms.

"Ben!"

"This must be yours," he said, smiling, tucking the corners of the sheet into the bundle as the wind seemed to jostle for control.

Jennifer glanced up at him then quickly looked to the ground, stepping forward to reclaim her sheet. Her heart was pounding. In her surprise and embarrassment, she could not look him in the eyes. Then, as she tried to look up again, she spoke quickly, nearly in a whisper.

"Yes, thank you," she said, reaching forward for the sheet.

She looked over his shoulder, left and right, to be certain they were alone before she added, in a much softer tone: "Ben, I'm so happy to see you. I've been hoping…"

He raised his eyebrows and turned his gaze to the corners of the fence, left and right, before she remembered herself and ushered him through the gate, closing it behind him. Alone, behind the privacy of her cedar fence, Jennifer tossed the sheet into the laundry basket. Turning back to him, she raised herself on her toes and threw her arms around him, kissing him with parted lips. He hugged her so quickly and so tightly, it took her breath away. After a few moments of kissing him, then looking again into his shining eyes, she felt faint. Deliciously dizzy in his gaze.

"I'm so glad to see you," she repeated, the fingers of one hand caressing the tufts of thick brown hair jutting from beneath his ball cap, her other resting upon his shoulder. "I've missed you so much. I can hardly breathe," she said. "And with everything that's been going on…"

"Me too," he said at last. "I can't stay long—"

He saw the basket of clothespins, which had scattered over the lawn in her rush to get to the gate. "Here," he said. "Let me give you a hand."

Before she could say no, he had crossed her yard and, on one knee, began to gather up the clothespins.

"Oh, you don't have to do that!" she laughed, hearing the embarrassment in her own voice. Then, with less urgency, "I drop them all the time."

"I don't mind."

She circled him and, pushing the sheet into the wicker basket, kneeled before him to help gather clothespins. She watched his eyes. The momentary happiness at seeing her had dissolved as he busied himself gathering clothespins.

"I heard about Anna," she said.

With those words, his brows furrowed, and the sadness in his eyes a moment before now became a much darker angst. He rose, watching her face. She had never seen his face so dark, so troubled, before. She wanted to hug him, but her feet, her arms, wouldn't move.

"I don't want to ask," she said. "But, Ben, I really need to know. She drowned, didn't she?"

He leaned forward, "No one told you?"

"Michael told me she had died…"

"Jen…"

She held her breath.

"She was murdered," he said.

"In the river?"

"No. Someone cut her throat. She was in the pump-house."

She exhaled, rushing into his arms, her face against his chest. "Oh, my god."

After several moments, very conscious of her breath, deep and measured, she asked, "Did you see her?"

"Yes," he said.

"You're sure she wasn't drowned?" she asked.

"I'm not certain of anything except that she was dead." He grasped her shoulders and moved her back so he could see her face. "Jennifer? What makes you think she drowned?"

"Nothing, I just thought…" She fumbled for the words. "I had a dream about the river the other night… "

"Why didn't your husband tell you?"

"You know he doesn't talk to me. And you know he doesn't like me to be upset."

"But he was with the police all day…"

"Ben. Please don't. You knew he wouldn't tell me. That's why you came."

"Mostly I needed a hug."

"Me too," she said, slipping back into his arms. His chest was so wide, his shoulders so high, and his stomach so flat, being in his arms was like being in a world apart from her husband. It was a world she knew now she never wanted to leave.

"I should get going," he said, once again nudging her out of their embrace.

She looked up at him. "You know he's golfing."

"But still, I've been here too long already."

"I don't care," she said.

"You will."

"No, I don't care about that any more. I think he's still going away for a few days."

"Then I'll get to see you soon," he said, caressing with his fingertips her chin, her cheek, her lips.

She kissed his fingers. "Maybe then we can finally leave this place."

He cocked his head, looking into her eyes. "So you've decided?" he asked.

"I think so, yes."

"You *think* so," he repeated.

"I want to go with you, Ben," she said. "And I think this is the right time, if you still want me."

"I wish you had decided two weeks ago," he said. "I may not be able to leave for a few days."

"But you said—"

"Jennifer, Anna was murdered. I can't run away right now."

"But it's not your fault, Ben!"

"I'm still a cop…"

"But you're not. You said you gave that up."

He shook his head. "This isn't the time or place. Put some

flowers in your window when he's left. *If* he's left. He might not be leaving now."

"He'll go."

"You can't be certain of that. This changes everything."

"I promise you he'll go."

"Then we'll talk about that in a couple days," he said. "We'll talk about everything, when we have more time, okay?"

"Okay."

With that he drew her chin gently towards him and softly kissed her on the corner of her mouth. She moved closer and squeezed him tightly. He pressed his lips to hers and she felt her body melt into his arms for one brief moment before he slipped through the gate and was gone.

NINE

Ben Taylor slept little that night, thoughts racing in and out of his mind faster than he could retain them. For the question of Anna's killer, he tried to convince himself that the matter would be resolved within another day. Inspector Kumar struck him as a capable man. Once he questioned the workers and spoke to the relatives of Anna's boyfriend, David Quiring would soon be located and the issue most probably solved. In fact, the case might have been solved already. Kumar might already have gone home tonight with a suspect in custody and with all the loose ends neatly tied in place. Just like everyone else at Tanglewood, Ben was not going to get any inside information on this case, not as he would if he were still carrying a badge in his pocket. He would have to check the newspaper in the morning, just like everyone else.

While it was certainly not as grave as the murder of Anna Wagner, Ben found it nearly impossible to put Jennifer out of his mind as he fought for sleep that night. Perhaps, he told himself, this was because he could not trust Michael with Jennifer's fate even for a day, the way he could trust Inspector Kumar with that of Anna Wagner's.

Her change of heart had surprised him, delighting him to a degree he could not admit to himself at the time, but had made his chest throb with hope and excitement all along his walk home.

"I want to go with you, Ben," she had said.

Except for his sister, Becky, in their short, infrequent phone calls every couple weeks, Jennifer was the only person in over a year who ever called him by his first name.

But he had also been unnerved by her sudden change of heart. After denying him for so many months, her words returned to him through the long humid night, like a familiar presence suddenly emerging from a fog-shrouded path, but instead of being a dozen yards away, was right in his face, nose to nose. This was a path he had been walking for months. He had become accustomed to the fog on the other side of Jennifer's cedar fence. He had become accustomed to the vague, ill-defined features of her intentions—her vague promises, and her hazy replies to his questions. After months of waiting, the last thing he'd expected today was for her to say she was now ready to leave her husband. In the solitude of his motel room, Ben's world had suddenly shifted forever, once again.

Unless she has a change of heart, he reminded himself through the night. *Unless she changes her mind yet again, and again, and again.*

His motel room was four miles from town and a mile and a half from the vineyard if he took a shortcut through a field and a thicket of trees at the edge of the vineyard. His was one of four small detached cabins, with white siding and bright blue trim. It reminded him of similar cabins he had seen as a child while driving on vacations with his parents and his sister Becky. Each summer as their father drove them through Quebec and the Maritimes towards Prince Edward Island, Ben would look out of the window with wonder at these tiny houses as they streamed past in the family car. They looked like doll houses, and he imagined such homes were where Tolkien's hobbits or fairies might reside. He had never been inside one until he'd found this one nearly eight months ago. Inside, despite the cheery exterior, there was nothing that could bring him to that feeling of excitement he had had as a young boy. It was just another grubby room with a kitchen sink and a bar fridge. The windows were warped and could not be opened more than a crack. The bathroom had only a toilet and a shower. Ben brushed his teeth and shaved at the kitchen sink with a small hand mirror. The walls were the dark faux-wood panelling that had been popular in the late Seventies, and the wall-to-wall carpeting was matted and stained. However, the room didn't really bother him. It was simply a place to sleep and a place to keep the rain off his head. Other than that, he spent little time here. However, he often reminded himself, it was better than the car Scotty Doherty lived in for nine months of the year, or the bungalow the migrant workers shared, sleeping six to a room.

This morning, after sleeping not much more than two hours, Ben grudgingly turned on the light beside his bed. His mouth felt strangely clean without the taste of tobacco, and after a night of contemplation, Jennifer's words to him now seemed more like a dream. In the first blush of dawn, he felt like a fool for letting himself become so obsessed with her words. She'd been overcome by the moment, by seeing him so unexpectedly, he decided. Most likely she didn't remember what she had said or realize the impact it would have upon him. He would wait for her to repeat her intention to leave her husband before he would take it to heart again.

And with that affirmation, his mind returned immediately, with the same effect as turning the channel on a television set, to Anna Wagner. Her pale face with its perfect ivory complexion was again foremost in his mind, staring at him with eyes as grey as ashes, her pale lips imploring him to make things right. It was a good idea to set the case aside so he could sleep at night, but now, in the light of day, he would not let it go until he was certain her killer was identified, charged, and behind bars.

With that, he rose from his bed and showered quickly, rinsing the salt from his skin and the sleepiness from his mind. Already, as he turned on the shower faucet, he began reviewing in his mind every detail he had seen in the pump-house, the condition of Anna's body, and the little information he was able to glean from Inspector Kumar, from Scotty and Juan, from Jennifer, and from Anna herself in the last conversations he'd had with her.

He remembered one conversation. They'd been eating lunch together, sitting side by side on a bench near the tomato sorter. A half dozen Mexican migrants were crossing the room to get from the east greenhouses to the west.

"No one cares about these people," she said. "They're in a world all by themselves. They come and go each year. No one cares where they come from. No one cares where they go. No one cares what happens to them."

"That's only because they don't speak English," Ben replied.

"No," she said. "It's the same for my friends and my cousins. The Mennonites, the Mexicans…we're all the same."

"I don't see it that way."

"Do you care where they come from?" she asked. "Do you care where they go?"

"I care," Ben had said then.

"I do care," he said again now as he pulled on his jeans and a clean t-shirt. "And I'm not going anywhere until I get to the bottom of this."

Ben took a breath of relief. Saying those words aloud seemed to help.

Since he had started working on the farm, he had learned to reverse his daily habits by taking his showers and shaving when he came home instead of in the morning. Unless he had worked too many double shifts and needed cold water to rouse him from his cabin, morning showers made no sense. He would be dirty again within an hour. He pulled on a plaid shirt and ran his fingers through his hair before pushing the ball cap onto his head.

It was best to get to work as soon as possible, he decided. His heart, in the worst possible timing he could imagine, was full only of Jennifer. Her voice, her eyes, her scent, her smile, her hair.

A horn honked outside. Scotty was early.

"How the hell are you?" Scotty shouted through a tire commercial being broadcast loudly from his speakers.

"Great," said Ben without enthusiasm. "Could you turn that down? Some people are still sleeping."

Scotty turned off the radio without argument.

"You look damn tired," Scotty noted as he put the car into gear. "Did you get any sleep at all?"

"Not much."

"I didn't either. I couldn't stop thinking about Anna. You know what's really freakin' me out?

Ben shook his head as he cranked down the passenger window.

"What if she was still alive when that pump-house caught on fire, you know? I mean…"

"It's a bit early for this shit. Maybe you should turn the radio back on."

Ben leaned towards the open window, getting the cool breeze on his face as Scotty accelerated well over the speed limit.

Scotty made their usual detour to the edge of Andover, where they stopped at Tim Horton's to pick up a coffee and some breakfast.

Ben was surprised to see Cindy, the waitress from Beck's Tavern, coming out as he opened the door. She was wearing a pair of tight faded jeans and a plain white t-shirt. Her blonde hair was down, framing her pretty face with windblown wisps of gold. Her body was slender and her breasts pressed against the fabric, begging for attention. Her mouth was open in a long, wide yawn. In one hand she was balancing both a coffee and a small bag with a doughnut or muffin inside. In the other was a newspaper, folded in half, which was occupying most of her attention. She was still peering at the paper when Ben came through the door.

His first reaction was to avoid her. He remembered the way he had been flirting with her, and now with Jennifer fresh on his mind, he simply did not want to talk to her. He stepped to the side as she walked towards him, hoping she would pass without looking up from her newspaper. She looked up at him.

"How are you this morning?" Ben asked as she stared at him.

She stepped back, looked at her newspaper again then raised her eyes, staring blankly at him, before stepping hurriedly through the door.

"Fine," she muttered as she passed. "I'm fine."

"She's kinda bitchy in the morning," Scotty offered. But Ben was only relieved.

There were few people inside this early in the morning, mostly farmers and farm workers. The office types would be in for the next shift in about an hour. On the counter, Ben picked up a copy of the *Andover Reporter* someone had left behind, hoping for the unlikely news of a midnight arrest last night. The town's own weekly paper, it was folded over to page three. Anna's death had made the top of the page, with a yearbook photo of the girl, and a press release photo of her father standing in front of a Tanglewood Vineyards oak cask. WINERY WORKER MURDERED, the headline read.

Ben scanned the article. There were few details. Her name, the fact she had been missing for a week, and the fact she was dead. There was no information about a suspect, or anyone in custody. Ben noted with disdain that the story had been bumped from the first page by an itinerary of the town's upcoming Canada Day festivities.

He realized this was the same article Cindy had been reading as she walked by. Evidently, if her reaction was any gauge, everyone who worked at Tanglewood was a suspect.

"Damn. See this?" he asked Scotty.

Scotty was not there. Ben turned around and caught a glimpse of the back of Scotty's shirt in the washroom as the door closed. Turning again, he saw Inspector Kumar stepping out of his Buick beside the front door. He was dressed in the same jacket and tie as the night before. Ben could not help thinking that Kumar looked nothing like a police officer. He looked more like a salesman on his way to call on a store here in town. Ben grinned with a deep sense of respect for this man.

"Taylor!" said Kumar. "I was hoping I'd find you this morning."

Ben faked a look of surprise. "Me? Here? That's good deducing."

"Yeah," Kumar admitted, "I was just on my way to the winery to find you. I actually just wanted coffee. But I prefer to think of it as good police work." He beamed. "It would have waited until later. But while I've got you now, I want to talk to you."

"See this?" Ben asked, holding up the paper. "Page three. Is it just me, or doesn't a murder in a small town usually get more coverage?"

"That's the only article you'll find," said Kumar. "Nothing on television. Nothing in the daily papers. The big news this morning is on those terrorist suspects they arrested in Toronto the day before yesterday."

"I hadn't heard about that," said Ben, suddenly feeling very much out of touch with the world.

"There was a local connection too, I heard. A couple people holed up in a farmhouse near Sacketville."

"I hadn't heard about that either," Ben said.

"Well, there's excitement enough for us here, isn't there."

Ben gritted his teeth. "Do you know how much this sucks?"

"Hey, don't look at me," Kumar replied as he accepted a large black coffee from the young girl behind the counter. "I don't control the press."

"No," said Ben. "Not you, nor me."

"Let me give you a lift," Kumar said. "We can talk."

Ben looked back for Scotty. There was no sign of him. "Sure."

"I'm glad to have someone here I can talk to. McGrath is getting on my nerves. And Patterson…well, I'm sure he's a good traffic cop."

He unlocked the door of his car. It was a Buick Regal, gun metal blue, less than a year old. It looked as though the back seat had never been used. Ben lifted a large manila envelope from the passenger seat before sitting down.

"Is the investigation going well, Inspector Kumar?"

"Please…call me Walt."

"Okay. Walt. How goes the investigation?"

Kumar tapped the envelope on Ben's lap, buckled up and started the car. He waited for a clearing in the traffic before pulling out. He made a quick right and then another. Andover was older than Confederation itself, and the streets seemed to wind themselves into tangles beneath the canopy of oaks and willows and maple trees. Kumar seemed interested in the houses bordering the streets and slowed to look at four or five before he spoke to Ben about the contents of the envelope.

"This would be a lot easier if McGrath would retire. I'll tell you, I could have used some of the evidence he trampled over."

"Well, there should be something on the body you can use. Small town cases don't all have to be small now, do they?"

Kumar laughed. It was a laugh of authority, deeper and louder than it had to be, Ben noted. He wasn't quite at ease with Ben yet, but he was trying. "I'm kind of glad to be getting some fresh air, to tell you the truth."

"You're based out of the London detachment office?"

"Not at all. I'm based out of Toronto, but I'm using the local OPP office, just a mile outside of Andover."

"Not the Andover Police Station?"

"They're not involved right now. They don't have the resources."

Kumar stopped at a stop sign. There were no other cars. He turned in his seat, facing Ben. "So your friend in Ottawa vouched for you." His tone had dropped dramatically. "He told me you're on a leave of absence, but you're able to return any time you want. I don't buy it, though. And I don't like it. It's too convenient. And I guess your real reason for being here is none of my business right now. However, if I find it has anything to do with my investigation, there will be hell to pay. You need to understand that."

"Did he tell you why I'm on leave?"

Kumar pursed his lips thoughtfully. He had not moved from the stop sign and waved to cars behind them to pass. "No," he said, "he wouldn't say. It wouldn't matter if he did. I still wouldn't believe you. This is a long way from Ottawa. This is the senator's family farm. There's been a murder here. And everything surrounding this farm reeks of trouble. It was the second thing I smelled when I got here."

Ben hated asking the obvious question, but ask it he did. "What was the first thing you smelled?"

"You. But that's okay. For now, do you want to assist in this investigation or not?"

"Yes. I owe it to Anna. I owe it to myself right now too."

"Then take your badge back."

"I don't need a badge right now."

"Fair enough," said Kumar. "I'm going to ask you one more time. Will you tell me what you're doing here?"

"I'm on a leave of absence. That's the truth."

"Fine. If you and your friends in Ottawa want me to play along with that, I'll play along for now. But don't expect me to believe you'd be working in a place like this voluntarily."

"What do you mean?"

"Working in the mud with a bunch of immigrant workers for farm minimum wage? What are you hiding from that could possibly be that bad? That you'd be here shoulder to shoulder with the transient element as you are."

Ben eyed Kumar before answering. "Right now, after what I've been through, I can honestly say I'd rather breathe some fresh air and walk through this mud compared to the shit *you* wade through day after day."

"Yeah, but we're both in the same pile of shit right now. We're both dealing with the same element. You're just standing shoulder to shoulder with them."

"What element? These people work harder than you and I ever will. There are easier ways to make a living. If they were criminals, they wouldn't be here. The way they're treated... It's like prison without the square meals or clean beds."

"Well, you'd know more about them than me, I'll grant you that. But don't assume I don't know what it's like. Right now it's none of my business..."

Kumar pressed the accelerator and they continued on their way.

Ben watched him icily, saying nothing. The tone of his words had made Ben feel itchy. In fact, he was beginning to feel like he wanted out of this car now. He clenched his jaw and made the feeling abate. He seemed to be pushing a lot of feelings aside today.

Kumar sensed the discomfort. "Listen," he said, "I apologize. You're right. I don't know what you've been through. Hell. What do I know about you, or you about me? Right? But in the meantime, Bob Krall said you were a man I could trust, with or without a badge. Is that true?"

"I believe so, yes."

"Then I need your help. While you're here, maybe you can keep your eyes and ears open for me. I know you liked Anna Wagner, and I just want to find her killer. It's a difficult case."

"Why is that?"

Kumar again tapped the envelope Ben held in his hand. "Someone killed that girl. Take a look, but keep it under your hat. McGrath hasn't even seen it yet. I'll show it to him when he asks, but I'm not counting on him asking for a while. He's too busy writing up jaywalkers." He shook his head. "Damn."

"By me looking at this..." Ben began.

"I'm trusting you, yes," said Kumar. "I was told I could trust you. So I am. But that doesn't mean you're in the clear. Everyone is a suspect right now."

"Certainly not everyone," Ben replied as he pulled the papers from the envelope. He leafed through the pages. Eight faxed pages, one fax of a photograph he didn't need to look at. Fortunately, the fax was poor quality, and the details of the photograph unrecognizable. "I thought you were looking for her boyfriend. Isn't he your man?"

"Maybe, if he's chaste."

"Chaste?"

Kumar pulled the car to the side of the road and put it in park. "McGrath got it all wrong. That girl wasn't raped. At least not by any man...or at least not by any man with a dick bigger than a grape."

Ben went cold at Kumar's ill-timed attempt at humour. No, he decided. Kumar was trying too hard to be a buddy now. Maybe he was desperate for a lead. Maybe he was lonely. Maybe he just did not know how to deal with people unless he was questioning them. Who knew? Ben looked at him, as if distracted from the report.

"She wasn't raped." Kumar pointed to a handwritten scrawl in the paperwork. "There was no sign of intercourse before her death.

119

And I mean at any time before her death. The girl was a virgin."

Ben's mind went blank. "A virgin."

"You got it."

"Then what the hell?"

"Precisely."

TEN

It had been nearly a year since Ben had slept through a sunrise. This morning he awoke a few minutes before eight o'clock, dislocated and confused, uncertain of where he was. In the bright light, the rented cabin took on a stark, empty quality. He could smell the dust and age of the room all around him as he lifted himself from the sheets and pulled on a pair of jeans.

Operations at Tanglewood were closed for the day, except for the shipping dock, so only Scotty and Randy Caines would be working. Officially, it was in honour of Anna's memory. Ben, however, couldn't help thinking that operations were usually closed down about this time anyway. There had not been many ripe tomatoes yesterday, and a production slowdown always came several days after a period of heavy cloud cover.

Ben had the day off. He had no plans, nowhere to go, but once he was dressed, he knew he needed to get out. For the months that he had been here, this room had been only a place to sleep. It was not Ben's home, and not a place where he felt at ease in the daylight. It was always better to be at work, better to have things to occupy his hands and his mind, before his mind had a chance to occupy itself with questions and memories. Now of course, there was another reason not to be here. The clues to Anna's death were not to be found in this room. They were at Tanglewood.

He decided to go to the warehouse. Even during a shutdown, there could be work. Randy Caines was always in a lather about something that needed to be done right away. A twenty-minute task could easily become a twelve-hour workday if he timed his appearance right and played on Caines' mood correctly. The path from the back of the motel parking lot led to an empty field and through a woodlot, emerging at the east end of the vineyard. It was a quiet walk, and Ben loved the smell of the evergreens and the touch of the maples and poplars brushing against his open palms as he passed.

The weekend had been uneventful. He'd had a couple of beers from Scotty's six-pack on Friday night. Saturday, he'd worked until midnight. Sunday he had worked until ten and shared another couple of beers with Scotty in the field behind the warehouse, which led him to today. He had not seen Jennifer all weekend, though his eyes had scanned each window of her house when he had an opportunity to pass. Those opportunities came frequently. He dumped garbage more often than needed and found a reason to move some propane tanks from the winery to the warehouse then back again. He thought of her constantly. His arms ached to hold her, and he longed to breathe in the scent of her hair, the scent of her skin, close, close to his face once again.

With a forced yawn, he emerged from the thick woodlot and passed between the tall rows of grape vines, considering for a moment that he would be willing to work for a day only for an opportunity to see Jennifer through her gate and to steal a few moments with her. Of course he would. That was, after all, the real reason he had come here. Ben grinned at himself, at how easily the heart can let the mind think it is in control, directing it so easily to the heart's will.

As he made his way up the gravel driveway, he saw the house was dark inside, the blinds and drapes all closed. Michael's truck was missing. Jennifer did not seem to be home either. There was, however, a great deal of activity by the loading docks. A red Kenworth tractor trailer with the name "Sonny" handwritten in yellow paint on the driver's door had pressed its trailer against the docking bay. Ben could hear the sound of a forklift bouncing around inside the trailer. Scotty's car was parked near the stairs, and Randy Caines' golf cart was visible from the next docking bay. There would be work at hand.

As he climbed the steel stairs towards the loading dock, Ben thought of Kumar's comments about the "transient element" he now worked with. Understanding the inspector had likely not meant it to be as disparaging as it had sounded, Ben was surprised at how little Kumar cared. Certainly it was true that this was not his element, but that was only because he had skills and opportunities they didn't. Ben genuinely admired these people he worked with. He enjoyed watching the easy fellowship that arose after normal working hours between the men who stayed behind to finish a long job. He liked listening to them sing as they worked.

Even men like Randy Caines and Scotty Doherty, who openly hated each other during the day, shared an understanding which would never be known by the men who punched out at the stroke of five. Even Ben had a better affinity with Caines after dark. He could never like the man, could not respect him for the kind of man he was, but he seemed to have a better insight into what Caines was about. Perhaps it was simply mutual respect between men who took pride in their work, who were willing to work sixteen hours if that's what it took to finish a job. On one occasion just a few weeks before, Ben remembered, Caines had disappeared just before midnight and come back with a case of beer and some pizza, for himself, Ben and Joe, the retired mechanic who worked there two days a week. The three of them had shared stories of women and gossiped about the other workers. Caines was as obscene as ever in his stories, and most lacked the detail to make them believable, but he had shown in a few longing silences that there was a heart beneath the flesh somewhere. A reminder that everyone is human.

Ben could see from the open loading bay doors that Scotty already had been busy cleaning up today. The palettes had piled up quickly in the last two days as the police were investigating. Workers were detained, generally on company time, to answer questions and a small uniformed cop with a ruddy complexion had taken over Caines' desk for almost two days to take additional witness statements and sort through company personnel records. The palettes had been stacked four or five deep all around him as he worked, except for a small three-foot corridor to give the police officer access to his chair. This morning, however, there were hardly more than a dozen pallets remaining.

A few hundred cases of wine had been loaded into a transport bound for Dallas. The usual driver, David Quiring, was still missing, and the company had hired the husband of one of the girls on the line to fill in for him. The rest must have been loaded by Scotty this morning. Ben could picture Caines arriving at dawn and rapping his key against the driver's side window of Scotty's car. "Hey, loser. You want some hours this morning?"

Ben was climbing the steel stairs beside the docking bay when Scotty emerged from the back of the trailer, wheels crashing the steel plate that connected the platform with the trailer floor. He braked and grinned.

"I thought you were taking the day off!" Scotty hollered.

Ben shrugged. "You too. How long have you been here?"

"That bastard woke me up at five thirty," Scotty yelled back over the sound of his engine. "Every time I'm about to leave, that goddamn Caines finds something else for me to do."

"Is there much left to do?"

Scotty shrugged. A handful of silver hoops dangling from his right ear sparkled in the sunlight. "Three trucks so far today. And it's supposed to be a fucking holiday. I don't know what's left."

"No rest for the wicked," said Ben as he mounted the steps.

Scotty nodded.

"Nor for the ugly," Ben added.

Scotty stuck out his tongue, letting it drape down over his bottom lip, a fleck of silver sparkling from the centre of his mouth. He laughed and snorted, displaying his extended middle finger before he lifted his forks a foot from the ground and sped away from the docking bay to fetch another pallet of bottles. Scotty was in a good mood. It was nice to see.

As Scotty sped past Randy Caines' desk, Ben could hear Caines shout: "And who the hell were you talking to?"

"Ben Taylor!" was Scotty's shouted reply.

Caines peered around the corner down at him. "Taylor!" he said. "Get your ass up here. I've got work for you, too."

"I'm off today," Ben said with a serious face. It was actually a relief to see Caines back in his blustery, bitter mood again. The docile Caines who did as he was told when Inspector Kumar was nearby was becoming old.

"Bullshit," said Caines. "If you had anything better to do, you wouldn't have dragged your sorry ass back here. Punch in, and I'll give you an extra hour."

"That depends on what you want me to do," said Ben.

"I want you to help load this truck. Then get rid of some garbage. It's a helluva mess back there."

"Yeeeehaaaaw!" yelled Scotty, who had dropped off his pallet. "A bonfire. I got the marshmallows!" He pressed the accelerator and spun the forklift's tires on the smooth cement.

Ben yawned and pulled his time card from its slot in the wall.

The next three trucks loaded easily. The rest of the day passed slowly as the pair moved some heavy steel shelving from one end of the greenhouse complex to the other. Caines stayed at his desk through the day, filling out paperwork and thumbing through his magazines.

The sun had crossed the sky and begun to set when the last expected rig arrived to take three pallets of tomatoes. Caines put his papers away once the truck had pulled away. From the loading dock, the sky looked heavy and bruised. It was nearly nine o'clock. The Voracci house was still in darkness. Ben stared idly at the glowing western sky as Scotty finished his cigarette.

"I marked you both for ten," Caines said as he passed. "Lock up before you set the fire. If you stay longer, it's on your time, not mine."

"Sure thing, Randy," Scotty said.

"Stay out of the greenhouse. I just let the dogs out to roam."

Scotty let out a loud, groaning sigh of relief once Caines had left. "I thought he'd never fuckin' leave!"

Walking by the greenhouse doors, they could hear Caines' dogs barking, probably chasing after a chipmunk that had gotten inside. Scotty shivered, his shoulders shuddering at the sound of the dog's growling and their nails on the cement.

"Fuck, I hate those goddamn mongrels!"

"I've never actually seen them," Ben said. He had been told they were large, mistreated and poorly fed. Randy Caines may have been as attached to those dogs as he claimed, but he apparently did not treat them any better than any human he knew. Ben had passed by their doghouse behind the greenhouses a few times, but they had always been asleep inside the blackness of their plywood house. The chain-link fence around the doghouse was wrapped with sheets of plastic and pieces of rough plywood to keep the wind away and to keep their contact with humans beside Caines to a minimum.

126

"Yep. Mean fuckers," Scotty frowned. "I don't go near them."

"Don't you help feed them?"

"Yeah, but I just stick the food in through the slot in the door. I make sure they're locked up if Caines isn't around, but they go back to their kennel by themselves. I'm glad. They scare the hell out of me."

"What kind are they?"

"Mean."

"Pit bulls?"

Scotty shook his head. "No. I think they're some mixed breed. They must be part Saint Bernard from the size of them. And part coyote. Red eyes like they've got rabies or something."

"I don't think rabies makes a dog's eyes red," Ben replied. "And I don't think they breed dogs with coyotes."

"Wolves then. I don't know." Scotty pointed his finger with a seriousness he seldom showed. When he was agitated or nervous, his long, bony arms moved sporadically, emphasizing his thin, gangly frame. "What I do know is you don't ever want to be alone with those dogs. I remember one of the pickers wandered in there one night after the dogs were let out. They messed him up bad. They went after his face. Chewed up his arms. Randy had to pull them off. He was there when it happened. But they still made a mess."

Scotty did not seem to remember telling Ben snippets of this story before. He was already caught up in his own disgust and outrage about it. The details were only a medium for the emotions they evoked.

"What happened to him?" Ben asked.

"I don't know. I figure he was in the hospital, then they shipped him home."

"No investigation?"

Scotty looked sideways at Ben. "What do you think?"

"I guess not?"

"No fuckin' way. Only a few of us knew about it. I shouldn't be telling you about it either."

"Who am I going to talk to about it?"

Scotty backed off. "I don't know why Caines likes to scare us with them anyway. Why would we go in the greenhouse?"

"I know you, Doherty," Ben grinned. "You'd set the forklifts, the dogs, even the tomato plants on fire if you could. You're a firebug."

Scotty rolled his shoulders and neck as his earrings jingled with silent laughter. "You know, that's true."

He was still grinning as they made their way across the warehouse.

"Anyway, I'm glad you showed up. Now that Caines is gone, we can have fun. I got some beer in my cooler."

There were three or four dozen broken pallets, a dozen old wooden soda bottle crates that Caines had tossed down from the mezzanine in the warehouse, several green plastic bags full of garbage from the picking crew, and several cardboard boxes of assorted paperwork that the police had poured through and dismissed as unimportant. Scotty poured a half gallon of gasoline on them and lit the fire. Within minutes, a thick column of blue smoke rose before them in the breezeless air. Ben and Scotty sat back in a pair of old aluminum folding lawn chairs with broken nylon webbing and put their feet up on the gouged and faded picnic table.

"We should burn this fucking table too," Scotty said as he stood up to scan the yard around them for anything else he could throw on the fire. He spied three old two-by-fours leaning against some pipes beside the greenhouse and ran over to get them. He chucked them like spears onto the flaming debris.

The pair settled down on the picnic table. Scotty tugged at a cement block and set his feet up on it, legs stretched towards the fire, sneakers silhouetted by the growing flames.

"Sucks we don't get overtime," said Scotty. "We'd be cleaning up by now."

"We *are* cleaning up," Ben observed, playing on Scotty's inadvertent double meaning, and watching it soar past his head, unnoticed.

"Money, I mean." Scotty stretched his arms and yawned loudly. "Eighteen hours!" He let his shoulders drop and repeated himself to be certain he conveyed his point. "It's a damn shame we don't get overtime, y'know."

He grinned and leaned back as his chair creaked under the shift in weight. He lit a cigarette and threw back his head to let a stream of smoke rise above his head. Ben tried not to gag and was thankful he was at least upwind from the bonfire.

"The cops talk to you?" asked Scotty, handing Ben a can of Bud.

"Yeah," he replied, popping the top from his can and quickly spreading his legs, leaning forward to drink it as white foam dribbled from the top of the can.

"Damn! I thought you said these were in the cooler." Ben put his mouth back on the end to suck back the foam.

"Yeah, but I think that's the one I dropped," Scotty laughed.

"Have you met with them?"

"Yeah." Scotty nodded. "Two hours with them."

"How'd it go?"

Scotty shrugged. "Mostly asked me the same questions the others asked when she disappeared. I really didn't have much to say." He looked at Ben from the corner of his eye. "They did ask a lot about you."

"Me?"

"Yeah."

Scotty guzzled the rest of his beer and tossed the can towards the fire. The can was light and soared only a few yards before dropping three or four feet short of the flames. He rose to retrieve it but then decided it was too close to the heat to go after.

Towards the horizon, a few wisps of clouds shone pink, like swirls of cotton candy beneath a darkening blue. Pinpoints of light were appearing now in the sky. Scotty leaned back and pointed at a light hanging low in the sky.

"Do you think that's a star or a plane coming towards us?" he asked.

"That's Venus," said Ben.

"Cool. How do you always know stuff like that?"

"I just learned it somewhere. You can tell it's Venus because it's bright and it's near the horizon. It's usually the first thing you see at night, besides the moon."

"How about that one near it?" Scotty asked.

"The red one? That would be Mars."

"And that one there?"

"I'm not sure," Ben said. "Could be Saturn or Jupiter."

"How do you know those are all planets?"

"Because," Ben said as he pointed at the half-moon rising from the east. "We're all on a plane," he said. "All the planets, the sun and the moon, more or less. So from the setting sun to the moon, you can make an arc and all the planets in the sky would be on that line."

Scotty nodded. "You're too smart to be working here on a job like this."

"What about you?" said Ben. "You don't have to be here, do you?"

"It's different for me. I can't do much else. I used to wash dishes. But I like this better. So what are you doing here?" Scotty asked as he watched a piece of broken irrigation pipe sag and melt as it was consumed in flames. "Were you in prison or something?"

Ben took his time answering. This was a serious breach of etiquette, asking something like this, and Scotty knew it. He, had

130

been studying Ben long and hard before posing the question. It seemed that Scotty was a man who needed to get something off his chest. For that reason, he considered the question carefully then decided to answer.

"I did something I shouldn't have done. Made a mistake. Pissed some people off."

"That'll do it. But you got off, right? You weren't there for long."

"Yeah, I guess I got off," said Ben. "But I didn't murder anyone either."

"Me neither."

"Ever been in jail, Scotty?"

Scotty shook his head. "Me? Nah... " He lit another cigarette. "And I want to keep it that way. It's just that fucking Randy pisses me off so much…"

"What about him?"

"You know. Same old stuff," said Scotty. "Caines is a bastard. Everyone knows that."

Ben finished his beer and crushed the can in his hand before tossing it into the centre of the flames. The bright sparks from the fire rose up with the smoke towards the stars, like failed stars themselves. Living in the city, he had not realized how much he missed watching the stars at night. Nor had he realized how dark it could get without streetlights until on a moonless night several weeks after he had arrived he had been walking along the path through the field beyond the vineyard, and he had been amazed to discover that once he was away from the lights of the loading dock, he was unable to see his hand in front of his face. That's what you missed in the city—the sky and all its facets from absolute darkness to the enormous galaxy above. That same feeling of wonder was beginning to come over Ben once again tonight.

Scotty had soon finished his second can of beer. This time he crushed it in his hands, the same way that Ben had done before. He tossed it into the flames.

"I should have tried that the first time," he said. "Works much better." Jumping to his feet, he raced towards his first can, crouching low and turning his head away from the heat. Retrieving it, he dropped it on the ground and crumpled the aluminum beneath his foot. He tossed it into the fire.

"I love fires," said Scotty.

"Why did you ask me about prison?" Ben asked once Scotty had sat down again. He hoped that coming at the question about Caines by retracing the conversation from its beginning might be more fruitful.

"Just thinking out loud," Scotty replied with a long, loud yawn, stretching both arms towards the sky. "All the stuff going on. Anna, y'know…" He drifted off until Ben nudged him with a pointed stare "…and because of my old lady, y'know? If I don't come up with that cash, I don't know what they might do to me. You got me to thinking about that at the diner the other day. I try not to give it much mind, but when it's in my head, I can't shake it. It's like being caught in a metal trap. You know what I mean?"

"I do," said Ben.

"It's just that we should be free to be what we want to be. It shouldn't matter what we do for a living, or how much money we make. Or how much money we don't have." Scotty took a long breath. "That fucking Caines!" he seethed.

"So that's what it is. How much money do you owe Caines?"

"Enough," said Scotty. He turned quickly, realizing that he had revealed more than he had wished. Then he shook his head. "Well, that cat's out of the bag."

"Why would you borrow money from Caines, of all people? If

you hate him so much…"

"I didn't borrow it…" Scotty caught himself this time before he finished the sentence.

Something in the bonfire began to pop and whistle. Sap began to ooze from the end of a green two-by-four. Ben scanned the base of the fire for any signs of aerosol cans, remembering that one had exploded one night after Scotty had dumped a load of garbage into the bonfire.

"So what is it then?" Ben asked.

"Sorry, dude. I can't talk about it."

"You know you can trust me," Ben replied. "Maybe I can help."

Ben watched Scotty's face reflecting the orange flames. His eyes sparkled as if they were moist. His voice in the darkness sounded choked up.

"Right now, all I want," said Scotty, "is to make enough money that I can get out from under his thumb and get the hell out of here. Just get in my car and drive away." He shrugged. "Where? Who knows? Who cares? I've been thinking about Arizona a lot. You liked it there, right? How long were you there?"

"A few days," said Ben.

"And why'd you go there?"

"I told you. It was just a road trip. I just headed south."

"Was it nice?"

"Hot. But, yes, the people are nice enough."

"Know anyone in Arizona?"

"Nope."

"They why'd you decide on there?"

"I didn't decide on it," Ben replied. "Like I said, I just started going south."

"Really?"

"It's the truth," Ben lied.

"I like that," Scotty said, nodding his head and gazing into the fire. "I like that a lot. You just felt like taking off south…and so you did."

"I guess, yeah."

"I think California would be nice. Or even Texas. Lots of jobs in Arizona, I hear."

"Yes, I hear there are."

"And Nevada too. Lately…I've just been thinking of taking off. Ever feel like that? Taking off like you did, but just not coming back again?"

Ben half smiled and nodded. "Just about every day."

"Maybe we should do that," Scotty suggested.

"And what would you do when you got there?"

"Same thing as I do here," Scotty sighed dreamily. "But I'd be on a horse farm. Or herd cattle. Riding a horse instead of a lousy forklift. Wide open ranges instead of being trapped in the warehouse all day."

"So just leave," said Ben. "Caines couldn't track you down if you went to Arizona."

"Maybe. Maybe not. I don't know about that. Besides, it's no fun going on adventure alone," he shrugged. "But I'll tell ya, man, if you want to get out of here with me, I'd go tonight. Y'know?"

Ben shook his head. "I can't. Responsibilities."

"Shit. We all do. But there's a time and a place to do what's important to you." Scotty sat up. "Hell. I'd go if you went too. It would be a lot different if you traveled with someone you knew. Someone you could trust to watch your back when you were sleeping."

"Yes, it would," Ben said.

"Well, think about it, okay? I mean…we really both should get out of here."

"But you don't trust me that much," said Ben.

"Sure I do."

"Then tell me about Caines."

"I'll tell you everything once we get across the border."

"I'll need a few days to think about that."

"Then tell me what's keeping *you* here."

"Anna."

A long, thoughtful silence hung between them as Ben gazed at the sky. Scotty remained fixated on the fire. Different thoughts. Different worlds.

"Think David killed her?" Scotty asked.

"I don't know."

"You know, McGrath asked if I noticed anything odd around there the few days before. I told him I didn't."

Ben yawned, carefully leaning back in the broken lawn chair.

"I'll share something with you," Scotty said, "seeing we're talking about trust and being partners and getting out of this dump and all. Know what they didn't ask me? The cops, I mean."

"What's that?"

Scotty was rocking back and forth, thoughtfully and with disdain. With his left hand, he was reaching into the front pocket of his jeans. "They were so fucking concerned with where I was and who I was with, those bastards didn't even ask if I knew anything that could help them."

Ben turned to Scotty and edged himself up again, listening attentively now.

"See this?" Scotty pulled out his car keys. He removed a small silver key and handed it to Ben. "I leeched this off the guy last year who put the lock on the pump-house door. I used to sneak in there to catch a few zees when things were slow and no one was around."

"Was that the same lock that was on the pump-house after the fire?"

"Yeah, sure," Scotty said. "I don't know about after the fire, but it worked fine the week before."

Ben leaned forward. "The week before? What day were you there?" He paused as he noticed a bullish expression come over Scotty's face. "Did you go in?"

"Yeah, but she wasn't there then." Scotty said defensively. "No one was there."

"What the hell were you doing there?"

"You know. Just catching some zee's."

"What day that week?"

"Thursday, I think."

"You didn't tell McGrath this?"

"He didn't ask."

"What about the OPP?"

"He didn't ask either."

Slowly, Ben shook his head, looking at the fire. "Of course he asked."

"Well, he didn't ask directly then."

"You still should have told them."

"Why? I hate that bastard, McGrath. I hate all of them. I told you. I have to keep a low profile."

"If you wanted to keep a low profile, you should have told them everything right from the start. Dammit. You should have told them, Scotty. They don't care about you right now. They're looking for Anna's killer."

"Well, that's why I'm showing you this. You can give it to them. Just tell them you were there, and you didn't see anything."

"I can't do that."

Scotty sat up. "You have the key. Tell them you had the key all along."

"Dammit, Scotty. I can't do that. I wasn't there." Ben stared at the key long and hard. "How many keys are there?"

"Jesus, I don't know. I figure two came with the lock. Plus my copy. Plus any other copies anyone else might have made."

Ben felt the smouldering anger in him begin to get hotter. He glared at Scotty.

"What? You think I'm lying? You think I did it?"

"No. But you should have told them you had been in the pump-house and then given them this. It's important."

"Yeah, and get myself fired." Scotty crossed his arms. "I don't even know if it's the same lock. Why would I be lying to you?"

"I believe you," said Ben. "It's just a touchy thing, giving this to me instead of the police."

"You have to believe me, Ben. There was no one there. No girl. Nobody. I didn't do it. Her boyfriend did it. David Quiring. Everyone knows that, right?"

"No. No one knows anything. Why are you telling me all this?"

"I needed to tell someone. I've been having dreams about it. Nightmares. I needed to get it out of my head, and you're the only person around here I feel I can trust, Ben." Scotty tossed his cigarette butt towards the fire. It came up short and landed only a few feet from the table. "I guess you trust people you feel are most like yourself. Do you think that's true?"

"I imagine," Ben said.

"We're a lot alike, aren't we?"

"I suppose," said Ben. He wondered if that was true at all. He wondered why Scotty would even feel they were alike.

A year ago, would you have thought that, Scotty? Can't you smell a wolf when you're beside one? Are you a fool, or have I really changed?

Scotty cracked open another beer. "After this, I'm sleeping in my car. You can have the back seat if you'd like."

"No, but thanks." Ben said as he stood and slipped Scotty's key into his pocket. "I'll give this to the police, and I'll try to do it your way. But I'm not making any promises."

"I trust you, Ben."

In his motel room, Ben flicked on the light switch without even thinking about it. Reflex made him pick up the phone. He had one message. Jennifer. Her voice was quiet, almost breathless. Michael was going away on business as he had originally planned. He would be leaving the next day for Chicago. Gone for two days, maybe three. She was inviting him for a late dinner at her place once the coast was clear. No one else would be coming by, so he shouldn't worry.

"Right. Don't worry," he said aloud. Jennifer was either going to tell him again that she wanted to leave her husband or was going to act as if she had said nothing to begin with. Ben had no idea how he was going to react to either scenario.

He dropped the phone onto its cradle and fell backwards on the bed. Fishing Scotty's key from his pocket, he held it tightly in his fist. He closed his eyes to keep the room from spinning. He was so tired, the two beers he'd drunk had gone straight to his head. The room was eerily silent except for the buzz of the light bulb overhead and the sound of a distant car approaching on the highway. He was asleep before the car had passed the motel. He was dreaming of Jennifer before its sound had faded away.

ELEVEN

You are responsible. For the second night in a row, Ben had fallen asleep with thoughts of Jennifer stirring thick in his mind, but woke in the morning with thoughts only of Anna Wagner. Anna had emerged into his dreams as he began to wake up, appearing to him as a shimmering silhouette at the edge of the vineyard, standing on a wooden palette, descending from a forklift, her golden hair glowing; face white, eyes of blazing light shining towards him. One by one, Ben watched himself stack box after box of tomatoes around her, imprisoning her. *You are responsible, t*he pale face whispered as he put the last box in place.

If Ben had remembered more of his dreams, he would have realized it was not uncommon that they be filled with repetitious aspects of his daily fourteen-hour shifts. Forklifts, boxes of wine, the bottling machines, the sorting machines were always in the background, through dream or nightmare, burnt into his psyche, whether he was awake or asleep.

Now he looked around his empty room, still dark except for a narrow shaft of moonlight through the window, fractured by a crack in the pane of glass. The pale light shone on the dresser mirror, angled down towards his bed, and on the white t-shirt draped across the top of the dresser where he had tossed it the night before. Ben pulled himself out of bed. The damp sheets clung to his legs as he slid away. The room was stale and stifling, unbearably hot. He focused on the absurdity of the boxes in his dream and tried to shrug the images away, but Anna's words still seemed to echo through the empty room, and he thought he could smell a lingering trace of smoke, thick with death, on his skin. He stepped towards the dresser, balled up the shirt and used it to wipe the sweat from his back and chest before tossing it into the basket in the corner.

You are responsible.

Leaning over, he picked up his clothes from the chair beside his bed. Even his jeans felt damp, and he had to tug hard at them to get them over his thighs.

Outside the air was a bit cooler, but still warm and humid. A single streetlight above the parking lot shone down with a steady buzz that was exaggerated by the silence of the night. A small swarm of insects and moths formed a frantic halo around the bulb. The moon was still high above the trees, and its aura gleamed. The air was lifeless, hazy and hot, even before dawn. It was going to be a muggy day.

Ben perched himself on the step and absently reached into his jeans pocket for a lighter. He found instead the key Scotty had given him the night before. He turned it between his fingers and watched its edges glimmer under the harsh lamplight above his head. He would have to call Kumar once the sun was up and give him the key. Until then, it was too hot to sleep, too early to go to work. There was not much left but to think, or try not to think.

Of course it had been a dream, he told himself now. A dream and a distortion of the light, of course.

It was not surprising to him that he seldom remembered his dreams. Ever since he had arrived here, without a past he was interested in revisiting and with no desire to plan for a future, Ben's attention had always been best focused on living in the present moment. It had been years since he had really considered whether he dreamed or not, or what they were about when he did. Except

140

recently. Except his recent daydreams of Jennifer, yes. She had evoked those dreams.

He stood up and slipped the key back in his pocket, pulling out his own set of keys to lock his door. It was only then that he saw the message that had been left on his door. Written on an old piece of cardboard with red magic marker, the message had been taped to his door with black electrical tape.

Morderer! Youll Pay!!

Ben let out a long, slow whistle. "Just great."

He peeled the electrical tape from the wooden door and examined the cardboard. The letters were thin and angular, inconsistent in their size and their spacing, written by an unpracticed hand. The cardboard was brown and corrugated, torn from a packing box similar to the boxes used at Tanglewood Vineyard, but not quite the same. Half of a printer's stamp was still intact, with a portion of a letter M, from a company name. This did not come from Tanglewood Vineyards. McCracken Farms, perhaps, which was only two miles farther up the road. The note had been left while Ben was asleep, of course, which meant that whoever had left the note had not been terribly eager to make good on the threat. Ben, after all, had been alone and asleep, and his door had been unlocked.

Ben locked his door now, however, before he walked through the shadows towards the vineyard. He enjoyed the quiet of the meadow in this hour before dawn, with only the moonlight to guide him along his path. Soon his jeans were drenched with the dew of the weeds he brushed past, and his legs began to itch with the friction of the wet denim as he walked. He relished the feeling.

Ever since he had moved back to Andover, up until the morning he'd discovered Anna's broken body, Ben had found himself reveling in the smallest daily moments of his life. Quite often throughout the day he would pause to close his eyes and focus more intently on the sounds, odours and textures that surrounded him. The variety of textures fascinated Ben: the smoothness of the steering wheel of his forklift, with a roughness on the left side where someone's ring had scratched into it repeatedly over the years; the texture of each tomato, differing with each shade of red; the metal burrs along the handles of the propane tanks; the rough edges of cardboard cases, the cool bottles of wine inside. It was a world of sensation: the coolness of the concrete on the loading dock in the morning; the heat emanating from the cement walls of the warehouse outside after sunset; then the warm pockets of air he walked through as he passed woodlots and meadows and small hills on his way to and from his motel room. The closer he approached the smallest details of the world, the more the world responded with a richness of sensations that seemed more and more each day like its beauty could have no end.

The Voracci house came into view as he rounded the end of the vineyard towards the warehouse, and Ben's thoughts edged their way towards Jennifer. He thought of their odd meeting last week in her yard then about his upcoming visit with her this evening. As he began work, he daydreamed of her. Time took on a heavy, damp consistency, and the details of the work slipped past unnoticed until his forklift slowed while carrying a stack of broken pallets and sputtered to a full stop. He had run out of propane, in a stalled forklift, at the farthest point from the locked iron cage that held the spare propane tanks.

The walk to the cage with the empty was fine, but the full canister began to feel heavy on the walk back. As he walked, a voice in his head said: *Just leave. Get out—now. You don't belong here. No*, he thought, *I can't do that*. He let the metal rim of the canister dig into the palm of his hand. The burning itch the canister coaxed from the skin of his hand took care of any urge to run, but his thoughts still revolved around Jennifer. He was surprised at how much he missed her now and how much he had missed her over the years. Maybe that was what Susan had seen and why she had left. Seeing Jennifer again had rekindled his feelings for her. But holding her in his arms, feeling her breath on his cheek and the way she said his name...the way her mouth, even if there were tears in her eyes, always ended in a smile as her tongue lingered on the last letter of his name. *Ben.*

It had been over six months since he had spent any reasonable amount of time with Jennifer, having basked in a full ten days alone with her, hidden away in her home in December while Michael had been away on business in California.

Ben had arrived at Tanglewood to work in September, but had not realized that Jennifer, his university love, was now married to Michael until he'd spotted her from a distance, across the warehouse parking lot, in mid-October. A week after that, he'd approached her. A few days later, she slipped a note in his pocket as she passed by in the warehouse on the pretext of bringing her husband some lunch to his office. They'd stolen a few hours together once every week or so when Michael was out of town. Then, one night in the last days of November, she had happily announced that Michael would be going to California for ten days in December.

"How would you like to spend Christmas with me?" she'd grinned.

While they missed Christmas itself by only two days, those were perhaps the happiest ten days of his life, hidden away in her home while her husband, his employer, was out of town. Ben did not venture outside once in those ten glorious days. Their hearts were blissfully saturated with one another's attentions, sharing themselves only with each other, dancing together behind drawn curtains, making love in her bed, and talking of their hopes and aspirations, as lovers do, in each other's arms beside the fire and in candlelight.

That had been the first time Jennifer had expressed her intention of leaving her husband and going away with Ben. They spoke of it often in the last days of their time together that December, of her coming back to Ottawa with him, or moving to British Columbia where they might create a new life together from scratch, each leaving their pasts behind.

But of course this was just an illusion, this small pocket of time they had carved together. Two days before Christmas, Michael called. Ben watched from the bed as she rose to answer the phone, her back towards him. He lay on his side, half-covered by the warmth of her blankets, watching the curve of her spine and the tender muscles of her thin shoulders as she arched away from him, leaning closer into the phone. All she said was, "Yes. Of course. You're probably right. Yes."

And with those four short sharp sentences, the bonds that had kept their mutual illusion together had been snapped in four places. Broken was the revision they had made of their histories. Broken were their dreams of the future. Broken was the illusion that their time together could last as long as they wished it to. Broken were the sweet lies they had been telling themselves through each long night in one another's arms. When she hung up and turned around, Jennifer reached for her robe and covered herself. Ben understood what had happened and began packing his bags.

Michael arrived home the next afternoon to take his wife to Arizona for two weeks, just in time for Christmas. But by dawn of that same day, Ben was already on his way out to British Columbia. Alone. He spent three weeks with his parents in Cranbrook before he decided to head back to Ottawa, to end his sabbatical, pick up his badge and his gun and to return to the world which, through Jennifer, he had hoped to leave behind. Instead of flying east, however, he rented a car and had driven south, finding himself in Arizona. There, he'd lingered through the streets of Tucson for several days, forcing himself to walk the same streets Jennifer would

144

have walked hand in hand with her husband only a few weeks before, as if he thought that by walking the same dry streets she'd walked, he could exhaust his feelings for her and pour them from his heart as one could pour dry sand from one's shoe.

When at last, sometime near the end of February, when he felt his strength had returned and his resolve was as steadfast as it had been a year before, he began making his way back toward the Canadian border, then, from a motel room in a small town just outside of Chicago, he'd called his sister Becky in Ottawa to tell her he would be home in two days.

"Where have you been?" Becky asked, her voice soft with concern. "What's going on? Do you know Jennifer has been calling every single day? She's out of her mind with worry…"

And with those few words, his resolve dissolved once again, and the newly won parole of his heart was suddenly revoked. Ben returned to Tanglewood.

Randy Caines had been as pleased to see Ben as he had ever been. In fact, he nearly smiled as Ben asked when he could begin work.

"As soon as you punch in," Caines had replied with a shrug.

It was the following day that Ben found a note stuck in the door of his motel room.

Please forgive me. Until we can speak know that each time you hear me play the piano, I'm playing for you.

In her discretion, Jennifer had neither signed the note, nor addressed it to Ben.

And now, as July was already well under way, it seemed like an eternity ago that they had shared that time together alone in her house. The memory of those nights and days with Jennifer haunted him with as much power and force as the memory of Anna's dead body, creating a counterbalance to his thoughts—a whisper of

145

happiness to balance the sorrow, a promise of hope to balance the despair, the anger, and regret he felt whenever he asked himself why he had not returned to Ottawa, to his real life, his real job, instead of returning here to this illusion.

Yet whenever he was working outside, Ben listened for her music and kept an eye out for her silhouette in the window. Even from a distance, her beauty captivated him to a degree he would have otherwise found embarrassing. She had a wide smile and a cascade of long lustrous brown hair that shone in the sunlight as she leaned back on her elbows on the stairs of the porch, eyes closed, soft smile greeting the warmth of the sky. He would find himself, many seconds after she had gone, standing in place, watching her door, immersed in vacuous thoughts and not aware that she had left until the slam of her back door drifted to him, arriving at his ears after she had gone from his sight. He would stand there, blinking, feeling a twinge of guilt at watching her while she was alone, unselfconscious and at peace with herself in her own backyard.

He shook his head. It was incredible. He was falling in love with her all over again; falling in love with a married woman. A woman who tonight might or might not decide to run away with him.

Jennifer and the farm were the only portions of his previous life here, as a child and teenager, that he had any interest in exploring. As for the rest of it, he took great pains to insulate himself from it. He had not had the slightest curiosity to return to Buckingham, where he had grown up, only twenty minutes over. He even avoided going into Andover, except when it was unavoidable, in case he might bump into old friends who had might have moved there from his hometown. He wanted to work and dissolve his identity for a while without distraction. He had missed the simplicity of his life when he'd lived here. That was the reason he'd given himself of returning, to have a few months, or maybe a year, to immerse himself in a simpler, more honest way of life for a while. A chance to reconnect with the part of himself that knew nothing of death, knew nothing of killing, knew nothing of the darkness that had surrounded his life for the past few years. But he had known since the first day he'd arrived that Tanglewood was not the place he had remembered. He had been working within himself to come to a place of honesty and innocence despite this realization—if only because he could think of no other place to go. Until Anna's death, it had almost felt like it was working. But the delicate illusion of peacefulness had shattered with the first whiff of the girl's charred body.

Ben had to question himself too. He should have known that Anna had not run away. And if he had not been so obsessed with trying to reconnect with the simpler days of his youth while working at Tanglewood, he certainly would have known something was wrong. Instead of leaving her fate to McGrath, who saw her as just another Mennonite, a life of little consequence, Ben would have questioned her disappearance further. He would have helped Abe Wagner look for her. He would have talked to her friends himself. He knew her. He cared about her. How could he have been so oblivious?

He made it back to his forklift now. He had neglected to lower his forks, and the load was high off the ground, so he pulled the hydraulic lever and released the pressure, letting the forks smack the cement platform. The pile of broken pallets, eight feet high, wobbled but stayed in place. The propane canister slipped easily into place behind the seat, and he secured the metal bracket and attached the line before turning on the tank. He climbed back into the seat, brought the load outside into the open sunlight and dropped it at the edge of the concrete platform.

Ben pulled his watch from the front pocket of his jeans. It was almost four. Time to call it a day. It was always nice when a shift ended early. He had been carrying his paycheque in his back pocket for four days. It would be best to snag a ride into town or borrow the company van for a half hour to deposit it then give Kumar a call to hand over the key.

Caines was on the phone, grunting and filling out a shipping label. He moved aside as Ben took the keys for the winery van from Caines' desk drawer.

"Hold the phone," said Caines. "Where the fuck are you going?"

"Heading to the bank and to grab some groceries."

"Get me some tea."

Ben hooked up the golf carts and the single electric forklift to the battery recharger and swept the floor, near the cooler, until the clock struck 3:59. By the time he walked over to the clock, it was exactly four o'clock, and he punched out.

Outside, he saw Voracci's truck still beside his house. He looked toward the kitchen window and saw Jennifer behind the glare on the glass. She grinned and waved. He waved back just before she suddenly stepped back from the window. He whistled aloud. Damn, she looked beautiful, even from here. With any luck, Voracci would be gone before dark. He couldn't wait to talk to her.

There was no air conditioning in the van, and Ben opened both windows before venturing inside. After being under a plastic roof every sunny day this spring, he was intent on enjoying this afternoon. The sky seemed more blue than usual, and the trees waved happily in the breeze. The smell of flowers and cut grass carried in the wind as he drove into town.

He stopped at Loblaws to deposit his cheque and pick up groceries including some tea for Caines, before pulling Kumar's card from his wallet and punching in the number at the payphone outside the store. Kumar did not answer his phone, and Ben was forwarded to his voicemail.

"It's Ben Taylor. I've got some information you'll want..."

As he said this, Ben turned around. Two young men were standing several yards away, watching him.

"Give me a call." He hung up.

Ben recognized the younger of the two. Markus was his name. He was one of the group that Anna had associated with and, if Ben remembered correctly, a cousin of Anna's boyfriend and now murder suspect, David Quiring. The second man, who looked ten years older, Ben had never seen before. Both wore jeans, worn-out running shoes and faded t-shirts. One wore a John Deere fertilizer cap, the other a Blue Jays cap.

He approached them. "You're David's buddies, aren't you?"

"His cousins. This is Sammy." Markus did not take the time to introduce himself. He seemed to know Ben already.

They were obviously tense, but Ben decided it was important to talk to them about David.

"Do you know where David is?" he asked. "Have you seen him?" He watched as they silently communicated with each other through glances to each other, to the ground, to the sky, to each other again. They knew something, but they were not going to trust Ben with this information. "You know the police need to talk to him."

"No one has seen him," Markus said. "It wasn't David. We know it wasn't him."

"That's fine. He still needs to talk to the police."

"We don't know where he is. And we know already that the police are looking for him. Someone put the police onto him."

"I think the police put the police onto him. If your girlfriend is murdered, it makes sense they would want to talk to you, doesn't it?"

The older cousin stepped forward, glaring at Ben. "No. David had nothing to do with it. You're the one who put the cops onto David. You should mind your own fucking business."

"Me? I don't even know David that well. He's *your* cousin. Do you think he could have hurt her?"

"No," said Markus, crossing his arms. "Not like that. But the police think he did. And we know what you said."

"I said nothing to make them suspicious. Who told you it was me?"

Markus smiled but with anger. "We just know."

"Even if we didn't," Sammy piped in, "Anna told us enough about you."

Ben should his head. This was getting much too confusing. "One thing at a time," he said. "Who told you I put the police onto your cousin?"

Markus shrugged his shoulders, still glaring at Ben.

"Then what did Anna ever have to say about me?"

Again, Markus shrugged his shoulders.

"But we only spoke a few times…"

"And you weren't seeing her behind David's back."

"Of course not. Again, we only spoke a few times."

"She thought you were an honest man. But listen to you lying to us now."

"Don't put too much faith in rumours," said Ben. "That won't help your cousin in the least."

"But it will help Anna when we…" Sammy began, before his cousin nudged him with his elbow.

Ben reached into his shirt pocket and took out Inspector Kumar's business card. "Here. I'm not saying you know where he is, but you have a much better chance of running into David than I will."

The cousin took the card, examined both sides as if he had never seen a business card before, as if he had no idea what he was expected to do with it. Ben could not blame him for being suspicious, for being angry. All they had were their families, although many did not even have that. These were not the Mennonites who had lived in this area for generations, had churches here, property, farms and businesses. These were the Mexican Mennonites. Although of German heritage too, they were not generally regarded by people in town as much more than white trash, if that at all. They were seen as drifters, refugees, forced from one place to another all their lives. Few people cared who they were. Many were born and raised in their own small communities and on farms in Mexico. Their parents and grandparents had pooled their money together to buy their own farms and moved from the Canadian prairies. They had now been forced to leave because of the years of devastating droughts in Mexico. Many, like Juan Reger, were just biding their time, hoping to some day return to their homes. Anna Wagner, whose family had come from Argentina, was one of the few who had hoped to build a life for herself here.

"Tell him to talk to Inspector Kumar," Ben said. "Maybe the local cops don't like your cousin, I don't know. But this guy's with the OPP, and he seems fair. David has to know it will only look bad if he hides from the cops."

The older cousin handed the business card back to Ben. "David wouldn't hurt her."

"I didn't say he did. And I don't know why you think I have it in for him. But police are trying to find out who did this to her. Maybe David knows something that might help them find the killer. Maybe he can remember something she said or did that means nothing to him, or you or me, but to the police it might point them in the right direction."

"We'll find out who it was ourselves," Markus said. "What do you, or the fucking cops' care who killed her? The cops don't care. No one cares about her but us and her family."

"That's not true. I care. The OPP cares. Her friends care."

"Yeah, right. And when we find out who did it, we'll take care of him ourselves."

Ben watched the two tense up. "Would that be a good idea?"

"To us it is."

"Do you know who did it?"

"I think I'm looking at him right now."

"Me?" Ben watched them both, their eyes gleaming with cold hatred. Then it clicked. "You work at McCracken Farms, don't you?" said Ben. He stepped forward, looking down at them both. "I got your note this morning. I'm going to warn you once, and only once. Threatening me will not help Anna. It will only hurt you. And if you really want to help your cousin, you should convince him to go to the police."

"David told us all about you. The way you were with her. Everything here was fine until you started shooting your mouth off around here."

Ben stepped back to keep them both in clear view. Their anger was about to get out of hand. "I don't know what you're talking about," he said.

"Doesn't matter. You want to blame David for it, though. And we know it wasn't him."

"I don't want to blame anyone."

"Save your trash for the cops. I'm not buying it." Markus had no interest in anything Ben would say. They had both made up their minds.

"Your words mean nothing," Sammy added. "*You* mean nothing."

Markus lifted his shirt. Ben saw a flash of silver. A small bowie knife concealed in its sheath and tucked under his belt. Markus put his hand on the handle of the knife.

"You better tuck your shirt in," said Ben.

He glanced around. There was no one around but the three of

them now. No innocent bystanders to get hurt in what was about to happen, but no witnesses either. Sammy stepped back, his anger dissolving with nervousness at seeing his cousin's knife. Sammy was not going to be a threat. Ben steadied his eyes on Markus as he tried to talk him down.

"You don't want to do anything rash right now," said Ben. "Now step back and tuck in your shirt."

Markus' eyes shifted quickly to Ben's stomach.

Without a moment's hesitation, Ben stepped forward before the knife was out of its sheath. As he moved, Ben lifted his elbow, catching Markus in the throat with his elbow while pinning Markus's own arm with his chest. Seconds later, Markus was on his back, his hand still on the handle of the sheathed knife. Ben had his arm pinned down with his knee, Ben's right hand also now on the knife, his left hand holding Markus's throat, keeping him down on the sidewalk.

"Let it go," said Ben.

The sudden drop to the ground had sapped Markus of all his resolve. He relaxed his grip on the knife and lay limp, docile beneath Ben's hold. Sammy had stepped away and was watching them, mouth gaping, palms up in front of his chest.

Ben pulled the sheathed knife from Markus's belt and slipped it into his own back pocket. "Approach me again," he said, "and you're going to the hospital, and then to jail. Do you understand?"

TWELVE

Jennifer preferred to brush her hair without the aid of a mirror. She turned off the vanity lights above the sink and turned to face the doorway, where the failing evening light filtered through the hallway. When she did look in the mirror, she saw only her silhouette. With the exception of putting on makeup, she could get through almost any chore without having to look at herself. And even when she put on her makeup, she didn't look into her eyes. It wasn't that she didn't like herself, or the way her face looked to others. It was just that she had become so accustomed to being a spectator in her own life over the years that it was easier to get through the day without reminding herself that she could be seen and heard as well.

This evening, Jennifer wore her hair down, naturally curled, the way it looked when she let it dry without blowdrying. She wore no makeup, the way Ben used to always like to see her, as she recalled. She wore a red blouse, black skirt, black shoes.

She looked at her fingers, now conscious of the deep shade of red she had painted her nails and the three rings she had carefully chosen earlier that afternoon. She rarely painted her nails and had done so this afternoon mostly as a way of occupying herself instead of counting the hours before he arrived.

"You look *fine*," she whispered to herself.

Downstairs, she dimmed the lights in the dining room and pulled at the drapes until she was satisfied they would conceal the light from any vineyard employees who might pass by in the evening.

A deep breath. "Everything is *fine.*"

She stepped back and pulled the rings off her fingers. Then she returned to the kitchen and checked the chicken in the oven. Once again, she peeked through the blinds down the laneway towards the warehouse. There was no sign of anyone. Ben should have been here by now.

She had no sooner gone upstairs to get a better look beyond the fence when there was a loud rap on her screen door. She hurried down the stairs and opened the door.

"You were supposed to just sneak in!" she laughed once Ben had closed the door behind him. He had showered and shaved and wore a clean plaid shirt and clean jeans for the occasion.

Jennifer hugged him tightly and breathed in the scent of his aftershave. "I remember that cologne," she said. "It's always been my favourite."

"Is it the same?" he asked, knowing full well that it was. "I picked it up today in town. I didn't want to smell *too* much like a farmhand."

"I think farmhands can be sexy," she replied. "Well, one farmhand I know, anyway." She touched the tip of his nose with a finger. "I can't believe we finally have this time together. I've missed you so much."

She hugged him again, even more tightly. "Dammit, Ben," she sighed, "I missed you."

He held her more tightly. When she stepped back again, the nervousness was gone. Ben looked into her eyes, as though he was intent on reading every thought in her mind, every feeling in her heart.

"Help me," she whispered, calmly, resigned. "I need your help."

Ben didn't know what she meant, not yet. But the depths of her need spoke to him more than her words.

"Anything," he said.

She turned away. He watched her profile in the darkness of the kitchen, backlit by the faint dining room light.

"I'm so glad you're here," she whispered quickly,

It was as if her husband could have been in the next room, listening in, as if she were not accustomed to speaking aloud in her kitchen. Years of silence had engrained itself in the room, as years of use had darkened the table she now leaned against. "I wanted to send you a note. I found your number in his day planner. I needed to let you know he was finally going away."

"His day planner?" he asked.

"Michael's," she whispered. She had not wanted to say his name, as if breathing the word aloud would invoke his presence in the room between them.

She slipped her arms around him again, placing her cheek on his shoulder. "That cologne," she said. "I just realized. Just now... I smelled it just before I saw you. Smell is the most powerful of our senses in bringing back memories, isn't it? Since I saw you, smelled you —" She giggled. "It's like, how could I have ever forgotten the man I loved most in my life? All my heart and my mind and my body have always known that you are the one I've loved most."

"Yes," he whispered. "I think I know what you mean."

He took her hands. She looked down where their fingers were touching. She felt warm and safe. Now, in her kitchen, she felt his arms come around her, holding her close to him. The same arms. Same man. Same love from so many years ago. At that moment, time seemed to have lost all meaning to her. The ten years seemed to dissipate as she took her next breath. They kissed, and the room seemed to recede from them, fading as they lost themselves in each other.

"Are you hungry?" she asked at last.

"I should be," he laughed.

"Yes," she said. "You work hard. I've seen you."

His eyes widened. "You've been spying on me?"

Jennifer nodded quickly, eyes beaming. "From my bedroom window. I like to watch you dump the garbage."

"Yes." He cleared his throat. "Fascinating work, I know."

"I like the way you raise the forklift up so high then climb right up. You're not afraid of anything, are you?"

"Not of heights. Not like that," he said.

"Are you afraid of anything?"

He seemed to think about that for several seconds. "What do you need help with?" he finally asked.

Jennifer shrugged, looking at the floor before looking into his eyes again. She could not help but smile. "Where do I even begin?"

"Where do you want to begin?"

She stepped to the kitchen counter and removed a bottle of Tanglewood Riesling. She held it towards him in one hand, a bottle opener in the other.

"Opening this wine?" she said.

He took the bottle. "That I can do."

THIRTEEN

Inspector Walter Kumar shut off his engine and pulled the keys from the ignition. Before stepping out of the car, he scratched the top of his head vigorously. His scalp was itchy and his skin felt dry. He was irritated. His legs were tired and his butt felt numb. He had been in his car for eight of the last twelve hours. A wasted day.

He had been on his way to Abe Wagner's house at eight o'clock this morning when his phone rang. His superior, the Detachment Commander, had summoned him to a meeting at the Commissioner's office in Toronto to discuss the progress of the case.

"There has been no progress," Kumar had protested. But that mattered little. It was a three-hour drive for a ten-minute meeting. He had only met the Commissioner twice before—neither occasion in the midst of an active investigation. He was a tall, grey-haired man with glasses that seemed too small for his long face, a man Kumar had always respected. A man everyone believed to be far above the politics his predecessor had been known for.

Kumar gave him a full report, and the Commissioner had listened in silence.

"I have full confidence in you, Walter," the Commissioner said afterwards. "I'm sorry to have dragged you in here today. I do appreciate you making the time. It was necessary. Under no circumstances will you allow anything to get in the way of solving this as quickly as possible."

The irony of that statement was understood by both men.

158

"I also want you to know that the local police will no longer be involved, except as requested by you."

"Thank you, sir."

Kumar was then reminded of the political sensitivity of dealing with the Voracci family. While he was not to let any such politics interfere with the case, he was not to involve any of the Voraccis themselves unless evidence warranted it. Obviously, Senator Anthony Voracci still had all the important connections to keep his family as far removed from the normal processes of justice as the law could allow. Anthony Voracci was one of the most active senators on Parliament Hill. He currently chaired three committees, including a recent bill on international police procedures and national security. He had a lot of connections throughout the government, in both houses, and on both sides of the political floor. His family carried a lot of political clout.

Kumar resented the need to treat anyone with kid gloves, but he had to agree there was no need yet to drag the senator or his sons into the case.

"Now, before you head back," the Commissioner said, opening his office door, "I'd like you to stop by the Forensic Centre. Talk to them. Go over everything they have one more time."

Kumar did not debate the pointlessness of that excursion. He had everything they had already.

The meeting there was longer—nearly two hours—but resulted in no new information.

The evidence documented by McGrath and his men was practically useless. While they had photographed everything and had dusted for fingerprints, they themselves had contaminated the entire scene. No fingerprints consistent with the crime had been found. Whoever had cut the girl's throat and poured gasoline on the body and folded her clothes neatly in a pile at her feet had probably worn gloves. There were no useful footprints on the scene

159

either, compromised by the rain and by the number of people who had been walking about the morning the body was discovered.

While the team was still trying to pull what they could from the collected evidence, Kumar had little hope that anything useful would be found that could help him right now. Once a suspect was in custody, there was a good chance something from the crime scene could be used to work towards a conviction. But as far as pointing Kumar to a suspect, the evidence they had was useless. Because he had no suspect, that meant, for now, that everyone was a suspect.

By the time he emerged from the Forensic Centre, Kumar found himself mired in the beginnings of rush hour traffic.

He had a single short voicemail on his cell phone from Andover's Chief of Police: "I'm taking some time off. My men will assist you as needed."

That was the only thing that gave Kumar a reason to smile all day.

He had no intentions of using the local police. He had already tasked the local OPP constables with locating David Quiring, the most obvious suspect, and in questioning Anna Wagner's friends at school. Kumar himself would deal with the employees at Tanglewood. The reports from the interviews were thorough, but unfortunately the girl's friends had little useful information to share. Anna Wagner had been a very private young woman. None of her friends seemed to know her well at all. As for David Quiring, he was still nowhere to be found.

While he had no reason yet to suspect Quiring over anyone else who had been in contact with the girl, he was the best person to start with. Whoever had killed the girl, Quiring might give him the information he needed to narrow down the search. He hoped the boy would be located soon, or he would have to handle that part himself as well. Only then would he know if this part of the case could be put to rest or not. Until that happened, Kumar needed to meet the victim—which meant visiting her room.

With the sun setting behind him, the inspector knocked twice on the wooden screen door of the Wagner residence and waited patiently. He watched the blue painted door, noting a large tear in the screen, before he saw some movement in the room inside. Abe Wagner, looking drawn, slowly opened the squeaking door and wordlessly invited the officer inside. He looked like he was half asleep.

Inside, it was Kumar who spoke first. "I appreciate you seeing me," he said. "I need to ask some more questions about your daughter's activities in the last several weeks before she disappeared."

Kumar helped himself to a chair at the kitchen table. Abe Wagner sat down across from him, elbows on the table, hands folded and supporting his forehead as in prayer. Exhausted. It was an old chrome kitchen set that had seen kinder days. The inspector looked around the room. The counter was clean, as was the floor. The room was sparse but orderly. This was not the home of a careless man.

"How well do you know David Quiring?" the inspector asked.

For a moment Wagner became the wine master who graced the brochures and pamphlets that detailed the long history of Tanglewood Vineyards. Kumar had learned much about the wine industry in his investigation. Much of the vineyard depended on the face that graced those brochures. Wagner, grey-haired and very German, in both his name and facial features, told a story of age, patient wisdom and time-honoured traditions handed down for generations. How much of this was true, Kumar neither questioned nor cared. His investigation did not hinge on the company's marketing. He was here to learn more about the real man and the real girl whose life was torn from her.

"He was my daughter's friend," said Wagner.

Kumar took a small notebook and a slim pen from his jacket pocket. "Do you have any idea where David may be?"

Wagner sighed and wiped his face with his hand. "None."

The old man sat back in his chair, looking up at the white plaster ceiling. "Is that why you are here? To ask the same questions McGrath asked me?"

"Not at all."

"No. I don't know where he is. No, I don't think he could do such a thing. No! I did not harm my daughter either."

Kumar remained calm, his expression sympathetic. "I didn't suggest you had."

He had read McGrath's report several times. He knew by heart the stupid, insinuating and insulting questions that had been asked of Wagner when he'd filed a missing persons report on his daughter two weeks before. McGrath had done everything but accuse the man outright of abusing his daughter and turning her out of his home.

"I'm not here to accuse you of anything," Kumar said. "Everyone has spoken highly of both you and your daughter. Right now we all want the same thing. I simply need more information to uncover more leads."

Wagner looked into Kumar's eyes, and in a few seconds his tired, tense expression clearly relaxed. It seemed Wagner had decided Kumar was an honest man, a man to be trusted. Kumar decided to make sure this decision was merited. He needed Wagner's help if he had any hope of moving the case forward.

"Frankly," he said, "I'm almost willing to bet my badge that the boy didn't do it."

The old man nodded.

"But I need to talk to him. He may have information about her that can help us. I need to find out what Anna did, who she spoke to, who she spoke about in the last two months, or the person who did do this to her is going to get away. I don't want that. Neither do you."

"I really don't know where the boy is," said Wagner. "I don't know anything about his family, except his parents are in Mexico. He has cousins here, but I don't know them."

"From what you do know of him, do you think he left the country?"

"No. I think he's around here somewhere."

Wagner dropped his hand on the table and looked up at Kumar, pleadingly. "Who do you think killed my daughter?"

"We don't know yet. We have a number of leads. We have eight men working on this case right now, Mr. Wagner. Most of them you will never see here. We're still gathering evidence from forensics, for example. But right now...I need to learn more..." Kumar hesitated.

"Yes?"

"Could I trouble you for a coffee?"

Wagner stood up. "I'm sorry. Let me get you a coffee."

"Thank you." He watched Wagner open cupboards, pour water, measure coffee with a tablespoon into a drip percolator. Daily rituals helped pull a victim's family from their grief and enabled them to connect with the days before the horror.

"We have a number of people still to talk to. Miguel Gonzalez, being one. Do you know him?"

"Yes. I told the officers about him too. The way he used to look at my Anna. He was a vile man."

The coffee machine began to churn and groan like an empty stomach.

"What do you mean, vile?"

"He used to stare at her. You know..."

Inspector Kumar nodded. There was a long silence as Wagner watched the coffee brew, running through memories, or running from memories, probably both.

"She'd tell him to stop. He'd look at her in a dirty way, or say disgusting things to her."

163

"That must have pissed you off?"

"Yes. I spoke to him about it when she told me. Randy Caines spoke to him as well. He denied he ever looked at her."

"Is there anyone else she complained of to you?"

"No."

"Anyone else she spoke to you about?"

"No."

"Anyone else who would look at her that way, that made you suspicious or made her nervous?"

Another long silence. "No," he said at last.

"Anyone in town?" asked Kumar softly. "Do you know of anyone following her?"

"No. She didn't know many people in town. She seldom went there. She would shop for clothes with a friend, but not often."

"Anyone at church? Or anyone from school? Anything stand out in your memory there?"

"No. I've been thinking of this too." Wagner shook his head sadly. "No one."

"Anyone here at the vineyard?"

Wagner set out the sugar and milk and two cups of coffee in mugs that bore the Tanglewood Vineyard logo. A silhouette of two clusters of grapes, a grape leaf and a wine bottle. Kumar had seen it often in the liquor stores in Toronto.

"Her friends in town; her friends from school; her friends at church—you have all those names. Here at Tanglewood? Mrs. Voracci was a good friend to her. She didn't have many friends here at the vineyard though."

"Mrs. Voracci?" Kumar leafed through his notebook. "Jennifer? Michael's wife?"

"Yes, that's her. Anna would go there to help with things. She talked to her. I don't know what about."

Kumar put some milk and sugar in his coffee. He took a sip. It was weak and tasted like an old dishrag. He set the cup down.

"What about her husband?"

"Mr. Voracci? No. He was polite to her. But his wife spoke to her more. Now that I think about it, they would sit together for lunch sometimes. I think Anna said something about keeping an eye on each other if her husband and I were away at the same time."

"Anyone else?"

"No."

"What about people she had problems with?"

"A few of the workers on the farm. That kid...Scotty. But he is a coward and a weakling. Anna was a strong girl. There is the new worker. He started here last fall. Taylor, Ben Taylor. I wonder about him."

"Why?" Kumar jotted Scotty's name in his notebook.

"He watches everyone. Everything. I can't read a man like him. Too quiet. Keeps to himself. If you can't read a man, you don't know what he may be capable of."

Kumar wrote Ben's name down. "Were they ever alone that you knew of?"

"Just once. They didn't know I saw them. They were talking, here—outside the door. I don't know what she was saying to him. She was upset."

Kumar underlined the name twice. "Why didn't you tell Chief McGrath this?"

"I just remembered."

"I can understand that. When was this?

"The day before she disappeared. I was surprised, because I didn't know she knew him. I meant to ask her about it, but I never had the chance. She seemed very upset. I don't know what about."

Kumar circled the name and closed his notebook. "I'd like to look in her room now, please."

Fourteen

Jennifer had prepared the most delicious meal Ben had tasted in months: roasted chicken, fresh garden salad, roasted potatoes and white wine. Ben tasted a few mouthfuls of each dish, hardly able to keep his eyes from her. Each time her hand reached across the table to reach for the salt, or a plate, or her glass of wine, he had to resist the urge to drop his fork and to take her hand in his.

She did not yet bring up the issue of leaving her husband, and he did not yet ask. Jennifer played with her food, pushing it back and forth on her plate, taking small bites. She watched him from beneath lowered lashes.

"I really should be hungry," said Ben. "But my appetite's been distracted, I think."

"Dessert?" she offered.

"If you're having some, other than that..."

"Maybe later," she grinned.

Ben helped her clear the table and loaded the dishwasher as she wrapped the leftovers and put them in the fridge. For several minutes they stood side by side, nearly touching, as she wrapped the food and he rinsed the plates in the sink. She turned to him, beaming, and he kissed her softly. Her breath was sweet with wine.

"Today," she said, her lips close to his, "for the first time in so many years, I feel optimistic. Like things might actually work out for the best after all. I love you, Ben."

Then, she quickly pulled away, before he could respond, before he could reply with a smile and a kiss, before he could reply with a frown, or stiffen in her embrace.

"Don't say a word," she said, blushing, her eyes glistening with tears. "It was so good to say that to you. But it's too soon for me to hear if you feel the same or not. Let me just savour the moment, okay?"

"But I need to ask you…" he said.

"I know. But wait just a minute. Wait right here."

She dashed out of the room and up the stairs.

Ben leaned back against the cupboard, closed his eyes and let out a deep breath. This was going far too fast. For a moment, he envisioned Jennifer returned wearing only her lingerie. He wondered how much coaxing it would take for him to get in that mood. His feelings for Jennifer had not faltered at all in the shadow of Anna's murder, but the mechanics of sex, here, now, would be something different.

No, he decided, that was not what she had in mind. There would have been more romantic atmosphere in the evening she had planned for them if she had been hoping to make love after dinner. A nice meal with a glass of wine might be any other woman's idea of a romantic evening, a lead towards sex, but this was not Jennifer's style—at least not the Jennifer that Ben had known. She had always been ultra-romantic, ultra-sensual, and exceedingly rich in her tastes for atmosphere. When they'd lived together in university, he would come home to find the apartment filled with dozens of candles for their special planned evenings together. There would be more dessert than dinner, chocolate fondue instead of chicken, champagne instead of wine, soft music in the background, perfume on her neck, and lingerie discreet but visible beneath her dress. No, Ben decided, she had something else in mind this evening. Realizing that, he relaxed considerably.

He waited for her in the kitchen, listening for movement upstairs, but heard none. He looked around the quiet country kitchen. The kitchen which had nearly seemed like home just seven months ago. It was a well-organized, well-used, and Ben could see Jennifer's style at every turn. A garlic braid hung from the edge of one cupboard, pans hung from an iron grate overhead, a large spice rack on the wall beside the fridge. The counters were clean, and above the window, between the white curtains, hung a glass witch's ball, hand-blown. Traces of the Jennifer he had always known—a woman who loved cooking and mysticism, and creating a protective, comfortable space around herself in her home to protect her from the cold world outside.

Jennifer returned in faded jeans and a black t-shirt, barefoot, her hair down. One hand was thrust into the front pocket of her jeans, and her eyes beamed. He saw the soft white skin of the underside of her arm. He saw her lips curled in a shy half-smile as if asking to be kissed.

"Hmmmmmm," she hummed happily, after he kissed her. "I have something for you. You know me. I don't get rid of anything."

"What is it?" he asked, looking at her closed hand to see what she was hiding.

"You gave this to me," she said, "long ago. I never had a chance to return it."

She opened her hand. It was a thin gold ring, strung on a simple silver chain. "Do you remember this?" she asked.

"No," he lied, grinning. They both knew that he remembered it very well.

"I think it was your grandmother's."

"The ring," he said. "Yes. I gave it to you."

She smiled. "You didn't actually give it to me. You let me wear it..."

"To keep you safe," he said as he lifted the chain from her hand, his fingers briefly touching her palm as he did. Carefully, he opened the clasp before slipping the chain around her neck.

"Keep it a while longer," he said.

Her eyes welled up with tears. "Oh Ben..."

"I can't believe you held onto my ring for all these years," he said as she rolled it between her fingertips. It was around her neck now, he thought. It was exactly where he most wanted it, keeping her safe. But he needed to know her intentions now.

"I need to ask you something," he said.

She seemed disappointed, as if she felt he was trying to distract her from something more important. She caressed the necklace with her fingers and looked down at the floor.

"What is it?" she asked.

"What do you want to do?" he asked.

"Tonight?"

"Tonight. Tomorrow. When your husband returns."

"For me?" she asked. "Or for us?"

"That should be the same thing."

"I want to be gone."

He waited a moment, waited for the awful "but" that was to follow.

Instead, she asked, "Is that still what you want?"

"You know it is. I wouldn't have come back here. I wouldn't have waited."

"Really, Ben? You can really forgive me for going back to Michael?"

"I'm here, aren't I?"

"But now you need me to wait a while longer for you," she said, wiping her eyes.

"Yes," he said.

"Because of Anna."

"Yes."

"But after that…"

"Yes. We'll go."

Jennifer poured the last of the wine into their glasses. The bottle wavered as she fought back the tears. "It's been so long since I've felt so loved, so understood," she said.

He clicked his glass to hers. "Here's to the girl who can't be shrugged away." He took a sip and put the glass on the cupboard beside her, one arm slipping around her waist as he did.

She wiped her face with the palm of her hand.

He kissed her once more. Slowly. Lingering. Her kiss tasted of salt and wine. He cupped her cheek with his hand and wiped away a remaining tear with his thumb.

"You haven't changed a bit since the first time I met you," he said. Before she could respond to the compliment, he hushed her with another kiss.

They had met in college during their first year. He had introduced himself to her mid-November in an overcrowded European History class. It had been an evening class, and afterwards she had let him buy her a beer at the pub. It turned out they lived on different floors of the same residence, and within a week she had all but moved into his room. They were inseparable. Slept together, ate together, studied together. The world stopped around them when they were together.

"I remember the first night we met," he said. "You wore your hair up in a loose ponytail. You were wearing a grey sweatshirt and black sweatpants. White running shoes."

She laughed. "That's because I'd gained so much weight from that awful cafeteria."

Ben nodded, thinking of the other reasons. Too much fast food was only one of the problems. Too much to drink, too many pills, too many joints were more reasons she would prefer not to dwell upon.

"How are your parents?" she asked.

"They're fine," he said. "I saw them for a couple weeks in January."

"And how is your sister?" she asked.

"Becky? She's doing well. I talk to her every few weeks."

"She loves you," said Jennifer.

"She really does," he said. "I don't know where I'd be without her." Jennifer looked into his eyes, pursing her lips. "What?" he asked.

"I was really lousy to you at the end," she said. "I'm so sorry about that."

They enjoyed a moment of silence. They both remembered all too well her drinking habits when they had been together. Living on campus had been her first experience living away from home. After the first month, she had thrown herself headlong into beer and marijuana. While most of her friends had kept their drinking to the weekends and after exams, Jennifer had made pot and alcohol a nightly event. Ben remembered often waking up to the chill of cold air in the middle of the night to find Jennifer standing in her terrycloth robe beside the open window, smoking a joint to help her get back to sleep.

As her grades continued to slide from average to poor, their arguments became worse. During midterms of their third year, Ben had taken to locking her in his room with him to get her to complete her readings. By the time final exams arrived, he had locked her out. The last time he saw her, he watched her from the window, on the street, stoned and drunk, out of control, her arm around the waist of her dealer, shouting up at him, giving him her middle finger and laughing, bewildered, angry and vengeful.

"You can't control me!" she had shouted up at him in the dead of night. It had been a dare, a shout of defiance.

Later, he'd looked for her everywhere. But that was the last time he saw her for ten years.

"It took me a long time to get over you," Ben told her now. "No one saw you, or heard from you. After three or four months, I joined the army."

"Because of me?" she asked.

"Yes," he whispered. "But only partly because of you."

"My god," she said. "I was so awful back then. I can't imagine why."

"I thought I could bring you back," he said.

Deep intake of breath. "You have no idea how much I wanted you to."

"But you disappeared," he said. "I asked about you. No one knew where you went."

"I know. I dropped out. But I didn't want to drop away from you. I came back in September to find you..."

"I had left by then," he said.

"I had no idea. I nearly called your parents, your sister, a dozen times a week. But I was too ashamed of myself. I thought it would be best for you if I stayed out of your life for good."

She turned away as the tears flowed again.

"I felt the same by then," he said. "I figured I had been the reason you went over the edge. I know I could be too—"

"No," she said, placing a finger on his mouth.

"We were so young," she said to summarize. "We were foolish with what we had. We took it for granted. I don't want to dwell on these painful memories, okay? Not tonight."

He sipped the rest of his wine and set the glass on the counter again, then put both arms around her.

"I stopped all the drugs. And I hardly ever drink any more." She turned her head away, trying to shake off the regret of past mistakes.

"I knew you'd grow out of it," he said.

"When I saw you here again," she said, "When you handed me

that sheet, I thought..." She took a breath. "I know it sounds silly, but I really felt like you had come for me," she said. "It didn't occur to me you came here just to work."

"A man needs to work, doesn't he?"

"But you don't make much money here, do you?"

"As much as anyone else," he said. "Farm minimum wage. No overtime. But money isn't the only reason one should work."

"Maybe for you," she admitted. "But why here? Of all the places in the world, why did you arrive here?"

"Who knows," he smiled. "I didn't really think about it too much. I got in my car one morning and started driving. By night, I found myself here. I thought it was because I had such good memories here. Life seemed so carefree in the summers when I worked here."

"We were so close to each other, a few dozen yards away from each other, behind the fence, behind the walls of this damn house, but we were both alone without knowing how close we were. And then, when we finally saw each other... I didn't care. I didn't care if you hated it here. I didn't care if he treated you badly, as long as you stayed here. I need you here. That's so awful, I know. But I can't help those feelings. I don't want you to leave here. Ever."

Ben stepped back and took both her hands in his, caressing her fingers, looking into her eyes as she searched for the words.

"This is all coming out wrong," she said, squeezing his hands as hard as she could. "Promise me."

"What?"

"Please," she said. Her voice was weak, barely audible as her throat was choked with the onset of new tears. "Promise you won't leave."

He looked at her.

"No." She shook her head. "I mean, promise that when you leave here, you won't leave me too."

"I can't leave yet," he said. "And maybe not for a long time."

"But I hate that you work here; that you work for him. I don't want you to be stuck here in this miserable place because you want to be with me."

"Believe me when I tell you I am not stuck here."

"Just promise me you won't stay here just for me."

"When we find out who killed Anna, I'll be ready to leave. Don't discuss this with anyone. I'm not going anywhere until I find out what happened to her."

"You really *are* a cop," she said. "I thought…"

"I can't talk about it, Jennifer. I'm not a cop right now. I was. Then I wasn't. I came here. Okay?"

"But I know you…" she protested. "You like to help people. You couldn't walk away…"

"Jennifer," he said firmly. "That's all I can say."

He found a napkin on the counter beside her and wiped her cheeks and eyes. She took it from him, turned from him to blow her nose and tucked the napkin into the garbage can beneath the sink.

"No more crying tonight," she said. "I promise that too."

He reached for her hand. "I'm not afraid of your tears."

"No. Really. I don't want to cry any more."

She kissed him.

"Know what I want to do?" she said.

"What's that?"

"I just want to kiss you."

She took his hand and led him into the living room, turning off each light as they passed until the house was dark, and they were finally removed from the light and present circumstances and past defeats. Alone in each other's arms, their breath mingled until their lips were almost sore.

FIFTEEN

Inspector Kumar stood at the threshold of Anna Wagner's bedroom. It was a small room with a single bed in the corner, white pillowcase, white sheets, yellow comforter folded along the foot of the bed.

"Is this how she left it?" he asked the girl's father, who stood down the hall with crossed arms, head bowed.

"Yes," came the reply. "Always. She was a very neat girl."

As he stepped into the room, Kumar was aware that he was stepping into the undisclosed life of an innocent Anna Wagner. To his right was a small wooden desk. A very basic design, it was well worn and had been repainted more than once. A light coat of yellow paint poorly covered the paint chips of previous coats of colour, and on the sides of its legs, a previous blue leaked through the yellow. Constructed before the advent of computers, it would have been able to support a typewriter and little else. There was no typewriter, no computer. At home, Anna had worked with pen and paper. Several textbooks were piled on the edge: geometry, calculus, and chemistry. A copy of *House and Homes* magazine lay beneath the texts. A red three-ringed binder lay beside the books. He flipped through it. Tabs separated it into eight sections—a section for each class. Her handwriting was neat, girlish loops, though her dots were pointed marks and t's were crossed with straight curt lines. She preferred black pen to blue. Kumar closed the binder. Inside the single shallow drawer was an assortment of pens and highlighters, blank papers, and a course calendar from Queen's University. Behind that were several crumpled chocolate bar wrappers.

Kumar took the course calendar out and thumbed through it. The pages on scholarships and bursaries were well-marked, many of the awards underlined with a black pen, several marked with stars. On the inside cover she had mapped out several course numbers, listing them under the headings Year One, Year Two, Year Three, Year Four. Courses in business and finance, courses in literature, history, philosophy, science and math. This was a girl thirsty for knowledge. A girl who had planned out the next four years of her life, which had nothing to do with running away to another farm, or to Mexico.

"Was Anna going to university?" Kumar called.

"Yes," Wagner replied from down the hall. "She was getting a scholarship."

"A smart girl," said Kumar.

"Yes. A very smart girl."

A thin jewellery box on the top of a fibreboard dresser contained silver and gold-plated earrings. Beside it was a small music box made of paper-covered cardboard. When opened, the box played Beethoven's "Für Elise". Kumar smiled momentarily, recognizing the tune. A shelf on the wall displayed an assortment of dolls and stuffed animals from her childhood. Under the bed was an old violin, in its case. The inspector stepped back to the doorway again.

Instead of asking what was in the room, it was often more productive to ask oneself what was missing. What was missing from this room? There were no certificates of achievement on the walls, despite the fact she was an A student. There were no trophies on her dresser, despite the fact that she excelled in volleyball and track and field.

There was only one photograph visible, without a frame, flat on the top of her dresser. Kumar picked it up carefully and looked at the poorly lit photo of a young woman holding a baby in a park somewhere Kumar did not recognize. The woman's dress and hair made it impossible to date the picture, but the inspector took an educated guess.

"Is this a photograph of her mother?" he called out.

"Yes. Her mother." Abe Wagner stepped towards her doorway now, though he refused to look in the room. "That is her, with Anna when she was six months old. That was taken in Argentina just before we left."

"Where are her other photographs?"

Reluctantly, Wagner stepped inside the room. He opened the bottom drawer of her dresser and took out a small photo album. It was a binder decorated by hand with strips of felt and cloth. Hearts and balloons cut of felt were glued on the cloth. Kumar looked through the six pages that had photographs in them. There were only two dozen photographs, most from school, some from birthday parties. A group of six-year-old girls seated around a cake with party hats on, saying "Cheeeezzzz" for the camera. Two photographs of her father. No other photographs of her mother.

"We lost most of our things in the fire that took my wife," Abe Wagner explained from the doorway. "This is the only picture of her mother Anna had. That was ten years ago now." He sighed wearily. "We lived in town then. The Voraccis gave us this home to live in after that fire. They were very generous to us."

Kumar returned the binder to its drawer. "Now that is odd," he said, not realizing he had said it aloud.

"What?" asked the girl's grieving father.

Kumar pretended not to hear him, quite embarrassed to have spoken his thoughts aloud. He clenched his jaw and continued to survey the room.

"What is odd?" Wagner asked again.

Kumar decided not to hide his thoughts. Wagner wanted to help him. He was not a suspect. And McGrath could be damned for his incompetence.

"It's odd that you should think your daughter ran away, when she did not take the only photograph of her mother she owned. It's right here."

"Yes," said her father. "That is what I told them."

Kumar scratched his cheek, vaguely aware that he was in need of a shave. "You did?"

"I told them she would not run away and leave her mother's picture here."

"They discounted that?"

"Yes. They told me not to think a teenage girl was as sentimental as her father." Wagner breathed deeply to control his grief.

"I wish I'd been here sooner." Kumar decided he should not say more. It was a hell of a position McGrath had put him in; the man was so blatantly incompetent. He did not like criticizing another cop—any cop—but McGrath's incompetence gave him little choice. It was damned embarrassing, and it made Kumar angry to think anyone would lump the likes of McGrath in with himself and the men he could respect and count on.

He continued to survey the room. He stayed for more than an hour, opening each drawer, looking through every paper, every note scrawled in every margin. What he had hoped for was notably absent. "She didn't keep a diary?" he asked.

"I don't know. Maybe. A father should know that, shouldn't he."

"Well, that depends."

Wagner began nodding his head. "When she was a little girl, she had a diary. But the fire destroyed that too. Now…I don't know. This was her room. She was a young woman. I let her have her privacy.

I've been in here more often now since…" He nodded again. "But I didn't come in here. Not before."

The father turned his face away. His shoulders began to shake as he wept silently. "I'm burying her in two days. I just wish I could have told her how proud I was of her."

"Please, Mr. Wagner. I know how hard this is for you. Go sit in the other room. I promise not to be too much longer."

Wagner raised his elbow and used his forearm to wipe his face. "Thank you." Lost in his own home, he turned left then right before heading down the hall. This could not be easy, Kumar knew, having lost a wife only a few years ago and now a daughter. He looked at the photo on the desk. Anna was the spitting image of her mother too. Beautiful women, both of them.

He sat down at the girl's desk and put his notebook on the desk beside the binder. He looked around the room, trying to get some sense of her and her life. She was intelligent, beautiful, but solitary in her nature. With the death of her mother, she had assumed the role of housekeeper and cook for her father. Her brother was an engineer and lived in Dallas, working for a company contracted to NASA. He had returned home for his mother's funeral, stayed a few weeks then left again. He had not been back since, not even with his sister's disappearance. With the death of his mother, he had estranged himself from the family. Kumar picked up his pen and made a note of that.

What else?

He closed his eyes, leaning back in the creaking wooden chair. She was responsible, caring and level-headed. But where was the teenager in all of this? He sat forward and turned on the desk lamp.

Then something struck his eye. Something about the red binder, something very subtle that had escaped his attention. He picked it up and grinned to himself.

On the cover of the binder were small indentations made from writing on paper that was laid on top. He tilted the binder and looked at the notes. Pieces of sentences written over each other. Dates and numbers. And a heart. He looked at the heart and could make out the initials inside it: BT & AW.

"So, who is BT?" he asked himself. Her boyfriend's name had been David Quiring.

Kumar reached for the girl's school yearbook. He went to her class and searched the T's. There were two boys in her class with names starting with a T, but neither had a first name beginning with a B. He turned through the pages and looked at the classes one year ahead and one year behind Anna's. One boy, perhaps. It could be Bill Thibodaux. He was a year younger than Anna and cursed with acne. His hair was long, and he seemed to be one of the party boys in the class. It didn't feel right, but perhaps he would check up on the boy anyway.

He opened his own notebook to jot down the boy's name. As he flipped to the last page, he saw the name he had written down only a few hours before. Ben Taylor.

"Well, I'll be damned," he said.

Inspector Kumar put away his pen and closed his notebook, leaving the girl's bedroom.

"Do you have something?" Wagner asked as Kumar made his way for the door. "Did you find what you need, or not?"

"I think so," Kumar nodded. "I'll know soon enough. Thank you for your time, Mr. Wagner."

He let the door slam behind him as he bounded down the wooden steps of the porch and hurried towards his car.

SIXTEEN

Kumar drove his car two hundred feet up the laneway and turned off his engine near the Voracci home. He sat in his car for several minutes. Crickets sang in the darkness. He checked his watch. It was nearly nine thirty.

The Voracci home was larger than most in the area, almost stately in its presence. While it was over a century old, it had been built well and had been nurtured over the years to ensure it remained comfortable. It had a charm that was not shared by the modest Wagner bungalow. It had the quiet air of wealth behind the familiar veneer of a modest lifestyle.

Aside from the fluorescent lights of the warehouse some five hundred feet away, the only light Kumar could see from this angle came from the back porch behind the fenced yard. He wondered if anyone was still up. The people here seemed to live by the amount of work that needed to be done, and the rising and the setting of the sun, with little regard for clocks. He had been thinking a lot of Ben Taylor's respect and affinity for the farm workers here, and he was beginning to understand why. The concept of an eight-hour day was as unfamiliar to the people here as it was to Kumar himself.

Michael Voracci's vehicle was not in the driveway, but a quick check in the window of the split-shingled garage revealed to Kumar a second vehicle, a light-coloured, late model Volkswagen Beetle—Jennifer Voracci's car. There was no sound from inside the house, but lights glowed faintly from two rooms. Kumar fumbled with the latch on the gate before stepping onto the porch. He knocked gently on the wooden screen door.

He could hear footsteps inside and a woman saying quietly, "I don't know," from behind the door. Then the inside door cracked open an inch, and a woman's eye peered up at him.

"Mrs. Voracci?"

"Yes?"

He extended his ID. "Police, ma'am."

The door opened another couple inches. He could see her full face from the porch light overhead. She looked as if she had just woken up.

"You're here about Anna," she said.

"That's right, ma'am. I'm Inspector Walter Kumar with the OPP. I'm investigating the death of Anna Wagner. I'm sorry for catching you at an inopportune time. Were you and your husband asleep?"

"No," she said. "He's out of town. I was just getting ready for bed."

"I apologize for that," he said. "I know it's probably late for you. Everyone in the country seems to get up earlier than we do in the city…"

"No, no," she said. "That's fine. Really. I don't usually go to bed so early, but it's been a terrible week, you know. But I thought I covered everything with the town police when she disappeared."

"Yes, I know. But this is a separate investigation."

"Well, can we do this in the morning?"

"I'm afraid not. It won't take much of your time."

The door opened further. "But there really isn't that much to tell you. I honestly don't know anything."

"You would be surprised at how helpful people can be, even when they don't believe they know anything at all."

"I guess that makes sense," she said, stepping back and tucking her t-shirt into the back of her jeans. "I don't mind helping at all. I just thought it would be kind of late for you."

"I don't work nine-to-five," he replied. "A girl has died. I want to find out why."

"I heard she was murdered."

"That's why I'm here," he said. "To find out what happened. This won't take long at all," he said, opening the screen door. She stepped back to let him in. The kitchen was dim, with only the light above the stove illuminating the room.

He looked down at the rug, noting the large pair of work boots beside the door. There were no other shoes in sight. They were well-worn, the leather scuffed on the toes, resting a foot from the wall, and one was on its side.

"Did you see or hear anything unusual in the last week?" he asked.

"You mean before they found her?"

"To start, yes."

"Nothing. I'm sorry. I wish I had. I don't go out of the house very often. But I've been thinking a lot about it. Wishing I'd paid more attention. Gone out or looked out the window at least."

"What about the night of the sixteenth or seventeenth?" he asked.

"I remember it stormed on the seventeenth. I did stand at the window looking out for quite a while." She sighed. "But even then, all I looked at was the rain and the lightning."

"So there was a lot of lightning that night?"

"Not a lot. A bit, yes. But it was mostly rain. Pouring rain."

"Did you go out for any reason on either day?"

"I think I went grocery shopping the day before."

"The sixteenth?"

"Yes." She took a moment to give it some thought, then crossed her arms and leaned against the counter. "Yes. I went to get some groceries. But that was in the morning."

"Did you see or hear anything unusual then?"

"Not at all."

"Did you notice anyone you don't usually see?"

"I saw some of the workers."

"Who were they?" he asked, retrieving his notebook from his jacket pocket. "Did you recognize any of them by name?"

"I don't know their names. My husband would know them. They were just walking from the greenhouses to the vineyards. They've worked here for a long time, I think."

"How well did you know Miss Wagner?"

"Not that well…"

"I was told you were close," Kumar pressed.

"Maybe for her. I'd hate to think I was one of her closer friends. She was a wonderful girl, but I don't think anyone knew Anna very well. She was very reserved. She was very quiet, and she liked to listen more than she liked to talk. We spoke a few times, but nothing very much." Her hand absently combed out the hair on the back of her head. "I liked her. I liked her a lot."

"Did she ever speak to you about any of her friends?"

"Not really. She talked to me about her boyfriend a few times."

"David Quiring?" he asked.

"Yes."

"Did they get along?"

"He was in love with her. Very much. But she didn't want to take the relationship very far. Mostly…" she paused, in thought, while Kumar waited. "Mostly," she continued, "she had her eyes set on going to college. She wanted to focus on her schoolwork. That was more important to her than any boy, I think."

"What is he like?"

"With her? Intense. He was always by her side; always touching her, holding on, in that way boys like to do."

"He was territorial towards her?"

"Yes. That's the best word, I think. Territorial."

"And how was she with him?"

"She seemed used to it. She'd let him hold her hand. If she pulled away to talk to someone, or eat something, she'd let go of his hand, but he'd always come back within a few minutes at the most. Then she'd pull away again. I don't know if he even noticed it was happening. But I noticed."

"Why did you notice?"

"Maybe it's something women notice. She liked him, but she didn't want to be with him like he wanted to be with her. Like you said, he was territorial."

"Was he likeable?"

"He didn't speak much. I didn't care for him. But I don't think he'd hurt her."

"Why not?"

"He wasn't really aggressive. He watched her all the time, but he let her have a bit of space when she needed it, I think."

"Why don't you go out very often, Mrs. Voracci?"

"What do you mean?"

"You seem like a healthy, active woman."

"I try to keep myself in good shape," she said, stepping to the side, away from the counter. "But I don't have many friends here. All my friends are in the city, and we don't get out very often. As a couple, I mean."

"I see." He handed her his card. "Anything else comes to mind, please call me."

She looked at the card, biting her lip. "I will. I really want to help you with this."

185

"You've been more help than you realize," he said.

Jennifer locked the door behind him, staring at his card as she stepped back into the living room.

Ben waited on the edge of the sofa.

"He saw your boots by the door," she said. "I don't know. It seemed like he kept looking into the living room. And every time I stepped back, he'd step forward, like he was trying to edge his way into the house."

"Well, that's his job," Ben said. "I'm sorry if me being here made it difficult for you."

"I'm okay." She sat down beside him. "Really." She was still looking at the card.

Ben smiled and put his arm around her. She leaned into him and tossed the card on the table.

"That damn card," she said. "When he handed it to me, it was the strangest feeling. It was as if when he handed it to me, he brought me right into the middle of all this."

"He's just asking questions," Ben said. "It's his job."

"I know. But I was trying to remember that dream as we were talking just now. Trying to remember more of it. There must be more. I wonder if I should have told him about the dream."

"It was a dream," he said. "The police are looking for evidence. They're not looking to analyze your dreams."

"I know. But it seemed so real. It's silly, really. I know that." She pressed her head against his shoulder. "It's silly. It's just a dream."

"About Anna."

"Yes."

"How well *did* you know Anna?" he asked.

"Anna?" She sighed. "The OPP Inspector just asked me about that too. You heard him, didn't you? I didn't know her very well at all. And when I told him, I realized how awful that was. That's

186

really awful, isn't it? I've known her for almost five years, but I really didn't know her well at all."

"Just because her father works here doesn't mean you had to be friends."

"I know… But..." she squeezed his hand. "It's awful because I spent time with her... but she was just a kid. Besides her dad, she was the only worker I really knew. She and her father would come here for dinner. But Abe and Michael did most of the talking. When we did talk, it was always about surface things. We talked about her family. Her father. The weather. She barely talked about David, her boyfriend. Actually, he didn't seem that important to her. Not as important as she was to him."

"What do you mean?"

"I'm not sure how to explain it. I only saw him a couple times. At the company picnic, he doted on her. When she passed by, his eyes followed her. When he was near her, she was fine. But when he wasn't, it was like, out of sight, out of mind."

"She wasn't in love?"

"He was madly in love with her. He would do anything for her. But she was cooler towards him. If they split up, I don't know how he would have taken it. She would have adjusted, you know?"

"I think so."

"I know she drowned, Ben."

"Jennifer, she didn't drown."

"How do you know?"

"I saw her."

"But how do you know how she really died?"

"I'm pretty damn certain she didn't drown."

"I don't want to talk about it now. Not tonight. This isn't what I wanted for us tonight at all."

She stood up and took his hands. He rose and she put her arms around him, pressing her head on his shoulder.

"What do you want to talk about?" he asked.

"It's not about talking. It's just that—"

'I know," he said. "Let's go for a drive. We can go to the beach. I know how you love the beach."

"Yes," she grinned. "I haven't been there for a long time. Michael and I went last year. Once. I insisted. I had a hotdog. Then we went home."

"The beach is less than a half-hour away. We can watch the stars. And it will get you out of the middle of all this." He picked up Kumar's card and placed it on the fireplace mantle.

"Can I drive?" she asked.

"Sure."

She beamed at him. "And we get to walk in the wet sand."

"Yes. Bring a towel then."

"Two. And let's bring something hot to drink."

"We'll pick up coffee on the way."

She went upstairs and came back with two grey sweatshirts under her arm. "This one's for you," she said, handing him a sweatshirt.

He unfolded it and recognized the Tanglewood Vineyard logo on the left breast. "No," he said, handing it back to her. "I'm not wearing your husband's clothes."

"It's not his!" she laughed. "It's mine. We got a whole shipment the year before last. I grabbed a few. It's a large, 'cause I like big sweatshirts. I don't think I've ever worn that one though."

She handed it back to him, and he pulled it over his head. "Perfect fit. Thank you."

The ride to the beach was silent except for the radio quietly playing classical music. They held hands above the console through the entire trip and did not even remember to stop for the coffee.

A rush of images flashed through Jennifer's mind, memories of their years together in university, the many times she had wondered what had ever become of him in the years since then. So many memories, none of which seemed worthwhile to discuss now that he was here beside her.

"It really isn't that long," he said to her. "Ten years really isn't forever."

But it had seemed like forever. She had never thought she could feel so old. No one should feel this old before they are sixty, she told herself.

She parked the Volkswagen near a beach she had never stopped at before. Climbing out of the car, she saw him watching her as she shook out her long brown hair. Ben took her hand and led her towards the water.

"Wait!" she laughed. "I want to take off my shoes."

He turned and waited.

"You can't walk on the beach with shoes!" she said. "What's the point?"

In the moonlight, they found an old log half buried in the sand where a campfire had recently been. The moon rose above the lake, nearly full. Sitting down, Ben put his arm around her, and they listened to the waves.

"I've almost left him a few times," she said, knowing they were thinking of the same thing.

"Why didn't you?"

"Actually, I really did." She snuggled against him. "Have you ever just disappeared?" she asked.

"That depends on what you mean by disappear."

"I did. Once. I disappeared completely. Without a trace. I'd been married to Michael for nearly two years. I already knew by then that marrying him was a mistake. I didn't know how to get out of it. I knew I had to. But how? He took me on a trip with him to

Montreal. I remember feeling very strange. We took a cab to the airport, and when he opened the door, I dropped my bag... I just wanted to turn and run down the street, run away as fast as I could. I didn't want to get on the plane. When they called us for boarding, my legs wouldn't move, and I remember having to say to myself out loud, 'Get up! Get up!' We barely spoke for the entire trip. We went on a carriage ride through the old part of the city. Cobblestone streets, old buildings, that kinda thing. It was beautiful, but I felt like I wasn't even there. I felt numb and I didn't know why.

"He was in such a good mood. It was the middle of the afternoon, and we were window-shopping at all the tourist shops. We sat down at a park bench. And he was talking about his business. The same stories he always told about how his grandfather worked the land and survived starvation to make it into something. How his father had built on that and turned it into an empire and how now it was his turn. The responsibility was on his shoulders to take it to the next step and how he was going to need me to help him do that.

"I didn't marry him for his family's money."

Ben nodded slowly, considering her words. "Why *did* you marry him?"

"That's a long story," she said after a long pause. "I was working for his father at the vineyard the summer after I left college. He was always in the papers then, y'know? He was dating actresses and these famous models. So when he asked me out...I guess I was swept off my feet."

"That makes sense," Ben replied.

"It was just dinner and a movie, but I had fun. We dated a couple times, then he took me to New York for a weekend. I met his friends. I met a lot of famous people. Some of the guys from Saturday Night Live, stuff like that." She sighed and squeezed Ben's hand. "I'm sorry...I guess I really was starstruck, and I let him sweep me off my feet. We seemed to click. He proposed about a year later, I accepted, and it seemed to work for a while."

"What happened in Montreal?" Ben asked.

"Well, that day on the park bench, it was like I just woke up from a long sleep. He was talking about all his plans, and he was going on about it all and suddenly... I just wanted to be sick. I just wanted to die. To disappear forever.

"So I stood up. He told me to sit down. Asked me where I thought I was going. I said I just wanted to see something, and I'd be right back.

"I just started walking. Down the street." She paused and looked up at the large moon edging its way above the lake.

"Where did you go?"

"I just walked. I didn't know where I was going. I just walked, then I came to a corner. And suddenly there were a lot of people around me. Lots of tourists. People holding hands. People talking and smiling and laughing. All of them seemed to be acting the way I'd thought Michael and I were going to be. The way I wanted to be. Happy, y'know?"

"I know."

"And at first I thought, 'Please, God, make him come and get me now.' But another part of me prayed he'd just sit there and wait. And I turned the corner. And then I turned another corner. Then I walked a couple more blocks. And then I turned another corner. And then I walked faster."

"You got lost."

"Completely lost. I *made* myself get lost. And suddenly, everyone was talking French. No one was talking English any more. They weren't tourists anymore. And the streets weren't cobblestone any more."

He held her tight, could smell her hair mingling with the sweet salt smells of the water. "You must have been so scared. What happened then?"

"No. Not scared. I was numb. I went to an ATM and took out all the cash I could. Then I walked some more. Then I found a bench and sat down. I knew I could find my way back to the hotel if I just found a cab. But it was too late for that. I remember wondering what he was doing. Was he still there waiting? Was he angry? I imagined he'd be angry at first. And he'd walk around looking for me. But when it got dark, I wanted him to be scared. I wanted him to worry and to hurt for me."

"You didn't want to be shrugged off."

She tilted her head, looking at him, taking in that phrase as if it was something that had never occurred to her before.

"Yes," she said at last. "I guess that was a big part of it. He came for me in the morning. Said he'd called the credit card company, and they told him where to find me. I guess he did that before he went to bed. He didn't lose sleep over it anyway. In the morning, I woke up. He was in my room. He had brought our bags and laid out some clean clothes for me to wear."

"What did you do?" Ben asked carefully. "How did you feel about that?"

"There wasn't much I could do. He had clean clothes for me. I took a long shower. I cried in the shower. And when I was dressed, he called a cab and we went to the airport. He found me and took me back all on schedule. He didn't even have to reschedule the flight." She shook her head, grinning with disbelief. "Then in the airport, he made me promise never to run away from him again."

"Did you promise?"

"Yes, I did."

Ben nodded thoughtfully.

"But you have to know something else," she added quickly. "He didn't worry about me. He didn't call the police when I disappeared. He didn't hug me. He didn't kiss me. He didn't cry for me. He never asked me why I did it. Even though I came back to him, I wasn't coming back to any man or husband. He gave me a stone wall to lean against. Solid, but cold."

"But you kept your promise," he said, watching her with sombre eyes.

"But that was a long time ago," she explained. "I don't feel bound to that promise any more. We're different people now. All of us. At the time, I guess I could have left or called someone to get him out of my room. But he had my clothes. I was in a strange city. Running away like I did was foolish. I was numb. I realized he didn't really care about me. Where would I run to? Where would I go? I kept thinking to myself, nothing matters any more."

She looked at him, searching his face in the moonlight. "That night when I was alone," she continued, "I remember thinking: this is my choice. To be with him, like we are. Or to be alone, like that."

"Some choice."

"Now," she smiled, "maybe I have new choices. I don't feel numb any more."

She leaned toward him, and he pressed his lips to hers, softly. Ben stood up and took her hand. She watched him curiously as he led her a few yards from the log. He slipped his arms around her waist. They danced together, slowly turning and rocking to the sound of the surf that seemed all around them in the shadows. All sense of time receded with the tide in the shadows. They said nothing, holding each other closely, eyes closed as the moon rose slowly above the water.

Ben slowed the car at the motel and parked outside of his own cabin.

She looked up at the yellow neon sign.

"Ohhh," she sighed, "this is perfect!"

"Home sweet home."

He unlocked the door and opened it wide for her. Inside, he left the lights off, and they kissed again as the moonlight spilled in through the window of his crowded cabin.

"This is all I ever wanted," she said. "I can't believe you came back for me. I can't believe I'm here with you now." She began to cry. "I'm so afraid I'm going to wake up, that this is all going to end."

Ben sat down with her on the bed and held her in his arms. He dried her tears with his hands.

They made love in the moonlight, hungry, thirsty for one another.

"I don't want to go back there," she said. "Why does our timing have to be so screwed up? Why can't we just leave now?"

"I know how you feel," he said. "Trust me. As soon as this is cleared up…"

"I know." She turned her head away, ashamed. "I feel so stupid. So self-centred. I'm sorry." She cried again. "I couldn't leave tonight anyways even if it weren't for Anna. I just wish I could."

"Why couldn't you?"

"There's something I didn't tell you about him," she began. "He doesn't love me. But he doesn't want me to be gone either. He needs me. I can't just leave. I have to talk to him first."

"You mean you need his permission to leave him?"

Jennifer nodded. He was surprised she looked him straight in the eyes, unblinking. "He doesn't love me. Not like you did. But he understands things. He accepts me for who I am."

"I accept you for who you are too."

"Do you? Do you really, Ben? Did you accept me for who I was ten years ago?"

"You've changed. We all change."

She held his shoulders. "Yes. That's it exactly. We all change. But you don't know what changes I've been through. You don't really know me. Not any more."

"I know by looking into your eyes," he said.

"Oh, Ben. Always the white knight. I love that about you too. Maybe you're the one who hasn't changed."

"I've changed," he said. "You have no idea."

"Then let me get an idea. And you too. I do want to be with you, and a part of me is scared, is terrified, that you may change your mind."

She threw her arms around him, holding him tightly, wanting to hide her tears from him, wanting to hide the conflict that tore at her heart as he spoke of taking her away. "I'm not the innocent girl I was ten years ago. Don't you think I want to tell you the terrible things about me? Don't you think I want to give you that chance to love me? I mean to love all of me? All of the good that is in me? All of the bad that is in me? All the good things I do. And all the bad?"

"What are you trying to say?" he asked, caressing her arm with his fingertips. "Just tell me. Whatever it is, I'm sure I can deal with it."

"I've been an awful person," she began.

"Don't say that, Jennifer. You're not. I can never accept that."

"But you have to. Don't you remember what I was like with you? Don't you remember at all?"

"I remember I loved you. I see nothing bad in you, Jennifer."

Suddenly, she turned towards him, glaring. "Don't say that!" she shouted. Her left fist struck his chest. Her right hand slapped his shoulder.

Ben grabbed her wrists with his hands. She tried to pull away, but he held her firmly. Then he pulled her against him. He glared back at her.

"I can accept anything you've ever done. Anything you've ever been. I know you, Jennifer. You can't say I won't accept you without giving me that chance."

"How can you?" she asked. "How can you possibly accept me when even I can't?"

"He does."

"Michael is different."

Ben lay back. "You're right," he said. "Then maybe I don't understand."

"Please," she cried. "I just need some time. We both need some time. There's so much I need to tell you. A few days. A couple weeks maybe. My god, you thrust your way back into my life just a few days ago, and already all I can think about is you." She caressed his cheek with her hand. "You have all of me. Just give me a few days to adjust, to share myself with you, before you tear me out of this life too."

Ben took a cleansing breath. "I just can't stand the thought of you being in that house with him."

"I know." She held his cheek in her hand. "I know. I love you for that too. Try to remember I'm really alone when I'm there. And you need to know one more thing, my white knight."

"What's that?"

"When you take me from here, it has to be forever. I'll have nowhere to go back to. You can't ever change your mind."

"I know," he said. "I know."

Later, as she drove away, he watched her, his hands thrust in his pockets.

Neither noticed the blue Buick that drove by once again as she turned from the parking lot to make her way home.

A half mile up the road, Inspector Kumar pulled over and took out his notebook to make a few notes on Ben Taylor.

SEVENTEEN

Randy Caines looked up at the clock on the wall behind the tomato sorter. It was almost two in the morning. He wiped the sweat from his forehead with the back of his hand and pulled a red box-cutter from his pocket. It had been a long day. Quickly, he slit the length of the shrink-wrap from the second pallet of tomatoes. He pulled away the plastic, balled it up to about the size of a football and stuffed it into the blue garbage bin in the corner. The pallets were stacked with five white boxes to a layer, three wide and two across, and fifteen layers high, to a height of nearly eight feet.

Caines dragged a wooden pallet across the warehouse floor and let it drop with a resounding slam onto the concrete. Then, box by box, he began pulling down the stacked tomatoes from the first palette and placing them on the second. The difference between the stacks was important—with the new palette, the boxes were only placed on the perimeter, leaving an open square in the centre.

David Quiring paced nearby, a large yellow backpack slung over his shoulder. Nervously, he smoked a cigarette as Caines began pulling additional palettes of tomatoes from the cooler. He watched Caines open the back of the truck and climb onto a forklift, starting it up.

"Are you sure that thing's not going to collapse on me?" Quiring asked. "I'm not going to suffocate in there, am I?"

"Relax!" Caines snapped back.

"But how do you breathe in there?"

"It's a truck, not a fucking tomb," Caines replied. "Air circulates. I'm not sealing the top of the palette."

Quiring stamped out his cigarette on the concrete floor.

"Hey!" Caines shouted over the noise of the forklift. "Use the ashtray, you pig."

Adjusting the backpack on his shoulder, Quiring stooped down to pick up his butt before placing it in the ashtray. The weight of the backpack made it shift uncomfortably as he leaned over.

"What do you have in that thing, anyway?" Caines asked. "I told you to pack light."

"Mostly pot," Quiring replied.

"And what are you going to do with that? You're going to Mexico, for fuck's sake."

"And how am I going to get there? I have to pay for my next trip too, you know. You have all my cash."

"Fair enough," Caines admitted, speeding away in the forklift.

Quiring watched Caines' thigh protruding from the seat of the forklift and his jowls jiggling as the machine went in and out of the cooler. It was no wonder, he decided, that no one had stopped Caines yet. The man was a bulldozer of flesh, pushing his way through life without regard for anyone, not even for himself. Assuming Caines never got caught and kept all his secrets intact, the best he could hope for was to live past age fifty. He was an engorged heart ready to collapse on itself.

Quiring was the Laurel to Caines' Hardy. He was young, tall, lanky and fair. At eighteen years old, he had just finished his last growth spurt of adolescence, and his shirtsleeves cut out an inch above his wrists. He had a difficult time finding jeans at Walmart that were long enough for his thin legs and could still grip his waist. His belt pulled tightly, and the buckle was off-centre from the constant tugging to keep his pants up. Standing next to Caines,

David Quiring was a matchstick.

As soon as he had finished his cigarette, he lit another. His hands would not stop shaking. He was exhausted and had not slept for days. His girlfriend had just been brutally murdered, and he was the prime suspect. An illegal immigrant with a murder hanging over his head. It did not matter that he was innocent. He was the perfect scapegoat, which meant he had to get out of the country and back into Mexico now, or he would be spending the rest of his life in prison.

Quiring hated this scene. He hated being here. He hated Caines. He hated the whole damn thing. Hiding in Caines' filthy bungalow for almost a week had been bad enough, but being trapped in this warehouse for the last day and a half, waiting for Caines to have an order ready to cross the border was almost more than he could bear. Caines had been smuggling people in and out of the country for years now, and he was not going to let a small matter like a police investigation rush him or cause him to change his methods. So Quiring had been squirrelled away behind several dozen bales of flat boxes on the third story mezzanine above the warehouse cooler until Caines was ready to let him leave.

There he waited, eating tomatoes, dry bread and cold french fries. He pissed into empty juice bottles during the day and snuck down to use the bathroom during the night before Caines locked up. Hiding in the centre of a palette of tomatoes for two or three hours was probably not going to be as bad as he feared. After all, his entire living space for the last day had been four by four by eight feet, in his own personal shanty made of stacked cardboard boxes.. For a week now, there had been nothing to do but to wait for Caines to arrange this shipment so he could get out of here. Nothing to do but to wait and to think and to remember.

Anna was dead. Murdered. And everyone seemed to think he had done this to her.

"I shouldn't be doing this. Not now," said Quiring. "Her funeral is in two days. I should be at the funeral."

"Don't give me that shit now," Caines said, his anger flaring. "After I arranged all of this for you. You stupid bastard. Just do yourself a favour. Shut the fuck up and help me with these boxes," said Caines.

Quiring helped Caines shrinkwrap the last palette of tomatoes, holding the tail end against the boxes as Caines began to walk the plastic around and around the palette.

"What do the cops want with me, anyway?" he asked. "It just doesn't make any sense."

"I'm not going through that again with you. Go turn yourself in if you want to. But I'm telling you, they've already pegged you with everything. They want your blood, you stupid fool."

"It's not right. They're after me, and that bastard is still out there walking around free."

"Don't worry about that," Caines replied. "He'll get his. Don't you worry. No one knows where you are. And I sure as hell ain't gonna tell them, am I?"

"No. I guess not."

"We're in this together. If they find out how you got across the border, my ass will be in jail along with yours. So relax. You'll be in Mexico by the end of the week."

Quiring grimaced and lit another cigarette. His legs were shaking now too.

"Just don't forget our deal," Caines said. "If the Americans pick you up, you've been there the whole time. They won't have a record of you crossing the border, so you don't have to worry about an alibi, right?"

"Right."

"And you have no reason to mention me, right?"

"I know. But won't they want to know how I got into the States, even if I tell them it was six weeks ago? Won't your name come up then?"

Caines stepped forward, glaring at him. He poked Quiring's shoulder with a fleshy finger. The thrust was hard enough to push Quiring a step back. "After all I've done for you," hissed Caines. "Don't you dare try to turn on me."

"It's not that —"

"You don't want to become a liability to me, do you, boy?"

"No, I don't. I just don't want to be blamed for Anna's death. Dammit all, I should be helping them find out who did it."

"Why? Will knowing who killed her help bring her back?"

Quiring peered at him, evidently surprised that even Caines would say such a thing. "It will help me. It will help her rest in peace."

"Whatever. You can read all about it in Mexico. Right now, you do it my way."

The cell phone on the desk began to ring. Caines cursed and examined the number before he answered. He turned back to Quiring, who was watching him nervously.

"No problem," he said after a few moments. "I figured as much." A short pause. "Naw, I already planned for that." And he put the phone down.

"What was that about?" Quiring asked.

"Nothing to do with you," Caines replied. "Shit!" He laughed. "What are you so testy about? You should be grateful I'm not charging you more for this, you miserable fuck. Normally this ride costs two grand a head."

"I do appreciate it, Randy. I really do. Who called?"

"Do you have a gun?"

"No."

"I'll give you one. Better take precautions. You don't know what's going to be waiting for you when you get to the Mexican border. I hid a Colt up on the mezzanine."

"I didn't see a gun up there."

"I hid it, moron."

"Who called?" Quiring asked again.

"So curious!" Caines laughed. "Just get on the forks. I'll give you a ride."

Quiring dropped his backpack on the floor before he hopped onto the forks of the forklift, a foot on each tong.

"Here," said Caines. "You can put this away while you're up there. It goes on that shelf on the left." In mid-sentence, he tossed Quiring an old grease gun that was perched on the floor beside his desk.

Quiring caught it, just barely, with his right hand.

"Damn," he said. "It's filthy."

"What do you expect, Einstein? It's a grease gun." Caines climbed into the forklift and started it up.

Quiring straddled the forks, holding the greasy machine away from his clothes, and Caines sped the forklift to the warehouse cooler end of the warehouse. The mezzanine was above the cooler, thirty-six feet from the platform. Caines pulled up beside a steel ladder, painted blue, which was bolted to the wall. No one used the ladder. It was common practice to use the forklifts as elevators for anyone needing to go up or down.

"Lift me up," said Quiring.

"Fuck you, you lazy ass. Use the ladder."

Quiring just stared at him. Caines laughed and put the forks parallel to the wall beside the steel ladder. He pulled the lever, and the forks ascended thirty feet to the top of the mezzanine. "The gun's in the canvas bag at the top," he said.

"Where?" yelled Quiring.

"Behind the barrels, you blind sonofabitch. In the canvas bag. The green one. The green canvas bag."

Quiring searched behind the empty barrels and found the bag.

"Hurry up!" shouted Caines.

"What the hell is in this thing?" asked Quiring, peering over the edge. "It's packed with hammers and screwdrivers and shit…"

"Well, it's not just going to have a gun in there, is it?" Caines was annoyed. "Just get the hell down here."

Quiring slung the bag over his shoulder and stepped out with one foot onto the forklift, using the top of the steel ladder for support.

"Why don't you want to tell me who called. Is it about this trip?"

"Not the trip you're thinking of," Caines said. "Another trip."

"Which one's that?"

Just as Quiring stepped onto the forks, Caines made his move. He pulled back the lever and let the fork fall three feet.

"Shit!" Quiring gasped in surprise and lurched forward.

His hand reached out and down to grab the bar between the forks. At the same time, Caines threw the machine into reverse. Quiring fell, but caught the left fork with his arm. He grabbed on with his hands, the canvas bag still slung from his arm, heavy, caught on his elbow, and the gun inside hit him in the head. His right hand, still greasy, slipped off. But his left hand kept its grip. He hung with one hand, thirty feet above the concrete platform.

"Randy!" he screamed again. He dangled from the fork. "What the hell are you doing? Hurry! Let me down."

"*This* trip, you stupid fuck. You think we'd let you drag us all down with you?"

Caines pulled back on the lever, raising the forks higher into the air, now six feet above the mezzanine. Quiring glanced at the mezzanine, but he was too far away to jump onto it. He tried to pull himself up onto the forks instead.

"Just fucking let go! Shit-for-brains, I don't have time to fuck around!"

"What the hell is wrong with you?" Quiring screamed. "Let me down!"

Caines laughed. "Just fall. You look like a fucking monkey hanging up there."

Quiring tried to regain his grip with his right hand. But his fingertips were grease-covered and slipped again from the smooth metal.

"Let me down!"

"Fine." Caines let the forks drop four feet and stopped them cold. Quiring's grip slipped, and he scrambled to get a better hold. His fingers were slipping.

"Randy!"

Caines raised the forks again, lifting him up another ten feet. He backed up and began to tilt the forks forward. They reached an alarming angle.

Quiring managed to get his right hand up and was trying to swing his legs onto the other fork, but both hands were slick with grease now. When the forks slowly tilted forward, his hands slid down the forks.

"You bastard! I'll get you for this!"

Those were his last words. He hit the cement, back first. His shoulders struck the floor only a fraction of a moment before the back of his head. His skull opened like a cantaloupe. The sound of the crack echoed through the warehouse.

Randy Caines lowered the forks and brought the machine back to the loading dock. He wiped the grease and the fingerprints from the forks with a cloth in his pocket and closed up the warehouse for the night. He shut the shipping doors. He would take the truck out himself tonight. The last thing he did before getting into the truck was to open the door that connected the greenhouses to the warehouse. He whistled for the dogs, held the door open as they rushed into the warehouse then stepped outside into the fresh night air.

On a normal day, the plant would go to a standstill with him being away and Michael Voracci being in Chicago on the same night. But Caines expected production might not be running all that well, anyway, once the police decided to close down the warehouse.

He climbed up into the cab of the truck. He took a moment to quickly go over the plan and its execution. There was no way he could risk David Quiring talking to the police and exposing the most lucrative part of Caines' private operation—smuggling immigrants across the border.

He put the key into the ignition and eased the truck into gear, taking the back road exit towards the highway on his way to Ohio. He stopped only once for a bag of doughnuts and a cup of hot black tea. He ate all the doughnuts before he reached Detroit. He would drink the tea after he crossed the border, once it was cold.

EIGHTEEN

Scotty Doherty's favourite place to go after work was a gas station on the north end of Andover's Main Street, where a cute girl he had become infatuated with usually worked the evening shift. He drove there tonight in his faded blue Camry and left the door open once he stepped out of the car. He pushed the driver's seat forward and began to scrounge beneath the seats for change. It was another two days until payday, and he was flat broke. It always amazed him how quickly the money vanished. Just one night with the peelers was always what wiped him out. Scotty had no self-control. It had been Candy last night, a tall blonde with big natural tits and a butt to die for. It took him less than an hour to give her the last of his week's cash. He needed a girlfriend. Desperately. Until that happened, he was doomed to blow every last dollar each and every week, one lap dance at a time.

So this had become a weekly ritual: scrounging for quarters and looking for long butts in the ashtray of his car. Tonight he was out of smokes, out of beer and without food. He had skipped lunch, and for dinner he had scooped a few tomatoes and eaten them like apples while he thought about going to the bank machine. He was almost certain his account was empty, but there was always a chance the bank had cleared his cheque a day early, or that he had miscalculated how much he'd withdrawn over the course of the week.

Beneath his seat he found four cents and an empty lighter.

"Dammit," he cursed as he went inside, pulling his bank card from his back pocket.

He smiled anxiously at the cute redhead with the pierced eyebrow and tattoos, who did not seem to notice him walk in. She was talking excitedly on the phone. Scotty grinned at her nonetheless and walked to the back of the store.

The bank machine always made him nervous, whether he knew he had a few dollars left in the bank or not. He approached the machine with the same anxiety as a gambler approaching a slot machine with his last dollar. The bank often made him wait a few days before he could take the cash from the paycheques he deposited. But they did not always make him wait. Last week he'd been able to take his cash right away. He could never trust the banks, and he knew they did not trust him. It made no sense to him, and he wondered momentarily who had been the first to mistrust whom. With a knot in his stomach, he punched in his pin and waited for the dreaded single beep of denial or the wonderful sound of the tumblers inside spinning out his money.

After a few moments of deliberation, the tumblers were set in motion.

"Sweet relief!" he sighed as the machine spat a single twenty dollar bill.

He turned away, stopped, and decided—what the hell—to see if there was another twenty in there somewhere. He slipped his card back in the bank machine and punched in his code. Again, the tumblers turned and the machine spat out a twenty dollar bill. Scotty squeezed his fingers into fists, rocking back and forth on his heels, trying a third time, to see if he could turn the forty dollars into sixty. No luck.

He kicked the machine before pulling a Coke from the cooler and a bag of chips from the rack and going to the counter.

He smiled again at the cashier, who was still talking to her friend on the phone. Scotty had been coming here for several weeks, once he'd found she worked the same shift every night. He liked flirting with her, and she seemed to like flirting too. Tonight she was wearing a red halter top, showing off the large eagle tattooed on her left shoulder, one wing spreading across her chest bone, the other sweeping across her bare shoulder. She had told him several nights ago that her name was Andrea.

He stood at the counter, waiting for her to make eye contact.

"Black Cats," he said. "King Size."

"Just a moment," she said into the phone before reaching behind her for the cigarettes. She set them on the counter, phone balanced on her shoulder against her ear. Scotty slipped the cigarettes into his back pocket as she rang up the sale.

"How are you doing?" he asked as he handed her his twenty.

"Fine," she grinned back. "Sec," she said to the phone before setting it on the counter. "It's you again. You're becoming a regular. How are you?"

"I'll be better when it's payday," he said.

She nodded and handed him his change. "Do you want a bag for that?" she asked.

"Sure. What are you up to tonight?"

"After my shift, I think I'm going home for a nice hot soak in the tub," she said.

"Sounds nice. Is there anything else you like doing after work?"

She tilted her head, eyes gleaming. "What did you have in mind?" Scotty liked the way her hair touched her shoulder when she did that.

"We could go for a drink," he said.

"Maybe," she said. "Why don't you come back if you want to? I'll see how I feel then."

"When does your shift end tonight?"

"Ten thirty," she answered.

"Did you give me my cigarettes?" he asked.

She hesitated a moment, looking at the bag. Finding no cigarettes there, she turned around and dropped a pack on the counter. "Sorry about that!" she laughed.

Scotty drove to the west end of town to stop at the beer store, where he picked up a case of Blue, before he drove to the park near the river and watched some kids play softball, smoking his cigarettes until twenty after ten. When he came back to the store, Andrea did not seem to recognize him.

"How are you feeling?" he asked.

"I'm fine," she said. "How are you?"

"Almost ready for that drink?"

"Oh," she said. "Yeah, yeah. I could use a drink tonight. It's been a madhouse here tonight. You wouldn't believe it!" She leaned forward, even though they were alone, and whispered, "And maybe a toke." She was grinning in that sly way he liked. He liked that smile a lot.

"And maybe we can make out," he grinned back at her.

"Ha!" she burst with a laugh and covered her mouth. "We'll see how it goes."

"Sounds good."

"What's your name again?" she asked.

"Scotty."

"Where's your car?"

"Over there," he said, pointing.

She peered out the window, standing on her toes to see over the chocolate bar display.

"Okay." She gave him a good look up and down. "I like your rings," she said.

He shook his head vigorously to make his earrings jingle. That made her laugh. "What do you like to drink?" he asked.

"Anything really. Beer and wine, mostly."

Her replacement stepped inside the store, an Hispanic teenager Scotty recognized as well, and she asked Scotty to wait outside.

"Sure thing," he said. She watched him with interest as he went out to the parking lot. He grinned at her as he leaned on the hood of his car, biding his time with a cigarette until she emerged from the store.

"Where do you want to go?" he asked when she stepped outside.

She looked around. "Damn, it's hot out here."

He waited with a smile.

"Anywhere with air conditioning," she said.

"I thought we'd go for a drive."

"Do you have some pot?"

"Yeah."

"Okay then."

He opened the car door for her, metal grinding on metal, but let her close it herself. It was a fine line between being a gentleman and a sexist, Scotty had decided, but this straddled that line quite well. Getting into the driver's seat, he rolled down his window.

"You don't have air conditioning?" she asked.

"It's not so warm when you get moving," he said. "And the beer's cold. Let's go to the park."

Andrea shrugged but did not offer the same smile. "Sure," she said at last.

When he pulled up by the river, he was glad to see most of the kids had gone home. He parked near the edge of the lot. He opened a beer for her and tried to get her to talk.

"So how long have you worked there?" he asked.

"Not long. Couple months, I guess." She looked out the passenger window at the shadows of the shrubs and trees. She sipped at her beer. "Know of any parties?" she asked.

"Not tonight," he said. "It's a Thursday. I don't know of many parties on a Thursday night."

"We can start our own party," she said. "So you said you have some pot."

"Yeah," he said. Scotty reached into the glove compartment, his hand brushing her knee, and opened it.

"Damn," he said. "I forgot. I'm all out."

"Do you have any at home?" she asked.

"No." He shifted in his seat and put his hand on her shoulder. "Do you live near here?" he asked.

"Yeah. You?"

"Yeah."

Scotty reached to kiss her. She let him but kept her mouth closed, refusing entry to his tongue. Then she sat back.

"Is there anywhere else we can go?" Andrea asked.

"You don't like it here?"

She shrugged and became quiet. After a few moments of awkward silence, she said she was more tired than she had thought. Scotty was not about to give up so easily, and when he tried to kiss her, she let him. He placed the flat of his palm on her breast, the one with the eagle above it. She pulled away and asked him to take her home.

"I'm sorry," he said. "I thought I had some pot."

"Maybe next time," she said with a shrug.

As he drove her home, Scotty tried to think of places to get some pot. Andrea pointed him to her street, when he remembered joking with Ben Taylor about Randy Caines' secret greenhouse. If there really was pot in there, he decided, he was sitting on a gold mine.

"I know where we can get some pot," he said. "But it's pretty green."

"It's late," she replied, looking out the window.

"It's only twenty minutes from here."

"Maybe next time," she said.

"I'll get it," he said. "I promise."

"Next time."

He took her to her apartment on Stacey Street, and she let him kiss her goodnight.

Scotty drove off, grinning. He loved the taste of her lips, still sweet with the gum she had been chewing earlier in the evening, and the touch of her soft breast under his hand. He turned on the radio and tapped his palms on the steering wheel to the beat of the Red Hot Chili Peppers before helping himself to another beer.

He drove back to Andover and cruised through the dark streets until he found he was out of beer. He stopped at the Gilded Tavern and hopped out of his car.

Scotty had been here a few times before, but not often. He was hoping to find a friendly girl. Looking around, he was disappointed to find only a few men gathered around a long table with several pitchers between them. Scotty palmed two loonies left behind as a tip on an empty table and found a chair against the wall. When the waitress came, he ordered a draft beer. The beer was not very cold, and the waitress was twice his age. He drank it quickly, deciding to leave.

"Another draft?" the waitress asked him.

He considered his options for a moment. "Damn straight," he said. "Why not."

He was feeling more liquid. Everything seemed to flow better, and his head was feeling light now. The weight of his troubles began to lift from him in the flow of alcohol. Soon he had drunk another two beers with his last dollars. A younger waitress was serving him now... or was it the same woman? She was lean and muscular, with wide hips and thin legs. Scotty watched her, distracted by her thighs as she bent over to clean a table. He finished another beer.

"Have you seen Andrea?" he asked her.

She stepped back, either disinterested or annoyed, Scotty could not tell.

"Who?" she demanded.

"Andrea."

"I don't know who you're talking about," she said as she took his money and put his change on the table. "You came here alone, remember?"

Scotty passed by the old men at the table on his way back from the restroom.

"What time is it?" he asked.

"Ten to one."

"Damn!" said Scotty. "I gotta get that pot! You guys wanna come?"

"Get the hell out of here!" someone shouted at him.

He spun around, knocking his chair over.

"Hey! Watch it!"

Scotty picked up the chair—it was lighter than it looked—and knocked it over again before putting it back.

He found his car and drove relatively straight through the streets on his way back to Stacey Street, trying to remember Andrea's last name. He read the names beside the intercom and decided she must be A. Parker. He pressed her buzzer, but there was no answer. He pressed it again.

"Who is it?" a woman's voice said.

"I know where I can get some," he whispered. "Less go...gettit."

"Who is this?"

"Is this Andrea?"

"No."

"Is she home?"

"Leave me alone. You've got the wrong number."

He stumbled down the steps towards his car and realized he was on the wrong street.

The best thing to do, he decided, was to call her first. He would ask the teenager back at her store for her number.

He walked inside, only to find a small middle-aged man behind the cash register.

"Where's Andrea?" he asked.

"Who's Andrea?"

"The girl...you know. The girl who was here before." Scotty looked around. This might not be the right store.

The clerk stared at him. "She's gone. And you'd better be gone too, cuz I'm calling the cops now."

"No," said Scotty. "I just want some beer. Did she go right or left?"

The clerk stared at him.

"Did she go left?"

"Yeah, yeah," the clerk said. "She left."

Scotty nodded and went outside, turning left. He stopped after a few paces and went back for his car.

He found her a block away, walking home, alone. He gazed at her tight jeans and her thin white blouse.

He pulled alongside her and slowed, talking through the open passenger window.

"Hey, hey," he said, His head was beginning to spin. "Hey, I know where I can get some pot."

The girl ignored him, walking faster.

"Hey!" he said. "I'm sorry! I thought you wanted to smoke."

"No, thanks."

"C'mon. I can get a lot."

"No, thanks," she said again, her legs moving as fast as they could without breaking into a run.

He leaned closer to the passenger window, his hand pulling the wheel too hard, and the car came over the curb, dinged a parking metre, and came off the curb again. Scotty didn't notice.

"Get away from me, you freak!"

She ran twenty feet and went into the Chinese food restaurant.

He decided she was not the girl he thought she was. Her hair was too light, and she looked a lot older than Andrea. And she didn't have Andrea's tattoo.

Nineteen

It had been a long night. Scotty had slept in the driver's seat of his car, parked behind the Tanglewood warehouse for two or three hours before daybreak. He awoke slowly to the cool morning fog, with the distant sunrise already beginning to burn orange through grey mist around his car. Scotty turned on his windshield wipers once, to clear the dew from his windshield. He stretched his legs as best as he could between the brake and accelerator, and rubbed his eyes. His mouth was stale, his stomach nauseous, and his head was as foggy as the morning outside.

"Shit," he said as he saw the flower petals on his lap.

He picked up a petal and examined the curious light pink colour and the strangely exotic shape, cursing Randy Caines.

Slowly, most of the details from the night before began to come back to him, although he did not understand why Andrea had snubbed him when he offered to get her some of Caines' marijuana. He shrugged that off now, however. It was just as well. Caines' big secret hidden in his forbidden greenhouse had turned out to be nothing but a couple of dozen freaky looking flowers.

Scotty had been convinced Caines' was hiding a small marijuana plantation in there. Still quite drunk, he had snuck inside with a knife and a flashlight, peeling back a corner of the plastic and sliding on his belly, to find the disappointment of a lifetime inside—a large table with a dozen or so pots of orchids.

"Caines, you fucking pussy!" Scotty had cursed, knocking several of the plants from the table.

He had made quite a mess of things for sure, he now recalled. He would have to try to repair some of the damage he had made to the greenhouse and do his best to cover his tracks, before anyone else arrived. He was going to lose this miserable job if Caines ever discovered he had destroyed the flowers in the secret greenhouse.

Scotty climbed the steel steps to the warehouse and unlocked the steel door to the shipping area. Crossing the platform, he picked his punch card from the rack and punched in. Within a couple seconds after that, the clock marked the next minute with a heavy click and a thud. Scotty grinned as he looked at his card: 5:30 a.m. His timing was perfect.

He replaced his card on the top of the rack and was about to turn on the overhead lights when he noticed the door to the greenhouses was open. That was his first clue that something wasn't right. His skin went cold.

"Ohhh, shit."

Where were the dogs?

The dogs patrolled the greenhouses at night but were never supposed to be in the warehouse. There was nothing of value in either the warehouse or the greenhouses, but the dogs were necessary to protect the greenhouses from vandalism. With everything under plastic, a couple of kids with a butcher knife could cost the farm a season's growth.

On the rare occasion when Randy Caines was not around, Scotty was responsible for locking the dogs back in their kennel in the morning, but under no circumstances was he to have contact with the animals. They were supposed to remember him; he was the one who sometimes fed them. But they were not there to protect him; they were to protect their territory inside the greenhouse walls. Finding that the door in the warehouse open was the closest he had ever come to the animals without a fence between them. These were not the trained guard dogs that would corner and detain a prowler. They had been neglected and abused as pups and were now essentially wild dogs. They were not to be trusted. One of these dogs on its own was more than a match for Scotty. The pair together could tear him to shreds if the mood struck them. He often wondered about that. What would they do if he wasn't on the other side of the fence?

Scotty backed out the door through which he had entered and walked around the shipping compound to where the dog kennel was attached to the last greenhouse. The dogs knew the routine well enough to be waiting in or near their kennel at dawn. But they were not in their kennel. Scotty opened a white pail and measured out three scoops of dog food, dumped it into their chute, and poured some water into their bowls. He rang their bell and waited. Nothing happened.

He rang the bell again.

Still, nothing happened.

He rang the bell once more and finally heard the hounds approaching, keeping a slow pace. As they entered the kennel, Scotty pulled the latch and locked them in. They sniffed at their food and finally began to eat, slowly, without hunger. Scotty peered at them in the shadows as they drank some water and licked their jowls. Their mouths and front paws were dark and matted, as if they had been in the mud.

This was not mud.

Scotty jumped back, nearly falling on his butt, before scrambling as quickly away from the dogs as his legs could take him.

TWENTY

With a yawn, Ben reached for the snooze button, and with the palm of his hand was able to push the morning away for a few minutes more. With the third alarm, he let the clock radio stay on and finally pulled himself out of bed. Somewhere in Detroit, the radio told him, traffic was moving swiftly, and he was told it was going to be another hot muggy day. It was hard to focus on the news. He felt groggy and his face looked bloated in the mirror as he washed and brushed his teeth. It occurred to him, vaguely, that he should feel more refreshed after spending such a wonderful evening with Jennifer. But his worries outweighed any sense of contentment, and he had awakened several times throughout the night with visions of blood and the lingering odour of wet ashes. His dreams were disturbed and disjointed. Anna's eyes haunted him through every dreamscape.

Outside, the air was cool and still. Fog lingered between the distant trees. The moon, which he had shared with Jennifer the night before, was now concealed in the grey morning mist, setting low somewhere anonymously in the western sky. Light mist and clouds clung to the eastern horizon as well, and the sun behind it gave the sky the colour of a ripening peach.

His shoes were soaked with the morning dew of the meadow and vineyard when he emerged in the parking lot behind Jennifer's house. There Ben recognized the familiar Buick parked alongside the laneway.

Kumar was asleep, reclined back in the driver's seat. Ben rapped on the window. Kumar opened one eye, looked at him and closed it again before pulling up his seat. He rolled down the window.

"Good morning," said Ben.

"Morning. I got your message. You have something for me?"

Ben pulled a key from his pocket and handed it through the window. Kumar held it edgewise, examining it closely.

"This key was used on the padlock to the pump-house a couple days before we found Anna. She wasn't in there then. I thought you'd want it."

The inspector handed it back. "That's the wrong key."

"How do you know?" Ben asked, startled.

"It's too small. Either he gave you the wrong key, or someone has changed the lock. Where'd you get it?"

"I didn't have it. Scotty Doherty gave it to me."

"I see."

"He went in there to catch some sleep one afternoon the week before. He wanted you to have it, but he was nervous about talking to you."

"He should be nervous. I'll be seeing him this morning."

The two men exchanged glances. Kumar was waiting. All Ben had to do was to ask.

"I don't think I want to know quite yet."

"Understood." Kumar nodded. "Where does he live, anyway?"

"Behind the warehouse," Ben replied. "In his car. Same as you."

The inspector forced a smile. "I need to get some paperwork first…grab a coffee…and wash up."

"You're welcome to use mine," Ben replied.

"Thanks, but I need to get some paperwork anyway." Kumar seemed to be watching Ben warily, as if he were studying him, or deliberating a question to ask.

220

"Anything wrong?" asked Ben.

Kumar smiled, but his eyes remained serious. "Nothing. Everything okay with you?"

"Just on my way in to work."

"Don't let me keep you then," the inspector said before starting his car.

"Shit," Ben said to himself aloud. There was more to this than just Scotty. "I should have asked."

TWENTY-ONE

When he went into the warehouse, Scotty turned on the overhead lights and quickly looked around. At the far end of the warehouse, near the mezzanine, he saw two bags lying on the cement floor, as well as a large bundle of laundry beside it. As he approached the mezzanine, he began to recognize that the bundle of laundry was really a human body, disfigured and torn. He saw the splattering of dog prints leading from the body, and his stomach lurched. But more than this, his eyes were drawn to the yellow backpack on the floor. Its contents had spilled out from the opening—a plastic bag with familiar green leaves inside.

Keeping his eyes only on the backpack, Scotty crouched forward until his hand reached the strap. He pulled it up. The bag was heavy, bulging with its contents—dozens and dozens of clear plastic bags stuffed with marijuana.

"Holy shit."

He looked again at the body, lying tangled in dried blood on the cement floor. Blank, open eyes staring at the ceiling, mouth open, tongue exposed, he recognized the face as that of David Quiring. The left leg was twisted harshly in the wrong direction, folded under the right thigh, jagged shinbone protruding through a tear in the jeans. But it was doubtful that it was the broken leg that had killed him, or even the dogs, whose pink paw prints formed a frantic circle in the dried puddle of blood around his body. He had fallen head-first on the cement, his skull cracked and flattened at the back, from where most of the blood had spilled.

Scotty glanced at the backpack full of marijuana and again at the bloody corpse before he slung the bag over his shoulder and ran for the door. He hopped down the metal stairs and was just turning the corner to head for his car when he collided with Ben Taylor.

"Dammit!" Scotty gasped. "You scared the hell out of me!"

"What's wrong with you?" Ben asked. "Are you stoned?"

Scotty laughed with fear and excitement. "Not yet, pal. Not yet. Let's get out of here. Just you and me. But we gotta get a move on. Right now."

Ben shook his head. "What's going on?"

"Somebody died in there last night. I think its David Quiring. The dogs chewed the crap out of him. C'mon, let's just blow this fucking place. We can make it now. Look what I found!"

Scotty lowered the bulging sack from his shoulder to let Ben take a look inside.

"Where did you get that?" Ben asked.

"Don't ask, man. Let's just go."

"Was this his?"

"Maybe. I don't know. Let's just go."

Ben would not let the bag free from his grasp. "I'm taking a look inside the warehouse. You're coming with me."

"Fuck that, man! If we're going to blow this place, we have to do it now."

Ignoring him, Ben climbed the stairs towards the loading dock, taking Scotty's newly found treasure with him.

"Just fucking hurry, and let's go!" Scotty shouted from the stairs.

A few minutes later, Ben emerged, his face determined and composed.

Scotty collapsed, head in hands and sat on the bottom step. "You called the police, didn't ya?"

Ben nodded and took a seat at the top of the stairs.

"This was our chance, you know. I gotta get out of here."

"You're not going anywhere," Ben replied, watching the back of Scotty's head, watching his shoulders for the twitch that would indicate he was about to get up and run away. That twitch never came.

"This goes far beyond either of us," Ben said.

"There's something you need to know," Scotty said, turning around. His eyes were red and his bottom lip quivered. "I don't belong here. I wouldn't have even stayed here if fucking Caines hadn't been such a prick about everything—"

"Wait a minute," said Ben. He spotted something gold dangling from the metal stair between them. "Did you drop anything?"

"No." Scotty twisted around to see what Ben was staring at.

Ben slid down two steps to get a better look. A long thin strand of gold was dangling from the centre grid of the metal step, on the end was a small gold cross. "Don't touch it. It's a necklace."

"Someone must have dropped it going home from work," Scotty offered.

"I think it's Anna's."

"Holy shit."

"Tell me what happened," Ben said. "Start with the moment you woke up. And what does you staying here have to do with Randy Caines?"

Scotty had just begun his story when the first OPP officer arrived. Constable Pat Patterson of the Andover Police arrived moments later, followed shortly by Inspector Kumar and three more OPP constables.

"Here's some evidence for you," Ben said, handing over the

backpack. "It was found with the body inside. Be careful. It's messy." He pointed at the necklace. "You'll want that too. You'll find it belonged to Anna Wagner."

The inspector nodded, saying nothing to Ben. "Collect that," he told one of the OPP officers. "Don't let these two slip away anywhere until I talk to them."

Kumar looked up the laneway and saw the first workers, on foot and on bicycles, on their way to the warehouse.

"Send everyone else home," he added. "There's no work today."

Inside, Kumar put on his rubber gloves and inspected the items in the duffel bag next to the body of David Quiring. Along with the Colt 45 revolver were several aluminum irrigation pipe couplers, a few lengths of rope, and various lengths of chains, a hammer, several screwdrivers, and a can of screws and nails.

The inspector dropped the backpack full of marijuana next to the duffle bag. "What does it look like?" he asked one of the OPP constables.

The officer was caught with his mouth full of coffee. He swallowed it quickly and spoke uncomfortably, his throat coated with hot coffee and cream. "Looks like he was climbing the ladder up to the mezzanine to escape the dogs and fell."

"But why with a bag of junk?"

"There was a gun in there," the officer replied.

"But he only needed the gun. What was he going to do with a bunch of pieces of pipe, or the hammers and nails?"

"No idea about that, sir."

Kumar shook his head, pacing back and forth alongside the two bags on the floor. "If he was up there, he would have put the gun in his backpack. There was still room in here for a gun. And it wouldn't get scratched in there the way it would with all that metal junk. Let's not even address the fact that he didn't have any bullets…" He shook his head again. "No. This does not make any sense. How did he get in here?"

The constable snuck another quick sip of coffee then tossed the half full cup in the trash. He cleared his throat and spoke more clearly now. "The shipping door on the loading dock wasn't locked."

"Who found the body?"

"Scotty Doherty. He was the first in here. He found the body and the dogs. He said the dogs weren't supposed to be in the warehouse. The door to the greenhouses was open. That's how the dogs must have got in."

Kumar paced a circle around Quiring's body. "Was the door left open last night?"

"It shouldn't have been. But he doesn't know. The guy who closed up shop was Ben Taylor. He's outside with Doherty."

Kumar set his jaw. "Taylor. Again." He sighed. "Bring Taylor here." He walked to the shipping door as an OPP constable brought Ben in.

"Ben!" Kumar pointed to the wooden door leading to the greenhouse. "Was this door secure when you left here last night?"

"Yes," Ben replied. "It's always closed."

"Why?"

"On account of the dogs. We can't punch in if the dogs are in the warehouse. And if we don't punch in, we don't get paid."

"Good. Thank you. Wait outside. We'll have more questions."

Once he was outside, the inspector told the constable. "Don't let them leave. Keep an eye on them."

Kumar looked around the shipping area. The body was in a large room set off from the rest of the warehouse by two sliding doors, each larger than a garage door. Both doors were half open right now, enough to get a large car through. At the other end of the room was another door, twenty feet high and twenty feet across, which led to the greenhouse. It was a storage room, about a thousand square feet in size, with brick walls painted white, and small windows for ventilation near the roof, which, Kumar estimated, was about three stories high. On the left was a mezzanine about thirty feet above the floor where pallets of unassembled cardboard boxes were stored. A metal ladder, bolted to the wall, gave access to the mezzanine.

"So," he said mostly to himself, pointing to the shipping door. "He comes in the shipping door. Then he walks over here and opens this door that leads to the greenhouse, and where the dogs are. The dogs chase him. He runs to the mezzanine. He begins climbing the ladder. He panics, slips, and falls to his death."

"Do you think he was hungry?" he asked the constable.

"Hungry, sir?"

"Why would he open this door? To pet the dogs? To grab some tomatoes? To hide the tools?"

He walked over to the ladder and began climbing to the top. Once on top, he surveyed the mezzanine. Behind the stacks of cardboard, he could see other pallets, some with old tools in wooden boxes, cables, chains, and some empty blue barrels used to transport wine juice. Some barrels contained equipment; loose hoses, rope and the like.

"Helluva fall from here. Why is there grease on the top of this ladder?"

"There was grease on his hands as well." The OPP officer pointed to the grease gun lying on the edge of the mezzanine. "We think it came from here."

"So. The bag was up here. He came in to get it. Got grease on his hands. Grasped the ladder. Here. His hand slipped. He fell to his death."

"Yes!" said the constable.

"Why did he let the dogs get in?"

"Maybe they pushed the door open when they smelled the blood?"

Kumar frowned. "I can't buy that."

"Maybe it wasn't closed all the way?"

"Why close it at all, if it wasn't closed all the way?"

"An oversight, perhaps?"

"Perhaps. That would be coincidence. Unless…"

"Unless what?"

"Unless Quiring wasn't alone."

Kumar looked at his gloved hands. They were covered with dirt. He re-examined the ladder.

"Why would he jump?" Kumar wondered aloud.

The constable stepped back. "What do you mean by that, sir?"

"Look at the smudges here. You can see the finger marks. Going down a ladder, you turn backwards, right hand on the right side of the ladder. His right hand was on the right side of the ladder, but the finger marks are on the opposite side. He wasn't going down the ladder, but standing adjacent to it."

"He jumped?"

"And look where his body has fallen. Over there. Not under the ladder. He jumped. Or he was pushed. Or… Bill!" he yelled down. "Are you getting prints?"

"Yes, sir!" the officer hollered out.

"Dust the forklifts too. Then bring those two workers in here. No. He didn't jump," Kumar added.

After several minutes, Scotty Doherty and Ben Taylor were led into the warehouse.

"Scotty!" shouted Kumar. "Beam me down from here. Someone give him a pair of gloves first."

Scotty nodded. The OPP inspector watched with fascination

as Scotty started a forklift and rode it over, lifting the forks to the mezzanine level.

"Why climb a ladder when you can get a ride?" the inspector shouted.

Kumar stepped onto the forks and Scotty gently brought him back down.

Once on the ground, Kumar nodded to the officer. "You can have him now."

The officer took Scotty's arm and turned him around, quickly cuffing his hands behind his back.

"Scotty Doherty, you're under arrest."

"Arrest?" said Ben. "For what?"

The police ignored the question.

"Why are you arresting him?" Ben demanded.

"Arrest him too," said Kumar.

Scotty sneered over his shoulder as Ben was quickly cuffed as well. "I told you we should have took off for the States when we could."

TWENTY-TWO

Jennifer Voracci sat on the back steps of her porch, arms wrapped around her knees, watching the OPP inspector's blue Buick roll past her gate and park alongside the two OPP cruisers and single Andover Police car beside the warehouse.

Her thoughts, full of apprehension, were on Anna. And of course Ben as well. She had watched the workers arrive as usual and watched them all leave again. There was no sign of Ben, and she wondered if he might be inside with the police officers as well. Several of the Mexicans had gathered near her gate and were obviously discussing the situation in Spanish.

Michael had been scheduled to be out of town for another two days, but with so many police officers here again now, she knew he would be compelled to return early. Something important was going on. She could not imagine so much attention for a break-in or a case of vandalism. It had to be something bigger. It had to have something to do with Anna. She thought of David Quiring and jumped at the notion that he had raped and murdered his girlfriend.

"I hope they fry the bastard," she said aloud, as if there was someone to hear her, as if that supposed person would not remind her there was no death penalty in Canada.

As she sipped at her morning half cup of black coffee, Jennifer watched a new black SUV come up the laneway and stop between the two police cars. Michael's father, Anthony Voracci, stepped from the vehicle as a uniformed OPP officer shook his head and pointed at the SUV. She watched Anthony and the officer speaking calmly at first. Then the officer pointed to Anthony's SUV again, obviously telling him to leave. Even from this distance that was clear.

Anthony, looking thin and fragile, leaned forward, silver hair gleaming in the morning sunlight, pointed a bony finger angrily at the constable and began shouting at him. He kicked a rock and stomped his foot. He had a temper like his son's, but Michael held his better these days, Jennifer reminded herself thankfully.

She continued to watch as her father-in-law turned on his cell phone and spoke to someone. He shook his fist as he shouted on the phone. Then he offered the phone to the police officer. The policeman, hands on his gun belt, shook his head. He raised his hand again and pointed at Anthony's vehicle once again. Finally, Anthony got back in his SUV. The truck was already in motion by the time the sound of the slamming door reached Jennifer's porch.

Jennifer watched the SUV wind up the laneway, and she waved at the black tinted windows, wondering if her father-in-law had even seen her. Perhaps waving at the blank window was silly. He rarely acknowledged her, even when he did see her. But Jennifer's wave was from a belief in kindness she had acquired long before she met the Voracci family. It was the one thing she was determined to never give up.

The only member of Michael's family she had been close to had been his grandfather Antonio, who had passed away several years ago. She had last seen the old man in his hospital room, where she had stood at his bedside. While Michael boasted to the tired old man about all that he had planned for the family's farm, Jennifer had held Antonio's withered hand. Slowly, she'd lifted his wrist and slipped his fingers into her jacket pocket, which she had filled with a cup of dirt from his beloved fields. She remembered with a deep bittersweet fondness Antonio's soft sigh and smile. His eyes gleamed at her with this small secret they shared as he felt the wonderful earth in his fingers for one last time.

Jennifer tried for a few moments to remember the last time she had actually had an honest understanding with either of her in-laws. It had been at least a couple years. Michael's parents were not very fond of the woman their son had chosen to marry. They all knew he could have done better, and Michael reminded her of this frequently. Jennifer sighed.

She often wondered what Michael told them about her. And what was true, and what he had embellished.

She was about to step back inside when she saw Ben approaching the police cars. She smiled at the sight of him, at how straight he stood, always self-assured and strong. She adored the way his hair was always just a bit tousled on the top, like he had just gotten out of bed.

Her smile suddenly collapsed when she saw the police officer behind Ben. Then she realized both of Ben's arms were behind his back. Then she saw the glint of silver near his hands in the sunlight as he was led to the OPP cruiser.

"Oh, no!"

The fear kicked in with a stab of adrenaline to her heart. Jennifer stood up, but as soon as she did, the blood rushed from her head as the fear pressed tightly at her chest. The breath left her, and she fell back onto the wooden steps. Her legs refused to move. The police car made its way up the laneway towards her.

She stood up again, her arms hugging her chest, biting her lip as she watched the police car. She watched Ben watching her, their eyes meeting as the car passed slowly by.

He grinned at her and winked as he passed.

Her heart sank. "I can't believe it," she said aloud. "Oh my god, Ben. What have you done?"

She turned around and climbed the steps into the house, barely noticing the slam of the screen door behind her, and retreated to her bedroom. She grabbed the ring he had given her from under her pillow and squeezed it tightly in her fist. The tears began to well in her eyes.

"Don't cry," she demanded. "He couldn't have done anything bad. Why would he?"

She imagined a fight between Ben and another worker. She imagined some missing inventory and someone pointing a guilty finger at him. She refused to let herself consider, not even for a moment, that this could be related to Anna's death. But the suspicion crept behind her willpower and seized her heart in its grip.

Jennifer opened her palm and glared at the ring, then threw it to the floor. It hit the baseboard instead and spun under her dresser. She clenched her teeth in anger at herself for her weakness and lack of faith in Ben and crouched down beside the dresser to retrieve it.

"Dammit!" The ring was just out of reach. She slipped back on her knees and pulled out the bottom drawer. She spotted the ring tangled in a small cloud of dust. She picked it up and tossed the dust into the trash basket. Lifting the drawer back into place, she took one more look for dust beneath the dresser.

That was when she spotted the small key she had misplaced and tried to banish from her memory nearly a year before. It lay on the floor beneath the dresser, so small and seemingly insignificant, she would have missed it entirely if she had not been looking for more dust.

She picked it up and held it in the palm of her hand, staring at it curiously. Her secret key. The key that had bound her here for so many years. The feel of it in her hand now filled her with dread. Her hand began to tremble.

"Why now?" she asked herself. "Why should it come back to me now?" She shuddered.

Quickly, she slipped the key into the drawer she had removed, tucking it behind her stack of sweaters. Then she replaced the drawer and fell back on the bed, holding the ring at arm's length above her eyes. She watched it until the key was all but forgotten. It was a simple ring, unmarked, plain and beautiful. Her arm extended above her, Jennifer watched it dangle before her eyes from the end of the silver chain.

This little ring was so precious to her. How could she have thrown it on the floor? No expensive piece of jewellery Michael had ever given her could come close to the feelings she had for the little ring on the end of a thin silver chain. It was a reminder of love unencumbered by possession, by guilt, by the weight of maintaining appearances. She wondered if her love for Michael had ever been so free. No, she decided, it had been encumbered by his need to maintain appearances from the start. She had been an accessory in the vast mural of his self-image from the first day she took his hand. She was not feeling sorry for herself. A part of her had seen what was happening, even as she'd agreed to become his wife, but for some reason, she had hoped it would change. But it never had.

Jennifer placed the ring on her belly and closed her eyes. Images of the ring glittering in the light filled her mind, interspersed with glimpses of the small key, which were then linked with vivid snapshots of the handcuffs on Ben's wrists.

When she was four years old, Jennifer had broken a small crystal vase. She had been colouring a picture in the dining room and reached for her box of crayons, still looking at her picture rather than what was on the table. She had pulled on the tablecloth by accident, seen the vase start to fall and jumped back with fright. Jennifer, her crayons, the vase filled with water and flowers, all had tumbled in silence through the air and landed with the crash of crystal on the hardwood floor.

Her mother had rushed into the room, more afraid and alarmed than angry. She rushed to her child, fearing she was terribly hurt, and when she'd picked her up, realizing she wasn't hurt at all, her panic had turned to anger and she'd yelled at her little girl.

"Go to your room! I can't believe you did this. Get to your room while I clean up this mess! Just wait until your father comes home."

Jennifer ran to her room, feeling dreadfully guilty for what she had done. She lay down on her bed and counted the seconds, waiting for the familiar sound of the front door opening that signalled her father was home.

She always waited for her father by the living room window, and he always came in and picked her up with a smile when he came in. Now, however, she could only imagine his anger at the mess she had made on the floor. Her mother would whisper in his ear, and his happy face would turn angry. She closed her eyes, trying to make the bad feelings go away. She hugged her pillow and, in tears, the little girl eventually drifted to sleep.

She had awakened some time later. The sun was setting outside, and her room had turned to a strange yellow hue she did not recognize. She sat up, feeling sleepy and uncertain what time it really was. The sunlight looked like morning, but as the light came in the wrong window, everything felt odd to her.

She sat on her bed, yawning, but suddenly she remembered the terrible thing she had done. After a very long time, Jennifer got up and peered through the doorway.

To her surprise, her parents were sitting at the dining room table, eating their dinner. The smell of chicken filled the air. A new vase held the flowers. The tablecloth was on the table, her crayons put away.

Magically, everything wrong that she had done had somehow been undone.

"I'm glad you woke up, sleepyhead," said her father.

"Yes," said her mother, caressing her head as she walked past. "I was just going to wake you before your dinner got cold."

She stood there, silently, waiting for either of them to mention what had happened. But apparently, they could not remember. Perhaps, she thought to herself, the broken vase had just been a dream.

She sat down at her chair and drank some milk. No, the vase was different now. It had really happened, but somehow it had been all undone.

As an adult, Jennifer remembered much of this, especially the odd feeling she'd had. Her parents had obviously talked about the accident. Her mother had overreacted, and they had decided not to bring up the subject again. But in a place in Jennifer's child-mind, a connection had been made. Going to sleep could change everything. As if by magic, her sleep had made the bad go away, and all was right with the world.

This morning, clutching her ring in her hand, Jennifer stretched out on the bed and rolled over onto her belly.

"Why would they arrest Ben?" she said again and again. "Why?"

This was not the way it was supposed to end. Not with him being arrested and going to jail. Perhaps they had decided Ben had killed Anna. But she knew that was impossible.

"It couldn't be Ben," she said. "I know it wasn't him. Why would they think it was him?"

Folding down her pillow and pulling it under her chin, she cried for Ben. Hoping to make all the badness go away, she closed her eyes. Going to sleep always made things better.

But this time, sleep did not come to take her troubles away.

Twenty-Three

Ben sat in the Andover Police Station, his left hand cuffed to the arm of a metal chair. He had spent the last six hours sitting in the station's drunk tank—a pathetic, squalid room with torn orange foam on the walls, designed to keep inebriated prisoners from smashing their heads. Pat Patterson had brought him into the office over an hour ago. None of the officers said a word to him as they came and went. No one would tell him what he was here for, or what he was waiting for.

At last, Inspector Kumar entered the station, ignoring the prisoner. He nodded at Patterson, who sat across the room from Ben, at his desk, typing at the computer terminal. Patterson seemed to relax with the inspector here. Obviously, Ben was waiting for Kumar.

"Is this a joke?" asked Ben, rattling his cuffs. "What am I under arrest for?"

"At the moment," Kumar replied, "possession of narcotics and suspicion of murder."

"That's a crock, and you know it."

"Maybe it is a crock," said the inspector. "We'll know that soon enough."

"You can't hold me here without a good reason."

Kumar cocked his head. "I don't need a *good* reason. You know that. *Suspicion* is all I need."

He said nothing more as he stepped into the men's room. A few minutes later he emerged again, drying his hands with a paper towel, which he tossed into the garbage can beside the coffee machine. He helped himself to a coffee as Ben watched him.

"I thought you were based out of the OPP office," Ben observed.

Kumar continued to ignore him and stepped into McGrath's office, closing the door behind him.

Ben breathed through clenched teeth and shook his head in disbelief. "How about a washroom break?" he shouted to the closed door.

Patterson's lean, pale face did not change expression as he continued to type. Ben watched the clock for forty-five minutes before Kumar opened the door. He stood in the doorway and nodded to Patterson.

The constable stood up, crossed the room and unclasped the cuff from Ben's chair. He cuffed his hands behind his back.

"Don't tell me this is really necessary," said Ben.

Neither cop replied as the constable escorted him into McGrath's office, where he was seated on a small metal chair in the centre of the room, four feet from the desk. Kumar closed the door as Patterson went back to his work. He had taken off his jacket and removed his tie. Now he rolled up his sleeves as he circled slowly around Ben's chair several times. Finally, he took his place behind the large, cluttered desk. He leaned back in the high-back chair, crossed his legs and stared at Ben long and hard.

Ben returned the stare. He wasn't angry as much as annoyed. His wrists were becoming sore, and his back and shoulders were becoming increasingly uncomfortable.

The inspector spoke at last. "Who am I?"

"An angry cop."

"Damn right."

Kumar leaned back. He had been expecting to hear his own name, but he was not surprised at the retort. It was two thirty. This could be a long day, he decided.

"You're not getting what you wanted from me," Ben continued.

Kumar watched, staring coldly.

"And you thought a couple hours in cuffs would soften up my tongue."

Kumar continued to stare.

Ben put on his most charming smile. "All you had to do is ask, Walt."

"You've been read your rights. Do you want a lawyer, or do you want to talk to me man to man?"

"I'll talk to you," said Ben. "We both know you don't have a thing on me. So tell me what this is all about."

"Okay, I'll tell you."

Kumar picked up his coffee mug and leaned back in his chair, legs stretched out. "I'm sick of this place," he said. "I'm sick of being here. I want to go home. But you're helping them keep me here. And it's pissing me off."

"What do you mean?"

"I mean…" Kumar seethed, "you withheld evidence from my investigation," he said. He took a sip of coffee before putting it on the table. Then he stretched his arms forward, happy to show Ben how nice a good stretch could feel. "You understand the repercussions of that."

"I didn't withhold anything from your investigation."

Kumar slammed his open palm on the desk in a sudden burst of anger. "You fucked with my investigation!" He rose and glared down. "*Nobody* screws with my investigations."

"Everyone is fucking with your investigation. McGrath screwed it up from day one. The local politicians I'm sure are screwing with it, or you wouldn't be having the problems you are. I've been helping you, remember? Maybe I'm the only one who's been helping you."

Kumar stepped out from behind the desk, leaning on it, still staring down at Ben. Instead of being angry, he now looked amused.

Ben was beginning to feel detached from his present situation. Under arrest, cuffed and perhaps awaiting charges. His sense of identity split between the participant and the observer. The observer in him was impressed with Kumar's versatility. Despite knowing he was being played, despite knowing each motion and word from Kumar was designed to evoke a certain reaction from him, Ben found himself reacting to them just the same. He was reacting to Kumar just as any suspect would.

"Whose office do you think this is?"

"Right now, it's your office."

Kumar pointed to the pictures on the walls, the collection of police badges from around the country and the United States. "Whose toys are these?"

"McGrath's"

"Whose office is it then?"

"McGrath's"

"Thank you." Kumar picked up his coffee and took another sip. "Now then," he continued, "do you see Chief McGrath here, in his own office?"

"No, I don't."

"Do you know why he is not in his office?"

"Because you're using it."

"More than that."

"I don't know."

"Have you seen him today?"

"No."

"Do you know where he is today?"

"No."

"Would you like me to tell you where he is today?"

He watched Kumar's hands as he put down the coffee cup. Kumar pulled another metal chair from beside the desk to a place directly in front of him.

The key was to understand that the inspector was fishing for answers, Ben reminded himself. He was the fish. Hooked on a line he couldn't resist when the line was pulled. He had to wait until it was slack then pull back. He detected that slack in the line now, as Kumar turned his attention from him to reach for his coffee cup again.

"I don't care where he is," said Ben.

Kumar hesitated for only a fraction of a second, just as his hands touched the cup. He had been expecting some affirmative, but hadn't gotten it. He had surprised the inspector by putting a kink in the line of questioning. He had just pulled another ten feet of line from Kumar's reel.

Kumar turned his attention back to him and began again. "Ben, you should care where he is."

"Why?"

"Because he is essentially in the same place you are going to be."

"How is that?"

"He fucked with me. And now he's gone. You fucked with me. And now you're going to be gone too."

Kumar shifted forward in his seat, drastically cutting into Ben's sense of personal space with his leg between Ben's knees, but not touching him at all.

"The difference," said Kumar, "is that Chief McGrath is going to be gone for a few days. He fucked up because he is a moron. You are not a moron. You tried to fuck with me on purpose. And if you continue, you're going to be gone for a lot longer than he is gone. And I'm going to send you to a place you will have a very hard time getting back from. And when I'm done with you," he smiled, "when you come back from that place you're going to be lucky to find a job as good as the one you have now."

Ben looked straight ahead. "So what did I do?"

"You withheld evidence."

"What evidence?"

"For starters, you failed to tell me about your personal relationship with Anna Wagner."

Ben did not move, did not blink, did not swallow or twitch a muscle, ensuring he neither admitted nor denied this accusation for now. "What else did I supposedly do?"

"You met with a key witness. You knew his whereabouts. You didn't tell me."

"Neither of those things is true."

"You spoke with Anna Wagner on at least one occasion, alone. You had a personal conversation with her. You were involved with her romantically."

"That's not true."

Kumar reached behind him and picked a file from the top of the desk. It was the same autopsy file he had shared with Ben a few days before. He took from the folder the autopsy photo Ben had refused to look at in the car. He held the photo in front of Ben's face. When Ben turned his head away, Kumar moved the photo to keep it in front of his eyes.

"I've seen this," said Ben.

"I want to make sure you don't forget it. Because you're telling me this girl was a liar. And that is pissing me off as well."

Kumar waited until he was satisfied Ben had had a good look at the photo. Then he put it down on the desk, on top of the open autopsy file so that Ben would know it was sitting there, right on top, the most important document of all the clutter of paper on that desk.

"She met with you," Kumar continued. "She had some kind of schoolgirl crush on you. She talked to you several times. Her boyfriend knew about it. And she told you that."

"How is that relevant?"

Kumar stood up. "How is that relevant?" he shouted. "You had a lengthy conversation with a murder victim the day before she disappears, in which she talked to you about problems she was having with the key suspect. How is that *not* relevant?"

"She flirted with me. She did not have a lengthy conversation with me. And I had no idea she was having problems with her boyfriend."

"What about him? Didn't he tell you about the problems?"

"No. I barely spoke to Quiring. And certainly not about his girlfriend."

"And you didn't tell me you spoke to him at all."

"I didn't think that was relevant."

"Are you kidding me? You know it's my job to decide what is relevant and what is not relevant. When you talk to someone wanted in connection with a murder, it is always relevant. You have an obligation to tell me where he is."

"I didn't know where he was after the murder."

"Then who gave him this?"

Kumar pulled a small card from his wallet. It was Kumar's business card. The one he had given to Ben with his cell phone number written on it in his own handwriting.

"I gave that to his cousin and told him to give it to Quiring if he ran into him."

"If I had arrested you last night, do you think David Quiring would still be alive?"

"What are you talking about?"

"David Quiring was never a suspect. The shipping manifests

243

showed him leaving the warehouse the evening she disappeared. Quiring crossed the U.S. border from Windsor two hours before she was last seen alive. While she was being murdered, David Quiring was still in the United States. McGrath and his boys never checked the shipping manifests for that information. So they never contacted Border Services to see if they had records of his crossing, or videos of him behind the wheel of the truck. I checked the manifests. My men checked with Border Services. And we have the video."

Ben shook his head. "Then why...?"

"First, you don't tell me you had a relationship with the victim. Second, you forget to mention you know about her relationship with the prime suspect. Third, you don't bother to tell me you had contact with that suspect. Fourth, I find police-issue handcuffs on the body of the victim. I find these cuffs twenty feet from a renegade police officer who is roaming around farm country for no other given explanation than he wanted to get some fresh air."

"I was given a six month leave. What was I supposed to do, watch TV for six months?"

"You could have told me yourself."

"I couldn't tell you."

"Yes, you could have. It's damn well time you get straight with me," Kumar said, "because right now, you are my primary suspect. We know Quiring was a drug trafficker. We know Anna Wagner was his girlfriend. I think maybe you got involved in their operation. I think despite what you and your friends in Ottawa keep telling me, that you're here undercover."

"For pot? That wouldn't be in RCMP jurisdiction."

"If they're taking it across the border, you know damn well it would be. I think this school girl had a crush on you. I think she found out about you being a cop. I think they got tipped off, and Anna Wagner was killed because they found out about you."

Ben glared at Kumar, his jaw set and eyes burning. "That's a load of shit," he said slowly, "and you know it."

Kumar leaned forward, his hand on Ben's arm. "If none of this is true, Ben, I think you would have told me the real reason why you're here, right from the start."

"I couldn't." Ben shifted in his seat.

"Maybe you can tell me now, since you seem to have a bit of time to kill. Want a coffee?"

"Can I use the washroom?"

"Not likely," Kumar said his face grim.

"Then, no, thanks."

Kumar rose to his feet and left the room, closing the door behind him. Ben rolled his eyes and shifted in his seat. After nearly twenty minutes, Kumar returned. He sat back in McGrath's chair looking steadily at Ben. It was a long minute before he spoke again. Finally, he leaned forward, his grey eyes studying Ben as if he were not quite sure what tact to take with him next. "Do you want to be open and honest with me, Ben?"

Ben sat up straight, returning Kumar's stare with a half smile. "All you had to do is ask. I'll tell you everything."

"I guess I'd hoped that I wouldn't have to ask."

"I'll tell you everything."

"Thank you, Ben," said Kumar. He pulled his keys from his front pocket and freed Ben from the handcuffs. "And while we're being friendly again, I'll get you that coffee."

"You'll want one too," Ben replied, rubbing his wrists. "It's a long story."

TWENTY-FOUR

This was not a story Ben Taylor had any desire to relive. His position then, as Sergeant Ben Taylor, had been much the same as Kumar's now. A young woman had just been murdered in the small town of Petersburg, Alberta, and he had been there for two days, working on the investigation. He had been driving back into town after conducting an interview when a call for assistance came over the radio. Shots had been fired and an officer was down.

A warrant had been issued for a forty-two-year-old man named Darryl Harris, who had breached a restraining order and had assaulted his ex-wife at a bar the night before. Two rookie constables had gone to the home Harris shared with his girlfriend and their two-year-old daughter to pick him up when something went terribly wrong. At the time, Ben did not know any of these details. He only knew someone had been shot and help was needed. Ben was nearby and arrived on the scene within a few minutes of the call.

It was a small four-room bungalow on a rural road on the edge of town. A chain-link fence surrounded the property. An RCMP cruiser was parked on the shoulder of the gravel road in front of the house. The driver's side door was open and one officer, Cheryl McKay, was on her back beside the cruiser, mortally wounded. Her partner, Anthony Sacchi, was lying outside of the front door, already dead, from a single gunshot wound to the face.

Ben pulled up alongside the cruiser, calling for an ambulance and more backup from his radio. Bending down, gun drawn, he

246

hurried to Constable Cheryl McKay. A shot was fired from inside the house, striking the fender of his car, just a foot from his head.

Keeping as low as he could, he checked McKay. She was bleeding profusely from a wound in her head. He peered above the hood of the cruiser at the house, and another shot was fired from the living room window. Then another, shattering the window of Ben's car.

Ben returned fire. Two shots, both aimed at where he had seen the muzzle flash from inside the darkened house. Those were the last shots fired that day.

Ben did his best to keep Cheryl McKay alive until the ambulance arrived, but she was pronounced dead on arrival at the hospital. There had been nothing, he was told, he could have done differently to have saved her.

By the time Ben got inside the house, four people had died. Both RCMP officers had died from shots fired by Darryl Harris's hunting rifle. He had shot Sacchi through the screen door before the officers even had a chance to knock. Cheryl McKay had died from her wounds before the ambulance even arrived. Inside, Ben discovered both his shots had hit Darryl Harris, the first in the shoulder and the second in the head.

The shot that hit his shoulder, however, had only grazed him, entering just above the bone. It exited slightly downwards and slightly to the right, striking the chest of two-year-old Samantha Jane Anderson, killing her. She had been sitting on the couch behind her father, a storybook in her hands.

"I heard about that shooting," Kumar replied after several seconds of silence. "Nobody blamed you for the child's death. Not the Mounties. Not even the press."

"Except me," said Ben. "And the child's mother. She was at work that morning."

Kumar leaned back in his chair, staring at the floor, expressionless.

"So you quit? You just walked away? I don't buy it."

"Not just then. But soon after. And I didn't quit. I took a leave of absence."

"You walked away," said Kumar pointedly. "When?"

"The end of September of last year."

Kumar looked into his mug, slowly swirling the last drops. "I'm sorry," he said, looking into Ben's eyes. "I couldn't even begin to imagine. I was told you're a good cop. Do you think you'll go back?"

"I was going to, yes. The next morning, I found Anna's body."

"You have to forgive yourself for what happened in Alberta, Ben."

Ben looked up, eyes blank. "It's not a question of forgiveness."

Kumar sipped his cold coffee.

"What did you speak to Anna about the day before she disappeared?"

Ben blinked, feeling as if he had just been plunged into a cold pool of water: present-day reality. "She was trying to talk herself into leaving for college," he said. "She was having second thoughts about leaving her father."

"Did she talk about her boyfriend?"

"Not at all. This was about school. She had a torn sense of responsibility towards her father."

"How so?"

"She wanted to work, to help take care of him. But she also knew if she got an education, she could help him even more in the long run."

"What did you tell her?"

"I told her she had to be true to herself. I told her that her father would need her more later than he does now. He's happy and working now. Later, as he aged, she would be in a position to help him more if she got a good education now. I asked her if he had any savings for his retirement. She said she had always thought so, but she had just found out he had nothing. That put even more pressure on her."

"Did you have an affair with her?"

Ben frowned.

"I know she was a virgin. I mean, were you getting romantic at all with her, Ben? Were you leading up to that at all?"

Ben shook his head. "For god's sake, she was a kid. I knew she had a crush on me. But I didn't encourage that."

"What time did you leave the warehouse last night?"

"Six."

"Did you let out the dogs?"

"No. Caines does it. Scotty does it. No one asked me to. I've never dealt with the dogs before."

"Did you know Quiring was hiding in the warehouse?"

"No. But I wasn't surprised."

"Why weren't you surprised?"

"I knew he was close. He had to be hiding somewhere. Now that I know, it makes sense."

"What can you tell me about Randy Caines?"

Ben gave the question some consideration. "He's a real asshole. He abuses his employees. He has no life outside of his warehouse. There's a greenhouse he keeps under lock and key. A lot of people think it's marijuana, but I checked it out some time ago. He just has a weakness for orchids. It's his hobby, and he keeps them in there."

"Does Scotty deal drugs?"

"I don't think so. He's a pot-head. He never has any money. I think he blows it on pot, beer and strippers. But if he was dealing, even on a small scale, he'd have more money on him." Ben shook his head. "No. He couldn't be dealing, not on any scale."

"Did you know Scotty is an American?"

"Well, I'll be damned."

"He's here illegally. He was nervous when I interviewed him, and he said he had lost his ID. Neither is he on the company payroll, at least not officially. So I pulled his prints from a can of pop when we were done talking. He doesn't know we're on to him yet. Then we got a call last night from a woman who said some drunk was soliciting her and almost ran her over. She gave us the license plate. It was registered under Randy Caines' name. But her description was your friend Scotty."

"No way."

"It's his car, all right. So your friend's name is Donald Scott. And there's a warrant for him in Ohio."

"That explains why he was in no rush to talk to you. He mentioned a woman was after him for child support."

"Maybe," said Kumar. "But the warrant was for armed robbery. He jumped bail in Cleveland. He was also charged with assault. A girlfriend, it looks like."

"Armed robbery?"

"It was a failed robbery. The store clerk recognized him and knew he was using a toy gun, plastic."

Ben could not keep himself from chuckling.

"Does that surprise you, Ben?"

"I guess not." Ben chuckled again, thinking about Scotty botching a robbery. "It really doesn't surprise me at all."

"He claims that Randy Caines smuggled him into the country with a shipment full of wine. Apparently Caines has been doing this for quite some time. Scott says he's been taking workers across the border for years, for anywhere between two and five grand a head. Scott himself has been working off a two thousand dollar debt to Caines, two hundred dollars a week since he started here. Plus big interest."

Ben nodded. "So that's why he was always broke. And that's why he couldn't leave."

"Yeah. He was almost paid up. Scott told us everything before he asked to make a deal. We might need him as a witness, but we'll have to ship him back to the States when we're done. A lawyer is what that kid needs."

"So you've got Caines?"

"For the smuggling if that pans out, sure. And Quiring's murder too."

"Shit!"

"Yep. Caines left his prints all over the crime scene. We may be able to tie him into Anna Wagner's murder as well, using the smuggling operation as the motive. Maybe she caught on to what was happening."

Suddenly—very suddenly—Ben's skin went cold. His limbs were numb.

You are responsible.

"You okay?" Kumar asked.

"Yes." Ben took a deep breath. "This is a lot to take in. Why didn't I see any of this?"

"It was all done in the night. Scott took a lot of time telling us how they hid it from everyone. From the Voraccis. From the workers. You especially, he singled out as not being involved. He seems to look up to you. Did you know that?"

"Yeah. So you think Caines took out Anna too?"

"It's looking likely. According to Scott, Quiring was a driver for at least a few of these runs. Maybe Quiring took the girl out, but I doubt it. More than likely it was Caines. And he took Quiring out to keep him from talking too, because he was our prime suspect. Everyone else involved, Caines seemed to have them pretty much in his pocket."

"What about the necklace we found on the stairs this morning?"

"Her father confirmed it's hers. That could tie Caines to her murder. He might have dropped it when he left the scene. Or maybe he was hoping to plant it on Quiring's body before he misplaced it. We'll find out soon enough. Fortunately, Caines doesn't know we're after him yet. He's on the road. He took a shipment out to Philadelphia. He filled out the dispatch log as such last night, and we confirmed with the warehouse there that he arrived this morning. We're expecting him back tomorrow. We'll grab him as soon as he arrives."

"Why not grab him at the border?"

"There's no reason to bother. He wanted it to look like an accident. He'll be on his guard at the border. Once he gets through the border, he'll think he's in the clear, and he'll be relaxed. Most importantly, there won't be any bystanders here if he proves to be armed."

Ben could not resist the urge to speak for Anna Wagner. "I can't imagine she was involved with Caines," he said.

"I think she just got in the way," Kumar replied. "We'll have to see what Caines has to say about it." The inspector paused. "Unless there's anything else you might like to add?"

"No," Ben replied blankly.

"You should get going, Ben. I want you to be my eyes and ears inside that vineyard. We'll get Caines soon enough. But call me if you see or hear anything. Don't wait for me to ask."

"So you believe me now?"

Kumar patted his shoulder. "Go home, Ben."

Ten hours after being brought into the police station, cuffed and escorted by the OPP, Ben was unceremoniously released without so much as a charge threatened against him. He turned down an offer of a ride home. He walked alone through the darkening tree-shrouded streets for the two miles back to his motel room. The sound of crickets made him uneasy. He could feel the eyes of small animals upon him as he walked. Raccoons and owls, perhaps.

He did not mind the walk. It gave him time to think. The news of Caines' smuggling operation and the possibility that this had been the motive behind Anna's murder had shocked him. In fact, it was not until he had walked a block from the police station that the clammy feeling of his flesh and the numb sensation in his limbs begin to subside. His legs seemed to move of their own volition as he turned the new pieces of information over and over in his mind. Oddly enough, as he'd scratched the week's growth of beard on his cheeks, he became aware, for the first time in months, how badly he needed a shave. He had not thought to shave in the seven days since he'd discovered Anna's body. He felt as if he had been wearing the same clothes all week, although he knew he had cleaned up for his evening with Jennifer. He had not eaten today, and all he'd had to drink was coffee. His throat felt raw from talking.

Before leaving, he had agreed to keep an eye out for Kumar while he worked at the winery. It only made sense for Kumar to have Ben on his side, despite the inspector's mistrust of a cop who'd walked away from his job to labour on a farm for a year. He could not blame Kumar for that. The inspector could have no idea who Ben had become since he'd walked away from the police force. Yet the local police, and even the OPP or RCMP, had limited access to the farm. As well, the Voraccis' political influence was always looming over the police. That could not be avoided under any circumstances. Ben could be Kumar's inside man. Now that Kumar had identified his primary suspect as Randy Caines, trusting Ben would be much easier.

Ben felt at peace with the information he had provided. The only item he had withheld was his relationship with Jennifer. It had nothing to do with Anna's murder. There was no reason for anyone to know about that, not yet. Jennifer could certainly not be a suspect in any crime that would interest a homicide detective. And yet, he wondered if that was a mistake, if there was some small scrap of information about his relationship with Jennifer that might have an influence on some other information Kumar had. Times, dates, motives. They all had to be taken into consideration. It was very seldom that a small observation had any effect on a typical police investigation: the eagle-eyed witness who remembers a glimpse of a license plate number seen two weeks before that will tie a suspect in with the crime scene. Typically, it just didn't happen that way. But this investigation was becoming less and less typical every day. Ben would have to be careful. He would have to be prepared to tell Kumar anything that might have the smallest chance of being important to the investigation.

His thoughts began to roam through the evidence he had seen. One thing was for certain. Neither Ben nor Kumar was convinced that Quiring had killed Anna. There was no evidence proving he had not done it, but there was no evidence proving he had. Everything was pointing to Randy Caines. Caines' murder of David Quiring made sense to Ben. But why would anyone, including Caines, feel the need to kill Anna?

Ben remembered his brief conversation with her the night before she disappeared. He had been lurking around the warehouse, waiting to catch a glimpse of Jennifer in the window, hoping to steal a few minutes alone with her, when Anna had come outside to talk. She had looked so tired and was looking forward to the end of the summer. The trucks at night, in the busier summer schedule, had been keeping her up late. She seemed lonely too as they talked about her moving away to go to university. Her words said she was looking forward to leaving, but there seemed to be a sadness in her tone at the same time. Ben had chalked that up to her being tired, but perhaps there was something more there, something he should have asked her about. If only he had not been so preoccupied with ending the conversation so he could spend a few minutes with Jennifer.

He was still pondering this tonight when he finally reached his motel room. Wearily, he unlocked his door and stepped inside. Once again, he had no sense of home. He turned on the light and looked around at the bed and furniture that came with the room. The room was an empty box. He would have to leave soon. This was not his life. It was only a retreat. He kicked off his running shoes and took a glass from the counter. While he was waiting for the lukewarm tap water to reach a threshold of coolness he could endure, Ben caught a glimpse of his face in the small shaving mirror on the counter. He recognized a fire in his eyes he had not seen for a very, very long time.

As if on cue, he turned off the cold water and turned on the hot. From the cupboard he pulled his razor and shaving cream and began to remove the whiskers from his face.

Welcome back, the new face in the mirror seemed to say.

The question Inspector Kumar had asked him over and over again today, the question Ben did not answer only because he did not have the answer—why did you come here?—was no longer relevant. It did not matter if he had come here to run away from his life, or to just take the time away his soul had been yearning for. He could worry about that later, if he felt the need. Was he going to stay here and help Kumar with his battle, now that it seemed that Randy Caines was ready to take the fall for both murders? Or should he return to Ottawa, pick up his badge and his gun and go back to the battles that waited for him there?

Ben washed his freshly shaven face with warm water. A decision needed to be made.

He set his glass of water down on the television and fell back on the bed. He didn't want to be here any more. He could feel that in every fiber of his being. It was simple: just get up and go home. Go home now; leave the local crimes to the capable hands of the OPP. But if it was that simple, he asked himself, why was he not already packing his bags?

Was it Anna's haunting voice that made him wait here with this last indecision, or was it Jennifer, or was it something still within himself?

Perhaps the fatigue was making it difficult to think clearly, he decided. Then, suddenly, there was a loud knock at his door. Don't answer it, the same voice inside warned him. He watched the door, warily. The knocking began again. Loud and urgent.

Ben pulled himself to his feet and warily approached the door. The knocking grew louder and did not stop until he turned the doorknob and opened the door.

Twenty-Five

Jennifer looked up at Ben, wide-eyed, rubbing her knuckles anxiously. "I was afraid you'd fallen asleep already," she said. "You must be exhausted."

"Almost." He held the door for her to step in. As soon as he had closed the door, he slipped his arms around her waist

"I was here before and I waited for you," she said. "But I couldn't stand sitting around, so I've been driving around, up and down the roads, circling back and hoping you were home again. I was so happy to finally see your light on."

"You shouldn't have waited," he said. "They could have kept me all night."

"But why? You didn't do anything wrong!"

"I know that," he said. "And I'm glad you know that too."

She flushed, remembering the doubts she had felt about that when she saw Ben being led into the police cruiser in handcuffs that morning. "Of course I do."

She sat on the edge of his bed, ankles crossed. Ben breathed in the scent of her hair—green apples. She was beautiful. White t-shirt and khaki shorts, canvas shoes, a small black purse slung over her shoulder. Her arms and legs were long, her thighs were smooth and tan. Her hair was down, framing her face, as if trying to hide the strain that showed itself in her features. She stared up at Ben, speechless, with a combined expression of sadness, exhaustion and relief. It was a combination he would not have thought possible to convey in one expression.

She opened her mouth to speak, staring up at him with watering eyes. No words came, and she cleared her throat, eyes pleading.

"What?" he asked needlessly.

"Why did they arrest you, Ben?"

"They had to," he said. "They needed information. And that meant stirring up the pot. See what comes to the surface."

"Ben, do they think you hurt Anna?"

"No. And if you thought that for a moment, you wouldn't be here," he said.

"I don't know anything any more." She stretched her legs and stared at her own feet.

"No," he said. "I didn't. And they didn't think I did. And I didn't hurt David either."

She looked up, confused. "David Quiring? What happened to David?"

"This morning," he said. "Didn't you know?"

"Know what?" She asked. "What?"

"David had an accident. They found his body in the warehouse this morning."

"Oh my god."

He sat down beside her, putting his arm around her, her head on his shoulder. A long sob was forced from her throat.

"I was so afraid," she said, tears spilling onto his shirt. "I was afraid you'd be gone. Gone forever. I saw you leave. Then the police left. I called Michael's father later on. He wouldn't come to the phone. His mother told me not to worry about anything. Said they found the bastard and not to worry. That's all she said."

"They questioned me," he said. "That's all. They arrested Scotty Doherty."

"How was he involved?"

"He wasn't," Ben said. "He was wanted for something else. The police have been looking for him for quite a long time. He was working here under a phony name, trying to stay low."

"So he had nothing to do with Anna?" she asked, trying to make sense of this. "You mean it was just a coincidence?"

"He had nothing to do with it. It's what happens when you stir up the pot. All sorts of shit comes to the surface."

Jennifer nodded over and over again. "I was afraid I wouldn't see you again," she said. "I couldn't stop thinking about it. I had to know what happened. That's why I waited here for you tonight. I couldn't face going home alone. Couldn't face never seeing you again."

"I was thinking of that too," Ben said. "Just before you knocked. I don't know what the hell I'm doing here. I don't belong here. We should both disappear."

Yes. To hell with Kumar and the police, he thought, suddenly angry. *Let's just get the hell out of here.*

"What do you mean?" she asked, hopeful and very frightened at the same time.

"Let's leave," he said. "Tonight."

"Tonight?"

"Tonight."

The sharpness of the word and its immediacy seemed to bring her to her senses. She looked around the room, her eyes darting left and right, quickly, as if she were looking for an open door. Then she pursed her lips and sighed.

"I can't," she said. "Not tonight."

"Why not tonight?"

She looked again around the confines of his dimly lit room. The yellow ceiling. The cheap particle board made to look like wood panelling. The filthy carpet beneath her feet betraying years of grime and stains of unknown origin.

"Why not?" he repeated.

"Michael," she said.

"What about him?"

"The police called him. He's got to come back right away. He'll be back by morning at the latest."

"So what? We'll go pack a bag for you right now. We'll be gone within twenty minutes. He'll never know where to find you unless you want him to."

"He'll catch me. I know he will."

"So what?"

"You don't understand," she said.

She shook her head and pulled the hair from her eyes. She still refused to look at him. "How can I do that?" she asked. "How can I just leave without telling him?"

Ben lifted her chin with his hand. He brought his mouth to hers, and she closed her eyes, pressing out her tears. Her lips were dry and cold. Some fear had gripped her. But fear of what?

He grasped her wrists and pulled her closer towards him.

"Jennifer."

She opened her eyes but turned to stare at the floor.

"Jennifer," he repeated.

"What?"

"This has gone on long enough," he said. "What the hell kind of hold does he have on you? You want to leave. But you don't. You can't get more than a hundred yards of him without worrying he's right behind you."

Jennifer looked down at the floor, nodding. "I don't want to lose you," she said.

"Then make up your mind. Come with me tonight. Or stay with him. That's your choice."

"I can't." She sat up, looking into his eyes. "Please don't make me choose. Not now."

"Not choosing," he said, "is still a choice."

"No."

"The time has come, Jennifer. What's it going to be?"

"I don't want to lose you," she said. "I want to come with you."

"Then you've decided."

She took a deep breath. "Yes."

"Good."

"But there's something I have to tell you first."

"Okay."

"It wouldn't be fair to either of us not to tell you now. Remember what I said about Michael accepting me for what I am?"

"Yes."

"I want to tell you what that is. Then you can decide to accept me or not to. If you still want to be with me, I'll follow you anywhere, if that's what you want."

Ben rose from the bed and crossed the small room. He pulled the wooden chair from the corner and, turning it around, placed it next to the bed. The joints creaked as he straddled the chair, his arms crossed on its back, watching her.

"Okay," he said. "I'm ready."

"He saved my life."

"How?"

"You remember what I was like."

"Yes," he said.

"I got worse. Booze. Pot. Coke. I was out of control."

"When was this?"

"Just before I met Michael. I settled down for a bit just before we met. I was working in retail sales. He came in a few times. He asked me out. We seemed happy. I stopped the drugs, most of the drinking..."

"Go on," he said.

They were married a year, she began to explain, the first time she'd run away. Michael had been gone for the weekend when her girlfriend Karen had come to visit from town.

"I was pretty bad by then. Back to the drugs again, you know. We got pretty tanked. I wanted some coke. So we went for a drive."

"Where to?"

"Toronto. Karen had an old boyfriend there. She called him. He could connect us, so we just hopped in the car. He lived in this tiny dump near the airport. But he had everything. Coke. Heroin. Meth. You name it. So when it came time for us to leave, I said, 'Nope. Not me. I'm staying.'

"Karen was pissed. But she couldn't force me to leave. And this dealer wasn't in any hurry for me to leave. I didn't care. Besides I knew I couldn't face Michael the way I was, and I thought…I thought if I stayed tanked, I wouldn't have to go back."

"How long did you stay?" Ben asked.

"I honestly don't know. I really don't remember anything after the first night. A few days, maybe? It was awful. He OD'd. I almost died."

"Tell me what happened."

"Michael came home, found out from Karen where I was and came to get me. I don't remember what happened, but he told me everything. He knocked and knocked on the door. No one answered. So he kicked down the door. This guy was on the couch, out cold. I was in the bedroom. Once I'd passed out, I guess he kept me that way. Pumped me full of crap."

"What?"

"Heroin…who knows? I'm not sure."

There was an audible intake of breath from between Ben's teeth. "Dammit, Jennifer." He clenched his fists.

"He'd hit me. I was bruised all over. He'd tied me to the bed, and I guess he'd used me for sex. Michael wrapped me in a sheet because he couldn't find my clothes anywhere. He took me home.

He told me everything that happened a few days later. But we've never discussed it since then. He's never brought it up to me again. What I put him through. What a horrible little person I can be."

"You're not a horrible person," Ben said. "You were the victim here, not your husband."

"That's just it. I can be horrible. You've no idea. Michael has seen me at my worst, and he still accepts me."

"So you're grateful to him."

"Of course!"

"Did you tell the police?"

"No."

"What was this scumbag's name?"

"I don't know. Snake, I think. That was his nickname."

"Snake? Are you sure?"

She considered the name. "No," she said. "I'm not sure of anything."

Ben closed his eyes tightly, listening.

"This guy was passed out," she said. "I think I would have died if Michael hadn't come and got me."

"Did he die from the OD?"

"I don't know. I think so."

"How do you know?"

Jennifer jumped to her feet. "Why so many questions? What else do you need to know? Isn't it enough you know what I am?"

"What are you?" he asked.

"A junkie. A drug addict. An alcoholic. An irresponsible woman who can't be trusted before she runs off to do the worst things to herself."

Ben contemplated all she had said for several minutes before he tried to respond to her question. "When's the last time you've done that shit?"

"That was the last time. It's been what? Seven years now."

"And nothing now? No popping pills? No sneaking drinks alone?"

"No. Just my vitamins and…" she paused. "And sometimes Michael gives me sleeping pills when I'm too wound up to sleep."

"Sleeping pills? What do you need sleeping pills for?"

Ben did not like the sound of this at all. Had her husband just substituted one set of narcotics for another, drugs that he could control?

"It's not often," Jennifer replied. "Just sometimes. And he doesn't need to be worrying about me when he's working late…"

Ben did not say a word.

"See?" she said. "I guess I still am a junkie…"

"That's not who you are," he snapped.

"You don't really believe that," she said. "You want to." He did. "But you're not sure." No, he was not sure of anything right now.

"I know you," he said. "That's not who you are."

"That's a part of me," she replied, shaking her head. "If you can't see that, then you're blind."

"No one is perfect. We all have our bad sides. We all have our pasts to get over. All I'm certain of right now is that I still love you."

"Then love really is blind," she said bitterly.

"No. It sees everything."

She touched his cheek with the palm of her hand.

"If you want me to go away with you, Ben, I will. But I'm just afraid of ruining your life the way I've ruined Michael's."

"You've not ruined his life. Look at him. He has everything a man could want."

"Except kids," she whispered, her eyes trailing away.

"Well, look at my life. There's nothing left to ruin. Maybe that's why I'm here. Maybe we can build something together."

Jennifer crossed her arms, angry at him for not facing the truth of what she just told him, even angrier at herself for telling him everything she had. "So tell me what to do," she said. "Should I go home? Should I stay with you? What should I do?"

"Let's go get your things," he said.

She blinked. Her face softened. She looked into his eyes, uncertain for a moment, for a moment not willing to believe her ears. His gaze was steady, serious. Her lips began to quiver, and her eyes filled with tears.

"You mean...you still want me?"

He took her hand, caressing her fingers. "It's not like you killed someone," he said. Slowly, he pulled his hands away, looking from her hands to his own. He took a breath. "You had an addiction problem..."

"I still do," she interrupted.

"But you've faced it," he said. "How can I condemn you for something that happened years ago? Do you think I'm perfect?

"You are."

"I'm not."

"I know that. But you think you need to be, " she said, forcing a smile.

"We all need aspirations," he smiled back. "Jennifer, you know I love you."

"I still don't understand how you could," she said. "It makes no sense."

"But it's the truth."

"What should I do?" she asked.

"C'mon." He took her hand and squeezed it between both of his. He kissed her fingers. "Let's just go."

"First," she said, "hold me for a bit. We have all night. I need to feel you. I've been so worried and anxious today. I need to feel your arms around me."

She began to pull the t-shirt over his chest, running her hands over his skin.

"I should wash up," he said.

"No, no, no," she whispered, biting his ear. "I don't want to wait. You're perfect just the way you are."

He lifted her in his arms and eased her back down upon the bed.

Twenty–Six

As the first blush of dawn began to seep through the slats of the motel room blinds, Jennifer rolled a naked leg onto Ben's naked calf and sighed happily. They had made love and had fallen asleep in each other's arms, legs intertwined above the sheets. Eyes softly closed, she listened to the traffic outside, steady but light, a car rushing past every half minute or so. And the sound of a large insect buzzing at the window, wings beating against the blinds, its solid insect body butting against the glass, trying to get to the daylight outside. She let herself feel Ben's sleeping body against her skin, opening her eyes to watch his face just a few inches from her own, his left cheek pressed into the soft pillow. She watched his body pulse steadily, his arm rising and falling with each breath, and listened to the soft flow of air from his nose. She wondered if he was dreaming or in some deeper or lighter state of sleep. And then she smiled.

"You're awake," she whispered.

"Yes."

"Letting me watch you," she said.

"Umm hmm," he nodded, eyes still closed, arm drawing her near.

"Tell me you love me," she said.

"I love you."

"No matter what," she added.

"No matter what."

Jennifer sat up and stretched her arms high in the air. She was watching the shadow of the fly behind the blind as it repeatedly struck the window. "Do you dream of her, Anna?" she asked.

"I think of her all the time."

"But there's nothing we can do for her now, right?"

Ben sat up. "There's nothing we can do for either of them now. Anna or David. Trust me. The OPP will be arresting the person responsible very, very soon. So put it out of your mind."

As she dressed, Ben stuffed a pair of jeans and a couple of t-shirts into his backpack. "All set?" he asked.

"Is that all you're bringing?"

"Yep!"

She stared at his bag sheepishly. "I've got a bit more than that, you know. And I wanted to ask you something, but I'm not sure how…" She swallowed and took a deep breath. "Will you have room for a piano?"

"I don't know. I hadn't thought of that yet."

"We should think about those things too, you know. I don't need it right away, but after a while…"

She leaned forward, staring at her toes.

He stared at her, trying to understand why her piano could be so important to her now. Certainly it was a big part of her life, but could it be so important that, of all the things she owned, she would worry about a piano? Suddenly—very suddenly—Ben wondered if he was making a mistake.

"Are you getting cold feet?" he asked. "Is that what this is about?"

"No," she said, shaking her head. "It's just hard to get used to. Running away like this…my piano is my life. I never considered what I'd do without it."

"Worry about it later, okay?"

"Of course. I'm sorry, Ben." She grasped his hand. "It's just a piano. It's just a *thing*. I know. I'm just nervous. That's all."

Jennifer's Volkswagen was covered in dew, the windows all frosted. She turned on the wipers to clear the windshield.

She drove fast, barely using the brakes as she rounded the turns, tires squealing with delight at her speed. Ben held the dashboard with one hand as the car bounced across the ruts in her gravel lane before they came to a stop beside her gate.

She grinned at him as she turned off the engine. Her eyes were wide. Too wide, it seemed to Ben. Too wild, as they looked at the house, circled in her sockets, looking at the fence, at the roof, at the trees.

"We're here!" she exclaimed.

"What do you need to bring?" he asked as they stepped through the gate.

"I was just thinking about that...I have so many things! I'm not sure where to start."

"How about a few clothes. Your purse. Anything important, like that."

Jennifer stopped. The screen door was closed. The dark oak door behind it was wide open by a foot or so. The molding around the lock was pale and splintered. Pieces of broken wood littered the threshold of the door.

"Someone broke down the door," she whispered.

Ben lifted his hand. "Get back to the car," he said.

Jennifer backed up to the gate. "Don't go in," she said.

"It's fine," he said. "Let's just make sure there's no one inside."

He opened the screeching door, listening hard for any noises inside. The kitchen was neat, as was the living room. He stepped softly through the rooms and found Michael's study. A large oak desk presented itself to him, solidly placed in the centre of the room. Papers and opened file folders had been poured out from the drawers, cascading across the top of the desk and onto the green carpeted floor. A monitor sat on the top of the desk, cables leading to nowhere. Michael's computer was missing. Portions of his bookshelf looked a lot emptier than they should have.

Ben quickly bounded up the stairs to discover that the bedrooms were clean, untouched. He returned to Jennifer outside.

"What happened?" she asked, dazed, uncertain.

"Someone stole Michael's computer, maybe some other things. But the house is empty. It's not too bad."

Jennifer shook her head.

He held the tight screen door for her as she stepped into her house. She looked carefully around the kitchen before venturing into the living room.

"They took some things from the mantel," she said. "Some silver. Nothing important. But it's gone."

"Let's get you packed," he said. "And we should call the police."

She was mounting the stairs when the sound of tires on packed gravel came up the laneway. Jennifer ran for the window.

"Oh my god. Ben! He's here!"

"Who's here?"

"He's here! Michael."

Ben nodded calmly and stepped outside as Michael Voracci climbed out of his SUV. Michael looked fresh and alert. Sharp pleats in his black pants. His teal golf shirt was unwrinkled. Spotting Ben on his porch, he stared, annoyed at first then with a look of uncertainty, some confusion.

"Taylor? What the hell's going on?"

"You've been robbed," said Ben.

Michael dropped his overnight bag on the gravel and rushed up the steps. "What happened?"

"Someone came through your back door last night. Pried open the lock." He felt Jennifer standing behind him. "They took some things."

"What did they take?"

"Your computer," said Jennifer, standing behind Ben. "The silver platter. I'm not sure what else."

"Dammit." He glared at Jennifer, running his hand over his chin. "You didn't hear anything?"

"No," she said. "You know those pills knock me out. I'm just happy they didn't come upstairs."

"Yeah," said Michael. "What are you doing here, Taylor?"

"He saw the door was broken open," Jennifer replied, following Ben down the porch steps and onto the lawn.

"Did you call the police?"

"Not yet," said Ben.

"You didn't notice a thing?" he glared at Jennifer again.

"No," she said, looking down. "Not a thing."

Michael stepped up to the doorway, examining the lock. Ben and Jennifer watched him from the lawn.

"Thanks for your help, Taylor," said Michael looking up at the lightening sky. "I'll call the police myself. You'd better get to work. Go punch in."

"Are we open today?" Ben asked.

"Yes."

"Did you hear what happened yesterday?"

"Of course," said Michael. "That's why I came back early."

"We're still open?"

"Yes. The police cleared everything with me last night. You better punch in."

Ben stood in place, watching Jennifer between them.

Michael nodded his head at Jennifer. "Get in the house."

She stood directly between the two men. She looked to Ben then to her husband, brown eyes pleading at Ben. Ben motioned to the car with a quick look of his eyes.

"I don't want to go inside," she said. Her husband and the kitchen door were to her right; Ben and the car were to her left.

"Ginny," her husband said, "get in the house."

Ben felt his breathing quicken as he watched Jennifer's face, watched her feet and hips, watched to see which direction she turned. For the moment she was frozen in place. The look of fear in her eyes, watching her husband, seemed to change, to become pleading.

"Now, Ginny. Don't make me tell you again."

The pleading expression washed away to sorrow as her shoulders dropped. She looked one last time, apologetically to Ben. Her hips turned towards her husband, then her feet, and finally her eyes.

Ben watched with disbelief as Michael held open the door for her, and she stepped under his arm and into the darkness of the house.

He looked away. He couldn't bear to face either of them. His head began to spin, and the ground beneath his feet seemed to betray his sense of balance.

"Taylor," said Michael with a grin. "Go to work."

Ben blinked. "What?"

"Punch in. Get paid for your time. I really appreciate your help here. I'll have Randy give you an extra hour, okay?"

Ben nodded. His mouth and throat were dry. His head swam, disoriented. She had just walked away from him. He turned and walked through the gate, not knowing which direction he had gone, his stomach aching now, as if he had just been punched in the chest. As if Jennifer had just punched him in the chest.

He turned away from the warehouse and walked into the orchard, his feet moving on their own, and his eyes staring blankly ahead. He was in shock. His mind and his body had abandoned him, exactly as Jennifer had done just now. He had not seen this coming at all.

Twenty-Seven

Michael stepped inside, finding Jennifer sitting at the kitchen table, bent forward, her face in her hands.

"What was that all about?" he demanded.

"Nothing." She did not raise her head.

"Don't give me that," he replied. His calm voice masked the anger seething inside. "Tell me where you were going with him."

"Nowhere," she said.

"You know I don't like you talking to the workers. Especially when I'm not around," he said. "Considering what is going on right now, I'd like to think you would have enough sense to stay away from that one, especially."

Jennifer lifted her head. Her eyes were red and her face pale. "Why? I told you, he helped us... He helped me."

"I don't believe that for a moment," Michael said. He pulled up a chair and sat across the table from her. "You do understand what is going on here, Ginny."

"What?"

"Anna Wagner. You know he is the prime suspect right now."

"No. I don't know any such thing. You don't tell me anything that's going on here."

"Maybe it is you who should be filling me in on what happened to Anna."

"What are you talking about?"

"You're doing drugs again," he said flatly. "You can't hide it."

She rose from her chair. "That's not true!"

"I know it's true. Admit it now."

"It's not true."

Michael nodded, rose and left the room. Jennifer listened to his footsteps up the stairs. A few moments later he returned. He dropped a plastic Ziploc bag in the centre of the table. Inside were several ounces of dried marijuana and an assortment of pills and capsules.

She stared at it, mouth gaping, horrified.

"I found this in your room."

"It's not mine," she protested.

"Not another word," he said. "I know it's yours. It was hidden in your drawer. You promised to stay away from this, Ginny. You know the cost of this behaviour."

She stared at it.

"I know Anna was involved in this. I know her boyfriend was involved in it too. Is that why you killed her?"

Jennifer went numb. "What?"

"Is that why you killed her?" he asked again, still calm.

"No. I didn't hurt Anna."

"I know it was you. I know what you were involved with. Did Ben help you?"

"I didn't hurt her," she repeated. "I can't believe you would accuse me of this."

"Did Taylor help you kill her?"

"Ben would never hurt her either. You don't know Ben."

"But you do. Is that why you call him Ben?"

"Yes. I knew him a long time ago."

"So he was involved with this too."

"No!" She shouted. "You don't know what you're talking about. I didn't hurt Anna. Ben wouldn't either."

"You know you've been talking in your sleep again," he said.

"No."

"You know you've been sleep walking again. Just like you did back then. You know what the drugs do to you. You know what you're like. Why would you do this again? Why would you do this to Anna? Why would you do this to me?"

"You don't know what you're talking about!" she protested. "I'd never hurt Anna."

"But you did. Did he help you?"

"No! You think Ben is just another drifting farmhand. But he's not. He's…" The words were on her lips. She nearly told him, *Ben is a cop*. But, even as the words were forming on her lips, she knew she could not bring Ben into this, not with her husband already accusing them both of Anna's murder.

"I didn't hurt Anna," she said. "Do you think I'd lie to you about such a thing?"

"Maybe not. But you would lie to yourself after the fact. Like before."

He reached forward, pushed the plastic bag to the edge of the table and took her right hand in both of his. "Ginny. Listen to me. I'll make this go away."

"You don't know what you're talking about."

"No?" he said, softly, looking deeply into her eyes. He looked sad and defeated. "I found more than this bag of dope, Ginny. I got rid of it for you. No one will know. But you have to promise me to stay away from Taylor. You have to promise to let the chips fall where they may. I can't protect you without your help."

Jennifer looked down at his hands covering her own.

"You know I'll protect you," he said. "I always have."

"I know," she said.

He picked up the plastic bag. "No more of this," he said. "You have to promise. I can't protect you forever."

275

"You don't understand," she said weakly. Even to her own ears, her words sounded hollow and fake.

"I do understand," he said. "Just promise to stay away from him. Promise not to touch this crap again. That's all that I ask."

She stared at him, mute. What good would it do to argue with him? What did she care what he thought of her now, anyhow? It was Ben who was in her thoughts now. She couldn't believe she had sent him away like that. Now she was alone.

"Promise me."

"I promise," she said. And with those two words, Jennifer felt as if her life, with her willpower, was now draining from her body.

Twenty-Eight

Ben made his way through the orchard, becoming increasingly aware of where his legs were taking him, of where he was heading. His mind had reached a point of near no-return as he entered the orchard. And yet, he marvelled, as bad as it was, there was still a part of his consciousness that remained detached, observing his reaction in a methodical, nearly clinical manner.

Notice how your chest hurts as much as your stomach, it said. *She broke your heart before. Years ago when she left you. And again this past Christmas when she ran to Arizona with her husband. Why would you expect it to be any different this time? Just be grateful she did it now, and not a week from now, or a month from now. You fool. See how your mouth is dry and how you want to speak, but the words don't come? You know this place. You have been here before. This is shock. Your legs are moving, and while you could stop if you wanted to, there is no desire to walk or stop. Notice how you have no sense of your arms. Now you're certainly flushed and sweating, but you did not feel it until I pointed it out...*

He focused on this voice, letting it run through his thoughts in a constant narration. It became louder and clearer in his mind, until he was able to shed that numbing sensation in his arms and legs. It was a long time before the voice began to fade and he began to feel more like himself again.

"Shit."

He sat down near the river, a stone's throw away from the pump-house, and watched the slow moving water through the thick trees. The water was silky green along the banks from the reflection of the trees, with a wide stripe of grey down the centre, reflecting the hazy sky. He watched the willows and maples, the poplars, all swaying in a gentle rhythm with the slow, steady breeze. The trees near the edge all leaned in towards the river, branches stooping to touch the water, as if they were reaching to cross to the other side. Yet, it was the pull of the river itself that drew them in over the years, pulling them, one by one, into its shallow death. Even from here, Ben could see a dozen trees that had come too close to the bank and had drowned, already beginning to rot in the water.

Again, the same questions that had been plaguing him for weeks came at him, renewed in the sudden reality of being rejected by Jennifer once again.

He picked up a smooth stone from the laneway, measured its weight in his hand for a moment, then reached back and threw it as hard as he could towards the river. It plunged into the water with an unsatisfying plop a few feet from the shore. Ben kicked some stones, looking for something larger.

What the hell are you doing here? he asked himself.

He thought of his sister, Becky, and the last time he had spoken to her. He had asked her the same question. He could have sworn he heard her laugh.

"I knew you'd go back to her," Becky had said. Ben could see her grinning at him all the way from Ottawa. "Just as long as you're running to something and you're not trying to hide, I have no worries for you. You can't hide from the world, because you're in it. You're always in it. And try as you might, you can't hide from yourself either, Ben. You're going to realize that too, and when you do, you'll come home. With her, or by yourself."

Becky of course knew all about Ben's reasons for leaving the police force. She knew his history with Jennifer. She knew more about Ben than anyone in the world. He wished she were not his sister, just for a day. Maybe then her words would have felt like they had more weight than they did.

He cast another stone into the river.

He picked up one more stone, watched the flecks of quartz reflect the sunlight. "Unless..." he said aloud. Unless there was a reason for being here that lay beyond his own puny hopes and expectations. Anna's voice seemed again to be calling to him...

You're still responsible for me, she said.

"I am," he replied.

Then start saying you are, and do something. Do something to help.

Then he thought he heard his sister's voice say alongside Anna's. *You're not someone who would run away, Ben. Stop hiding.*

He turned the stone around in his hand. There was something about the stone that triggered a memory from high school. "The witnesses of eternity," his science teacher had said. Ben dropped the stone and began to look at the rocks around his feet.

"Taylor!"

Ben jumped at the sound of his name and spun around. Michael Voracci was approaching on foot, his face stern behind dark glasses.

"What are you doing here?" Voracci asked. "Why the hell aren't you working? I came by the warehouse to thank you for helping Jennifer, but you weren't anywhere around. What the hell are you doing out here?"

Ben looked up at the sky and saw that the sun was nearing its peak. He had been here much longer than he had realized. He watched Voracci without expression, wondering why he could not feel the hatred he knew he should have for this man, wondering why he felt so numb.

The heat was rising, and Ben was dehydrated. His head was spinning, and his thoughts were muddled, but his instincts had told him there was something important here, something he had missed before...but what? He paused, hands on his hips, looking at the brick pump-house and the door that was barred with yellow police tape. He stared idly at the notice stapled to the door, warning of the consequences of tampering with a crime scene. Ben turned around, bent forward, looking down at the gravel.

Voracci walked a slow, wide slow circle around him, watching him closely. Voracci had never liked Ben. He saw Ben as someone who could not be controlled as easily as most of his workers. But he would be damned if he would let him get away with this. A quick showdown, a few well chosen words, and Ben would be on the road again, and he'd know who was in control around here.

"I asked you a question, Taylor."

Ben continued to ignore his employer, blocking out the sound of his voice, pushing away the image of Jennifer retreating into the house at Voracci's command. He ventured towards the pump-house, still kicking stones as he walked over the gravel. Voracci followed slowly ten feet behind. Ben tried to clear his mind of everything except what he was here to look for. If he just knew what that was. Hair? A key? A personal item? Anything.

"What are you looking for?" Voracci asked.

"I don't know."

"I still can't believe she died here," Voracci said. "So horrible. She was such a bright girl."

"Yes, she was," Ben agreed, almost absently, still kicking stones and walking slowly around the gravel.

"Can I help you look for something?" Voracci asked.

Ben looked up, distracted. "I'd appreciate it if you just stood back right now."

"It really would help if you gave me some idea what you were looking for."

"Anything that isn't grass or gravel," Ben said.

"Didn't the police already do this?"

"Maybe."

"I thought they had to."

"They do. The question is whether they did it well or not."

"Any ideas of what to look for?" Voracci asked.

"I don't know. Hair? A key? A personal item. Drag marks. Anything."

"A key? To what?"

"A key to the lock on that door? Someone changed the lock. Maybe they tossed the old lock into the weeds. Maybe their key didn't work, and they threw it away. I don't know. Anything can be important."

"Why?" Voracci asked.

"Why, what?"

"Why would he drop anything on the ground?" Voracci shook his head as if trying to comprehend. "Wouldn't he throw it away? In the river? In the garbage someplace else?"

"He wouldn't drop it on purpose," Ben said. "But in a struggle, or in moving her."

Voracci nodded and began to survey the gravel around his feet. "I'm looking," he said. "All I see is stones and glass."

Ben nodded. He was looking at glass too.

"If there's something here, you shouldn't be around here at all. Leave it to the police, Taylor."

"Our friend made a couple mistakes," said Ben without taking his eyes from the ground. "You see, I think he wanted her body burned with the pump-house. He doused the pump-house with gasoline, expecting it to burn the building. But it didn't. The vapour ignited

281

an explosion. It blew out the window and blew off the plywood covering the roof. The rain got in, putting out the fire. He didn't intend that to happen at all. That was one mistake."

"What was the other?" Voracci asked.

Ben examined some discolouration on the gravel between his feet. He squatted down to get a better look. It was a small piece of glass in the coarse gravel, three sided, about the size of a quarter. It lay nearly flat against another large stone. It was covered by a small dark red stain. Blood.

"I asked you a question. What's the other reason?" Voracci repeated, stepping closer. "Returning to the scene of the crime?"

Ben pointed to the stone. "Looks like someone got cut," he said.

"Blood?"

"Yeah." Ben carefully picked up the broken piece of glass. "I think this is blood."

"Anna's."

"Not out here. She was inside."

"Put it down," Voracci growled. "And answer my question."

Ben stopped and looked up, blinking. "What?" Then he saw the growing rage in Voracci's face.

"Why did you come back here?"

The heat of the sun was getting to him. Ben's head was beginning to ache. He wished he had a hat, or even a pair of sunglasses. He wiped the sweat from his brow and blinked. His eyes stung from the salt of his sweat. For a moment he wondered if he was getting sunstroke, but it was still just the shock of Jennifer's decision, the lack of sleep, everything that had happened to Anna, everything that had happened in the last two weeks pressing down on him, adding to the weight of the sun.

"I had a talk with the OPP inspector before I left town," Voracci said. "I told him everything I know. How I saw you and Anna slip away from the warehouse the day before she disappeared."

"We were just talking about her plans for college," Ben said. "I'm not a suspect."

Voracci laughed, angry. "That's bullshit. You're the primary suspect! I'll be damned if I'm going to let you screw around with the crime scene. Put that down."

Ben peered at his employer. "That's why you followed me out here, isn't it?"

"You're damned right it is. I wanted to thank you again for taking care of Ginny this morning," said Voracci. "But when I saw you hadn't punched in, I remembered seeing you walking out this way. I wondered what you were up to."

"Looking for evidence."

"Or looking to cover up evidence," Voracci replied, glaring. "Ginny told me everything. How you stopped by when you saw the door was open."

Ben said nothing, still searching the ground. He did not want to hear about this, did not want to talk about Jennifer. Not with her husband. Not here, not now.

"Yeah," said Voracci, watching Ben carefully, his face stern, jaw set as he paused. He took a step closer. "And then she told me what really happened."

"What do you mean?"

Voracci cocked his head to the side, glaring at Ben from behind his sunglasses.

"I guess I should thank you for that too, shouldn't I?"

Ben looked down at the ground again, then back up at Voracci. Voracci's face was red, his cheeks rosy with rage, getting angrier by the second.

"Shouldn't I?" Voracci demanded.

"What do you mean?"

"She told me everything." Voracci took another step, his hands clenched at his sides. Tight, angry fists. He had been letting his anger build since he'd come out here, and now it was time to let Ben Taylor feel the weight of his rage.

"I trusted you, you sonofabitch. I gave you a job, I took you in. I gave you a place to live. And you sneak around behind my back? You kill my partner's daughter? You fuck my wife? You get her involved in this shit?"

Ben blinked. His head was swimming from the heat. He looked at the small stone in his fingers.

"Put it down, you bastard. I don't give a damn about some stone you found, you sonofabitch. You fucked my wife. *My* wife."

"You're making a mistake," said Ben. "Step back."

"She told me everything. Sitting in my house, at my table, in my living room, the beach, your bed, the sex, the plans to take her away from me. Where did you get the fucking nerve to think she would leave me for you?"

"She didn't tell you anything..."

"Shut the fuck up. You're the one who doesn't understand. She's not going anywhere. You are."

Ben blinked again. He did not see the punch coming. A full, clumsy right hook to the side of his head. If he had not been so confused about Jennifer's betrayal, so preoccupied with the evidence that was here on the gravel beneath his feet, he would have been able to dodge it. But as it was, Voracci's fist connected squarely on Ben's mouth.

Ben dropped to the gravel.

"Get up."

His arms were already pressing his body from the hot stones. But Voracci's shoe caught him in the stomach. All the desire to get to his feet again was forced from him. His face pressed against the stones, vaguely aware that the small stone had fallen from his fingers.

"Don't —" Ben began.

The next kick caught him in the ribs, silencing him. He couldn't breathe, couldn't think to breathe.

Another kick just below his left kidney.

You're gonna feel that in the morning, that same cool rational voice said in response.

Another kick, this time to his face, and something in Ben let go. The rational voice in his head took control, and he stepped back in his head to watch what would happen next.

Somehow, he saw the next kick coming, headed directly for his face. Ben, on his side, spun around, kicking Voracci's ankle and knocking him to the ground. Ben was on his feet before Voracci, who was breathless himself now, could rise.

"You made a mistake," Ben said without emotion. "Don't get up."

Voracci began to rise. Ben placed his knee in the small of Voracci's back and let his weight do the rest. A grunt from beneath him as Ben grabbed his wrist and pinned it between his shoulders.

"You fucker..." Voracci groaned.

Ben grabbed a handful of hair, lifted his head and smashed Voracci's head against the ground.

"Stay down," said Ben.

"You fucking sonofabitch," Voracci sobbed. "I'm gonna —"

Ben cranked his arm and twisted the man's wrist hard. "Shut up. Don't talk. Don't move."

"I'm going to have you for this too. I'm calling the cops, and when they get through with you —"

"*I'm* a cop, you stupid bastard."

Those words did more to silence Michael Voracci than any further beating could have.

Ben leaned back and wiped the blood from his mouth. His head and his ribs were searing with pain. His body was numb. He looked around and almost laughed. "Why the hell didn't you bring your car?" he asked. "This is too far to walk back like this."

The buzz in Ben's head was getting louder as he fought the urge to lie down or close his eyes. But then he realized that it was the sound of the Kubota tractor slowly approaching from between the trees. Ben waved and he heard the tractor engine bear down before speeding up.

Soon, Juan was standing beside him.

"Taylor! What happened? What are you doing to him?"

Ben was breathing heavily. "Get me to a hospital," he said.

Juan squinted at him, confused. "What?"

"Just give me a hand."

Juan helped Ben to the flatbed trailer. Ben was reeling, trying to keep his eyes open now. *Broken ribs, concussion,* the rational voice explained. The air around him turned to a white haze.

"Leave him there," he said, seeing Michael Voracci slowly get to his feet. "Get me to a doctor. Get out of here. I'm going to pass out."

"You got it, Taylor."

And then even the rational voice stopped talking for a while as Ben fell backwards into a pile of rolled up rope on top of several sheets of plywood. The haze dissipated, and he saw that the sky was dark blue, and the leaves of the peach trees danced above him before darkness fell in the midst of the sunlight.

TWENTY-NINE

Ben squinted in the presence of blunt pain and bright lights. His shirt was off, his belt unbuckled and his pants loose around his hips. His head felt like a cracked egg.

A bright-eyed woman in a blue scrub shirt, with tangles of dark hair tied behind her head, was looking into his eyes. She smiled warmly at him.

"Hospital?" he asked with a parched whisper, blinking. He coughed hard, and his chest flared with pain. He felt like he had been kicked in the stomach. Then he remembered he had been.

"Yes," she said. "Andover General. I'm Doctor Olivera."

She stood on his left, pressing his side with cool latex-clad fingers, looking for signs of abdominal injury. Another woman was preoccupied with some equipment on his right. The lights were too bright. He closed his eyes.

"No, no," Dr. Olivera said. "Keep your eyes open, Benjamin."

"My head hurts," he said.

"That's what you get for starting fights," she said absently.

"What?" He tried to push himself up, but his arms were rubber. "What are you talking about?"

The doctor spoke with the nurse, but Ben could not pick out more than a word or two. The words he did hear seemed jumbled, and he could not put them in any sensible order.

There was a police officer standing a few yards behind the doctor. He stepped forward when Ben tried to up sit again.

"The kid who called said you were in a fist fight with someone."

"Yes."

"You broke into his home."

"What?"

"You kicked down a door in his home."

"That's ridiculous..." He tried again. "That's not true."

She grinned. "You just lie back and relax."

Ben could not lie here helplessly and let himself be accused of attacking Voracci, let alone breaking into his house.

"I'm a cop," said Ben.

Now the officer smiled. "Is that right? Where's your badge?"

"In my desk. Ask Walter Kumar. He's the OPP Inspector on the Wagner case." Ben laid back and resisted the urge to sit up again, resisted the urge to say more to the officer before Kumar arrived.

The police officer looked at the doctor. The doctor nodded.

"He's not going anywhere for a while," she assured him.

The officer untangled his way through the blue privacy curtain.

"How are you doing?" the nurse asked.

"My face hurts," said Ben.

"Just don't smile," she replied with a wink.

He coughed again, violently, to the point he felt bile rising in his throat. The pain in his chest stabbed him again. "My ribs hurt too."

"I'm sure they do," the doctor replied. She shone a bright light into his eyes . "You've probably broken one or two."

"Guessed that much," he said. His thoughts seemed to be clearing up slowly. Very slowly.

She examined his ears.

"Your ribs may just be bruised," she said casually. "We'll know soon enough."

Ben coughed loudly several times. He thought he was going to vomit this time. He tried to keep his breathing shallow and closed his eyes in an attempt to escape the pain.

"Uh, uh, uh," she said. "Keep your eyes open."

"Concussion?" said Ben. "I'm woozy."

"Dollars to doughnuts," she said. "I want to get some X-rays. Looks like you've fractured some bones in your face."

"Let me see."

"You're still pretty," she smiled. "You can look at yourself in the mirror later."

This time he couldn't resist the pull of his eyelids. When he opened them again, the doctor was writing in her chart, and the officer had returned.

"Did you talk to Kumar?" Ben asked.

"Yeah. He vouched for you. He's also on his way in."

"Thank you. I had a small stone with me. Do you have it?"

The officer looked at him curiously. "A stone? No."

"When's Kumar getting here?"

"He should be here soon. He said he was coming right away."

"I had a small stone with blood on it. It was evidence for the Wagner murder."

The officer stood up and sorted through some keys and change on a blue tray beside the observation bed.

"Nothing here, sorry."

"Dammit!" Ben clenched his teeth, which made his face hurt some more. "Send somebody back to Tanglewood Vineyards. You have to cordon off the area around the crime scene. At the pump-house. There's blood there. I must have dropped the stone when he hit me."

"Who hit you?" the cop asked.

"Michael Voracci."

"Michael Voracci?" The cop looked even more puzzled. "No kidding. You got beat up by Mr. Voracci?" He squinted at Ben.

"Yes."

"You've been hit pretty hard, sir."

"Yes. But there's still evidence at that scene."

"Blood?"

"Yes."

"Your blood?"

Ben remembered sitting on top of Voracci, knocking his face into the gravel. The gravel would probably have blood smeared on it from north to south after that fight.

"Dammit."

"Relax," said the doctor, suddenly beside him. "It's time to take some pictures."

The process seemed to take forever. Walter Kumar came to the gurney while Ben waited for the X-ray results.

Kumar wore a blue suit and a green tie. His white shirt was wrinkled. He looked like he had been sleeping in his car again. He carried a coffee and a small paper bag in his hand. "We've cordoned off the pump-house area," he said.

"Are they looking for the blood?"

"Ben." Kumar balanced his coffee cup as he tore open the lid. "There's blood all over there. From the looks of you, I'd guess much of it is yours. I wouldn't have thought he could take you. He's kinda out of shape, you know."

"I know. He surprised me."

Kumar grinned. He set the coffee on the gurney beside Ben's knee and pulled a doughnut from the bag. He crumpled the bag and set it on the table beside the gurney. "Don't mind me. I haven't eaten yet today." He took a bite of his doughnut. "Voracci said you broke into his home."

"He's lying."

"Why?"

"He caught me with his wife."

Kumar tried to suppress a smile, not very successfully. As a last resort, he bit his cheek. "I was wondering when that would catch up to you."

"You knew too?"

"Of course. You like to keep your secrets, Ben. But it's my job, remember?"

Ben looked at the bright blue wall behind the OPP inspector. White ceiling. One blue wall. One red wall. Fisher Price toys on the table beside his bed. Ben wondered if he had been placed in the children's ward.

Kumar took a big bite from his doughnut. Chocolate stuck to his lower lip, but he didn't seem to notice. Ben's stomach protested at the sight. He felt repulsed and hungry at the same time. He looked away from the crumbs on the detective's lips, back to the ridiculously bright blue wall.

"What did you find at the pump-house?" Kumar asked.

"The murderer's blood."

"How did you come to that?"

"When he set the fire, the gasoline blew the window out. It cut him. He bled on the gravel. There was a piece of glass. From the window. It was bloody."

"That area was combed. Maybe it was dropped there after the fact."

"Combed," said Ben. "Maybe with a trowel. There was more blood at the scene. I'm sure you can find it if I can. It had been raining that night, remember? But it hasn't rained since."

Ben watched the realization wash over Kumar's face as he swallowed his coffee. "Morons," Kumar cursed. "Why couldn't they do that right?"

"I tried telling you."

"True. I didn't know I could trust you then. I thought you were just some redneck making waves. You really should have told me right away who you were."

"Probably."

"You know, if you had told McGrath who you were, he would have been more careful with the evidence. He's a fool, but he's not stupid."

"Or he would have sat back and let me do it myself."

Kumar nodded. "I'll go back myself in a few minutes."

"Good idea."

"It doesn't look likely, though. I don't know what Voracci did to you, but he left a mess."

"It's not all my blood," said Ben. "Did you get a look at him yet?"

Kumar grinned. "Yeah. Looked like someone took a cheese grater to his face. He hasn't pressed charges yet. Do you want to charge him with assault of a police officer?"

"Not yet."

Kumar sipped at his coffee.

"Voracci said he spoke to you just before his trip."

"That's right," Kumar nodded.

"Did you tell him I was a suspect?"

"Of course."

"Why?"

"Because you are."

"Thanks."

Kumar patted Ben's shoulder. "He said he was going to let you go. I suggested he keep you around for a while. I needed your help, remember?"

"That makes sense," said Ben.

"Any idea whose blood you found at the site?" Kumar asked.

Ben considered this question. "Not really. Not any more of an idea than you have. Who are you betting on?"

"Randy Caines is my prime suspect right now. Miguel Gonzalez might be number two."

"Not David?"

"Doesn't make sense. He may have been hiding, but that doesn't mean he took out his girlfriend."

"Gonzalez doesn't make sense either."

"Maybe not. That's why he's number two."

"Has Caines returned?"

"We called the warehouse in Philadelphia. He's on his way back. We'll catch him unawares."

"Have you tried the church, looking for Gonzalez?"

"No."

"Give it a shot, if you want to speak to him."

"How do you know he's there?"

"Sunday is their only day off. Almost everyone works Sunday, except the migrants. They never work Sunday. I think it's in their contracts. Most of them are practicing Catholics. They go to Mass then socialize at the church grounds afterwards."

"I'll go there too. Do you know who the priest is?"

"Me? No idea."

"Any other clues, hotshot?"

Ben's head was beginning to throb again. "Not at all. I wish they'd hurry with the X-rays. I could use a pill right about now."

Kumar leaned against the rail of Ben's gurney. "The call I got said you were a Peeping Tom from the farm, sneaking around the house. Voracci apprehended you for the break-in. One of his employees called it in. Didn't get his name."

"It was probably Juan."

"So you were hunting around for evidence, found some blood. Then what happened?"

"Voracci came at me. He was furious. He abuses his wife, you know."

"I didn't know."

"He suckered me. Started kicking me. That's when I must have dropped the evidence. I managed to subdue him. Then Juan showed up. He gave me a ride back to the warehouse. I remember getting onto the wagon, but not much else after that."

"We'll need a statement from you. But that can wait a bit." Kumar sipped his coffee. "You really screwed up, Ben. I hope she was worth all this."

The doctor returned and planted three X-rays onto a lighted screen above Ben's head. She studied each film before saying a word. A few hums and hahs escaped her lips, barely audible to Ben.

"Looks like a small crack on your cheekbone there. Nothing else is broken."

"You obviously didn't X-ray my ribs."

She smiled. "Didn't have to. You broke a rib. But we don't treat rib injuries of that degree."

"No tape?"

"No tape. That will just restrict your breathing and leave you prone to a lung infection. Best thing to do is lie still when you can. The same thing with your face. If it hurts, don't do it. Other than that, take some Advil if you need it."

"That's it?"

"No. I want you to force yourself to breathe deeply three times, twice a day. Just to clear your lungs out."

"How long will it take to heal?"

"Again, both fractures are similar. It should heal quickly. Give yourself a week after it stops hurting before doing anything strenuous. Some heal within two days. Others take a month."

Ben tried a smile. It hurt, so he stopped. "Good. Then I can get out of here."

"Not so fast, Ace," she said. "You're staying the night." He could tell she called many male patients Ace. Nicknames helped when you saw too many people to remember their names. Nicknames for boys and girls, young men and young women, old men and old women. Six names to remember instead of a hundred or more given names each shift. It was a good system. It made each patient know that they were special. Ben could tell from her bedside manner that the care she felt for each patient was sincere. She must be a good doctor, he decided. But that did not mean he was going to blindly take her advice.

"Why should I stay?" he asked.

"Because I told you to."

"That's not necessary," he told her. "You should save the beds for the real patients."

"Do you have someone to stay with? No? We don't want you falling asleep alone. We're going to have to wake you up every hour on the hour."

Ben nodded. "I know, I know. To make sure I didn't die in my sleep. I used to play hockey. I know about that. My girlfriend is a pro at that," he lied.

"I still want you here."

Ben started up. "I'll be fine. If I'm not, I'll have her rush me back here, straight away."

The doctor looked in his eyes. She could see he was serious. The odds of a complication were remote. Her decision had been based on the rules of necessary procedure, for no other reason than the procedure.

"Every hour on the hour. Tell her that."

"I will," said Ben. His smile lasted only a second before the pain became too much.

"And no smiling!" she added with a smirk.

"I won't." Ben sat up. "Where's my shirt?"

"It's shredded," she said, nodding to a nurse, who nodded back and went down the hall.

"Where are you off to?" asked Kumar.

"I'm coming with you."

"No, you're not," he said. "I can look for blood all by myself."

"I suppose you can. But I can save your knees and point out where I found the one I did."

"Well, my knees might be grateful," said Kumar.

The nurse returned with a t-shirt for Ben. It had a big yellow smiley face with the words, "I volunteer at Andover General" beneath. Ben pulled it over his head with much discomfort.

It was mid-afternoon by the time they emerged from the hospital. The sky was heavy and grey with the heat of the day bearing down on them. Walter Kumar drove with apparent disregard for traffic as he guided his Buick through the shaded streets of Andover.

Coming down the gravel laneway of Tanglewood Vineyard, Ben noticed the lack of activity, the empty parking lot. A sole raven was perched on the telephone wire above the Voracci home. Kumar drove between the apple orchard and vines towards the river.

Emerging from the car, Ben noticed all the gravel surrounding the pump-house was wet. Puddles lay in the low spots. The entire area had been drenched. Swirls in the sand and damage to the grass revealed the water had been sprayed with some pressure.

Kumar pointed to the hose protruding from the trees. "Looks like someone's been irrigating this morning," he said.

"They've violated the crime scene," said Ben.

"Not exactly. The shed is taped off. Not the road."

Kumar's cell phone rang. He pulled it from his jacket pocket and stepped away from Ben.

He grinned at Ben as he turned around. "Thank you," he said to the caller and put his phone away.

"Let's see if we can find out who's been playing with the hose," said Kumar.

"Let's go."

"Not yet," said Kumar, eyeing the bandage on Ben's cheek. "I bet that smarts."

"Only when I laugh."

"Well, you need some rest. You're half-bagged."

"I'm fine," Ben replied as he wiped the sweat from his forehead with the back of his sleeve. He could not resist touching the white gauze that had been plastered to his cheek. The flesh beneath it was swollen and raw. Fortunately, that seemed to be the worst of his injuries, apart from a few nicks beneath his hair where the doctor had pulled bits of gravel embedded in his scalp.

"You're really not fine. A few hours sleep." Kumar paused, looking at Ben with concern.

"What?"

"If you look better, and only if you look better, I'll bring you with me to pick up Caines. The call I just got was from the New York State Police. He'll be here in a couple hours. He doesn't know we'll be waiting for him. Wanna come?"

"Of course."

"Then get some rest."

Ben nodded. "It's a deal."

"I'm thinking he's our man."

"I'm thinking you're right."

Thirty

Kumar drove through the winding streets of Andover, looking for St. Paul's Church at 1475 Maple Street. The address had sounded easy enough to find, but Kumar had been driving in circles for about twenty minutes before he realized some kids had twisted the street sign at the corner of Maple and Rochester. He spotted the stubby white-washed steeple a few blocks away, set behind a row of small houses at the end of a long laneway. Without an address, Kumar doubted he would have spotted it.

It was a small church hidden behind several trees on a crooked side street in the midst of a residential neighborhood that had sprouted in the late 1940s. The church was a stucco-style building reminiscent of an old Spanish mission Kumar would have expected to see in a western movie, not in a small southern Ontario town. A relatively modern office building was connected to the church by a covered walkway.

Inside, Kumar felt like he was in a school office. Three women worked at their desks behind the reception counter. The inspector approached the counter and rapped on it with his knuckles. All three women jumped with surprise.

The woman closest to him slid out of her chair, approaching him earnestly. The air conditioning was cool, and she pulled her white sweater across her chest. She looked to be about fifty years old. She was tall and pointed, her nose thin and long, and her glasses hung from her neck with a small plastic chain. The intensity of her gaze made the inspector realize most people did not knock at her counter. They would simply wait patiently until someone looked up. Being a cop sometimes made him look pushy. He was not a pushy man. He simply spoke to so many people in the course of an investigation that he could not afford the time for that kind of etiquette.

"I hope I didn't startle you," he said. "I'm looking for the parish priest."

She looked at him, thoughtfully.

"Which priest?" she asked "Any priest?"

"I'm not sure," Kumar said. "Who speaks Spanish?"

"That would be Father Bill."

"Can I speak with him?"

"He's on the phone at the moment. If you'd care to take a seat, I'll tell him you're waiting."

Kumar thought it curious that she did not ask him who he was or what it was regarding. If he had showed her his badge, she might have just let him in. But there was no telling who the priest was talking to on the phone. Someone ill or dying, a teenager in trouble. Even if she did interrupt him, Kumar would prefer to give him a minute or two.

He looked at a large painting in the lobby beside the door. It showed a man falling from a donkey. St. Paul at Damascus, the Patron Saint of the Church. Although he was not a Christian, Kumar knew the story from his childhood. Paul had been travelling down the road to break up the early Christian church when a vision of Christ had appeared to him. He was illuminated, and the brightness of the illumination caused him to lose his eyesight for several days. Kumar thought of Ben being beaten by Michael Voracci. He wondered what changes in Ben's worldview that must have made. In all his years of service, Kumar had never been shot at. Certainly he'd had his scuffles and had to bring down suspects resisting arrest. Once he had been nearly stabbed by a woman while he tried to arrest her husband for beating her with a whiskey bottle. But she had missed. When he looked back on his career, despite his successes, he often felt more like a clerk or a bureaucrat than a cop.

"Father Bill will see you now," the woman said gravely.

She was about to open the door, but the young priest was already ahead of her. He looked to be about thirty years old, with a trimmed beard and short black hair that appeared not to have been washed in a few days. There were dark circles under his eyes. The beard and the black robes gave him the look of a Jesuit, Kumar thought, though he had no idea what a Jesuit priest might look like today. More images from western movies. *Fistful of Dollars. A Few Dollars More. The Good, The Bad and the Ugly.*

"Yes?" said the priest.

Kumar finally took out his badge.

"Father, I'm Inspector Walter Kumar, Ontario Provincial Police. I'd like to ask you some questions regarding one of your parishioners."

"You are welcome to ask," said the priest. "Please, come into my office, Walter."

His office was small and quite cluttered with hand-painted signs and books stacked on the floor that would not fit on the bookshelves. The signs were face down so Kumar could not read what they said. The priest's desk was stacked with various papers. He seemed to be a busy man. The priest moved a megaphone from a chair and offered Kumar a seat.

"Pro–Life protest?" Kumar asked, pointing to the megaphone and the signs.

Father Bill grinned as he sat down. "No. Student pep rally. What can I do for you, Walter?"

"It's about a man who attended mass here. His name was Miguel Gonzalez."

The priest considered the name. "I'm not good at last names, I must confess." He ran his fingers along his chin. "And we have a number of parishioners named Miguel. Perhaps you could tell me something about him?"

"He disappeared about two weeks ago, Father. He worked at Tanglewood Vineyards. He was an illegal alien. We doubt Miguel was even his real name."

"Yes. I know the man you're talking about. That is his real name."

"Do you know where he is?"

"No. I've not seen him in several weeks. My hope is he returned home, but I've not heard anything."

"He's wanted for questioning in a murder investigation."

The priest leaned back in his chair, trying his best to stifle a yawn. "Yes, I heard. The young girl. And Miguel is wanted for questioning because...you think he witnessed something?"

"Actually, Father, he is a suspect."

"Miguel Gonzalez? Why?"

"He was described by his employer as a violent man, prone to aggression. He was also anti-social. He disappeared at the same time the murder occurred."

"I'm sorry," said the priest. "Tell me more. I must be thinking of the wrong Miguel Gonzalez."

"He came here four months ago. Reportedly from Mexico. Worked as a common labourer for Tanglewood Vineyards."

"Yes, that's Miguel. But I can't see him committing a crime like that. Any crime from him would surprise me, but certainly not something like that."

Kumar chuckled. "With all due respect, Father, the man assaulted his employer prior to the crime being discovered."

301

"Oh no." The priest folded his hands beneath his chin, sitting forward, his elbows on the desk. "What happened?"

"There appeared to be no provocation. He attacked his employer and was fired on the spot. He was never seen again."

"That still doesn't sound like the Miguel Gonzalez I know. Why would a man attack his employer without reason?"

"I don't know," replied Kumar.

The young priest looked up at the ceiling, but this time was unable to suppress his yawn.

"I'm sorry," he said, "you'll have to excuse me. I just returned from the hospital with an ill woman. I've not slept in the last day. Was there any provocation for this attack?"

"Apparently not."

"So you're telling me Miguel attacked his employer, the man who controls his financial well-being, without any reason at all? Does that sound like any man you know of, Walter?"

"I've met many men," replied Kumar. "I believe anything is possible. In this instance, there is a possibility that drugs were involved."

"Certainly, anything is possible. He could have been described as a desperate man. But I can't see him jeopardizing his job unless he had been provoked."

"Perhaps he was. I'm certain if I spoke to him, we could clear that up as well. For the time being, what can you tell me about him?"

"He is an honest man. One of the most honest and kind men I've ever known."

"Why do you say that, Father? I've been told he worked here illegally. And that he was a drug user."

"He may have been here illegally. And I know he was taking drugs, but certainly the drugs were not illegal."

"Why do you say that?"

The priest sighed. "Because he is sick. Listen, I know Miguel is not a very well-liked man. He does not talk much. He doesn't socialize with anyone. He is always sneering. People see that, and they think the worst of him. I've heard the stories. He does act strangely, but he has never been violent. And the reason he acts strangely is because of the drugs he takes, in combination with his drinking. And the drinking is for the pain. Miguel has cancer. For that reason he lost his immigration status to work here on a seasonal basis. But he has a wife and three children. He worked here to send money to them, to care for his wife and daughters. He was desperate, but not violently desperate. In fact, we were working with the government to try to get him medical attention while he was in this country, through the little influence the church has with the government. Without an operation, he had little chance of living another year. Leaving here ended his chances of getting that operation. Do you understand?"

"Perhaps there was a darker side to him you were not aware of?"

"Possibly. But I consider myself a good judge of character."

"With all due respect, Father..." Kumar adjusted his chair. "Couldn't it be possible he was pulling the wool over your eyes?"

"No. You are the one mistaken, Walter. He is a good man with limited resources and limited options. He worried for the welfare of his family, so he sacrificed everything. You yourself have never met the man. Everything you know about him is only based on hearsay. As a police officer you should know how unreliable that is. If something is missing, Miguel is blamed for it. If there is a fight, Miguel is blamed for it. But Miguel will not defend himself. Despite his demeanour, he is a devout man."

The priest stood up and began to pace between his chair and the wall. "He sacrificed everything he had, including his health,

303

including the luxury of being with his family in his final months, to try to give them some hope, some money to live on when he was gone."

"I'm sorry, but there is no proof he is even sick."

"Walter, I have seen his X-rays. X-rays I arranged to have taken, here by our doctors in front of my eyes. So don't tell me I don't know what I'm talking about. He is a good man. I know his being here is against the law. But that does not make him a bad or a violent man."

"But Mr. Voracci has said..."

"Mr. Voracci leaves his company to be run by Randall Caines. Mr. Caines is renowned for the neglect of the safety of his workers. Living conditions for his workers are intolerable. Men sleep two to a bunk in some cases, with over twelve people stacked up in bunks in a room no bigger than twelve-by-twelve feet."

"I didn't know that."

"The man who is silent in the face of accusation is that not something that naturally arouses suspicion, Walter?"

"Sometimes justifiably so."

"But it seems to me, such a man also makes a perfect scapegoat, does he not? In my opinion, if you are looking for a criminal, you should be looking at Randall Caines, not his employees."

Thirty-One

Ben had tried to rest but was unable to relax. A couple of painkillers had taken care of some of the pain, but his head and ribs still ached. He winced at the sharp pain in his chest as he bent down to tie his shoelaces. By the time Kumar arrived to pick him up, Ben had been sitting on the step of his door in excited anticipation of arresting the man they suspected of killing both Anna Wagner and her boyfriend, David Quiring. Grudgingly, he waited as Kumar drove back into Andover to go through the McDonald's drive-through.

"We can't do anything until Caines gets here anyway," said Kumar. "Try to relax."

"I know," said Ben.

"It's been a while since you've been on the job," Kumar replied.

"It's more than that," said Ben. "This is personal."

The sun descended behind the large white greenhouses as Kumar parked his Buick out of sight of the laneway and loading dock. Ben opened his window as Kumar turned off the ignition. The air outside was still warm but was considerably cooler now than it had been a few hours ago.

After finishing his french fries, Kumar climbed out of the driver's seat and left the door open to increase the circulation in the car. He strolled around the front of his car and leaned against the frame of the open passenger window.

"He should be here any time now," he told Ben. "Customs officials in Windsor let him pass about an hour ago. Now, I want you to stay in the car until we apprehend the bastard."

"You're in charge," said Ben as he slurped his Coke.

"I've got men in place out of sight all around here. In the warehouse and in the orchard over there," Kumar said, pointing to the edge of the vineyard.

"Understood."

Kumar watched Ben thoughtfully. "Caines troubles me. There's no telling how he is going to react. We know he may be armed..."

"I've told you everything I know about him," said Ben.

Kumar reached into the car and unlocked the glove compartment. Ben saw a badge and a .45 and holster.

"If you want to pick those back up, those are yours," said Kumar.

"I was just thinking today of going back for those," said Ben in surprise.

"You're a cop, Ben. And I know you're a good one. I had a long conversation with your friend from Ottawa, Bob Krall, yesterday."

"But how did you get these?" asked Ben.

"They were shipped from Ottawa. Police express. The Assistant Commissioner thought you might want them back now. I agreed."

Kumar put his hand on Ben's shoulder. "Pick them up, Ben."

Ben picked up the badge and looked at it a moment before putting the badge in his wallet and slipping it into his back pocket. He held the gun in his hand, looking at it, feeling its deadly weight in his hand.

"You're not well. Wait here. Stay low. If we need the help, I'll let you know."

"Understood."

Kumar patted his shoulder through the window. "Welcome back, Ben." He continued to circle his car, waiting, listening to the OPP officers on his radio.

Two officers waited behind the trees to the south of the loading dock. Two were behind the greenhouse to the west. Two more men waited inside the warehouse. Kumar and Ben were parked behind the warehouse covering the possibility of a rash south exit attempt by Caines.

Across the road, four uniformed police officers were already in place, waiting for Randy Caines to make his move.

Kumar said, "We know Caines wanted Quiring's death to look like an accident. He thinks no one has been after him, so he thinks we fell for that. Now that he's on his way back, we want him taken here. When he is least worried. When his guard is down."

"How did you know Quiring's death wasn't an accident?" Ben asked.

"We matched fingerprints at the scene of Quiring's death to fingerprints on file from Caines."

"I'm not saying he's not the man," Ben replied. "But his fingerprints would be all over that warehouse anyway."

"Both Caines' and Quiring's prints were on the grease gun itself. From Caines' greasy fingerprints, we surmised he was there shortly before, during, or after Quiring's death. We think someone tossed it to Quiring. Quiring caught it. The same grease was found on the light switch, forklift controls and the door Caines used to exit the warehouse. More evidence is coming, but it would simplify everything if we can just get this prick to admit it."

"So you need a confession."

"I want a confession, yes."

"That's why you're not stopping him at the border," Ben said.

"I want him to feel safe. At home. In his lair."

Twenty-five minutes later than they expected him to appear, Randy Caines brought his stake truck up the gravel laneway towards the Tanglewood warehouse. Covered by the darkening shadows of the trees, Kumar stood on the edge of the treeline to watch the truck come in while Ben waited in the car.

Caines backed his stake truck to the loading dock and opened the driver's side door. The officers were poised to move in once he was out of the truck and halfway between the cab and the warehouse door.

"He's just sitting there, grinning," a voice said over Kumar's radio.

"Just wait," said Kumar.

Keeping himself hidden from Caines' view and keeping the body of the truck between them, Kumar stepped from the orchard.

"He's stepping out of the truck."

"Wait until he is at the halfway mark," said Kumar.

The police, except for Kumar, were in protective gear. They wore helmets, masks and bulletproof vests. Pistols were sufficient. Caines was alone and lightly armed, if armed at all. Six men were sufficient. Kumar drew his weapon, though he was there to supervise and stay out of the way. They worked as a team, and it should go down quickly.

"Is he armed?" Kumar asked.

"Don't see a weapon."

"He's there."

"Move in."

The two men behind the trees came in quickly down the slope of the driveway towards the truck, behind Caines.

The steel entrance door burst open as Caines was at the bottom of the stairs.

"Police! Don't move!"

In a shocking burst of speed, Caines dove sideways and rolled under the truck. By the time the two officers came out of the building and down the steps, he was on his feet again. He had left the driver's door open. Now he leapt back inside, diving onto the cabin floor.

By the time the officers came in from the trees, Caines had pulled out a revolver. He was up on the seat, starting the engine.

Caines closed the door and fired once through the open window. The two men were exposed and went for cover behind the large garbage hopper. The officers from inside the warehouse split up and approached from both sides, weapons raised and ready to fire.

Meanwhile, at the first sound of trouble, Ben was up and running from the car, pistol low, ribs and face tearing with pain as he rounded the corner to the shipping platform.

At that moment, Caines had seen the police in his rear mirror. He leaned through the window and fired at the officer closest to him. One of the men behind the dumpster fired once, striking Caines in the shoulder.

He screamed and tried to put the truck into gear. Three guns were now aimed at his head. With his shoulder bleeding, his right arm was useless. He couldn't work the gearshift.

He raised his left arm and tossed the gun onto the hood of the engine through the broken windshield.

"Okay, okay, okay. You got me!"

"Turn off the engine."

Caines obliged, reaching around the steering column with his left hand.

"Now step out of the vehicle. Keep your hands in sight."

Caines obliged once again. Slowly he lumbered out of the truck and knelt, hands raised high above his head, in the gravel. His shirt was covered in blood. The bullet had gone right through his shoulder. Hands placed behind his back as he grimaced in pain, Caines was pushed to the ground, cuffed and searched.

Inspector Kumar holstered his pistol. "Randall Caines, you're under arrest."

"No fuckin' kidding," said Caines.

"We have you for David Quiring," said Kumar. "We have you for drug possession, trafficking, and for Anna Wagner."

Caines, breathing heavily, seemed to be adding up this list in his head as one of the OPP officers read him his rights. "That was Quiring's pot, not mine," he blurted. "I didn't even touch that bag. And I sure as fuck didn't touch Anna Wagner."

The inspector hid his satisfaction from the suspect. By admitting he knew about Quiring's bag of marijuana, Caines had just made Kumar's job a lot easier. Having given the police this much, Caines would not have far to go to give them a full confession.

"Why did you have to kill him?" Kumar asked.

"I didn't kill him!" Caines bellowed. Spit was drying on his chin. "He fell. And I didn't touch that girl. We all know it was him. We all know he raped her. So his accident just saved you some work, right?"

"No. He didn't rape her, shit for brains."

"Well, he killed her. What the hell do I know what he did to her? Dead is dead enough."

The constable began to help Caines to his feet. It was then that Caines saw Ben Taylor.

"What the fuck are you looking at, Taylor?"

"I'm looking at you about to go to prison for the rest of your life," said Ben.

"Well, you look worse than I do. What the fuck happened to your face?"

That was when Ben held out his badge for Caines to see.

"Christ!" Caines rolled his eyes and spat on the ground. "You're a cop? You're a fucking cop?"

"Yes."

Caines turned to Kumar. "I guess you got me for all of it then. Everything you said. You win. Let me see a lawyer now."

"You've got it."

"Not so fast," Ben said. "Tell me about Michael Voracci's involvement with this."

"Strike a deal, right? I wish I could." Caines breath was laboured. Ben stepped to the side, expecting the man to throw up. "Michael?" said Caines. "He didn't know anything about this. This was all my work. I don't bother him with minor details like what's legal and what's not. You might have me for the trafficking, but he had nothing to do with it."

Ben and the inspector exchanged glances.

"How can we believe Voracci wasn't involved with the trafficking?" Kumar asked. "He runs this place, doesn't he?"

"*I* run this place!" Caines bragged. "As long as they don't end up working here, I don't have to tell him who I take across the border, or why."

Kumar understood now. Caines had picked up on the charge of trafficking, mistaking the drug trafficking Kumar had used as a threat with human trafficking.

"You mean like Miguel Gonzalez?" Kumar asked quickly.

Caines looked stunned. "That was different. And I'm not saying anything else. Get me to a fucking doctor now!"

He turned to the side and puked. He grinned, pleased with himself.

"You're going to die in prison," said Kumar.

"I don't give a fuck. I don't have much time left. Look at me. I'm lucky to have made it this far. I don't care where I die. I just want to enjoy the ride."

Kumar motioned to the officer beside him. "Give him his ride."

Thirty-Two

Michael Voracci found his wife in her room, stuffing a pair of running shoes into a large suitcase already bulging with clothes and shoes. Her hair was tied back and even from behind, he could see her ears were bright red. From that, he knew she was angry or was crying, or both.

"What the hell is going on?" he demanded.

She turned around and he could see the tears. Her eyes were swollen and dark from crying. She opened her mouth, about to speak, then it closed again. She shook her head sadly, with resignation and began to close her suitcase.

"Answer me," he said. "What the hell is going on here?" He pointed to the suitcase and to the two open, empty drawers of her dresser. He knew exactly what was going on.

"I'm leaving," she said.

"No, you're not," he replied, calmly now.

"I'm going to find Ben."

"No, you're not," he repeated. "You promised to stay away from him. After everything that has happened. After all the grief and trouble you've caused..."

"I didn't do anything!" she screamed.

"You forget too quickly."

"That was years ago. And you had just as much to do with Snake as I did. I know I hurt you, but you can't make me pay with the rest of my life."

"If I hadn't helped you, you would be in prison for the rest of your life," he said.

"Well, you did help me. And I'm grateful to you. But I can't go on living like this. It's not fair to either of us."

"And what of Anna? What was fair to her?"

"I didn't kill her."

Michael watched her for several seconds before replying. "I know you probably don't remember what you did. But you have to understand, if the police had all the evidence, you would be the one behind bars right now, not Randy Caines."

"I think Randy killed her," she said.

"I know otherwise, Ginny. In your heart, you do too. You and I both know the truth."

"I'm leaving."

"I can't let you. You're not thinking clearly."

With that, he calmly left the room. Jennifer stood in place, momentarily stunned, wondering what he was going to do. She put her hand on the suitcase, deliberating whether or not she should finish zipping it up and make her way downstairs. She listened for his voice, wondering if he was calling the police. She heard only silence.

Michael returned to the room with a glass of water in one hand. In his other hand, in the centre of his open palm were two pills. "I think you need to settle down," he said.

She stepped back, pointing at the pills. "You're not serious! I'm not taking those!"

"They're mild sedatives. Take them. Then you can think clearly."

He stepped forward, holding them out to her. She took the glass of water in one hand and snatched the two pills with the other.

"No!" she shouted and threw the glass and pills against the wall. The glass punched a hole in the drywall and shattered, water

313

dripping down the wall and pooling beside the baseboard. The pills were lost on the floor. She marched past him and made her way down the stairs.

"Ginny!" he called after her, with a voice so calm it sent a shard of terror down her spine. "You can't do this," he said.

Jennifer gulped a breath of air. Then she turned on her heels in the centre of the living room as he raced down the stairs.

"I *can* do this, Michael. And I am. And I hate to say it, but you can't stop me. If you want to call the police, go right ahead, but I know they'll find you just as guilty as I was. At least what I did was by accident. What you did was deliberate and intentional. Just to protect your father's reputation."

"*My* reputation," he corrected her.

He smiled, calmly, condescendingly as he approached her.

It was then that she realized that she should never have stopped walking. She should never have turned to face him. If she had just kept going, she would be outside, visible and safe.

He grabbed her shoulder with his left hand, and as she tried to fight him off, the fingers of his right hand gripped her firmly around the wrist.

"Owwwww!" She screamed as he bent her wrist down. "Let go!"

"You need me to keep you from harm, Ginny."

"You can't keep me from leaving," she shouted, trying in vain to pull her hand free from his grip.

"That's just where you're wrong. I *can* keep you from leaving. And that is just what I'm going to do."

He turned, her wrist still in his grip, and began to drag her up the stairs. A few moments later, the bedroom door slammed behind them, and the house was quiet for a very long time.

Thirty-Three

In a pair of grey sweatpants and a scruffy white t-shirt, Ben Taylor set a glass of orange juice on his sister's coffee table and sat down on the floor. Stretching his left leg out and tucking his right foot behind him, in a hurdler's pose, he stretched forward, hands towards his toes. He was dismayed that he still could not touch them, but was pleased that he could now extend his reach beyond his ankle before his ribs began to hurt. Still, there was little pain in the stretching now, even when he breathed deeply. The gauze on his cheek had been replaced with a single Band-Aid. Other than that, there were no signs of the injuries he had suffered at the hands of Michael Voracci. A week of rest, it seemed, was enough to heal most of his wounds.

"It's odd how your surroundings affect the way you think and feel about yourself," he said.

"Especially when you're in denial," his sister said without missing a beat.

Becky was sitting on the edge of the couch, mug of coffee in hand, watching her brother stretch. She was still in such a state of surprise at seeing him in her home, she could not suppress a grin. Ben had come to the door three nights before, just before midnight. She'd been so happy and shocked to see him that she had thrown her arms around him and squeezed him until he winced from the pain in his ribs. He had looked tired, thin and drawn. His face was bruised, and his eyes looked as sad as a lost child.

"Have I told you," she began, "just how good it is to have you back?"

"A dozen times now?" he grinned.

"Well..." she yawned happily, "it really is. For some reason I thought working on a farm would be safer for you. Who'd have known?"

"I suppose I just attract trouble wherever I go. I'm kidding," he added quickly in reply to her frown.

"Have you come to terms with all that happened?" she asked.

"No. It doesn't make sense."

She picked up yesterday's copy of the *Ottawa Citizen*. The story had made the bottom half of page one: "Murders Expose Human Smuggling Ring".

"I'm still proud of you," she said.

He looked over his shoulder and saw she was reading the story once again. "It's all a fabrication, you know."

"A joint investigation," she read, "between RCMP, OPP and Michigan State Police has exposed a human trafficking ring that has helped over one thousand illegal immigrants cross the Canada-U.S. border for the past eight years. An undercover RCMP officer had been investigating the ring, based on a farm near Andover, Ontario, for the past eight months..."

"See?" he said. "You can't believe anything you read. I'm just glad they gave the OPP most of the credit."

"Well, there was obviously a reason for you being there, Ben. And you *were* undercover, even if you didn't know it."

Ben pulled himself from the floor and sat down on the couch beside her, taking the newspaper from her hand and dropping it onto the coffee table.

"Does it bother you there's no mention of Voracci, or the farm?" she asked.

"Not really. There was no proof anyone in the Voracci family knew what was going on. The papers saved themselves some lawsuits by not mentioning them. The thing that really bothers me is that nothing explains why Anna Wagner would be murdered over it."

"I thought you said she was going to blow the whistle on them."

"I know. And that's certainly what they're going with against Caines. But it just doesn't sit well with me. I told her I used to be a cop. And it makes sense that if she knew what was going on that she'd want to tell me about it. But how would Caines know before she told me?"

"She must have confronted him," Becky offered.

"That's what doesn't sit well," he replied. "It makes sense, but it still feels like there's a missing piece. That's the only thing that really gnaws at me."

"Jennifer doesn't bother you?"

Ben flinched. "No. She doesn't bother me at all."

"Right." She patted his hand before gulping the last of her coffee. "I have to get to work."

Becky went into the kitchen and put her coffee mug in the sink. Passing Ben in the living room again, she could not resist mussing his hair as she walked past. She paused at the door then turned around.

"I've been thinking about Jennifer," she said. "I really think you should call her."

"She made a choice."

"That wasn't a choice. It was a reflex, Ben. You were two or three minutes from turning her entire life upside down. You knew she was afraid of that man. She didn't turn away from you. She *was* afraid. Deathly afraid. And she turned to what she knew was safe."

"I'm not safe? If she didn't want to go with me, she could have just said no."

She laughed. "Just say no? What woman could say no to you?" She rubbed the top of his head and caressed his cheek, her fingertips lightly brushing the bandage. "Who could say no to this face?"

Ben nodded, hardly amused.

Becky was six years older than him. As children, she had been his protector when he'd found himself in trouble. She was probably the only person in the world who could still see the emotionally reactive child in Ben. Now, with a caress of her hand, she smoothed back the hair she had mussed a moment before.

"Seriously," she said, "I think you should call her. I have an idea she probably regrets a moment of panic. Don't let her pay for that for the rest of her life. Just call her."

"Do you really think we would have a future together?"

"Honestly? No, I don't. But there's something between you. And I don't think it was supposed to end like this."

Ben weighed her words carefully. He generally trusted her advice and would give her the benefit of any doubt. But she had been so far off the mark with her assessment of Jennifer this time; it did not seem she really had any idea of what had happened. He had told her everything, sitting for hours at her kitchen table, rambling in a stream of thought with anything and everything that came to his mind. But a year of such nightly confessions would not be able to portray the mixed feelings he had about Jennifer, or Anna, or his year at Tanglewood Vineyards.

"Just call her, Ben," she repeated. "I think if she knew where you were, she'd have called you herself by now."

"Maybe."

"Then call her!"

He nodded. "Maybe."

Ben leaned back on the couch and closed his eyes. In fact, he had been thinking of calling her all last night. He played out scenarios in his mind, trying to find an explanation for everything that had happened that would make sense. Nothing made sense. Countless times, he had to resist the urge to get in a car and go back to her. Four or five times he had found himself at the door, searching for car keys, before he came to his senses again and stepped away from the door.

The very worst part of it all, he kept reminding himself, was that Jennifer probably hated herself for what she had done. He knew she loved him. He could understand she had panicked. He could also understand how she could not forgive herself for betraying him in what most probably amounted to only a few seconds of uncertainty.

He lifted Becky's portable phone from the end table and dialed Jennifer's number. He had memorized it but had never actually dialed it since he'd come to Ottawa. Now, he listened to it ring six times. He hung up as soon as the answering machine kicked in on the seventh ring.

After a quick shower, he put on a jacket and tie. He pulled his gun from the cupboard above Becky's fridge and put it in his holster. He had picked up a Ford Taurus at Hertz two days before, regretting that he had sold his car the year before He started the car and made his way down Riverside Drive to his desk at the RCMP Headquarters on the Vanier Parkway.

Technically, he was on desk duty. But Bob Krall had encouraged him to come and go as he pleased to ease himself back into his old life. He had gone to the office for a couple of hours yesterday and wanted to do the same for the next several days to ease his way back to a routine. Becky had a wonderful house in Ottawa's South Keys, but it was not a good place to be all alone with nothing but a television and your own thoughts for company.

Inching through traffic, which always seemed to be congested as he approached the expressway near the train station, Ben began again to pore over every detail Jennifer had told him. He dwelled on the way her husband had spoken to her. "Get in the house...don't make me tell you again..." And he recalled the way she had been treated by that drug dealer six years ago. Ben wondered what really had become of the drug dealer.

He knew the area she had been in while she was in Toronto. Near the Jane-Finch corridor—she could hardly have looked for a neighborhood more ripe with trouble. Perhaps a few calls to the 31 Division of the Toronto Police could fill in the grey areas of her story with detail.

From his desk, he made a call to a detective he knew there, John Hirsh. Less than an hour later, Hirsh returned his call.

"Snake?" the detective asked. "You've got to be kidding me. That's all you have to go on?"

"Six years ago. A woman was assaulted and confined there. He may have been stabbed, or OD'd. I was hoping the name might ring a bell."

He could hear typing on a computer keyboard on the other end, accompanied by a series of sighs and grunts. "Wait a minute."

More typing. Ben waited nearly a minute.

"Yeah. We had a stabbing there six years ago. Charles Brogan. Snakehead Brogan. I remember that now. Nice name. Stabbed repeatedly with a syringe. Kicked and beaten. Had his throat cut open. Lots of suspects. No witnesses. No leads."

Ben thanked the detective and stared at the phone. "His throat was cut too..." he said aloud.

Something was beginning to come together. After another hour at his office, he went back to his sister's house and decided to work on his bike for a while. She had stored it in her garage for him for most of the past year, along with a few boxes of clothes, some books and some assorted keepsakes. Her garage, like the rest of her home, was neat and well kept. He had plenty of room to work. His bike was an old Honda that did its best to look like a Harley, but the sound was tinnier, less robust than any Harley. But the price had been right. Twelve hundred dollars, with a toolbox thrown in. When he was trying to work out the details of a case, he liked to work on his bike. Sometimes he felt he liked taking apart the machine and putting it together again more than he enjoyed riding it. In a pair of grubby torn jeans and a black t-shirt, sitting crosslegged beside it, he opened his toolbox and began to disassemble it. He thought of nothing but steel, bolts, screws, sparkplugs, fuel and oil. The details of the Wagner case, the haunting images of Anna and Jennifer, receded beneath the surface of his consciousness, where his mind would best sort them out. To someone else, it may have felt like some sort of mystical process, but thinking about the process would take away from its effectiveness Ben had decided long ago. He preferred to let the bike do the thinking. He just used his hands.

Becky came home and slipped him a cheeseburger and fries shortly after six. It was after seven before he remembered to eat it. The fries were stone cold. Shortly after eleven, Ben was tired enough to stop. His bike had been reduced to its base components. His hands were black with grease, and the smell of oil was thick in the air.

He crept into the quiet house. Becky had gone to bed. He washed and changed his jeans for a pair of track pants to bed down on her spare bed for the night. As he passed the kitchen on his way to the guest room, he noticed the light flashing on the answering machine. A small rush at the thought of Jennifer calling him, but the message was brief: a second or two of silence. Perhaps the sound of someone breathing, a slight rustling noise. He deleted the message and turned to go to bed.

Then he turned back again and picked up the receiver. He checked the last number calling in. Long distance. The Voraccis' home telephone number. Ben stared at the phone a long time, deliberating before deciding there was nothing that could not wait until morning. He turned off the lights and went to bed. He had worked too hard to keep his mind open to let this new entanglement interfere. He would know what to do in the morning. For now, he needed to turn off his thoughts and get some rest.

THIRTY–FOUR

Ben awoke shortly before five o'clock, feeling refreshed and alert. For the first time since his brawl with Michael Voracci, he had slept through the entire night without waking in pain. He sat on the edge of his bed and touched his cheekbone with his fingertips. Tender, but not painful. He took a breath and felt fine. Then he fully exhaled before carefully filling his lungs as full as he could. His chest on the right felt tight, but the pain was completely gone. He mustered a half-smile and stood up. He had nearly forgotten how good it felt to take a deep breath.

Snapshots and vignettes of vibrant dreams lingered in his mind, but there was no need to focus on them too intensely. They felt close to him in their vividness but detached from him emotionally. He could sense them, as if they hovered in the air to the right and just behind his head as he pulled on his old jeans. A flash of Anna, smiling. He buckled his belt. Another flash of her walking away from the bottling machine, pulling a college brochure from her back pocket, studying it intently as she walked. An image of Jennifer, naked and drugged in some unknown apartment years before, as he pulled his t-shirt over his head. Another flash of Michael Voracci's distorted sneer above him as his foot connected with Ben's chest. A memory of a raven, on the ground beneath a willow, plucking grass from the ground.

Quietly, making sure he did not wake Becky, he slipped into the garage and began to work on his motorcycle.

He let the images come and go. It was all a part of the process of piecing the clues together, letting his thoughts flow without restriction in a stream of memories and suppositions. The pieces of the puzzle would arrange themselves then scramble before rearranging themselves again in a different order. There was something here. Something very close to becoming resolved, becoming clear to him, if he just kept them at their distance and let them sort themselves out without any cognitive interference from him.

As he fitted his bike back together, he continued to sense pieces of information fitting themselves together in the back of his mind. Shortly after seven o'clock, the bike was complete. He stood up, wiping the grease from his hands. He knew exactly what he needed to do.

By then, Becky was already up, in her white terry cloth housecoat and fuzzy slippers, pouring milk into a bowl of Cheerios at the kitchen counter. "Want some?" she asked.

"Yes, please."

She pulled a large blue bowl from the cupboard and filled it with cereal. "Have you been up all night?" she asked, pouring milk into his bowl.

"No. Just got up early."

She grinned as she handed him a spoon. "You look a lot better."

"Yes," he said. "I feel more like my old self again. I'd been coming back to myself slowly, but now I'm back."

"I've seen that," she said. "I'm so glad, Ben."

She cocked her head and gave him that warm smile he never tired of. He knew exactly what was on her mind.

"Yes," he admitted sheepishly. "I'm going back today."

"I'm glad. Would you like some company for the drive down? It's Friday, and I could take the day off."

"No, thanks," he replied. "It's going to be a long drive. Besides, I should go back alone, if that makes any sense."

"Actually," she said, "it does. Let me know how it goes, okay?"

He agreed and finished his breakfast as she got ready for work. Once Becky was dressed and out the door, Ben picked up the phone, getting Walter Kumar's voice mail.

"It's Ben Taylor," he said. "I think I'm onto something here. I'm on my way back to Tanglewood."

He showered quickly and pulled his clothes from the closet. He replaced his jeans and t-shirt with a tie and jacket, running shoes with his well-worn brogues. He holstered his gun and slipped his badge and wallet into his jacket pocket. The reasoning for the suit came after the fact. He did not really think about it while he changed. It just felt like the right thing to wear, and it made sense to dress appropriately. Once he looked at himself in the mirror, lightly touching the small scar on his cheek, he realized that hardly anyone in Andover had known he was a cop except Michael Voracci and Jennifer. In a critical situation, he did not want that misconception to present a problem. It was one thing to see a cop draw a gun. It was another thing entirely to see a farmhand draw a gun. The weight of his pistol felt good. A year ago, even a week ago, he did not think he could ever wear a gun again. It was reassuring to know how wrong he had been.

Lunchtime rush hour through Toronto slowed his drive. It would take him over seven hours from Ottawa to return to the vineyard. He did not feel that was a problem. If anything, the drive would strengthen his resolve.

There had been something about Jennifer's story that shook him. She had told him she did not know if Snake had been dead or alive when she'd left. In Ben's dream it had been himself, not Michael Voracci, who'd burst through the door of that apartment.

He saw Jennifer passed out on a bare mattress, handcuffed to the radiator. He saw Snake passed out on the couch in the next room. As he reached for the keys to the handcuffs in the man's front pocket, the rage over what had been done to her filled him. The same rage Michael Voracci had shown at the pump-house when he'd kicked Ben in the head.

Wouldn't it be easier, that calm voice said to him, *to take the keys from a dead man than a sleeping man? Wouldn't it feel better having beaten the shit out of him first? Wouldn't that be the easiest thing to do?*

Yes, in a state of anger, in a rage, of course it would.

Stopping for gas off of the 401, just outside of Woodstock, Ben spotted a short stocky man climbing out of his white SUV, and he thought of Michael Voracci. Stepping out of his vehicle, the man dropped his sunglasses from a tiny front pocket of his white short-sleeved golf shirt. Before he could see that they'd fallen, he crushed them under his heel. Ben heard him grunt as he bent over to pick them up. The frames were ruined, and the left plastic lens had popped out. He grunted again to pick up the lens and held it up to the sky to see if it had been scratched.

Ben blinked. The image seemed to tie into his dreams and thoughts of this morning...

Ben shook off a sense of déjà vu and got back in his car. Merging back onto the 401, the image of this clumsy man holding up the lens to the light, thinking of Michael... and the way he had attacked Ben near the pump-house continued to play in his mind.

Michael had been angry just before he'd struck Ben, certainly, but he had controlled that anger quite well. In fact, he had camouflaged it so well that Ben had not detected the depth of this anger until it was too late. Or had he really been that angry? He had offered to help Ben look for evidence in the gravel. Why?

Ben searched his memory of those moments alone with Michael.

Had he really shown any signs of rage at first? Had he not seemed rather calm until the moment Ben showed him that blood on the gravel?

"Dammit. That bastard set me up."

Ben accelerated and pulled his cell phone from his pocket to call Kumar. Once again, he got the detective's voice mail.

"It's Ben Taylor again. Voracci is our man. I'm sure of it. I'm on my way. I'll be there in a couple hours. Give me a call. I'll explain everything."

THIRTY–FIVE

Ben arrived in Andover at four thirty. Once he was in town, he listened to a voicemail left by Kumar, suggesting they meet at the vineyard. Kumar was already waiting for him when Ben arrived, at the end of the Voracci laneway, leaning against the hood of his Buick, arms crossed, black tie waving in the breeze.

"Good timing," said Kumar, stepping forward to shake Ben's hand as he climbed out of his car. "I just got here a few minutes ago. Received your message just before lunch. It was interesting that you called when you did. I was just about to call you when I got your first message this morning. I've had a few sleepless nights about this mess as well. There's a missing piece. It doesn't fit."

"Exactly," said Ben.

"We need to speak to Jennifer," said Ben.

"Neither of them are here," Kumar replied.

"Where are they?"

"No idea right now. I've got an officer making calls as we speak. I want to look around."

"You mean you haven't?"

"I just got here. I was at home when I got your call, remember? In Toronto." Kumar put his hand on Ben's shoulder as they began to walk. "Relax."

"I'm worried about her."

"I know."

"Congratulations on the bust," Ben said. "You made the national papers. And thanks for not mentioning my name."

"Not at all." Kumar suddenly grinned.

"What?"

"I almost didn't recognize you all dressed up. You look good. Almost like a cop."

Ben smiled. "Is Abe Wagner home?"

"Let's find out."

As they walked down the laneway, the warehouse, the trees, all seemed smaller than the last time Ben was here. He felt taller, stronger than he had ever felt while working here. How much of himself had he lost while trying to find himself, he wondered.

Abe Wagner seemed to have aged ten years in the last three weeks. The grey hair and sombre eyes that had gone so well with his reputation for craftsmanship and vineyard wisdom had quickly eroded to the stereotype of a tired, worn, old man. The features on the left side of his face seemed sagged. Ben wondered if the heartbroken old man had suffered a mild stroke in the last week. He wondered if Wagner would have known to see a doctor if he was not in pain. He looked like a man waiting to die.

Wagner shuffled to the door so slowly that the men let themselves in through the torn screen door to save him the walk. He nodded to Kumar and watched Ben for a moment. Apparently, Ben decided, Wagner did not recognize him and was expecting an introduction. However, neither Kumar nor Ben offered one. Ben's identity was not the issue this afternoon.

As the three men sat down at the kitchen table, Ben noticed the obvious signs of neglect around the kitchen. This was not the legacy Wagner's devoted daughter would have wanted to leave behind. The poor man was alone and falling apart. More than a dozen dirty dishes sat in the sink, along with a half dozen coffee mugs. Empty cans of beans and vegetables lined the counter. Toast crumbs littered the floor and the counter near the toaster. A butter knife lay on the edge of the counter, to which a housefly was helping itself.

Sitting down, Ben put his hand on the table. The formica was sticky to the touch. Sitting straight in his chair, he let Kumar take the lead.

"Mr. Wagner..." Kumar began slowly, "we wanted to ask you some questions. A few questions about Michael and Jennifer Voracci."

"What about them?" Wagner answered with a dry, tired voice.

"To begin with," Kumar began, "when was the last time you saw Jennifer Voracci?"

Wagner considered the question before replying. "A few days ago, I think."

Kumar took his notebook from his jacket pocket and began to write in it. "Do you know where they went?"

"I didn't know they went anywhere," said Wagner.

"Do you think they went to visit family, or on a business trip? A vacation, perhaps?"

"No, I don't think so," Wagner replied. "He usually tells me if he leaves town."

"What about Mrs. Voracci? Do you always know when she's left town?"

"She doesn't go out, except with her husband."

"When you last saw them, were they together?"

"No. I've not seen her for a long time, actually. She rarely leaves the house."

"Are they a happy couple, would you say?"

"I don't know. He seems happy. I don't know about Mrs. Voracci."

"Do they quarrel?"

"No."

"Have you ever seen any signs of abuse in their household?"

He shrugged. "No. Never."

"What was the relationship between your daughter and Jennifer Voracci?"

Wagner sat back and took a long deep breath. He let it out slowly. "They were friends. She confided in Jennifer sometimes, I think. About women stuff. Anna's mother died some time ago. Jennifer wasn't really like her mother. She's too young. She was like a big sister to her. They seemed to get along."

"Did Anna spend much time in the Voracci household?"

"Not really. When they talked, it was in their yard. At the picnic table. We would go inside for dinner occasionally. But Anna didn't go into their house very often."

Kumar nodded and made another note.

"Why are you asking these questions?" Wagner said, showing an edge of anger behind his tired eyes.

"Please bear with me."

"Fine. What else do you need to know?"

Kumar moved his chair a bit closer to the table. This was the sensitive part. "What was the relationship between your daughter and Michael Voracci?"

Wagner's brow furrowed. "She worked for him."

"Were they friends as well?"

"Not the way she was a friend with Jennifer. Jennifer really took to Anna. Michael did not seem to have time to say hello to her when he walked by, let alone be friendly towards her."

"You're certain?" Kumar asked.

"I'm certain, yes. Don't misunderstand me. Michael Voracci is a good friend to me. He put up the reward money when Anna disappeared. But that was as a friend to me, not to her. He helped get my son into a good college. That was as a friend to me. Not to my son. He barely knew my children. But he knows they are important to me. And I am important to him. So that's how it worked out."

"What do you mean by your importance?" Ben asked.

"I'm the wine master here. His grandfather used to be the wine master. He made this winery what it is. His father tried his hand at it, but he did not have the patience, or the attention to detail. His grandfather trained me, just as I will train another apprentice. I thought that would be my son. And then I thought it might be my daughter. But now I don't know."

"I understand your importance to the Voracci family," said Ben. "What would happen if you left Tanglewood to work somewhere else?"

"I wouldn't do that."

"But if you did?"

"I wouldn't. The business is partly mine. I have a stake in it."

Ben pushed his chair back a few inches from the table.

"Hypothetically speaking?" said Kumar.

"The business would not last long unless he found someone quickly. But at the wages they pay here, that would be very difficult."

"You don't earn much then?"

"I am a humble man. I don't need much to live. I do not own a fancy car or a boat or a cottage on the Seine. I am a Christian man. I put God before money."

"That's why he can afford you?"

"I suppose. But money is not important to me. I would prefer we used the money to care for the vines we do have."

"Was there any time when you thought of going somewhere else?" said Ben.

"A few years ago, yes. After my wife died, I considered moving back to Argentina. That is where my family is from. I have family there."

"Why did you stay?" Kumar asked.

"That was when Michael promised to get my son into a good

school so he could learn to become an engineer. I agreed to stay. That was also when I invested my wife's insurance into the winery as well."

"Why?"

"That was the agreement. I would stay and be his business partner. He would help get my son into a good school. As a sign of good faith, I took the money I was going to use to buy a farm in Argentina and invested it into our business."

"But what if you changed your mind?"

"I'd simply get my investment back."

"Who handled this arrangement on your behalf?"

"Michael's lawyer. Bill Devers"

"Who is your lawyer?" asked Ben.

Wagner smiled. "Bill Devers. We have the same lawyer."

"Isn't that a bit odd?"

"No. He's a trustworthy man. I'm not a fool."

"We understand that, sir," said Ben.

"It's funny you should ask about that," said Wagner. "I was going through my papers. I keep them in a small file box in my bedroom closet. I found my contract with Michael in the front of the files. It used to be in the middle. I couldn't find it at first and thought I'd lost it. Then I found it there."

"When was this?"

"Couple days ago. I think Anna might have taken it out before she disappeared."

"Why?"

"She must have been looking it over. You know, she was thinking of becoming a lawyer."

"Yes, sir," said Ben.

"May we see the contract?"

"I think I know where it is."

Wagner stood slowly. His joints creaked loudly as he stepped slowly from the table. Ben wondered if his back or his legs or both were bothering him.

"Have you seen a doctor recently?" Ben asked, getting up to clear some room as Wagner passed.

"I'm due to see him tomorrow. Then I'm going to Argentina for two weeks."

"When are you leaving?"

"In a few days. I haven't booked the ticket. My son in Argentina is arranging it. He wanted to come here, but I asked him to stay so I could go see him there." He shook his head. "Too much pain here for an old man right now."

Once Wagner left the room, Ben leaned towards Kumar and whispered. "I told you Anna spoke to me about going to school."

"Yes."

"She mentioned law school to me. I told her if that's what she wanted to do, she should do it."

"Does this help us?"

"I think so." He heard Wagner opening a closet door in the other room and leaned closer, whispering more quietly. "She was concerned about her father's finances. I said she'd be better able to take care of him later if she had a good career. I asked her if her father had been saving for a retirement." He paused, remembering the thoughtful look on her face then.

"Yes?" Kumar said impatiently.

"She said he had invested all his money into the winery. And I remember then the look on her face. I didn't think anything of it until now..." He took off his sunglasses and put them on the table. "It was like something clicked. She didn't say anything more, but if she went back to look at that contract her father signed..."

"You think Voracci screwed him, and she found out about it?"

334

"I don't know."

"We'll soon find out."

Wagner stepped into the kitchen with a small bundle of legal-sized letters folded in half and wrapped with an elastic. "It's in here," he said, setting it on the table in front of Kumar.

Then Wagner took a step back and looked at Ben closely. "You're Ben!"

"Yes."

"Are you helping the police?" he asked.

"Actually, I am the police."

Wagner stepped forward and suddenly slapped Ben across the face. Ben did nothing to protect himself, even as he saw the old man lift his arm back to take the swing. He winced as the hand hit him. There was surprising force to the blow, and he was grateful it was not the side of his face that was still healing.

"You're a cop?" Wagner spat on his kitchen floor in disgust. "You were here the whole time. It was your job to protect Anna. You should have protected her from the monster who killed her."

"I know that. That's why I'm here today. To find out who did this."

"With you here…" Wagner faltered for words. "You should have protected her."

Kumar stepped between them. Ben was not going to defend himself at all. "If Ben could have, he would have. I know it's tearing him up about what happened. We all feel terrible. But he had no idea your daughter's life was in danger. None of us did, not even you."

Tears began to flow from the old man's eyes. He put his face in his hands. "I'm so sorry. I don't know what came over me. I don't… I just don't know what to think any more. This is just a nightmare that doesn't want to end."

Kumar put his hand on the old man's shoulder. "She is with God now."

"Yes, yes, she is."

"Please see your doctor. Anna wouldn't want you to get sick."

"I know. I will see a doctor. You catch her murderer."

"We will."

"Do you know who did it?'

"Yes," said Ben. "We believe we do. We just have to prove it now."

The old man cleared his eyes with a Kleenex from the counter. "Proof is always in a man's eyes," said Wagner.

"Yes," said Ben. "I've seen those eyes before."

THIRTY–SIX

In the car, Kumar turned on the console light and began leafing through the contract Wagner had given them.

"What do you think we're looking for here?" he asked.

"I'm not sure," Ben replied. "Was there any physical evidence on the body that could potentially tie Voracci to the murder?"

"Not really," said Kumar, "unless you want to count the small amount of tannic acid found. They even found some under her fingernails and toenails. Tannic acid is a form of tannin, a soluble, astringent, phenolic substance found in—guess what? —wine."

"Under her toenails? That's odd."

"Unless she was pressing grapes," said Kumar.

"What about this document?"

"I can't make much out of it."

Ben watched out the window as Kumar read the papers.

"Seems to be something in the fine print at the end," said Kumar after several minutes. "You'd think I'd know to read the fine print first. There does not seem to be a clause for repayment, except in the event of the death of Michael Voracci."

"So how could he get his money back?"

"He can't."

Ben nodded. "That would help if Abe had been murdered. But how does that fit with Anna?"

"I'm not sure. But there is one person who might know."

"Who's that?"

"Randall Gilmore Caines. He's still in lockup." Kumar pressed his tongue through his teeth in a gleeful grin and started the car. "He couldn't make bail."

Ben followed Kumar in his own car, enjoying the feel of the gravel beneath his tires as he stepped on the gas. If he never had to come back here, it would suit him just fine.

"Have you searched Voracci's house?" Ben asked as they walked across the parking lot of the Andover Police Station.

"No. Caines copped to everything regarding Quiring's death and the drugs. He swears Voracci had no idea. We have no way of showing Voracci did have any idea. We spoke to him, and he denied any knowledge. From Caines' story, it doesn't seem likely."

"But it was on his property."

"There's something you have to remember. We can't push him that hard. You can't forget who his family is."

"I don't give a damn who his family is."

"Half of this province *does* give a damn who his family is, Ben. You can't just bully your way around the Voraccis. Not without due diligence. Not to mention a farm is not public property. It's private property and he's protected by enough agricultural laws to fill a dozen books with."

"What about the necklace? Can you tie it to Caines?"

"You're kidding me. Not by itself, no. That necklace was as thin as a spider web. No prints. No partials. No hairs. No fibres we could identify. Anyone could have dropped it there. Including Anna Wagner two months ago."

"Do you remember the last day I was here, when we went to the pump-house? After Voracci kicked me. Remember all that water from the irrigation pipes?"

"Yes."

"Caines was out of town that day. Who else would have known that

338

would be a good time to flood that crime scene that particular day?"

"Voracci."

"He knew! That bastard knew. He didn't pick a fight with me because of his wife. He needed to distract me from the crime scene! And the break-in into his house the night before. What if that was Voracci too?"

"He was in Toronto." Kumar leafed through his notebook. "His flight arrived the day before, he spent the day and that night with a female friend, Linda Stolley, who verified this."

"Toronto's only a few hours away. He could have snuck out in the night. He could have arrived here a half hour before he said did. What if he and Caines worked on this together..." Ben's thoughts raced quickly, putting the pieces together. "Or what if he came back while Caines was getting ready to leave? He could have been the one to drop that necklace. And he could have been the one to break into his own home. Nothing was missing but the computer, right?"

"A few incidentals, but that's right."

"Who breaks into a home just for a computer? This doesn't make any sense. There's definitely more going on here than just Randy Caines."

Caines had been held in lockup at the Andover police station since he'd been released from the hospital for his gunshot wound six days before. He wore a denim shirt and jeans, blue flip flops; his right arm was in a sling. The fingers of his right hand were dark purple.

"You bastard!" Caines said slowly in disbelief as Ben stepped towards the cell. "You're really a cop?"

"No kidding," Ben replied.

"I thought I imagined that, what with the shooting and all."

"Where's Jennifer Voracci?"

Caines sneered at him, and an amused gasp escaped his mouth. "I don't fuckin' know where she is. Try her house, shit for brains."

Ben resisted the temptation to rush forward and kick Caines in the groin. Instead he poked Caines in the shoulder with the point of his index finger.

"Fuck!" Caines bellowed in pain.

Ben poked him again. Same place, an inch from the bullet wound.

"Stop it!" Caines hollered. He stepped back to avoid a third poke. "Okay, I take it back," he gasped. "But I don't know where the fuck she is."

"We know you killed Quiring. But we also know you didn't kill Anna Wagner. It was your boss."

Caines replied with a smug grin. "Like hell."

"He was setting you up to take the fall," Ben said. "He was the one who dropped that necklace on the stairs while you were finishing off David Quiring."

"Like hell."

"Are you admitting then that you dropped it, Randy?"

Caines shook his head. "No."

Ben decided it was time for a bluff. "Then how do you explain the tea?"

"What tea?"

"There were slight traces of a tea stain on the clasp of the necklace. Maybe from your fingers. Maybe your boss dipped it in your cup. We know she didn't drink tea. Did Quiring drink tea?"

"I don't know."

"Well, he didn't. Who do you know who drinks Earl Grey tea, Randy?"

"Sonofabitch! Me?" Caines shook his head vigorously, spit escaping his nose and lips. "You can't tell what kind of tea it is from a necklace."

"I can't," said Ben. "But our forensics experts in Toronto can."

Caines slammed his good hand down on the table. "No!"

"Where is Jennifer Voracci?"

"I told you. Check the house."

"There's no one home."

"Oh, she's home."

Ben glared at him.

"How do you know she's home?" asked Kumar.

"She's always home. He used to joke about it. She never left the house."

Ben picked up the Bic pen from the table and jabbed it into Caines' shoulder.

"Jesus Christ!" Caines howled, spittle flying from his mouth. "I admitted my part in this. I can't help it if you don't know to check her house. I'm telling you that's where she is, you bastard!"

Ben dropped the pen and walked away.

When he stepped out of the station, he had worked himself into a fury. Kumar was twenty yards behind him, trying to catch up.

It was getting dark, and the sky was being drained of colour. The air was cool, and the breeze seemed to wake Ben's senses as he walked quickly to his car.

"Where are you going, Ben?"

"I'm going to get her."

"You can't go in there. We can't go in without a warrant."

"I don't need a warrant. She's in danger."

"It'll only take us an hour to get a warrant."

"I'm not waiting another minute."

"You can't do that, Ben."

Ben turned on his heels. "I can't *not* do it."

"Okay." Kumar held up his hands. "Just wait a few minutes. Let me get some backup. We'll petition endangerment, and we'll get the warrant right away."

Kumar doubled back to the station. But Ben was already in his car, on his way to Voracci's house.

THIRTY–SEVEN

Dusk had settled over the vineyard as Ben parked his car in the laneway, about fifty feet from Jennifer's house, behind a hedge and safely out of sight. Neither Jennifer's Volkswagen nor Michael's pickup truck were in sight. He pulled on the closed garage door, but it would not budge.

From a distance, from somewhere near the river, came the sound of a bulldozer or a tractor hard at work. Ben paused a moment to identify the sound of the hydraulics in motion and the familiar steady warning beep as it backed up. An excavator.

He quickly crept up the creaking back steps. He had no idea what to expect. The house could be empty. Michael Voracci could be barricaded behind the kitchen table with a shotgun aimed at the door, packets of heroin stacked on the counter. At this point, Ben was beyond surprise. He hoped Michael was anywhere rather than in the house. And, whatever had been happening in the days since he had left, Ben hoped he was not too late.

He opened the screen door and tried the inside door. It was locked. He decided not to knock. The top half of the door was pane glass. He drew his gun from the holster and tapped the glass closest to the lock with the butt. The glass snapped, pieces falling to the doormat inside almost soundlessly. He listened for movement before putting his hand through the window to unbolt the door.

He pulled his flashlight from his pocket and held it against his drawn gun. Cautiously, he entered the house.

The kitchen was dark and silent. He approached cautiously around the corner, past the point where Jennifer had kissed him in the doorway, past the stove where she had cooked chicken for him.

"Police!" he shouted as he reached the living room.

Nothing.

"Is there anyone inside?" he shouted to the empty room.

Silence.

"Jennifer!"

Again, no reply.

He made his way up the stairs, watching carefully for the slightest movement. He seemed to be alone.

Gun poised and ready, he pointed the flashlight into the first bedroom. The beam of light revealed it was a seldom-used guest room with an ornate wooden frame bed, a sofa and a large coffee table in the centre of the room. He had been in there before but hadn't noticed the details. The low moon was shining in through the sheer drapes of the bedroom. He turned on the light of this room and stepped back into the hall.

The door of the master bedroom was open, and the light from the guest room gave him a good view. Empty. The bed was unmade, the sheets spilling onto the floor. Two pillows were piled in the centre of the bed. Someone had slept here alone last time.

Ben lowered his gun. Perhaps Jennifer had left town after all. He suddenly wondered what he had been expecting to find. Was this really the process of sound investigative procedures, or was it the temper tantrum of a spurned lover? Then he became aware of the faint, foreboding sound of the excavator working hard in the distance. Perhaps he was too late. Perhaps Michael had dealt with her one last time already. Ben clenched his teeth and stepped back into the hall.

Unlike the first two rooms, the door to the third bedroom was closed. He listened for movement.

Silence.

He turned the brass handle. The handle turned, but the door was locked.

He listened again.

Silence.

Ben raised his gun and lifted his leg back to kick. "What the hell," he thought. "In for a penny..."

He kicked the door open.

Wood splintered away from the latch, and the door swung open, slamming the wall.

In the darkness, Ben could make out the form of a body on the bed. A billow of hot air came at him, scented of urine and sweat. He stepped forward, and in the dim light could see it was Jennifer. She was on her belly on the bed, her head at the foot of the bed, her feet at the headboard.

A foot was tied to each corner of the headboard. Her hands were behind her back, secured with several feet of white cotton rope. Her jeans and her t-shirt were soaked with sweat. The sheets were stained beneath her. There had been no circulation in this room at all. It was unbearably hot. Jennifer was barely conscious, peering at him as he pulled at the knot in the rope around her right hand.

Between the closet door and an oak dresser draped with a crocheted doily, was a large blue barrel used for transporting wine. He began to loosen the knots in the rope on her wrists, staring at the barrel.

You could fit a body in there, the calm voice explained. *And that would explain the traces of wine on Anna's body...*

Ben holstered his gun. He saw a phone had been torn from the wall beside the bed and thrown across the room, the cord frayed, receiver busted.

A sudden flash as he remembered the silent phone call he had received at Becky's house. Then he recalled his own calls to Jennifer, imagining her listening to the phone ring and ring and ring. He swallowed the rage and knelt beside the bed, checking her breathing and putting his finger on her neck to check her pulse. Her left eye opened. An exhausted smile drifted across her lips and slipped away.

He pulled the rope from her wrists before untying her legs from the bedposts. He rolled her over and moved a thick wet lock of hair from her face.

She opened her eyes, tried to talk. "Water."

He found an empty glass on the nightstand and stepped into the adjoining bathroom to fill it. He lifted her and put the glass to her lips.

She drank quickly, coughing.

"I'm going to get you to the hospital," he said.

"No..." she whispered, shaking her head. "Want to lie down."

He laid her down again and put the empty glass on the nightstand beside her bed.

"Michael did this to you."

She nodded, closing her eyes. "I'm so..."

"Hush," he said, touching her parched lips with his finger. Her lips were chapped and white, deeply cracked.

Ben turned on the bedside lamp. Then he saw the bruises on her arms and on her shoulder where her shirt had been torn, like purple stains on her skin. A large welt on her left arm. Finger marks on her right forearm, left upper arm. Then he saw the bruise around her left eye. He clenched his fist. Seeing her like this, wondering how long she might have been lying here like this, his rage was growing.

"He beat you."

She nodded and coughed hard.

"How could you let him do this?" he asked, feeling his anger rising from his throat, pulsing at his temples.

She closed her eyes and turned away.

"How?" he asked again.

She turned to him and he could see the remorse and shame in her eyes. She said nothing and seemed to shrink from his concern and his anger, staring at him with tear-filled eyes.

"How long have you been here like this?"

"Don't know..." she said. "Made me take pills..."

"How many pills? Sleeping pills?"

She nodded, yawning. "While ago," she answered. "They're wearing off... Just groggy now, I think."

"Oh, Jennifer," he said. "Why did you stay here?"

"I had to."

"I was going to take you away from this," he said, hearing his voice getting louder. His fear for her life and his anger had climbed the summit of his own guilt for leaving her behind, all his emotions converging. He tried to control his voice. "Why the hell did you stay here?"

She sat up on her elbows, more awake now, recognizing the anger in his eyes.

"Kiss me," she whispered.

He pressed his mouth to hers. Her lips were dry as toast crust.

Then the room seemed to come back to him. "I'm going to get you some clean clothes," he said. "I have to get you out of here."

She pulled herself up and was sitting on the side of the bed when he returned from her bedroom with a t-shirt and track pants he'd found on her bed.

He helped her peel the wet shirt from her skin, covering her with the fresh t-shirt. He helped her pull the jeans from her legs and replaced them with a pair of cotton track pants. Whatever she had been drugged with, he decided, the dosage was weak enough, or she was accustomed enough to it, that it was quickly wearing off.

346

Clarity of thought was returning to him. "How long have you been here like this?"

"Don't know..." she shrugged, her words trailing away and inaudible. Then she beamed at him. "You came to save me."

"I'm only glad I'm not too late," he said, staring again at the blue barrel beside the bed.

He took her hand and led her down the stairs and out to the car, leaving the door open behind him.

"Where are we going?" she asked as he helped her into his rental car.

He got into the driver's seat. "I'm taking you to the hospital," he said as he fastened her seat belt.

"No," she said. "Take me home."

Ben looked at her in disbelief. "Home?"

"Your home," she said. "Take me home."

He thought about that for a moment.

"The motel?"

"Okay."

The cabin was still his for another three days. He had rented it until the end of the month. He had his cabin key on his key chain. He turned left at the end of the laneway and made his way there.

He took her hand and led her inside, laying her down on the bed.

"Can I have some water, please?" she asked, coughing.

Ben filled a glass with water and handed it to her. He pulled his cell phone from his jacket and dialed Kumar's cell phone.

"I found her. Voracci drugged her, but she seems to be okay. He was keeping her prisoner in her own home."

"Where are you?"

"My old cabin at the motel."

"Get her to the hospital," Kumar said.

"I tried that," Ben replied, watching Jennifer sit up. "But she feels safe here." He saw her nod, smiling contritely at him. "She seems to be coming out of whatever he had drugged her with," he added, seeing her nod again. "I'm watching her. I don't know why he was hiding her. But until he's caught, I don't want to chance him getting near her."

He put his phone back in his pocket. "This isn't home," he replied. "But it's safe for now."

She smiled sleepily and closed her eyes, leaning back on her arms on the bed, stretching and bending her legs.

Ben went back outside and moved the car onto the grass behind the cabins, out of sight from the roads.

When he returned, she had curled up in a ball on the bed.

"You have to tell me everything," he said, once he had closed the door.

"I'll tell you everything I know. But first…"

"Yes?"

"I really need a shower."

THIRTY–EIGHT

Once Jennifer emerged from the bathroom, wrapped in a large white towel, Ben handed Jennifer a glass of water and waited as she drank it. She lay back on the bed as he set the empty glass on the counter and returned to sit beside her. Then he examined each bruise.

"I knew you'd save me," she said. "I knew you would."

"Why did he have you tied up?" Ben asked at last.

She sighed. "I told him I was leaving. I was going to find you, to see if I could still be with you."

Ben almost smiled. "To be with me?"

"Yes. I love you, Ben. He said I couldn't leave. I said he couldn't stop me. He tried to make me take a sleeping pill to settle down, but I wouldn't. I threw the pill and the water against the wall. Then he grabbed me and brought me up there and tied me to the bed. He talked to me a long, long time. Told me I had no right to leave him like this, that I belonged to him, and that I owed it to him to see it through to the end."

"Why?"

"Because of what happened with that drug dealer," she said. "I don't know how long I was there. He came to check on me, but he drugged me, and I was so out of it. Once, I managed to get free enough to get the phone. I'd tried calling you and hoped it was still on speed dial."

"My sister's phone rang," he said. "I knew it was you."

She smiled, tired, relieved. "I knew you'd come for me, Ben. I knew it."

"Why did he keep you drugged?"

"He said he was going to make me stay till I stopped being irrational. But I never gave up, Ben. Never."

"Why was the blue barrel beside your bed?"

"I don't know. I didn't really see it until you came. I wondered about that. Maybe so I could use it as a toilet? I don't know."

He shook his head in disagreement but did not reply. "Tell me why he thought you owed him."

Her smile faded. She stared at him, biting her bottom lip as her eyes once again filled with tears.

"I don't know if I can tell you everything, Ben. It's really bad."

"You have to tell me."

Jennifer pushed herself up on one elbow and drew in her knees to curl her body around him.

"I think I might have killed her."

"Who?"

"Anna."

He touched her face, cupping her cheek with the palm of his hand, looking into her reddened eyes.

"No, Jennifer. You didn't."

"I don't know. I really don't know any more."

"Why do you think you did?"

"Sometimes, Ben..." She wiped a tear from her cheek. "Sometimes, I think I'm going crazy. Michael told me he knew I killed her. He said I disappeared a long time the night Anna disappeared. And I've been having dreams since the first day she disappeared. About her body in the river. I can't shake it. I could hear her, could feel her dying. She drowned in the river. I know it, Ben."

"That's not how she died," he said. "She was strangled. She was dead before she was put in the pump-house. Near the river. But she was never in the river. She did not drown."

"Michael told me she drowned."

"Jennifer, I hate to tell you this, but I think Michael killed her. I think he killed her and hid her body in one of the blue vats they have, just like the one beside your bed tonight. Then he brought her there and tried to set the pump-house on fire to burn the evidence."

"You never thought it was me?" She looked at him hopefully.

"No," said Ben. "Never."

"But you think it was Michael." She shook her head. "That makes no sense..."

"Doesn't it? Doesn't it make sense, Jennifer?"

"Maybe," she replied. "I don't know. I've been thinking I've been going crazy suspecting him, suspecting myself."

"Does it make any less sense than you telling me you drowned her? Why would you think that?"

"Michael told me she drowned. He said he was afraid I'd killed her. He's never lied to me..."

Ben stood up, flaring with anger. "Do you honestly think you killed her? If you thought you did it, why didn't you tell the police that?"

"I thought I just did, Ben. Aren't you the police?"

"Not right now. Not here with you, no. I'm too involved, and I'm not within jurisdiction…"

"Yes," she said. "You are. Being here now, saving me tonight, proves you are."

"Just tell me."

"I don't think I did. I liked her a lot. But for a while I thought it was possible. And then when Michael told me she drowned..." She looked away.

"What?" said Ben. "What did he tell you?"

"I want to tell you," she said. "But I don't know if it will make any sense to you."

"Try me," he said blankly.

Jennifer sat up, facing him directly. "Did you ever know something but not know it at the same time? I knew he hurt her, but I couldn't believe he could do that. But once I started to believe he could really have hurt Anna, I began to doubt everything else he had told me. And then the more I doubted him, the more I felt I had to believe him. I mean..." She leaned towards him emphatically. "It couldn't have all been lies, could it?"

"I don't know what you're talking about," Ben replied. "Try starting from the beginning."

She pulled a lock of hair from her face. "That goes back to Snake," she said.

"Snake or Snakehead?" he asked.

Wide-eyed, she stared up at him. "Snakehead, yes. But how did you know?"

"It's my job to know," he replied. "Now tell me everything you remember."

"I don't remember much," she said. "Michael told me almost everything I know about it. But I never told you everything. I always hoped it wasn't true..." Jennifer's eyes began to fill with tears once again. She took a breath and wiped her eyes, refusing to give in to the tears. "He was attacking me while I was high, and I stabbed him with a needle. In the neck. I killed him."

"With a syringe?"

"Yes."

"How would you kill someone with a syringe?"

"Drug overdose?" she said. "Bled to death, maybe? I don't remember that part. But his girlfriend was there too. She started hitting me. I kicked at her, and I guess I knocked her down."

"While you were handcuffed to the bed."

"Just one hand, I think. But, yes. She hit her head..." Jennifer wiped at the tears once again.

"Then what happened?" Ben asked impatiently.

"That's when Michael got there. He found out where I was from my girlfriend. The friend who brought me there to begin with. Michael kicked down the door. I was asleep then, I think. I remember the crash of the door when the lock broke open and the door crashing back against the closet. I remember leaning over to see what was going on. At first, I didn't even recognize him. I'd never seen him like that before. That, I remember very well. He was furious. His face seemed all distorted, and his eyes looked black and cold. I thought he was going to kill me. But he wasn't angry at me. He kicked Snake three or four times, shouting at him to get up. But he was already dead. Then he saw me, and the anger left him. He took the keys from Snake's pocket and uncuffed me from the bed."

"Then what happened?"

"He said we had to get out. Right away before someone called the police. He wasn't worried about Snake. But the girl... She was dead too. She had hit her head when she fell. Michael said anyone could have killed him for drugs or money. But he was worried about her, he said. The police would be more concerned if they found her dead too. He wiped his prints from the door and from the things in the room he had touched. Then he wrapped her up and made me watch the back door, he wrapped her in a blanket and dragged her down the steps and put her in the trunk of the car."

"What did he do with her body?"

The tears were flowing from Jennifer's face. "I remember now… when we got home…." She wiped her face with the back of her hand.

Ben stared at her a moment then gently squeezed her elbow with his fingers. "Tell me."

"I could hear her when he stopped the car. Oh my god, Ben. I didn't think she was dead. I told Michael to check. He did. He said she was dead. It was just my imagination. She must have been dead. But I don't know, it sounded like a little girl hurt and crying for help."

"Did you see her for yourself?"

She shook her head vigorously. "No. I was in the car. He got out and opened the trunk. I couldn't hear anything then. Then he closed the trunk and took me inside. He laid me down in bed, then he left."

"What did he do with her?"

"I don't know. Not really. He never told me, and he never spoke to me about it. But I always thought he buried her near the river or put her body in the swampy land near the river. There's a small inlet there by the orchard where the current is stagnant. If he weighted the body..."

"Why do you think that?"

"About two years later, it was a very dry summer. The waterline at the river went down, and he got very concerned. He had it bulldozed and filled in with dirt and rocks and chunks of cement. Anything he could find. And there was something else too. Michael never liked anyone going near that part of the river. Before that summer or after. You may have seen it. It's where the bank is very stony, and there aren't any trees."

"I've seen it," said Ben. "It's a large mound near the riverbank. There is a lot of old concrete and stones. Tall weeds."

"Yes. It's all wild there, and he won't let anyone do anything there. He said it's hazardous. No planting there. You know he's planted trees and grapes on every square inch of the vineyard."

Ben nodded, deep in thought.

"And what of your friend?" he asked. "The one who introduced you to these people and brought you there. What happened to her?"

"I don't know. After that night, Michael told me never to talk to her or her friends again. I never did. I don't know what she's doing now."

"Did you ever hear from her?"

"Never."

"And what does this have to do with Anna Wagner?" Ben asked.

Jennifer held the edge of the bed sheet to her chest, kneading it into a ball with her fingers.

"I killed Snake, and his girlfriend," she replied. "And then I did the same to Anna. I killed her."

"That's one hell of a jump," said Ben. "What happened to Snake and this girl was in self-defense while you were intoxicated with god only knows what kind of drugs."

"That's just it," she interrupted. "I'd been taking these pills. I'd go to bed and black out and wake up the next morning without remembering anything. You don't know what I'm like when I'm taking pills. I black out. I lose control. I'm completely out of control!" She pounded the edge of the bed with her fist, full of self-loathing now.

"When Michael found me in that room, he undid the handcuffs from the bed, but he left them on my wrist because he was in such a hurry to leave. Before anyone came by, you know? He didn't take the cuffs off me until we were home. And he kept them."

"Why?"

"To remind me. He kept them out of sight mostly. But once we were fighting and I threatened to leave him. He took them out to remind me. He said he'd handcuff me to my own bed if I didn't calm down. He never threatened to tell the police, but I was afraid."

"Is that why you were afraid to leave with me?"

355

"Oh, yes. You have to know that is the only reason. Because I owe him so much for how he helped me. What I put him through. God, what I made him do to protect me. I don't think he would turn me in to the police, but he always could, you know?"

"I know. But the guilt hanging over your head was enough to scare you into staying."

"Yes. That's it exactly."

"So what about Anna?" he asked.

"A few days after they found Anna in that pump-house, I was cleaning, and I found the key to the handcuffs. But the handcuffs were missing. I looked everywhere for them, but they were gone. I didn't add it up until you told me poor Anna had been handcuffed to the bed in the pump-house..." She took a breath and wiped her eyes with the edge of the sheet. "The same way I had been, Ben. They were the same handcuffs. I used them on her. I know it. Then I started to think about the dreams I'd been having. Hearing her crying. Strange, crazy dreams about her drowning in the river..."

"Those are dreams," said Ben.

"But if I really had killed her then blacked it out, wouldn't it make sense that she would come back to my dreams to haunt me?"

"No," he said. "It doesn't make sense. You liked her. You had no reason to do her harm."

"I know. That's what I told Michael too. She was such an amazing girl. So happy. Michael said I must have been jealous of her. Being so good and so strong for her father, when I've always been so weak and dependent..." She shook her head. "It makes sense in a way, doesn't it? Doesn't it?"

"Never mind what Michael told you," Ben replied coldly. "He's been lying to you for six years."

"Why?"

"First tell me more about your friend who introduced you to

this Snake person. When was the last time you saw Karen Gilles?"

Jennifer stared at him, wide-eyed.

"Yes. But I never told you her last name. My god, Ben. Who told you about her? How did you know her last name?"

"There is something you need to know," said Ben. "You've been misled about this the whole time."

Thirty-Nine

Inspector Walter Kumar received the search warrant a half hour after Jennifer was safely out of harm's way. Kumar and a young OPP Constable, Phil McLean, were the first two in the house.

After a quick search of the first floor, they went upstairs. There, they found the rope and the large blue barrel beside Jennifer's bed.

"Looks like someone was in trouble," said McLean.

Kumar looked at him with disbelief. "You think?"

McLean shrugged, not detecting the sarcasm. "Just look at this shit."

Kumar said nothing and led the constable down to the basement. The search appeared to be uneventful at first. There were several rooms in the basement. A pool table occupied the main room, with a fully stocked bar, a leather couch and three leather chairs. Adjacent to that room was another room, guarded by a thick oak door.

McLean looked at Kumar expectantly. "It's locked."

"Do you have a key?" Kumar asked redundantly.

"No."

Kumar waited as McLean stared at him.

"Well, open it," Kumar said.

"Kick it down?"

Kumar said nothing.

"Okay," said McLean. "I'll kick it down."

With a boyish grin, he stepped back and raised his leg. After four sound kicks, the latch gave way. Inside was Michael Voracci's personal wine cellar. It was twenty by twenty, with racks eight feet high. Most of the racks were empty, but Kumar estimated there were at least three hundred bottles of wine. The room was well insulated, with a thermometer and a humidity gauge mounted on the wall beside the door.

On the far wall was a second door. It too was locked.

After making a light attempt to find a key, Kumar kicked this door in himself. A bare light bulb hung from a wire in the ceiling. He pulled the cord and discovered a bare mattress in the centre of the room. The room still smelled faintly of sweat and urine. The stench of suffering and death.

The mattress was stained with a variety of fluids, which, Kumar was certain, would match DNA samplings from the remains of Anna Wagner. Kumar crouched towards the mattress with his flashlight, examining it closely. Strands of long blonde hair were readily visible on the mattress.

"What did I tell you?" said McLean. "Sadistic fuckers."

"You said it was Quiring who killed her," Kumar recalled.

"That was before," McLean said.

"Before we stepped in here?" Kumar said. "Before you saw this?"

He removed his cell phone from its belt clip and stared at it for a moment. No service.

He walked through the cellar, up the steps, and through the kitchen. He was on the back porch before his phone had a signal. Outside, it felt much cooler compared to the stagnant air in the house. The night stars had begun to show themselves one at a time, and a welcome breeze combed through Kumar's hair.

He pressed the redial button on his phone as McLean ambled onto the porch.

"Damn, it smells in there," McLean said.

Kumar turned away once Ben picked up the phone on the other end.

"Ben. We found where Anna had been kept. Voracci's wine cellar. I don't know. Probably from the day she disappeared until the night the pump-house caught on fire."

He paused.

"I don't think that's a good idea, Ben. We've cordoned off the entire property. I want you to bring her in too."

Another pause.

"Yes, I'm certain he's our man. But I also think she might be our woman. They kept her in their house. How could she not know about it?"

A third pause.

"I'll check it out now. Ben, it looks like they may have been in this together, both of them."

He hung up and turned to McLean. "Let's jump in your cruiser. We need to check the riverbank. Ben said someone was digging over there a half hour ago."

McLean drove them quickly to the end of the laneway where the weeds became thick near the riverbank. He turned on his brights, illuminating a small orange excavator perched in the midst of the weeds and stones. Flashlights and guns drawn, they climbed up the slope. The excavator was silent. There was no one in sight.

At the base of the small mound was a freshly dug hole, six feet deep and six feet in diameter.

Kumar dialed his phone again. "He's not here, Ben. Get her to the station now. We'll find Voracci."

There was no feeling quite like solving a case. Soon he would be back in his own bed every night, sitting at his own desk during the day, spending time with his wife, at least for a few days until the next case was handed to him.

"Get on your radio," he told McLean. "I want Voracci found tonight."

Kumar was already planning where he would go when he took the next few days off as he waited for the phone to be picked up on the other end. "Good news," he said. "We're close to wrapping this up. Bring in the forensics. We've found our suspects."

Forty

B en put down the phone, relieved that the police were now searching for Michael Voracci, but concerned that Jennifer was also now a suspect. He watched her apprehensively for a moment, deliberating how to tell her she was wanted for questioning, that she and her husband were both suspected of Anna's murder.

"Who was that?" she asked. "What's wrong?"

"We have to go," he said.

"Where?"

"Police station."

"Why?"

"Do you have a lawyer, Jennifer?"

"Michael has one."

"You need your own now."

She looked up at him, eyes wide. "I don't understand. Why do I need a lawyer?

He opened the dresser drawer. He had some work clothes still packed away here. For a moment, Ben wondered why he had not given this cabin a second thought all the while he was in the city. It was just as well. He pulled a pair of track pants from the drawer and tossed them onto the bed. He threw a clean t-shirt on top of that.

"You can wear these for now," he said.

Jennifer stared at him.

"Get dressed."

"No."

"Get dressed."

"I don't want to go. I want to stay with you."

"You can't stay with me. They want to know about your involvement in Anna's death."

"I wasn't involved. I know that now and so do you."

"I know you didn't kill her. But how could you not have known she was being kept in your house?"

Jennifer stepped back, her fingers pulling at her damp hair. "What do you mean?"

"She was kept in your wine cellar."

She shook her head. "No."

Ben stepped forward. "She was in your wine cellar, in your basement, for almost a week. How could you not know?"

"No! I didn't know that. I never go down there. He keeps it locked... Oh my god." She turned around, hands still on her face, and turned back to Ben. "The nightmares, Ben. I kept hearing someone crying in my sleep. When the house was quiet. That was Anna. Oh my god. That was Anna calling for help. I thought I was dreaming that!"

"That makes sense," Ben said, as he put on his jacket. "But I'm not the one you need to convince. You need to get a lawyer, and you need to make a statement. But first you have to tell me, Jennifer. You have to tell me everything. I'm bringing the car around front. Put some clothes on, or I'll take you in as you are. Understand?"

"You have to tell me about Karen. What did you find out about? What do I need to know?"

"I made some enquiries into this guy, Snake. It didn't happen the way you think. Michael has been lying to you."

"Tell me," she said. The fear had left her eyes. She was concerned, hopeful and also apprehensive.

"Snake was found in his apartment," he continued. "Dead, like you said. But he wasn't stabbed to death with a syringe. He didn't die of a drug overdose."

"How did he die?"

"He was beaten to death and had his throat cut. By a man wearing black leather shoes. He was kicked in the head repeatedly. After he died, a needle was stuck in his neck."

Jennifer shook her head, trying to comprehend. "That makes no sense," she said. "Who would have done that?"

"Who do you think?"

"Michael."

"Yes, Michael."

"Not me."

"No. But there's more."

She backed up to the edge of the bed, leaning forward, elbows on her knees.

"I made more inquiries when I found that out. There was also a report of a missing woman at the same time. She was never found."

"Snake's girlfriend?" she asked.

"No. Her name was Karen Gilles. No other woman was missing."

"I don't understand..."

"Jennifer. How did Michael know where to find you? Karen was the only one who knew where you were. Wouldn't it make sense that he would have her bring him to you?"

"But that would mean..." Her breathing quickened.

"He covered her body. You never saw her face, did you?"

"No."

"Michael killed him. Then he killed her so there wouldn't be a witness. It made no sense to remove his girlfriend's body from the scene, but it would make sense to remove Karen Gilles from the scene. Permanently."

"You mean that body was Karen?"

364

"That is what I believe, yes."

"Oh my god," she said, pulling at her long brown hair. "That was Karen!"

"Yes. Do you understand now? You didn't kill either of them. Michael did. And then he convinced you that you did it. So no one would know."

The realization flared in her eyes. "And," she said, "so I'd never leave again."

"Yes," he replied. "That is probably part of it too."

"He told me if I ever left him, or did anything like that again, he'd turn me in to the police."

"I know," said Ben.

She wiped her nose and mouth with the corner of the sheet.

"Yes," she said at last. "Maybe he could kill someone. If he's going to lose something, he'll do whatever it takes to make sure he doesn't."

She wiped her face again with the palm of her hand. "Michael always says...which would you rather do, win a thousand dollars, or keep someone from stealing a thousand dollars from you?"

"Keep the thousand you have," said Ben.

"Yes."

"But most people feel that way," he said.

"But Michael felt this way more."

"How do you mean?"

"He would ask this same question over and over again. Dinners. Parties. Even with me when we were home alone. It was like his motto or something. He has what he has and he's not going to let anyone take it away. Never. To him, it was better to die protecting what is yours than to let anyone take it away from you."

"Does that include his wife?"

"Maybe."

"Why was Michael digging a hole near the river tonight?"

"I don't know."

"Why was that blue barrel beside your bed tonight? What was he planning to do if you didn't promise to stay with him?"

"I don't know," she repeated. "I don't know. I don't know. When he came into that crack house looking for me..." She stopped.

"What?"

"I know I told you something else before. But the truth is. That man was dead. I didn't see him. But I remember seeing the blood on Michael's face when he took me home. I know he killed that man. So maybe he did kill Anna too. I'm so confused. Why would he hurt her? She was no threat to him."

"Maybe not yet. Maybe she was finding something out about him," said Ben.

"Like what?"

"Do you know much about the business relationship between Michael and Abe Wagner?"

"Not much."

"Was Anna involved in their business discussions at all?"

"I don't know."

"Would you know if she was?"

"No. She was a very responsible girl, though. She looked after her father's interests whenever she could. And I always suspected Michael took advantage of Mr. Wagner."

"Maybe she found out he had been."

Ben swung open the cabin door and took another glance at Jennifer to see if she was getting up or not.

"Get dressed," he said.

When he turned back to step outside, Michael Voracci, still dressed for a game of golf, was in the doorway, arm extended, pointing the end of a revolver at Ben's face.

"Get back inside," he said to Ben.

Ben stepped back into the cabin, and Voracci closed the door behind him. It stayed slightly ajar, but Voracci didn't notice.

"Where were you taking her?" he asked Ben.

"I was taking her to see you," Ben replied. "Don't move, Jennifer. Stay on the bed."

Jennifer did as she was told, staring wide-eyed at Michael and the gun he was pointing at Ben.

"Sit down," Voracci ordered.

Ben sat down on the kitchen chair next to the bed. He turned to the side to ensure the weight of his gun was not obvious to Voracci. Perhaps Voracci had forgotten he was a cop. Perhaps he had not considered that his former employee might have a .40 calibre SigSauer pistol holstered to his side.

"What is your plan, Michael?" he asked.

"That's my question to you. Where are you two going?"

"The police are in your wine cellar," said Ben.

"Why?"

"They're combing through the evidence you left behind. We know you kept the girl there for the whole time she was missing."

Jennifer began sobbing.

"We know you killed her. We think it was an accident," said Ben.

"It wasn't an accident. I couldn't keep her there forever, could I? She couldn't be missing forever."

"Why did she have to be missing at all?"

"She was trying to get her father to leave the country. She thought I was ripping him off. She wanted to ruin me. Have Abe pull out and leave me with nothing. I couldn't let her do that.

"She came to me. I offered to pay him more. I offered to cut him in on Caines' operations. That made her angry. She knew

367

Caines was moving people across the border, but she didn't know I knew about it, or that I was getting a cut. Then she started asking questions about the contract. She was looking into it. Questions about the termination clause. She knew there wasn't one. She knew I'd locked him in tight. I offered to change the contract. Then she slapped me. I slapped her back."

He shook his head, becoming angry again.

"Stupid bitch. It left a mark. I couldn't let her go home like that. Tell her father I was stealing from them and beating his daughter too. So I tied her up in the wine cellar. I was going to keep her there, in the cellar, till I could figure out what to do with her."

"You mean, till you could figure out how to kill her."

Voracci was swaying from left to right. It looked like he had not slept in days. This wave of anger had practically sapped the last of his energy.

"I didn't want to kill her. She was a little bitch, but I didn't want to kill her. I had no choice. I had to do it sooner or later. I kept her sedated, but then that started not to work so well. She started waking up and making noise. It wasn't very loud. But at night..."

He turned to Jennifer.

"Ginny must have heard her in her sleep. She started dreaming about the girl calling her for help. I knew it was only a matter of time till she started to figure it out. So when the storm came, I doped Anna up good, put her in a barrel and put her in my truck. It was supposed to look like a rape. You were supposed to think her boyfriend did it."

Ben saw a shadow in the crack of the doorway. He pressed for more. "Why didn't you dump her near the river like you did Karen Gilles?"

Voracci cocked his head. "Abe needed closure. If her body didn't surface, he was going to go to Mexico to find her. That would have defeated the whole purpose, now wouldn't it?"

"We know you were both in it together," Ben said. "It wasn't over money. We know you and your wife were using her for your sex slave."

"That's a disgusting lie!" shouted Voracci. "I didn't touch her. Ginny didn't know a thing about her. I fucking moved her out of there to keep Ginny from finding out."

Jennifer moaned. "The dreams. I really did hear her."

"Of course you heard her. I didn't want you to find out. What kind of husband do you think I am?"

"A sloppy one," Ben replied. "We also know about how you killed that drug dealer in Toronto. We've been looking for you for years on that. That was sloppy too."

"That wasn't my mistake."

"Why did you kill him?"

"What's mine is mine. He wanted to take everything I had from me."

"Everything?"

"My wife. My wife is everything to me, yes."

"You're not stupid, at least." Ben pressed on. "So you framed your wife for his murder to ensure your wife's loyalty to you. Forever."

"Yes. Forever."

"Until now."

"No. Now too. I'd rather have her dead than not belong to me any more..." He appeared to be thinking through a plan.

"Put your gun down," said Ben.

"No. I think you killed Ginny tonight. I think she pulled a gun on you, and you killed her, right here, before she escaped."

Voracci thought some more. "Get up, Ben. Turn around. This has to go in your back."

As Voracci turned, Kumar kicked in the door. Voracci turned, and Ben jumped him, knocking him to the floor.

The gun went off.

Kumar dropped his pistol, falling back in the doorway, his shirt suddenly red. Voracci knocked Ben from him and reached for the gun he had dropped in the scuffle.

Voracci, on his back, legs spread, aimed the gun at Ben, who already had his sights on Voracci.

Ben fired. The bullet pierced Voracci's heart.

Ben rose to his feet. Kumar sat slumped against the doorway. Ben picked up the phone and dialed 911. "There's a police officer down…"

Forty-One

Walter Kumar's injured arm healed quickly. Ben had wrapped it by the time the ambulance arrived and the bleeding was minimal. If it had hit him a few more inches to the left, the bullet would have missed his arm and would have opened his gut wide enough to hide a football. As it was, he was back on his feet within three days.

After a few days deliberation, the Crown Prosecutor decided not to press charges against Jennifer. Michael Voracci's boastful confession, combined with the forensic evidence presented by the police, which showed Jennifer had never been in the back room of Michael's wine cellar, helped to make certain of that. He had apparently removed his computer from his home, staging it to look like a robbery, only an hour before Ben and Jennifer arrived. They found the hard drive in the glove compartment of his pickup truck. In it were the accounts of every person Randy Caines had arranged to take in or out of the country—a total of 443 people, at an average fee of two thousand dollars a head. Voracci and Caines had been splitting the profits fifty-fifty.

Ben was preparing to leave for Ottawa but wanted to spend a few more days with Jennifer, to be certain she was going to be okay. The night before, they went for a long drive and found themselves once again at the beach. They sat side by side on the same log they had sat on together a few weeks before. It seemed like another lifetime.

"There was one part of this I didn't tell you," he said to Jennifer.

She squeezed his hand. "You can tell me anything now. You know that."

"I'd had dreams about Anna, much like yours. I kept hearing her voice. She kept telling me I was responsible."

"That's ridiculous," she said.

"Not really. I didn't realize it until much later, but I think I was. I talked to her a couple days before she disappeared. She was trying to decide whether or not to go college, because she didn't want to leave her father alone. I told her if she went to school she could be a bigger help to her father. I suggested she could help him with his business dealings."

"So?"

"So I also told her I was a retired cop. She said she wanted to talk to me about that. About Randy Caines and some of the workers he hired. But she wouldn't get into details. She said it would wait. A few days later, she found her father's contract with Michael. That's why she went to Michael. That's why she was killed."

"But that wasn't your fault."

"No. It wasn't. But I was responsible for starting what happened. And I was responsible for finding out the truth."

"And you were responsible for helping me," she added.

"Perhaps, yes."

"No 'perhaps' about it, Ben Taylor. You saved my life. You saved my soul from the guilt that I'd been hiding all these years. You showed me it was really Michael's guilt all along. He used me to justify everything he did. He used me to help hide what he did. You saved me, Ben."

Ben was pensive, thoughtful. He watched Jennifer looking out at the dark sea beneath the star-filled sky. He looked at the sky and she looked at him.

They watched the water and listened to the waves washing up onto the beach. Faint white strings of foam could be seen cascading on the sand. Jennifer took his hand, squeezed it and lifted it to her lips. She kissed his fingers.

"You were so concerned about saving me, you never considered you needed to save yourself too," she said.

"Are you going to stay here?" he asked.

"I don't know where I would go. Are you sure you wouldn't like to stay here?" she asked.

"I can't," he said. "Not right now. I've been away from my life for a year now. I need to go back for a while."

"I know," she said.

He watched her for a moment, the breeze in her dark hair, the moonlight reflecting on her eyes. He took a deep breath before he asked her.

"Would you like to come to Ottawa?" he asked.

"Maybe," she said. "I think we both need a bit of time before we look at what may lie ahead."

He nodded and squeezed her hand.

"Oh, Ben," she sighed. Her sigh mingled with the melody of the waves in the darkness before them. "What do you think will become of us now?"

"I'm not sure," he said. "But whatever it is, it will be what we both need. I'm sure of that."

Now she squeezed his hand. "Me too, I think." But she seemed much less certain than he was.

"Let me take you home," he said.

"Not yet," she said. "I want to stay here with you for a while. When I'm with you, I know I'm at home."

She slipped her arm around his waist and nuzzled into his shoulder as he put his arm around her. Together they looked out at the dark horizon. As the earth slowly rotated beneath them, they watched the stars emerging one by one from the blackness of the water.

The ghosts of their lives rested peacefully tonight.

Acknowledgments

There are many I would like to thank for their help with this novel, including but by no means limited to the following people: Clode Deschamps, Allister Thompson, Sylvia McConnell, Verna Relkoff, Morty Mint, Bill Flindall, Abby Hampton, Lori Flood, Maureen McGreavy, David Chalmers, Sandy Duck, and Heather Norman. Thank you.

David Weedmark, who was born and raised in Ontario, has lived and worked throughout Canada. *The Tanglewood Murders*, his first novel, comes from his experiences working with migrant farm workers in southwestern Ontario.

His first poetry collection, *First Stirrings*, was honoured with a 2004 Governor General's Award nomination. *Postcards from Paris* followed, a second collection of poetry, prose and sketches.

David lives either in downtown Ottawa or at a remote cabin in the Gatineau Hills of Quebec, depending on the season.